DEMON FIRE, DEMON DOOM!

Tall, thin, brown and ivory, like a lightning-blasted tree, an eerie, ugly creature solidified in front of Brann and reached for her.

Brann dropped to a squat, then sprang to one side, slapping against the floor and rolling onto her feet. The thing looked stiff and clumsy, but it wasn't, it was fast and flexible and frighteningly strong. When Brann kicked out, rough, knotty fingers got half a grip on her leg but slipped off as she twisted away. She bounced onto her feet, then gasped with sudden fear as a second set of hard, woody arms closed about her and started to squeeze.

Even as Brann struggled to free herself, another Treeish solidified from air and stench. And another. Desperately, Brann slapped her hands against her captor and began drawing its life into her—and as that corrosive firestuff poured into a body not meant to contain demon energies, Brann screamed in unbearable agony. . . .

BLUE MAGIC

JO CLAYTON

DAW BOOKS, INC.
DONALD A. WOLLHEIM, PUBLISHER

1633 Broadway, New York, NY 10019

DAW Book Collectors No. 743.

First Printing, May 1988

1 2 3 4 5 6 7 8 9

Printed in the U.S.A.

Hilde saved me from a major error
so this book is dedicated to her
and her sharp wits.

1

THE KINGDOM OF JADE TORAT. A MOUNTAINSIDE NEAR THE WESTERN BORDER.

Broad and yellow and heavy with the silt it carried, late summer low in its banks, the river Wansheeri slipped noiselessly past the scattered mountains of the Uplands, driving to the Plains and the vast city that guarded its mouth, Jade Halimm.

On one of those mountains, one close to the river and its deposits of clay, an old woman finished unloading her kiln onto a handcart and started downhill with the cart, old and broad and in her way as slow and heavy and powerful as the river. The sun was low in the west; the air moved slowly and smelled of dust, powdered bark, pungent sticky resins from the conifers, a burning gold haze filtered through lazily shifting needles; the shadows were dark and hot; sweat gathered on the old woman's scalp beneath strong white hair twisted into a feathery knot to keep it off her neck and poured in wide streams past her ears. Ignoring sweat and heat, she plodded down a path her own feet had pounded into the mountainside during the past hundred years. She was alone and content to be alone, showed it in the swing of her heavy body and the work tune she was whistling. The pots rattled, the cart creaked, the old woman whistled, here and there in the distance a bird sang a song as lazy as the sluggish air.

She reached a round meadow bisected by a noisy creek and started pulling the cart over flat stones she had long ago muscled into place for the parts of the year

that were wetter than this; the cart lurched, the pots
thudded, the iron tires of the cartwheels rumbled over
the stones. She stopped whistling and put more muscle
into moving the cart, her face going intent as she focused mind and body on the pushpole. When she
reached the bridge across the creek, she straightened
her back and drew an arm across her face, wiping away
some of the sweat. A breeze moved along the water,
cool after the still heat under the trees. She unhooked
the pushpole and shuffled to the siderail, lingering in
that comparative coolness, leaning against the top bar,
head bent so the breeze could run across her neck.
Across the meadow her house and workshed waited,
half hidden by ancient knotty vines, their weathered
wood fitting with grace into the stony tree-covered slope
behind them. She was pleasantly tired and looking forward to fixing her supper, then consuming a large pot
of tea while she re-read one of the books she'd brought
up from Jade Halimm to pass the evenings with when
the children were gone. Yaril and Jaril were due back
soon; she smiled as she thought this. They'd have a
thousand stories to tell about what they'd seen in their
travels, but that wasn't the only reason she was beginning to grudge the hours until they came; she was more
attached to them than she liked to admit, even to herself, they were her children, her nurslings, though their
human forms had grown older in the years (about two
hundred of them now) since their paths collided with
hers on the slopes of Tincreal. Recently she'd begun to
wonder if they might be approaching something like puberty. Their outward forms, to some extent anyway, re-
flected their inward being, so if they seemed to be
hovering on the verge of adolescence when they took on
the appearance of human children, what was that supposed to tell her? What was adolescence like for a pair
of golden shimmerglobes? How would she deal with it?
They'd been restless the past several years, ranging over
much of the world, coming back to her only when their
need for food was so demanding they could no longer
ignore it. She wrinkled her nose with distaste. She
wanted them back, but it meant she'd have to go down
to Jade Halimm and hunt for victims she could justify

sucking dry of life. High or low, it didn't matter to her, only the smell of their souls mattered. The folk of Jade Halimm who were ordinarily honest (which meant having only small sins and meannesses on their consciences but no major taint of corruption) were afraid at first when they knew the Drinker of Souls was prowling the night, but experience taught them that they had nothing to fear from her. She took the muggers, the despoilers of children, the secret murderers and such folk, leaving the rest alone. Many in Jade Halimm had reason to be grateful to her; the mysterious deaths of certain merchants and moneylenders made their heirs suddenly inclined to generosity and improved their patience wonderfully (for a while at least and never to the point of losing a profit). She frowned at the stream. How long have I been here? She counted the year names to herself, counted the cycles. Tungjii's tender tits, I'm letting myself go, time slips like water through my fingers, it seems like yesterday I came up the riverpath and argued old Dayan into taking me on as his apprentice.

The western sky was throwing up rags of color as the sun dropped stone quick behind the peaks; the old trout that lived under the bridge drifted out, a dark dangerous shade in the broken shadows of the water. She sighed and pushed back onto her feet. If she wanted to get the pots stowed before full dark there was no more time for dreaming. She set her hand on the pullpole, meaning to lock it back in front of her, turned instead and stood gazing toward the river as she heard the hurried uneven pound of hooves on the beaten earth of the riverpath. Whoever it is, he's pushed that poor beast to the point of breakdown. Leaving the cart where it was, she walked off the bridge, up the paving stones to the road and stood waiting for the rider to show.

For a moment she thought of climbing to the house and barring the door, but she'd been settled in contentment too long and had lost the wariness endemic in the earlier part of her life. Who'd want to hurt her, the ancient potter of Shaynamoshu? Besides, it might be a desperate landsman running from the whipmasters on one of the cherns along the Wansheeri. She'd hid more than one such fugitive after Dayan died and left her the house.

The horse came out of the trees, a dapple gray blackened with sweat, a black-clad boy on his back. When he came even with her, the boy slid from the saddle, leaving the beast to stand behind him, head down and shivering, a thin wiry boy, fifteen, sixteen, something like that, dark circles of fatigue about his eyes, his face drawn and showing the bone, determination and terror haunting his eyes. "Brann born in Arth Slya, Drinker of Souls?"

She blinked at him, considering the question. After a moment she nodded. "Yes."

He fumbled inside his shirt, jerked, breaking the thong she could see about his neck. A moment more of fumbling, him swaying on his feet, weary beyond weariness, then he brought out a small packet, parchment folded over and over about something heavy, smeared copiously with black wax. "We the blood of Harra Hazani say to you, remember what you swore." He pushed the packet at her.

She took it, tucked it in her blouse and caught hold of him as he fell against her, fatigue clubbing him down once the support of his drive to reach her was gone. A flash of darkness caught the corner of her eye. A tigerman popped from the air behind the boy. Before she could react, he slipped a knife up under the boy's ribs and vanished as precipitously as he came with a pop like a cork coming from a bottle.

An icy wind touched her neck.

Something heavy, metallic slammed into her back.

Cold fire flashed up through her.

Heavy breathing, broken in the middle. Faint popping sound.

Her knees folded under her, she saw herself toppling toward the boy's body, saw the hilt of the knife in his back, saw an exploding flower of blood, saw nothing more.

the one such fugitive after Davin died and left her the
trouble. Food and some fruit—it was either poor black...

—— **2** ——

TWO MONTHS EARLIER AND A THOUSAND MILES SOUTH AND WEST ALONG THE COAST FROM JADE HALIMM.
IN OWLYN VALE OF THE FIFTH FINGER, EVENTS PREPARE FOR THE KNIFE IN BRANN'S BACK.

SCENE: Late, the Wounded Moon in his crescent phase, just rising. One of the walled households in Owlyn vale. A small bedroom in the children's wing. Three narrow beds in the room, one sleeper, a girl about thirteen or fourteen, the other beds empty. The door opens. A boy of seven slips through the gap, glides to the girl and takes her by the shoulder, shakes her awake.

"Kori. Wake up, Kori. I need you."

The whisper and the shaking dragged Kori out of chaotic nightmare. "Wha . . . who . . ."

The shaking stopped. "It's me, Kori. Tré."

"Tré . . ." She fumbled her hands against the sheets, pushed up and turned in one move, her limbs all angles, her body with limber grace, the topsheet and quilt winding around her until she shoved them away and dropped her legs over the edge of the bed. She swept the hair out of her eyes and sat scowling at her brother, a shivering dark shape in the starlit room. "Ahhh, Tré," she said, keeping her voice to a murmur so AuntNurse wouldn't hear and come scold them, "shut the door, silly, then tell me what's biting you."

He hurried over, pulled the door shut with such care the latch went home without a sound, hurried back to his sister. She patted the bed beside her and he climbed up and sat where her hand had been, sighing and leaning his weight against her. "It's me now," he said. "Zilos came to me, his ghost I mean. He said I pass it to you, Trago; the Chained God says you're the one. They'll burn me too, Kori; when the Signs start, they'll know I'm the priest now and HE'll know and HE'll order his soldiers to burn me like they did Zilos."

Kori shivered. "You're sure? Maybe it was a bad dream. Me, I've been having lots of those."

Trago wriggled away from her. "I said he put his hand on me, Kori. He left the Mark." He pulled his sleeping shift away from his shoulder and let her see a hollow starburst, dark red like a birthmark; he'd had no mark there before, he was born unflawed, she'd bathed him as a babe, part of girls' work in the Household of the Piyoloss clan. And she'd seen that brand before, seen it on the strong sunbrown shoulder of Zilos the woodworker when he'd left his shirt off on a hot summer day, sitting on the bench before his small house carving a doll's head for her. Zilos, Priest of the Chained God. Three weeks ago the soldiers of the Sorceror Settsimaksimin planted an oak post in the middle of the threshing floor, tied Zilos to it, piled resinous pinewood about him and burned him to ash, standing around him and jeering at the Chained God, calling him to rescue his Priest if he counted himself more than a useless ghost-thing. And they promised to burn all such priests wherever they found them, Settsimaksimin was more powerful than any pitiful little local god and that was his command and the command of Amortis his patron. Amortis is your god now, they announced to the stubborn refusing folk of Owlyn Vale, Amortis the bountiful, Amortis ripe and passionate, Amortis the bestower of endless pleasure. Rejoice that she consents to bless you with her presence, rejoice that she calls you to her service.

Warily, feeling nauseated, Kori touched the mark. It was bloodwarm and raised a hair above the paler skin of her brother's shoulder. The first sign. He could hide that, but other signs would appear that he couldn't hide. One day mules might bray and rebel and come running from fields, dragging plows and seeders and wagons behind them, mules might jump corral fences, break through stable doors, ignoring commands, whips, all obstacles, they might come and kneel before him. Some such things would happen. He couldn't stop them. Another day he might be compelled to go to every adult woman in Owlyn Vale and touch her and heal all ills and announce the sex of each child in the wombs that were filled and bless each such unborn so it would come forth without flaw and more beautiful than the morning. A third time, it would be something else. The one certainty in the situation was that whatever signs were manifested would be public and spectacular. Kori sighed and held her brother in her arms as he sobbed out his fear and indignation that this should happen to him.

When his sobbing died down and he lay quiescent against her, she murmured, "Do you know when the signs will start? Tomorrow? Next week?"

Trago coughed, sniffed, pushed against her. She let him go and he wriggled away along the bed until he could turn and look at her. He fished up the edge of her sheet and blew his nose into it, ignoring the soft spitting of indignation this drew from her. "Zilos his Ghost said the Chained God gives me three months to get used to this. Then he lets everyone know."

"Stupid!" She bit down on the word, not because she feared the God, but she didn't want AuntNurse in there scolding her for staining her reputation by entertaining a male in her bedchamber, no matter that male was her seven-year-old brother, how you start is how you go on Auntee said. "Any hope the god will change his mind?"

"No." Trago cleared his throat again, caught her glare and swallowed the phlegm instead of spitting it out.

She scowled at her hands, took hold of the long flexible fingers of her left hand and bent them back until

the nails lay almost parallel to her arm. Among all the
children and young folk belonging to the Piyoloss clan,
Trago was the one closest to her, the only one who
laughed when she did, the only one who could follow
her flights of fancy, his dragonfly mind as swift as hers.
If he burned, much of her would burn with him and she
didn't like to think of what her life would be like after
that. She smoothed one hand over the other. "We've got
to do something," she murmured. She hugged her arms
across her shallow just-budding breasts. "I think . . ."
Her voice faded as she went still, her eyes opening wide,
staring inward at a sudden memory. A moment later, she
shook herself and turned to him. "I've got an idea . . .
maybe . . . You go back to bed, Tré, I have to think
about it. Without distraction. You hear?"

He wiggled back to her, caught hold of her hand and
pressed it to the side of his face, then he bounced off
the bed and trotted out of the room, leaving the door
swinging open.

Kori sighed and went to shut it. She leaned against it
a moment looking at the chest at the foot of the bed.
She crossed to the chest, pulled up the lid and fished
inside for a small box and carried that to the window.
She rested her elbows on the sill, turned the box over
and over in her fingers. It was old and worn from much
prior handling, fragrant kedron wood, warm brown with
amber highlights. It was heavy and clunked as she
turned it. Harra Hazani's gift to her children and her
children's children, passed from daughter to daughter,
moving from clan to clan as the daughters married into
other families, each Harra's Daughter holder of the
promise choosing the next, one of her own daughters or
a young cousin in another clan, she took great care to
chose the proper one, it was a serious thing, passing the
promise on and keeping it safe. And it had been safe
and secret through all the two centuries since Harra
lived here and bore her children. Kori set the box on
the sill and folded her hands over it as she gazed through
the small diamond-shaped panes of glass set in lead
strips. She couldn't see much, what she wanted was the
feel of light on her face and a sense of space beyond
the narrow confines of the room. There were times when

she woke restless and slipped out to dance in the moonlight, but she didn't want to chance getting caught. Not now. She opened the box, took out the heavy bronze medal with the inscrutable glyphs on front and back, ran her fingers over it, set it on the sill, took out the stick of black sealing wax and the tightly folded packet of parchment, ancient, yellowed, blank (she knew that because after Cousin Diyalla called her to her deathbed and gave her the box and a hoarsely whispered explanation, she took the box up onto the mountain behind Household Piyoloss, opened it and examined the three things it contained). *Send the medal to one called Brann, self-named Drinker of Souls*, Diyalla whispered to Kori. *Say to her: we, the line of Harra Hazani, call on you to remember what you swore. This is what she swore, that if Harra called on her, she would come from anywhere in the world to give her gifts and her strength and her deadly touch to protect Harra or her children or her children's children as long as the line and she existed. And this Harra said to her daughter, the Drinker of Souls will live long indeed. And this Harra said, trust her; she is generous beyond ordinary and will give without stint.* All very well, Kori thought, but how do I know where to send the medal? She smoothed her thumb over the cool smooth bronze and gazed through the wavery glass as if somewhere in the distortions lay the answer to her question. The window looked east and presently she made out the shape of the broken crescent that was the Wounded Moon rising above the mountains that curved like protecting hands about the mouth of Owlyn Vale where the river ran out and curled across the luscious plain that knew three harvests a year and a harder poverty for most of its people than even the meanest would ever face in the sterner, more grudging mountains. Absently caressing the medal, warming it with her warmth, she stared a long time at the moon, her gaze as empty as her mind. There was a small round hole near one end of the rectangle, she played with that a while. Harra must have worn it about her neck, suspended on a chain or a thong. Kori set it on the sill, raised her shoulders as she took in a long breath, lowered them as she let it out. She went to the chest and

took out a roll of leather thonging she'd used for something or other once and put away after she was finished
with it in a rare burst of waste-not want-not. She cut a
piece long enough to let the medal dangle between the
tiny hillocks of her to-be breasts, slipping it beneath her
sleeping shift. She went back to the window and stood
a moment longer watching the moon. I have to go out,
I can't think in here. I have to plan how to work this.
The other times she'd sneaked out, she'd pulled on a
pair of old trousers she filched from the ragbag and a
sleeveless tunic that was getting to be too small for her.
Somehow, though, that didn't feel appropriate this time.
In spite of the danger and the beating she'd get if she
were discovered, the disgrace she'd bring on kin and
clan, she went like she was, her thin coltish body barely
hidden by the fine white cloth she had woven herself on
the family loom. She glided through the house silent as
the earthsoul of a murdered child and out the postern
gate, remembering the doubletwelve of soldiers quar-
tered on the Vale folk only after she was irretrievably
beyond the protection of the House walls. Like a startled, no a frightened, fawn she fled up the hillside to a
small glade with a giant oak in the center of it, an oak
that felt to her as always old as the stone bones of the
mountain.

She drifted onto dew-soaked grass; her feet were aching with cold but she ignored that and danced slowly
around the perimeter of the glade through the dappled
moonlight, around and around, singing a wordless song
that wavered through four notes no more, singing herself deeper into trance, around and around, gradually
spiraling inward until she spread her arms and em-
braced the tree, circling it a last time, drinking in the
dark dry smell of it, breasts, belly and thighs rubbing
against its crumbly rough bark. When she finished the
round, she folded liquidly down and curled her body
between two great roots pushing up through layers of
dead and rotting leaves. With a small sigh, she closed
her eyes and seemed to sleep.

As she seemed to sleep, a dark thin figure seemed to
melt from the tree and crouch over her, long long gray-
brown hair drifting like fog about a thin pointed face,

androgynous, with an eerie beauty that would have been ugliness if the face were flesh. Long graceful fingers of brown glass seemed to brush across Kori's face, she seemed to smile then sigh. Brown glass fingers seemed to touch the leather thong, seemed to slide quickly away quivering with distaste, seemed to draw the medal from under the shift, seemed to stroke it smiling, seemed to hold the medal in one hand and spread the other long long hand across Kori's face.

HOW HARRA HAZANI CAME TO OWLYN VALE.

Gibbous, waxing toward full, the Wounded Moon shone palely on a long narrow ship that sliced through the windwhipped, foamspitting water of the sea called Notoea Tha, and touched with delicate strokes the naked land north of the ship, a black-violet blotch that gradually gained definition as the northwestering course of the smuggler took her closer and closer to the riddle rock at the tip of that landfinger, rock pierced again and again and again by wind and water so that it sang day and night, slow sad terrible songs, and was only quiet one hour every other month.

On the deck by the foremast a woman slept, wrapped in blankets and self-tethered to the mast by a knot she could pull loose with a quick jerk of her hand. All that could be seen of her was the pale curve of a temple and long dark hair confined in half a dozen plaits that danced to the tug of the wind, their gold beetle clasps tunk-tonking against the wood, the small sounds lost in the creaks, snaps and groans of the flitting ship. A man sat beside her, his back against the mast, a naked sword across his thighs. Now and then he sucked at a wineskin, the pulls getting longer and more frequent as the night turned on its wheel. He was a big man and in the kind darkness had the athletic beauty that sculptors give to the statues of heroes; even in daylight he had the look of a hero if you didn't look too closely for he was at that stage of ripeness that was also the first stage of decay.

The night went on with its placidities and tensions intact; the Wounded Moon crawled up over the mast and began sliding toward the heaving black water with its tracery of foam; the groaning song of the riddle rock grew loud enough to ride over the noises of the sea, the wind and the straining ship and creep into the fuddled mind of the blond hero who stirred uneasily and reached for the empty skin. Remembering its emptiness before he completed the gesture, he settled back into the muddled not-sleep that was a world away from the vigilance he was being paid for. The woman stirred, muttered, moved uneasily, on the verge of waking.

Shadows began converging on the foremast, dark forms moving with barefoot silence and confident agility, Captain and crew acting according to their nature, a nature she'd read easily enough when she made arrangements to leave Bandrabahr on that stealthy ship, needing the stealthiest of departures to escape the too-pressing attentions of an ex-friend of her dead father, a man of power in those parts. Having no choice in transport and understanding what a swamp she was plunging into, she hired the hero as a bodyguard and he'd done the job well enough up to this moment but her luck and his were about to run out.

The hero's throat was cut with a soft slide, the sound lost in the moan from the riddle rock now only a few shiplengths off, but since most of the crew were here, not tending the ship, she lurched in annoyance at being neglected and sent the hero's sword clanging against the deck. Half awake already, the woman jerked the knot loose and was on her feet running, knives in both hands, slashing, dodging, darting, slipping grips, scrambling on her knees, rolling onto her feet, creating and reading confusion, playing her minor whistle magic to augment that confusion, winning the shiprail, plunging overside into the cold black water.

She swam toward the land, cursing under her breath because she was furious at having to abandon everything she wasn't wearing. Especially furious at losing her daroud because her father had given it to her and she'd managed to keep it through a lot of foolishness and it was her means of earning her keep. She promised herself as soon as she reached the shore and could give her mind to it she'd lay such a curse on the Captain and crew, they'd moan louder and longer than that damn rock ahead of her.

Getting onshore without being battered and torn into ground meat and shattered bone proved more difficult than she expected; the smaller rocks jutting from the sea around the base of the riddle rock were home to barnacles with edges sharp enough to split a thought in half while water was sucked in and out of the washholes in the great rock, flowing in powerful surges that caught hold of her and dragged her a while, then shoved her a while, then dragged her some more. Half drowned, bleeding from a hundred cuts, she caught a fingertip hold on a crack in a waterpolished ledge and used will and what was left of her strength to muscle herself high enough out of the water to roll onto the ledge where she lay on her side, gasping and spitting out as much of the sea inside her as she could. When she was as calm as she was going to get, she began the herka trypps that were meaningless in every way except that they helped her focus mind and energy and got her ready to use the more demanding levels of her magic. Blending modes she learned from her father with others she'd picked up here and there in her travels since he died, she began to draw heat from the air and glamour from the moon-light and twisted them into tools to seal the cuts where blood was leaking away and taking strength with it and when that was done, she pulled heat and glamour into herself and stored it, then used it to shape the curse and used her anger to power the curse and shot her curse after the ship like poison arrow, releasing it with a flare of satisfaction that turned to ash a moment later as a net of weariness settled around her and pinned her flat to the cold stone.

Cold. She wasn't bleeding any longer, but the cold was drawing the life out of her. Get up, she told herself, get on your feet, you can't stay here. Struggling against the weight of that bone deep fatigue, searching out holds on the face of the riddle rock, she forced herself onto her knees and then onto her feet. For a minute or an hour, she never knew which, she stood shivering and mind-dulled, trying to get her thoughts ordered again, trying to focus her energy so she could understand where she was and what she had to do to get out of there. The riddle rock moaned about her, a thousand fog horns bellowing, the noise jarred her over and over from her fragile focus and left her swaying precariously on the point of tumbling back into the water. The tide began following the moon and backed away from her, its stinging spray no longer battered her legs. Once again she tried the herka trypps, closing her numb hands tighter in the cracks so the pain would break through the haze thickening in her head. Slowly, ah so slowly she regained her ability to focus, but the field was narrow, a pinhead wide, no more. She drew power into herself, plucking it from tide and moonlight, from the ancient roots of the rock she stood on, a hairfine trickle of strength that finally was enough and only just enough to let her *see* the way off the rock, then shift her clumsy aching body along that way until she was finally walking on thin soil where grasses grew gray and tough, where the brush was crooked and close to the ground. Half drowned still, blind with effort and fatigue, she walked on and on until she reached a place where there were trees and where the trees had dropped leaves that weren't fully rotted yet, where she could dig herself a nest and cover herself over with the leaves and, at last, let herself sleep. . . .

She woke late in the afternoon of the following day, stiff, sore, hungry, thirsty, sea salt and anger bitter in her mouth. The summer sun was hot and the air in the aspen grove heavy with that heat. Her aches and bruises said stay where you are, don't move, but the clamor in her belly and the sweat that crawled stickily over her body spoke more strongly. Gathering will and the remnants of her strength she crawled from her nest among the leaves and used the smooth powdery trunk of the nearest aspen to pull herself onto her feet.

She leaned against the tree and drew a little on its strength though all her magics had their cost and her need would always outpace the gain; as soon as her will weakened she'd pay that cost and it would be a heavy one. Stupid and more than stupid wasting her strength heaving that curse after the Captain and his crew; what she'd thrown so thoughtlessly away last night might mean the difference between living and dying this day. She grimaced and gave regret a pass, few things more futile than going over and over past mistakes; learn from them if there was anything to learn, then let them go and save your strength for today's problems which are usually more than sufficient. Yesterday banished, she turned her mind to present needs.

Food, water, shelter, and where should she go from here? Food? It was summer, there should be mushrooms, berries, even acorns if those dark green crowns farther inland were oaks. She touched her arms, felt the knives snugged under her sleeves; she kept hold of them when she went overside and didn't start swimming until they were sheathed. There were plenty of saplings near to hand. She could make cords for snares from their fibrous inner bark, for a sling too, if she sacrificed a bit of her shirt for the pocket and found a few smooth stones. There were birds about, she could hear them, they'd feed her, their blood would help with her thirst, though finding fresh water was becoming more urgent as time slid past, not just for thirst, she needed to wash the dried salt off her skin. She pushed away from the aspen and turned back her cuffs. Where do I go from here? After working stiff fingers until she could hold a knife without fear of dropping it, she began slicing through the bark of a sapling as big around as her thumb. No point in calling water and using that as a guide, she was surrounded by water and she wasn't enough of a diviner to tell fresh from salt. Ah well, this was one of Cheonea's Finger Headlands, salt sea on one side, salt inlet on the other; if she paralleled the inlet shore she was bound to come on streams and eventually into a settlement. The folk in the Finger Vales were said to be fierce and clannish and quick to defend themselves from encroachment, but courteous enough to a stranger who showed them courtesy and generous to those in need who happened their way. She sliced the bark free in narrow strips, peeling them away from the wood and draping them over her knee, glancing at the sky now and then to measure how much light she had left. No point in making snares, she didn't have time to hunt out game trails, she wanted to be on her way come the morning. She left the first sapling with half its bark, not wanting to kill it entirely, moved on to another. A sling, yes, I'm rusty, have to get close and hope for a bit of luck. . . .

She finished the cords, made her sling, found some pebbles and some luck and dined on plump brispouls roasted over a fire it took her some muscle and blisters to make, a firebow had never been her favorite tool and she was even less fond of it now. The pouls had a strong taste and the only salt she had was crusted on her skin, but they were hot and tender and made a pleasant weight in her stomach; she finished the meal with a bark basket of mourrberries sweet and juicy (though she had to spend half an hour dislodging small flat seeds from between her teeth). By that time the sunset had faded and the stars were out thick as fleas on a piedog's hide. Sighing, her discomforts reduced to a minimum, she got heavily to her feet, stripped off her trousers and shirt (leaving her boots on as she had the night before because she knew she'd never get her feet back in them), she wadded up her trousers and scrubbed hard at all the skin she could reach. The scum left behind when the sea water dried was already raising rashes and in the worst of those rashes her skin was starting to crack. When she'd done all she could, she dressed, dumped dirt on the remnants of the fire, smothering it carefully (she didn't relish the thought of waking in the center of a forest fire). A short distance away, she made a new sleeping nest, lay down in it and pulled dry leaves over her. Very soon she sank into a sleep so deep she did not notice the short fierce rain an hour later.

She woke with the dawn, shivering and feeling the bite at the back of the eyes that meant a head cold fruiting in her. She rubbed the heel of her left hand over the medal hanging between her breasts. Ah Brann, oh Brann, why aren't you here when I need you? With a coughing laugh, she stretched, strained the muscles in face and body, slapped at her soggy shirt and trousers, knocking away the damp leaves clinging to her. She shivered, feeling uncertain, there was something. . . . She looked at the three saplings she'd stripped of half their bark, shivered again as an image popped into her head of babies crying in pain and shock. Following an impulse that was half delirium, she scored the palm of her left hand with one of her knives and smeared the blood from the wound along the wounded sides of the little trees. She felt easier at once and almost at once found a clean pool of water in the rotted crotch of a lightning blasted tree. She drank, washed her wounded hand, then set off along the mountainside, keeping the morning wind in her face since as far as she could tell, it was blowing out of the northeast and that was where she wanted to go.

She walked all morning in a haze of growing discomfort as the cold grew worse and her cut hand throbbed. Twice she stopped at berry thickets and ate as much as she could hold and took more of the fruit with her pouched in the tail of her shirt. A little after the sun reached zenith she came to a small stream; with the expenditure of will and much patience combined with quick hands, she scooped out two unwary trout, then stripped and used the sand collected around the stones in the streambed to scrub herself clean, she even let down her hair and used the sand on that though she wasn't too sure of the result and never managed to get all the grit washed out of the tangled mass. After she pounded some of the dirt out of her clothing and spread it to dry over a small bushy conifer, she cooked the trout on a sliver of shale and finished off the berries. The sun was warm and soothing, the stream sang the knots out of her soul and even the cold seemed to loose its hold on head and chest. Her shirt and trousers were still wet when she finished eating, so she stretched out on her stomach on a long slant of granite that jutted into the stream and lay with her head on her crossed arms, her aching eyes shut.

The sun had vanished behind the trees when she woke. She yawned, went still. Something resilient and rather warm was pressed against her side. Warily she eased her head up until she could look over her shoulder. A large snake, she couldn't read the kind in the inadequate view she had, lay in irregular loops on the warm stone, taking heat from it and her. Its head was lifting, she could feel it stirring as it sensed the change in her. She summoned concentration, licked her lips and began whistling a two-note sleepsong, the sound of it hardly louder than the less constant music of the stream, on and on, until the snake lowered its head and the loops of its body stretched and loosened. She threw herself away from it and curled onto her feet, her heart fluttering, her breath coming quick and shallow. The snake reared its black head, seemed to stare at her, split red tongue tasting the air. For a moment snake and woman held that tense pose, then the snake dropped its head and flowed from the stone into the water and went swimming off, a ripple of black, black head lifted. She dropped her shoulders and sighed, weariness and sickness flooding over her again. She pulled her trousers and shirt off the baby fir and shook them out more carefully than she would have before the snake. Shivering with a sudden chill she strapped on her knives, pulled on her shirt and trousers, swung the long double belt about her and buckled it tight. She checked about the rock, collected odds and ends she'd emptied from her pockets when she washed her clothes, went on her knees and drank sparingly from the stream, then started on. There was at least an hour left before sundown and she might as well use it.

For seven days she moved inland, gathering food as she went, enough to fend off hunger cramps and keep her feet moving up around down as she patiently negotiated ravines and circled impossible bramble patches or brush too thick to push through, up around down. It was summer so the rains when they came were quick to pass on and the nights were never freezing though the air could get nippy around dawn. By the end of those seven days she was on the lower slopes of mountains that were beginning to shift away from the inlet, moving ever deeper into the great oak forest, walking through a brooding twilight with unseen eyes following her. The ground was clear and easy going except for an occasional tricky root that broke through the thick padding of old leaves. There were a few glades where one of the

ancient oaks had blown over and left enough room for
vines and brush to grow, but not many; getting food for
herself was hard and getting wood to cook it would have
been harder if she hadn't decided to dispense with fire
altogether. As soon as she stepped into that green
gloom, she got the strong impression that the trees
wouldn't take to fire and (though she laughed at her
fancies, as much as she could laugh with the persistent
and disgusting cold draining her strength) would deal
harshly with anyone burning wood of any kind here,
even down deadwood. She spent an hour or so that night
scooping wary trout from a stony stream, then gutted
them and ate them raw. And was careful to dig a hole
and bury the skins, bones and offal near the roots on
one of the trees. The next morning she went half an
hour upstream, got herself another fish and ate that raw
too and buried what she didn't eat. Urged on by the
trees who weren't hostile exactly, just unwelcoming, she
hurried through that constant verdant twilight, walking
as long as her legs held out before she stopped to eat
and sleep.

Late afternoon on the seventh day she stopped walking and listened, finding it difficult to believe her ears.
Threading through the soughing of the leaves and the
guttural creaks from the huge limbs she heard a steady
plink plink plink. It got gradually louder, turned into
the familiar dance of a smith's hammer. The ground
underfoot got rockier, the trees were smaller, aspen and
birch and myrtle mixed with the oak and the sunlight
made lacy patterns on the earth and in the air around
her. Even her cold seemed to relent.

She came out of the trees and stood looking down
into a broad ravine with a small stream wandering along
the bottom. It was an old cut, the sides had a gentle
slope with thick short grass like green fur. The sound
of the hammering came from farther uphill, around a
slight bend and behind some young trees.

She walked around the trees, moving silently more
from habit than because she felt it necessary. He had
his back to her, working over something on an anvil set
on an oak base. It was an openair forge, small and convenient in everything but location. Why was he out here

alone? His folk might be around the next curve of the mountain, but she didn't think so, there'd be some sign of them, dogs barking, cattle noises, she knew the Finger Vale folk had cattle, shouts of children, a thousand other sounds. None of that. He wore a brief leather loincloth, a thong about his head to keep thick, dark blond hair out of his eyes, and a heavy leather apron, nothing more. She watched the play of muscles in his back and buttocks, smiled ruefully and touched her hair. You must look like one of the Furies halfway long a vengeance trail. She touched her arms, the knives were in place, loose enough to come away quickly but not loose enough to fall out; she unbuttoned her cuffs and turned them back, a smith was generally an honest man not overly given to rape, but she'd lost her trusting nature a long way back and the circumstances were odd. A last breath, then she walked around where he could see her.

He let the hammer fall a last time on the object he was shaping (it seemed to be a large intricate link for the heavy chain that coiled at his feet) and stood staring at her, gray green eyes widening with surprise. "Tissu, anash? Opop'erkrisi? Ti'bouleshi?" He had a deep musical voice, even though she didn't understand a word, the sound of it gave her a pleasurable shiver.

"I don't understand," she said. "Do you speak the kevrynyel?"

"Ah." He made a swift secret warding sign and brushed the link off the anvil to get it away from her prying eyes. "Trade gabble," he said. "Some. I say this, who you, where you come from, what you wish?"

"A traveler," she said. "Off a ship heading past your coast. Its captain saw a way of squeezing more coin out of me; after a bit of rape he was going to sell me the next port he hit. I had a guard, but the lout got drunk and let them cut his throat. Not being overenchanted by either of the captain's intentions, I went overside and swam ashore. Aaahmmm, what I want . . . A meal of something more than raw fish, a hot bath, no, several baths, clean clothing, a bed to sleep in, alone if you don't mind my saying it, and a chance to earn my keep a while. I do some small magics, my father was a scholar of the Rukha Nagg. Mostly I make music. I had

a daroud, the captain has that now, but I can make do
with most anything that has strings. I know the Rukha
dance tunes and the songs of many peoples. If there's
the desire, I can teach these to your singers and music
makers. I cannot sew or embroider, spin or weave, my
mother died before she could teach me such things and
my father forgot he should. And, to be honest, I never
reminded him. There anything more you want to
know?''

"Only your name, anash."

"Ah, your forgiveness, I am Harra of the Hazani,
daughter of the Magus Tahno Hazzain. I see you are a
smith, I don't know the customs here, would it be dis-
courteous to ask a name of you, O Nev?"

"For a gift, a gift. Simor a Piyolss of Owlyn Vale.
If you would wait a breath or two beyond the trees there,
I'll take you to my mother."

And so Simor the Smith, priest of the Chained God,
took the stranger woman to the house of Piyoloss and
when the harvest was in and the first snow on the
ground, he married her. At first the Vale folk were dis-
mayed, but she sang for them and saved more than one
of them from the King's levy with her small magics
which weren't quite as small as she'd admitted to and
after her first son was born most constraints vanished.
She had seven sons and a single daughter. She taught
them all that she had learned, but it was the daughter
who learned the most from her. Her daughter married
into the Faraziloss and her daughter's daughters (she
had three) into the Kalathim, the Xoshallar, the Bach-
arikoss. She heard the story of Brann and her search,
she received the medal, the sealing wax and the parchment, she had the box made and passed it with the
promise to the liveliest of her granddaughters, a Xosh-
allarin. As she passed something else. Simor who could
read the heart of mountains found a flawless crystal as
big as his two fists and brought it to his cousin, a stone-
worker, who cut a sphere from it and burnished it until
it was clear as the heart of water; he gave this to Harra
as a gift on the birth of their daughter. She knew how
to look into it and see to the ends of the world and

taught her daughter how to look. It is not difficult she said, merely find a stillness in yourself and out of the stillness take will. If the gift of seeing is yours, and since you have my blood in you, most likely it is, then you can call what you need to see.

To find the crystal, daughter of Harra, go to the secret cavern in the ravine where Simor first met Harra, the place where the things of the Chained God are kept safe. Find in yourself the stillness and out of the stillness take will, then you will see where you should send the medal.

In the morning Kori went before the Women of Piyoloss. "The Servant of Amortis has been watching me. I am afraid."

The Women looked at each other, sighed. After a long moment, AuntNurse said, "We have seen it." She eyed Kori with a skepticism born of long experience. "You have a suggestion?"

"My brother Trago goes soon to take his turn with the herds in the high meadows, let me go with him instead of Kassery. The Servant and his acolytes don't go there, the soldiers don't go there, if I could stay up there until the Lot time, I would be out of his way and once it was Lot time, I'd be going down with the rest to face the Lot and after that, if the Lot passed me, it wouldn't be long before it was time for my betrothing and then even he wouldn't dare put his hands on me. I tell you this, if he does put his hands on me, I will kill myself on his doorstep and my ghost will make his days a misery and his nights a horror. I swear it by the ghost of my mother and the Chains of the God."

AuntNurse seached Kori's face, then nodded. "You would do it. Hmm. There are things I wonder about you, young Kori." She smiled. "I'm not accustomed to hearing something close to wisdom coming out your mouth. Yes. It might be your ancestor, you know which I mean, speaking to us, her cunning, her hot spirit. I wonder what you really want, but no, I won't ask you, I'll only say, take care what you do, you'll answer for it be you ghost or flesh." She turned to the Women. "I say send Kori to the meadows with Trago, send them tomorrow, what say you?''

"So I told the Women that that snake Bak'hve had the hots for me, well it's true, Tré, he's been following me about with his tongue hanging down to his knees, and I told them I was scared of him, which I was maybe a little, yechh, he makes the hair stand up all over me and if he touched me, I'd throw up all over him. Anyway, they already knew it and I suppose they'd been thinking what to do. Unnh, I wasn't fooling AuntNurse, not much, chain it. She just about told me she knew I was up to something. Doesn't matter, they let me go, almost had to, what I said made sense and they knew it.'' Kori flung her arms out and capered on the path, exulting in her temporary freedom from the constraints closing in on her since she'd started her menses.

Trago made a face at her, did some skipping himself as the packpony he was leading whuffled and lipped at the fine blond hair the dawnwind was blowing into a fluff about his face. "So," he said, raising his voice to get her attention, "when are you going to tell me that great idea of yours?''

She sobered and came back to walk beside him. "I didn't want to say anything down there, you never know who's listening and has got to tell everything, what goes in the ear comes out their mouth with no stop between.''

"So?''

Speaking in a rapid murmur, so softly Trago had to lean close and listen hard, Kori told him about Harra's Gift and the not-dream she had under the great oak. "Owlyn Vale can't fight Settsimaksimin, we've got the dead to prove it. Chained God can't fight him either, not straight out, or he'd 've done it when they burned Zilos. Maybe he can sneak a little nip in, maybe that's what he was doing when he picked you for his priest and made that oaksprite give me a dream. 'Cause I think he did, I think he wants the Drinker of Souls here. I think he thinks she can do something, I don't know what, that will turn things around. So I had to get loose, otherwise how could I get to the cave without making such a noise everything would get messed up? And I thought I'd better be with you, Tré, since if you don't know where the cave is, Zilos will come and tell you about it like the oaksprite did me. She said it's in the ravine where Simor met Harra, but who knows where that is? Only the priest and that's Zilos. He'll have to come to you again, like he did last night. Maybe tonight even. Drinker of Souls could be anywhere, the sooner we get the medal to her, the sooner she could start for here.''

Tré sniffed. ''If she comes.''

''It's better'n doing nothing.''

''Maybe.'' After a moment he reached over and took her hand, something he usually wouldn't do. ''I'm scared, Kori.''

She squeezed his hand, sighed. ''Me too, Tré.''

The packpony plodding along behind them, and then nosing into them as they slackened their pace, they climbed in silence, nothing to say, everything had been said and it hung like fog about them.

They reached Far Meadow a little after noon, a bright still day, bearable in shadow, but ovenhot in the sunlight. The leggy brown cows lay about the rim of the meadow wherever there was a hint of shade, tails switching idly, jaws moving like blunt soft silent metronomes, ears flicking now and then to drive off the black flies that summer produced out of nothing as if they were the offspring of sun and air. A stream cut across the meadow, glittering with heat until it slid into shadow beneath the trees and widened into a shady pool where Veraddin and Poti were splashing without much energy, like the cows passing the worst of the heat doing the least possible.

''Loooohaaa, Vraaad.'' Trago wrinkled up his face, squinted his eyes, shielding them from the sun with his free hand; when the two youths yelled and waved to him, he tossed the pony's halter rope to Kori and went trotting across to them. Kori sighed and led the beast up the slope toward the cabin and cheesehouse tucked up under the trees, partially dug into the mountainside, a corral beside it, empty now, a three-sided milking barn, a flume from the stream that fed water into a cistern above the house then into a trough at the corral. When Trago's yell announced their arrival, a large solid woman (the widow Chittar Piyolss y Bacharz, the Piyoloss Cheesemaker) came from inside the cheesehouse and stood on the steps, a white cloth crumpled in her left hand. She watched a moment as Kori climbed toward her, swabbed the cloth across her broad face, stumped down the steps and along to the corral, swinging the gate open as Kori reached her.

"You're two days early." Chittar had a rough whispery voice that sounded rusty from disuse. She followed Kori into the corral, tucked the cloth into the waistband of her skirt and helped unload the packs from the saddle and strip the gear off the placid pony; as soon as he was free, he ambled to the trough and plunged his nose into the water. "You take that into the house." She waved a hand at the gear. "I'll see this creature doesn't founder himself. And if that clutch of boys isn't up to help you in another minute, I'll go after their miserable hides with a punkthorn switch."

Kori grinned at her. "I hear, xera Chittar. Um, we are early and it's me because AuntNurse thought I should get away from the Servant of Amortis who looked like he was entertaining some unfortunate ideas."

"That's the politest way I every heard that put. Panting was he, old goat, no—I insult a noble beast, by comparison anyway." Chittar wrapped powerful fingers about the cheekstrap of the halter and pulled the pony away from the water. "I see the truants are coming this way; you get into the house right now, girl, those ijjits have about a clout and a half between them and that's no sight for virgin eyes."

The first night Kori slept on a pallet in Chittar's room while Trago shared Poti's bed (he was the smaller of the two boys). Whatever dreams either may have had, they remembered none. In the morning, as soon as the cows were milked and turned out to graze, Veraddin and Poti left, warned not to say anything to anyone about Kori until they talked with the Women of Piyoloss. Chittar

went back to the cheesehouse, leaving Kori and Trago
with a list of things to do about the house and instructions to choose separate rooms for their bedrooms, get
them cleaned up and neat enough to pass inspection, to
get everything done before noon and come join her so
she could show them what they were going to do until
they could get on with their proper chores. Since neither
of them had the least idea how to do the milking, she
was going to have to take that over until they learned,
which meant they'd have to do some of her work, like
churning butter and spading curd, the simpler things
that needed muscle more than skill or intelligence. Ah
no, she said to them, you thought you were going to
laze about watching cows graze? not a hope, l'il ijjits,
I'm working your tails off like I do to all the dreamers
coming up here.

By nightfall they knew the truth of that. Kori fell into
bed, but had a hard time sleeping, her arms felt as if
someone heavy was pulling, pulling, pulling without
letup; they ached, not terribly sore, just terribly uncomfortable; she'd done most of the churning. Eventually
she slept and again had no dreams she could remember.
She woke, bone sore and close to tears from frustration.
At breakfast she looked at Trago, ground her teeth when
he shook his head.

A week passed. They were doing about half the milking now and had settled into routine so the housekeep-
ing chores were quickly done and the work in the
cheesehouse was considerably easier. Sore muscles had
recovered, they'd found the proper rhythm to the tasks
and Chittar was pleased with them.

On the seventh night, Zilos came to Trago, told him
where to find the cave and what to do with the things
he found there.

The hole they were crawling through widened suddenly into a room larger than Owlyn's threshing floor.
Kori lifted the lamp high and stared wide-eyed at the
glimmering splendor. Chains hung in graceful curves,
one end bolted to a ceiling so high it was lost in the
darkness beyond the reach of the lamp, the other end to
the wall. Chains crossing and recrossing the space,

chains of iron forged on the smithpriest's anvil and hung
in here so long ago all but the lowest links were coated
with stone, chains of wood fashioned by the woodwork-
erpriest's knives, chains of crystal and saltmarble chis-
eled by the stonecutterpriest's tools, centuries of labor
given to the cave, taken by the cave to itself. The cold
was piercing, the damp crept into her bones as she
stared, but it was beautiful and it was awesome.

In the center of the chamber a square platform of
polished wood sat on stone blocks a foot off the stone
floor, above it, held up by intricately carved wooden
posts, a canopy of white jade, thin and translucent as
the finest porcelain, in the center of the platform a chest
made from kedron wood without any carving on it, the
elegant shape and the wonderful gloss of the wood all
the ornament it needed. ''I suppose that's it,'' she said.
She shivered as her voice broke the silence; it was such
a little sound, like a mosquito's whine and made her
feel small and fragile as a mosquito, as if a mighty hand
might slap down any moment and wipe her away. She
set the lamp on the floor and waited.

Trago glanced at her, but said nothing. After a moment's hesitation he moved cautiously across the uneven
floor, jumped up onto the platform. Uncertain of the
properties involved, Kori didn't follow him; she waited
on the chamber floor, leaning against one of the corner
posts, watching as he chewed on his lip and frowned at
the polished platform with its intricate inlaid design. He
looked over his shoulder. ''You think I ought to take off
my sandals?''

She spread her hands. ''You know more than me
about that.''

Nothing happened, so he walked cautiously to the
chest. He turned the lid back, froze, seemed to stop
breathing, still, statue still, inert as the stone around
him. Kori gasped, started to go to him, but something
slippery as oiled glass pushed her back, wouldn't let her
onto the platform. She clawed at the thing, screamed,
''Tré, what is it, Tré, say something, Tré, let him go,
you . . . you . . . you. . . .''

Trago stirred, make a small catching sound as if his
throat unlocked and he could breathe again. Kori shud-

dered, then leaned against the post and rubbed at her throat, reassured but still barred from the platform. He knelt before the chest and began taking things out of it, setting them beside his knees, things that blurred so she couldn't tell what they were, though she knew the crystal when he held it up; he brought it over to her, reached through the barrier and gave it to her, solemn, silent, his face blurred too (the look of it frightened her). Seeming to understand her unease, he gave her a smoky smile, then he returned to the chest, seemed to put something around his neck, (for Kori, impression of a chain with a smoky oval hanging from it) and he seemed to put something in his pocket (a fleeting impression of a short needleblade and an ebony hilt with a red crystal set into it, an even more evanescent impression of something held behind it). He returned the other things to the chest and shut the lid.

Abruptly the barrier was gone. Kori stepped back, clutching the crystal against her stomach, holding it with both hands. Trago sat on the chest and kicked his heels against it. "Come on, Kori, it's not so damp up here. Or cold. And bring the lamp."

Kori looked down at the crystal, then over her shoulder at the lamp. She wasn't happy about that chest, but this was Tré's place now; she was an intruder, but he belonged here. Holding the sphere against her with one hand, she carried the lamp to the platform, hesitated a breath or two, long enough to make Tré frown at her, managed to step up on the platform without dropping either the lamp or the crystal sphere. "You sure this is all right, Tré?"

He nodded, grinned at her. "It isn't all bad, Kori, this being a priest I mean. Anything I want to do in here, I can. Um . . ." He lost his grin. "I hope it doesn't take long, we got to get back before xera Chittar knows we left."

"I know. Take this." When he had the lamp, she settled to the platform, sitting cross-legged with her back to the chest. She rubbed the crystal sphere on her shirt, held it cupped into her hands. "Find the stillness," she said aloud, "draw will out of stillness, then look." She closed her eyes and tried to chase everything

from her mind; a few breaths later she knew that wasn't
going to work, but there was a thing AuntNurse taught
her to do whenever her body and mind wouldn't turn off
and let her sleep; she was to find a Place and began
building an image of it in her mind, detail by detail,
texture, odor, color, movement. When she was about
five, she found a safe hide and went there when she was
escaping punishment or was angry at someone or hurt
or feeling wretched, she went there when her mother
died, she went there when one of her small cousins
choked on a bone and died in her arms, she went there
whenever she needed to think. It was halfway up the
ancient oak in a crotch where three great limbs separated from the trunk. She lined the hollow there with
dead leaves and thistle fluff, making a nest like a bird
did. It was warm and hidden, nothing bad could ever
happen to her there, she could feel the great limbs moving slowly, ponderously beneath and around her like
arms rocking her, she could smell the pungent dark
friendly odor of the leaves and the bark, the stiff dark
green leaves still on their stems whispered around her
until she felt she almost understood what the tree said.
Now she built that Place around her, built it with all the
intensity she was capable of, shutting out fear and un-
certainty and need, until she rocked in the arms of the
tree, sat in the arms of the tree cuddling a fragment of
moonlight in her arms. She gazed into the sphere, into
the silver heart of it and drew will out of stillness.
"Drinker of Souls," she whispered to the sphere, in
her voice the murmur of oak leaves, "Show her to me.
Where is she?"

An image bloomed in the silver heart. An old woman,
white hair twisted into a heavy straggly knot on top her
head. Her sleeves were rolled up, showing pale heavy
forearms. She was chopping wood, with neat powerful
swings of the ax, every stroke counting, every stroke
going precisely where she wanted, long long years of
working like that evident in the economy of her movements. She set the ax aside, gathered lengths of wood
into a bundle and carried them to a mounded kiln. She
pulled the stoking doors open, fed in the wood, brought
more bundles of wood, working around the kiln until

she had resupplied all the doors. Then she went back
to chopping wood. A voice spoke in Kori's head, a male
voice, a light tenor with a hint of laughter in it that she
didn't understand; she didn't know the voice but suspected it was the Chained God or one of his messengers. *Brann of Arth Slya,* it said, *Drinker of Souls
and potter of note. Ask in Jade Halimm about the Potter
of Shaynamoshu. Send her half the medal. Keep the
other half yourself and match the two when you meet.
Take care how you talk about the Drinker of Souls away
from this place. One whose name I won't mention stirs
in his sleep and wakes, knowing something is happening here, that someone is working against him. Even
now he casts his ariel surrogates this way. If you have
occasion to say anything dangerous, stay close to an
oak, the sprites will drive his ariels away. Fare well and
wisely, young Kori; you work alone, there's no one can
help you but you.*

Kori stared into the crystal a few moments longer,
vaguely disappointed in the look of the hero who was
supposed to defeat the mighty Settsimaksimin when all
the forces of the King could not, nor could the priests
and fighters of the Vales. Brann was strong and vital,
but she was old. A fat old woman who made pots. Kori
sighed and rocked herself loose from Her Place. She
looked up at Trago. "Did you get any of that?"

Trago leaned toward her, hands on knees. "I heard
the words. What's she like?"

"Not like I expected. She's old and fat."

He kicked his heels against the chest, clucked his
tongue. "Doesn't sound like much. What does it mean,
Drinker of Souls?"

"I don't know. Tré, you want to go on with this? You
heard the Voice, HE's sticking his fingers in, if HE
catches us . . . well."

Trago shrugged. His eyes were frightened and his
hands tightened into fists, but he was pretending he
didn't care. "Do I don't I, what's it matter? You said
it, Kori. Better'n nothing."

"I hear you." She moved her shoulders, straightened
her legs out. "Oooh, I'm tired. Let's finish this." She
pulled the medal from around her neck, dropped it on

the platform. "Think you could cut this in half like the Voice said?"

"Uh huh. Who we going to give it to?"

"I thought about that before I went to see the Women of Piyoloss and wangled my way up here." She rubbed at her stomach, ran her hand over the crystal. "Moon Meadow's down a little and around the belly of the mountain. The Kalathi twins and Hervé are summering there with a herd of silkgoats. And Toma."

"Ha! I thought the soldiers got him."

"Most everybody did. I did." Kori pulled her braids to the front and smoothed her hands along them, smoothed them again, then began playing with the tassels. "Women talk," she said. "It was my turn helping in the washhouse. They put me to boiling the sheets; I expect they forgot I was there, because they started talking about Ruba the whore, you know, the Phrasin who lives in that hutch up the mountain behind House Kalath that no one will talk about in front of the kids. Seems she was entertaining one of the soldiers, he was someone fairly important who knew what was going on and he let slip that they were going to burn the priest next morning and throw anyone who made a fuss into the fire with him. Well, she's Vale folk now all the way, so she pushed him out after a while and went round to the Women of Kalathin and told them. What I heard was the Women tried to get Zilos away, but the soldiers had hauled him off already. Amely was having fits and the kids were yelling and Toma was trying to hold things together and planning on taking Zilos' hunting bow and plinking every soldier he could get sight of. What they did was, they took Amely and the young ones away from the Priest-House and got Ontari out of the stable where he was sleeping and had him take them over to Semela Vale since he knows tracks no one else does. And they gave Toma sleeproot in a posset they heated for him and tied him over a pony and Pellix took him up to Moon Meadow and told the Twins to keep him away from the Floor. They said he's supposed to've calmed down some, but he's fidgety. He knows if he goes down he gets a lot of folk killed, so he stays there, hating a lot. What I figure is, if we tell him about this, it's something he can do when it's just him could get killed and if it works, he's going to make you know who really unhappy. So. What do you think?''

Trago rubbed his eyes, his lids were starting to hang heavy. "Toma," he muttered. "I don't know. He . . ." His eyes glazed over, his head jerked. "Toma," he said, "yes." He blinked. "Aaah, Kori, let's get this finished. I want to go to bed."

"Me too." She got stiffly to her feet, sleep washing in waves over her. "Put this away, will you." She held out the crystal sphere. "Um . . . We're going to need gold for Toma, is there any of that in there? And you have to cut the medal before we go. I don't want to come here again, besides, we already lost a week."

Trago slid off the chest and stood rubbing his eyes. He yawned and took the sphere. "All right." He blinked at the medal lying by his foot. "You better go back where you were before. I think the god's going to be doing this."

" 'Lo, Hervé."

" 'Lo, Tré, what you doin' here?"

" 'S my time at Far Meadow. Toma around?"

"Shearin' shed, got dry rot in the floor, he was workin' on that the last time I saw him."

Trago nodded and went around the house, climbed the corral fence and walked the top rail; when he reached the shed, he jumped down and went inside. Part of the floor was torn up. Toma had a plank on a pair of sawhorses; he was laying a measuring line along it. Trago stood watching, hands clasped behind him, as his cousin positioned a t-square and drew an awl along the straight edge, cutting a line into the wood; when he finished that, he looked up. "Tré. What you doing here?"

"Come to see you. I'm over to Far Meadow, doing my month, 'n I got something I need to say to you."

"So?" Toma reached for the saw, set it to the mark, then waited for Trago to speak.

"It's important, Toma."

Muscles moved in the older boy's face, his body tensed, then he got hold of himself and drove the saw down. He focused grimly on his hands and the wood for the next several minutes, sweat coursing down his face and arms, the rasping of the teeth against the wood drowning Trago's first attempts to argue with him. The effort he put into the sawing drained down his anger, turning it from hot seethe to a low simmer. When the cut was nearly through and the unsupported end was about to splinter loose, peeling off the edge of the plank as it fell, he straightened, drew his arm across his face, waved Trago round to hold up the end as he finished sawing it off. "Put it over by the wall," he told Trago. "I think it'll come close to fitting that short bit."

"Toma . . ." Trago saw his cousin's face shut again, sighed and moved off with his awkward load. When he came back, he swung up onto the plank before his cousin could lift it. "Listen to me," he said. "This isn't one of my fancies. I don't want to talk to you here. Please, stop for a little, you don't have to finish this today. I NEED to talk to you."

Toma opened his mouth, snapped it shut. He wheeled, walked over to stare down into the dark hole where he'd taken up the rotted boards. "If it's about *down there* . . ." His voice dripped vitriol when he said the last words, "I don't want to hear."

Trago looked nervously around; he knew about ariels, knew he couldn't see them unless they chanced to drift through a dusty sunbeam, but he couldn't help trying. He didn't want to say anything here, but if he kept fussing that would be almost as bad; AuntNurse always knew when he was making noise to hide something, he suspected the Sorceror was as knowing as her if not worse. He slid off the plank, trotted to Toma, took him by the hand and tugged him toward the door.

Toma pulled free, stood looking tired and unhappy, finally he nodded. "I'll come, Tré. And I'll listen. Five minutes. If you don't convince me by then, you're going to hurt for it."

Trago managed a grin. "Come on then."

He led his cousin away from the meadow into the heart of an oak grove.

Kori stepped from behind a tree. " 'Lo, Toma."

"Kori?" Toma stepped back, scowled from one to the other. "What's going on here?"

"Show him your shoulder, Tré."

Trago unlaced the neck opening of his shirt, pushed it back so Toma could see the hollow starburst.

Kori dropped onto a root as Toma bent, touched the mark. "Sit down, cousin. We've got a lot of talking to do."

". . . so, that's what we want you to do." She touched the packet resting on her thigh. "Take this to the Drinker of Souls and remind her of her promise. It'll be dangerous. HE'll be looking for anyone acting different. Voice told us HE's got his ariels out, that's why Tré didn't want to say much in the shed, he wanted to be where oaksprites were because they don't like ariels much and chase them whenever they come around. Um, Tré got gold from the Chained God's Place because we knew you'd need it. Um, We'd kinda like you to go as fast as you could, Tré's got less'n three months before the Signs start popping up. Will you do it?"

Toma rubbed his face with both hands, his breathing hoarse and unsteady. Without speaking, he rested his forearms on his thighs and let his hands dangle as he stared at the ground. Kori watched him, worried. She'd written the message on the parchment, folded it around half the medal, used sewing thread to tie it shut and smeared slathers of sealing wax over it, then she'd knotted a bag about it and made a neck cord for it out of the same thread, and she had the gold in a pouch tied to her belt. Everything was ready, all they needed was Toma. She watched, trying to decide what he was thinking. If she'd been a few years older, if she'd been a boy, with all the things boys were taught that she'd never had a chance to learn, she wouldn't be sitting here waiting for Toma to make up his mind. She moved her hands impatiently, but said nothing. Either he went or he didn't and if he went, best it was his own doing so he'd put his heart in it.

A shudder shook him head to toe, he sighed, lifted his head. His eyes had a glassy animal sheen, he was still looking inward, seeing only the images in his head.

He blinked, began to cry, silently, without effort, the tears spilling down his face. "I . . ." he cleared his throat, "You don't know . . . Yes, I'll go. Yes." He rolled a sleeve down, scrubbed it across his face, blew his nose into his fingers, wiped them on his pants. "Was Ontari down below? I'll go for Forkker Vale first, see if I can get on with a smuggler. He knows them." He tried a grin and when it worked, laughed with excitement and pleasure. "I don't want to end up like Harra did."

Kori looked at Trago. Trago nodded. "I was talking to him the day before we come up here. He was working on a saddle, he won't be going anywhere 'fore he finishes that."

Toma nodded. "I'll go down tonight. He still sleeping in Kalathin's stable?"

"Uh huh. There's usually a couple soldiers riding the House Round, but they aren't too hard to avoid, more often than not they're drunk, at least that's what Ontari said."

"Wouldn't be you were flitting about when you shouldn't?"

Trago giggled and didn't bother denying it.

Kori got to her feet. "We have to be back in time to milk the cows or xera Chittar will skin us. Here." She tossed the packet to Toma, began untying the gold pouch. "Be careful, cousin." She held out the pouch. "Oaks are safe, I don't know what else, maybe you can sneak out, I'm afraid . . ."

He laughed and hugged her hard, took the pouch, hugged Trago. "You get back to your cows, cousins. I'll see you when."

". . . Crimpa, Sparrow, White Eye. Chain it, Tré, Two Spot has run off again. You see any sign of her?"

Trago snorted, capered in a circle. "Un . . . huh! Un . . . huh! Slippy Two Spot. Lemme see . . ." He trotted off.

"Mmf." Kori tapped Crimpa cow with her switch and started her moving toward the corral; the others fell in around her and plodded placidly across the grass as if they'd never ever had a contrary thought between their horns. A whoop behind her, an indignant mmmooo-aaauhh. Two Spot came running from under the trees, head jerking, udder swinging; she slowed, trotted with stiff dignity over to the herd and pushed into the middle of it. Trago came up beside Kori, walked along with her. "She was just wandering around. I don't know what she thought she was doing." He yawned extravagantly, rubbed at his eyes, started whistling. He broke off when they reached the corral, slanted a glance up at her. "So we wait."

"So we wait."

3

ANOTHER MEADOW,
THE SHAYNAMOSHU POTTERY
ON THE RIVER WANSHEERI,
AT THE MASSACRE.

SCENE: Late. The Wounded Moon a fat broken
crescent rising in the east. A horse streaked
with dried foam, trying to graze, having difficulty with the bit. A black-clad youth dead
in a pool of blood. Another figure, a
woman, crumpled across him. A pale translucent wraithlike figure lying upon her, a
second squatting beside them.

An icy wind touched her neck.
  Something heavy, metallic slammed into her back.
  Cold fire flashed up through her.
  *Heavy breathing, broken in the middle. Faint popping
sound.*
  *Her knees folded under her, she saw herself toppling
toward the boy's body, saw the hilt of the knife in his
back, saw an exploding flower of blood, saw nothing
more.*

A light weight on her, fire burning in her, pain . . .
  "Wake up, Brann. Come on. Yaril needs you, she's
fading." Jaril's voice, urgent, pleading.
  She blinked, her eyes felt grainy, sore. She fumbled
about futilely for a minute, found purchase for her
hands, managed to straighten her arms. They trembled.

She was horribly weak, it frightened her how weak she was. The frail weight slid off and Yaril rolled over twice, lay face down on the grass beside the rutted dirt road, very pale, almost transparent. Jaril was colorless too, though he had more substance to him. Brann looked down at herself. She'd lost almost all her flesh, her skin was hanging on her bones. Her hands were shaking and she felt an all-over nausea; chills ran through her body. "What . . ."

Jaril clicked his tongue impatiently. "No time for that. There's the horse, Brann, feed us before we go to stone, Yaril's hanging on a thread. The horse. You can reach it, come on, stand up, I can't carry you. Hurry, I don't know how long. . . ."

Trembling and uncertain, Brann hoisted herself onto her feet. Stiff with blood, feces and urine, too big for her now, her skirt fell off her, nearly tripped her; grunting with disgust she dragged her feet free, tottered down to the grazing horse. He started to shy away, but froze when her hand brushed against his flank. She edged closer, set her other hand on his back by the spine, hating what she was doing since she was fond of horses, but she was a lot fonder of the children so she drew the horse's cool life into herself, easing down beside him as he collapsed, sucking out the last trickle of energy.

Jaril drifted over, dropped to his knees beside her. "We brought some tahargoats," he said. "They're around somewhere, when we saw you down like that we forgot about them. I'll chase them over in a while. Horse won't be enough." He leaned against her, fragile and weightless as a dessicated leaf.

Brann straightened, twisted around, touched the tips of her fingers to his face, let him draw energy from her. Color flowed across him, pastel pinks and ivories and golds, ash gray spread through his wispy shirt and trousers, from transparent he turned translucent. He made a faint humming sound filled with pleasure, grinned his delight. Brann smiled too, got to her feet. "Get your goats," she said and started walking heavily up the grassy rise, heading for the road and Yaril. Jaril shifted to his mastiff form, went off to round up the goats.

Yaril lay on the grass, a frail girlchild sculpted in

glass, naked (she hadn't bothered to form clothing out
of her substance though she clung to the bipedal form
and hadn't retreated to the glimmersphere that was her
baseshape, Brann didn't know why, the children didn't
talk all that much about themselves) and vulnerable,
flickering and fading. Frowning, worried, Brann knelt
beside her, stretched out hands that looked grossly vig-
orous in spite of the skin hanging in folds about the
bone, and rested them gently on a body that was more
smoke than flesh, letting the remnant of the horse's energy trickle into it.

The changechild's substance thickened and her color
began returning, at first more guessed at than seen like
inks thinned with much water, but gradually stronger as
Brann continued to feed energy into her. When a dog
barked and goats blatted, Yaril's eyes opened. She
blinked, slow deliberate movements of her eyelids,
managed a faint smile.

Jaril-Mastiff herded the goats over to her. Brann fed
their energy to him and Yaril until they lost their frailty,
then used the last of it to readjust herself, rebuilding
some of the muscle, tightening her skin, shedding the
appearance of age until her body was much what it had
been when she and Harra Hazani had played Slya's
games so long ago. The changechildren had grown her
from eleven to her mid-twenties over a single night back
then and all her hair fell out. Remembering that, she
shook her head vigorously; most of her hair flew off;
she wiped away the rest of it. Bald as an egg. She
rubbed her hand over skin smooth as polished marble.
Ah well, maybe it'll grow back as fast this time as it
did that. She looked down at the dead boy, stooped,
grunting with the effort and took the knife from his
body, straightened with another grunt, held it up. A
strange knife, might have been made of ice from the
look of it. As she turned it over, examining it in the
dim light from the moon, it melted into air. She whistled with surprise.

Jaril nodded. "The one that was in you did the same
thing."

Brann laughed, wiped her hand on her blouse. "They
weren't souvenirs I wanted to keep." She started for

the house. "Shuh, I need a bath." A sniff and a grimace. "Several baths. And I'm hollow enough to eat those goats raw what's left of them." Another laugh. "I didn't know how hungry it makes you—dying, I mean. It's not every day I die."

"You weren't actually dead," Jaril said seriously. "If you were dead, we couldn't bring you back."

"Was a joke, Jay."

He made a face. "Not much of a joke for us, Bramble. Starving to death is no fun."

"You made me, you could find someone else and change them."

"We made you with a lot of help from Slya, Brann, we didn't do it on our own. I doubt she'd bother another time."

"Mmm. Well, I'm not dead and you're not going to starve. Uh . . ." She clutched at herself, started to turn back.

Yaril caught her arm, stopped her. "This what you want?" She held out a small bloodstained packet. "I found it lying beside me. You think it's important?"

"Seems to me this is what got the boy killed and me . . ." she smiled at Jaril, ". . . nearly." She closed her fingers about the packet. "It stinks of magic, kids. Makes me nervous. Somebody called up tigermen and whipped them here to make sure I didn't open it. I don't like mixing with sorcerors and such."

"Who?"

Brann tossed the packet up, caught it, weighed it thoughtfully. "Heavy. Hmm. No doubt the answer's in here. While I'm stoking up the fire under the bathtub and scrubbing off my stink, the two of you might take a look at this thing." She held out the packet and Yaril took it. "And I wouldn't mind if you fixed me a bit of dinner."

Jaril chuckled. "Return the favor, hmm?"

After scrubbing off the worst of her body's reaction to its own violent death, cold water making her shiver, and adding more wood to the fire under the brick tub, Brann climbed to the attic and pulled the gummed paper off the chest that held her old clothes. When she stopped wandering nearly a century ago and moved into the shed behind the house, she had to bow to Dayan Acsic's prejudices and pack her trousers away. She was a woman. Women in Jade Torat wore skirts. His one concession was this chest. When she came back with the proper clothing, he let her put her shirts and trousers and the rest of her gear in the chest, gave her aromatics to keep moths and other nuisances away and gummed paper to seal the cracks, then he shouldered the chest and carried it to the attic, tough old root of a man, and that was that.

She turned back the lid, wrinkled her nose at the smell; it was powerful and peculiar. She excavated a shirt and a pair of trousers, then some underclothing. The blouse was yellowed and weakened by age, the black of the trousers had the greenish patina of decades of mildew. "Ah well, they only need to cover me till I reach Jade Halimm." She hung the clothing in the window so it would air out and with a little luck lose some of the smell, retied the sash to her robe and climbed back down.

The water was hot. She raked out the firebox, tipped the coals, ash and unburned wood into an iron brazier and climbed into the water.

When she padded into the kitchen, sleepy, filled with well-being, the changechildren had salad and rice and goat stew ready for her and a pot of tea steaming on the stand. Jaril had dug out Brann's bottle of plum brandy; he and Yaril were sitting on stools and sipping at the rich golden liquid. The parchment was unfolded, sitting crumpled on the table, held down with a triangular bit of bronze.

Brann raised a brow, sat and began eating. Time passed. Warm odorous time. Finally she sighed, wiped her mouth, poured a bowl of tea and slumped back in her chair. "So. What's that about?" She smiled. "If you're sober enough to see straight."

Yaril patted a yawn with delicate grace; since she didn't breathe, the gesture was a touch sarcastic. She set her glass down, licked sticky fingers, brushed aside the chunk of metal and lifted the parchment. "First thing, these are Cheonea glyphs."

"Cheonea? Where's that? Never heard of it."

"A way west of here. A month by ship, if it's moderately fast. On the far side of Phras." Jaril sipped at the brandy. "Almost an island. Shaped like a hand with a thready wrist. We were there a year ago. Didn't stay long, one city the usual sort of seaport, farms and mountains and a smuggler's haven. Not very interesting. They kicked their king out a few decades back, from what I heard, he was no loss, but they got landed with a Sorceror who seems to think he's got the answer to the riddle of life." He reached for the bronze piece, tossed it to Brann. "Take a good look at that."

She caught it with her free hand. "Why not just tell me. . . ." She set the tea bowl down, began examining the triangle. Temueng script. On one side part of the Emperor's sigil, on the other part of a name. ". . . ra Hazani. The boy said something, um, let me remember . . . Harra . . . no, we the blood of Harra Hazani say to you, remember what you swore. This is half of one of those credeens the Maratullik struck off for Taguiloa and the rest of us. You remember those?"

Jaril grimaced. "We should."

Brann rubbed her thumb over the bronze. "I know." She'd had a choice then, Slya's sly malice set it for her, she could protect Taguiloa and the other players or send the changechildren home. She chose the players because they were the most vulnerable and accepted responsibility for keeping the children fed, though she hadn't really realized what that meant. Her own bronze credeen was around somewhere, likely at the bottom of the chest with the rest of her old clothes. "What's the letter say?"

Yaril lifted the parchment. "Took us a while to decipher it, we didn't pay that much attention to the written language when we were there. So, a lot of this is guess and twist till it seems to fit. We think it's a young girl writing, there are some squiggles after her name that might be determinatives expressing age and sex. She seems to be called Kori Piyolss of Owlyn Vale. She calls on the Drinker of Souls to remember her promise, that she'd come from the ends of the earth to help the Children of Harra. Harra married Kori's great great etc. grandfather and passed the promise on. Kori says she wouldn't use Harra's gift on anything unimportant, that you, Brann, must believe that. Someone close and dear to her faces a horrible death, everyone in the Vale lives in fear of He who sits in the Citadel of Silagamatys. That's the city Jaril was talking about, the only settlement in Cheonea big enough to call a city, a port on the south coast. She asks you to meet her there on the seventeenth day of Theriste. Mmm. That's thirty-seven days from now, no from yesterday, it's almost dawn, um, if I remember their dating system correctly. Meet her in a tavern called the Blue Seamaid. She'll be along after dark and she'll have the rest of the credeen. She can't write more about her plans in case this letter falls into the hands of Him. Got a heavy slash of ink under that *him*. You made the promise, Brann.'' She grinned. ''And very drunk out it was. You remember, the party Taguiloa threw for the whole quarter when we got back from Andurya Durat.'' She pushed ash blond hair off her face. ''Going to keep it?''

''Doesn't seem I have much choice. That sorceror, what's his name?''

''Settsimaksimin.''

''Right now he probably thinks I'm dead. That won't last long.'' She sipped at her tea, sighed. ''And there's another thing. I've put off thinking about it, but those tigermen cut through more than my flesh. I've stayed here about as long as I can. Much more and folk are going to start asking awkward questions about just what I am.'' She looked round the room, eyes lingering on surfaces and cooking things her hands had held, scrubbed, polished, shook, brushed against for the past hundred years; it was an extension of her body and leaving it behind would be like lopping off an arm.

Eyes laughing at her, Jaril said, ''You could turn into a local haunt, remember the old man on the mountain across the bay from Silili?''

''Hunh. And what would you be, Jay, a haunt's haunt?'' She smiled, shook her head. ''It might come to that, but I'm not ready for godhood yet, even demi-godhood.''

''What about this place?''

''Have to leave it, I suppose. Put the things I want to keep in the secret cellar you and Yaril burnt out for me, leave the rest to the wind and thieves.'' She yawned, finished her tea, rubbed her thumb against the bowl. It was part of the Das'n Vuor set that was one of the last things her father made before the Temuengs took him and the rest of Arth Slya to work in the pens of the Emperor. ''Mmmm. Either of you see a riverboat heading west when you flew in?''

''There was one leaving Gofajiu, you know what that means, it'll be here two or three days on. You really planning on flagging it?''

Brann's mouth twitched to a half smile. ''Yes no; Jay, I haven't made up my mind yet.'' She smoothed the teabowl along a wrist little more than bone and taut skin, half what it'd been a day ago. ''I don't look much like I did the past some years.'' Chuckle. ''Young. And bald. That's not the Potter. Couldn't be the Potter. On the other hand,'' she grimaced, ''that's the Potter's landing, what's she doing there, that woman, who is she, where's the Potter? Riverboat's comfortable and safe as you can get on the river, the two of you aren't up to much, me either.'' She set the bowl on the table and slumped in the chair gazing into the mirrorblack of the pot, her image distorted by the accidents of texture that gave the surface half its beauty. ''I don't know . . . I know I'd rather take the riverboat but. . . .'' She sighed. ''The river's low, the summer's been hot and dry, it's still a monster, I've never sailed the skiff that far, but. . . . Ah, Slya's teeth, I keep thinking, the Potter's dead, leave her dead, no loose ends like strange females hanging about. My father always said the hard way's the best way, it means you're thinking about what you're doing not just drifting with no idea where you're going.'' A long tired sigh. ''We'll forget the riverboat and take the clay skiff and hope old Tungjii's watching out for us.'' She sat up. ''I'm too tired to work and too itchy to sleep. Probably shouldn't have drunk that tea. Ah well, we can't leave tomorrow anyway, too much to

do.'' She yawned, then poured herself another bowl.
''So. Tell me more about Cheonea. When you were
there did you happen to visit Owlyn Vale?''

Brann slid into the harbor at Jade Halimm after sundown on the third day, threading through a torchlit maze
of floating life—flowerboats with their reigning courte-
sans and less expensive dancers, horizontal and otherwise, gambling boats, hawkers of every luxury and
perversion the foreign traders and seaman might desire, scaled to the size of their purses. The wealthier
passengers were left untroubled; they'd find their pleasures in more elegant surroundings ashore. The Jade
King's mosquito boats buzzed about to make sure these
last were not troubled by offers that might offend their
sensibilities. Too shabby to attract the attention of the
hawkers or the mosquito patrol, too busy managing the
skiff to notice much of this, Brann got through the water
throng without accident or incident and tied up at a
singhouse pier, the small old skiff lost among the other
boats. The tide was on the turn, beginning to come in,
but it was still a long climb to the pier, half of it on a
ladder slimy with seamoss and decaying weed and the
exudates of the lingam slugs that fed on them and the
weesha snails that lived in them. She wiped her hands
on her trousers when she reached dry wood, not appreciably worsening the mess they were already.

She stood on the edge of the pier looking down at the
boat, feeling gently melancholy. It was the last thing
left of her life as the Potter of Shaynamoshu. She stood
there, the harbor raucous about her, remembering . . .
a slant of light through autumn leaves, the sharp smell
of life ripened to the verge of decay, the last firing that
year, what year was it, no she couldn't place it now, it
was just a year, nothing but a collection of images and
smells and a deep abiding sense of joy that came she
didn't know why or from where, coming down the track
with the handcart loaded, the children playing in otter-
shape running and tumbling before her . . . another
time, the firing Tungjii blessed, texture moving in sacred dance over the surface, color within color, like an
opal but more restrained, subtle earth hues, and most

of all the feel of it, the weight and balance of it in the hollow of her hand when she almost knew the triumph her father felt when he took the last of the Das'n Vuor drinking bowls from the kiln on Tincreal and knew that three of them were perfect . . . another time after a snowfall when the earth was white and the sky was white and the silence whiter than both.

The onshore wind tugged at her sleeves, sent the ends of her headscarf whipping beside her ear. She thrust a finger under the scarf, felt the quarter inch of stubble. Growing fast, Slya bless. She settled the scarf more firmly, clicked her tongue with impatience as a horned owl swooped low over her head and screeched at her. "I know," she muttered, "I know. It's time to get settled."

She found a room in a run down tavern near the Westwall, a cubicle with a bed and not much else, blankets thin and greasy, bedbugs and fleas, a stink that was the work of decades, stain on stain on stain never insulted by the touch of soap; its only amenities were a stout bar on the door and a grill over the slit of a window, but these were worth the premium price she paid for sole occupancy. Her base established, she found a lateopen tailor and ordered new clothing, found one of her favorite cookshops and ate standing up, watching the life of the Harbor Quarter teem around her.

The next six days she prowled the night, in and out of houses, winding through back alleys, following the stench of corroded souls, killing until her own soul revolted, drinking the life of her victims, feeding the children, renewing her own vigor, drinking life until her flesh gave off a glow like moonlight. As the children edged in their slow way toward maturity, their capacity to store energy increased. Now they needed recharging only every second year, but it took many nights of hunting to fill their reserves. Back when Slya forced the choice on her she hadn't realized the full implications of her decision. She was, despite her appearance and the compressed experience of the past months, only twelve years old when that decision was made; she hadn't known how weary she could get of living (admittedly not every day, many of her days were contented, even joyful, but the dark times came more often as the decades passed), she hadn't known how crushing the burden of feeding the children would become, she hadn't known how much their appetite would increase, how many lives it would take to sate their hunger, how loathsome she would look to herself no matter how careful she was to choose badlives. Kings and mercenaries, counselors and generals, muggers, pimps and assassins, all such folk, they seemed able to live contentedly enough though they killed and maimed and tortured with exuberance and extravagance, but at the end of her bouts of gorging, she was so prostrated and self-disgusted that she wondered how she could bring herself to do it again; yet when the children were hungry once more, she found the will to hunt; they began as innocent victims of a god-battle they hadn't asked to join and finished as victims of her confusion and her preference for her own kind; to let them starve would be a greater wrong than all the killing lumped together.

On the seventh evening when her prowling was done for a while and her new clothes had been delivered, she moved from the tavern to a better room in a better Inn in a better neighborhood, close to the wall that circled the highmerchant's quarter, a four-story structure with a bathhouse and a pocket garden for eating in when the days were sunny and the evenings clear.

Brann gave a handful of coppers to the youth who carried her gear and showed her to the room she'd hired for the next three nights; she watched him out, then crossed to the single window and opened the shutters. "Hunh, not much of a view."

Jaril ambled over and leaned heavily against her. "Nice wall."

Yaril squeezed past them and put her head out as far as she could; she looked up and around, wriggled free and went to sit on the bed. "Should be bars on the windows. Bramble, our Host down there obviously didn't think much of you, putting you in this room. Should we leave the shutters open to catch a bit of air, anyone could get in here. The top of that wall is just about even with the top of the window and it's only six feet off, if that.''

Brann smiled. "Pity the poor thief who breaks in here." She left the window, prodded at the bed. "Better than the rack in that other place. My bones ache thinking about it. Uuuh, I'm tired. Too tired to eat. I think I'll skip supper and spend an hour or so in the bathhouse. Yaro, Jay, I'd appreciate it if one of you gave the mattress a runthrough before you bank your fires, make sure we've got no vermin sharing the room with us. I can't answer for my temper if I wake itching.''

Unlike Hina Baths, the House was divided, one side for women, the other for men and the division was rigidly maintained. The attendant on the women's side (a female wrestler who looked more than capable of thumping anyone, male or female, who tried to make trouble) didn't quite know what to make of Brann; she wasn't accustomed to persons claiming to be females who wore what she considered male attire. Half annoyed, half amused, too tired to argue, Brann snorted with disgust, stripped off her shirt and trousers. Demonstrably female, she strolled inside.

The water was steamy, herb scented, filled with small bubbles as it splashed into a sunken pool made of worn stones, gray with touches of amber and russet and chalky blue. Nubbly white towels were piled on a wicker table near the door into the chamber, there were hooks set into the wall for the patron's clothing, a shallow saucer of soap and a dish of scented oil sat beside the pool beneath a rail of smooth white porcelain, scrubbing cloths were draped over the rail. Brann hung up her shirt and trousers, dropped her underclothing beside the towels, tugged off her boots and put them on a bootstand beside the table. Stretching, yawning, the heat seeping into muscle and bone, she ambled to the pool and slid into water hot enough to make her bite on her lip and shudder with pleasure when she was immersed. She clung to the rail for a moment, then began swimming about, brushing through the uncurling leaves of the dried herbs the attendant had dropped into the water as she opened the taps that let it flow from the hot cis-

tern. She ducked her head under, shook it, feeling the
half-inch of new hair move against her skull. Surfacing,
she pulled herself onto the edge of the pool and began
soaping her legs, taking pleasure in her body for the
first time in years; she'd lived a deliberately muffled life
up on her mountain, centering her pleasures in her work
and the landscape around her; a longtime lover could
have learned too much about her, there was no one she
trusted that much, no one she wanted enough to chance
his revulsion when he learned what she was; even a
short-timer would have made too many complications.
Now, she was a skinful of energy, tingling with want,
and she didn't quite know what to do about it. Cultures
change in a hundred years; the changes might not be
large but they were enough to tangle her feet if she
didn't move with care. Laughing uncertainly as her nipples tautened and a dagger of pleasurable need stabbed
up from her groin, she pulled a scrub cloth across her
breasts, watched the scented lather slide over them, then
flung the cloth away and plunged into the pool, sub-
merging, sputtering up out of the water splashing herself vigorously to rinse away the remnants of the soap.
Later, as she stood rubbing herself dry, she began running through her plans for the next day. It was time she
began looking about for a ship to take her south. Better
not try for Cheonea from here, better to change ships
. . . she knew little about the powers of the limits of
sorcery, she hadn't a guess about how Setsimaksimin
had found her . . . she was reasonably sure he was her
enemy, she'd made enough others in her lifetime, though
most of them had to be dead by now, besides there was
the boy and the packet with its plea for her help . . . so
she didn't know if he could locate her again, but breaking one's backtrail was an elementary tactic when pur-
sued by man or some less deadly predator. Hmm. She'd
always had a thing for ship captains . . . she grinned,
toweled her head . . . maybe she could find herself another like Sammang or Chandro. . . .

The night was warm and pleasant, the garden between the bathhouse and the Inn was full of drifting
perfume and small paper lanterns dangling on long
strings; they swayed in the soft airs and made shadows

dance everywhere. On the far side of the vinetrellice that protected the privacy of bathers moving to and from the Inn she could hear unobtrusive cittern music and voices from the late diners eating out under the sky, enjoying the pleasant weather and the fine food Kheren Zanc's cook was famous for. She thought of going round and ordering a meal (more to enjoy the ambiance than because she was hungry) but did nothing about the thought, too tired to dredge up the energy needed to change direction. She drifted into the Inn, climbed two flights of stairs and tapped at the door to her room.

Not a sound. She waited. Nothing happened. She tried the latch, made a soft annoyed sound when the door opened.

The children were both in bed, sunk in their peculiar lethargy. As Brann stepped inside, one pale head lifted, dropped again. She relaxed. Trust Jaril to leave a fraction of himself alert so he wouldn't have to crawl out of bed and let her in. She stopped by the bed and ruffled his hair, but he didn't react, having sunk completely into stupor; she smiled, looked about for the key. It was on the bed table, gleaming darkly in the light coming through the unshuttered window. She locked the door, stripped and crawled into bed. A yawn, a wriggle, and she plunged fathoms deep in sleep.

A noise outside woke her from a restless, nightmare-ridden sleep. She pulled a quilt off the bed, wrapped it around her and got to the window in time to see a dark head and shoulders thrust out from the top of the wall, close enough she could almost touch them. Beyond the wall she heard shouts and dogs baying. Without stopping to think, she leaned out, caught the fugitive's attention with a sharp hiss.

The head jerked up.

"In here," she whispered. She saw him hesitate, but he had little choice. The hounds were breathing down his neck. She moved away from the window, jumped back another step as he came plunging through and whipped onto his feet, knife in hand, eyes glittering through the slits in his knitted mask. "Don't be silly," she said, no longer whispering. "Close the shutters or get away from the window and let me do it."

He sidled along the wall, keeping as far from her as he could. After a quick glance out the window, she eased the shutters to, careful to make as little noise as she could, pulled the bar over and tucked it gently into its hooks. That done, she set her back against the shutters and stood watching him.

He was over by the door; he tried the latch. "The key."

She hitched up the quilt which was trying to untuck itself and slide off her. "On the table." A nod toward the bed. "Go if you want. You could probably break loose. Or you can stay here until the chase passes on. Your choice."

"Why?" A thread of sound, angry and dangerous.

"Why not. Say I don't like seeing things hunted."

He lowered the knife, leaned against the door and thought about it, a small wiry figure, with black trousers and black sweater, black gloves, black busks on his feet and a knitted hood that covered his whole head except for the eyeslits. The dim light coming through diamond holes in the shutters touched his eyes as he moved away from the door, pale eyes, blue or hazel, unusual in Jade Halimm; he stared at her several seconds, glanced at the sleeping children. "Who are you?"

"Did I ask you that?"

"They aren't breathing." He waved the knife at the children.

"Nor did I make comments about your person."

He hesitated a moment longer, then he dragged off the mask and stood grinning at her. "Drinker of Souls," he said, satisfaction and certainty in his voice. "You knew my grandfather." He was a handsome youth, sixteen seventeen twenty at most, straight thick hair, heavy brows, flattish nose and a wide thinlipped mouth that could move from a grin to a grimace at the flash of a thought. Mixed blood. Hina stature, Hina nose and tilted almond Hina eyes (though they should have been dark brown to be truly Hina), the dark blond hair that appeared sometimes when Hina mixed with Croaldhese, his mouth and chin were certainly Croaldhese. He had the accent of a born Halimmer, that quick slide of sound impossible to acquire unless you lisped your first words in Jalimmik.

He slipped the knife up his sleeve and went to sit on the bed. "My mother's father was called Aituatea. You might remember him." He waited a moment giving her a chance to comment; when she said nothing, he went on. "You're a family legend. You and them." A wave of his hand at the two blond heads.

"Hmm. This seems to be the month of old acquaintances."

"What?"

"Wouldn't mean anything to you. Yaril, Jaril, wake up." The covers stirred, two sleepy children sat up blinking. "Forget it, kids, the lad knows all about you." She turned back to the young thief. "How serious were they, those folk chasing you?"

He scratched at his jaw. "I'm still here, not running for the nearest hole. Those Dreeps know all the holes I do, and they'll be going down them hunting blood. Not just them." He thought a moment, apparently decided there was no point being coy about his target. "Highmerchant Jizo Gozit, it was his House I got into, he's a vindictive man and he's got more pull than a giant squid; by now the king's Noses are in the hunt."

"I see. They'll be searching this place before long. We could shove you under the bed or hide you in it . . . no, I've got a better idea . . . maybe . . . you think they know it's you they're hunting?"

"Doubt it. I usually keep well away from that quarter. The hounds have my scent, though; if the Dreeps bring their dogs. . . ."

"Jaril, let him take your place. Mastiff, I think, hmm? Any dogs stick their noses in the door, you take their minds off our friend here."

Jaril patted a yawn, slid out of the bed, a slim naked youth. For a moment he stood looking at the thief out of bright crystal eyes, then he was a mastiff standing high as the boy's waist, muscle rippling on muscle, droopy mouth stretched into a grin that exposed an intimidating set of teeth. He went trotting around the room, came back to the rug at the foot of the bed, scratched at it until he was satisfied, turned around once and settled onto it, head down, ready to sleep until he was needed.

"Get into the bed beside Yaril," Brann said. "You'll be Jaril. Kheren will tell them I came in with two children, a boy and a girl, you're older and taller and not so fair, but that shouldn't matter."

The mastiff lifted his head, whined softly.

"Move it, friend." Brann whipped the quilt off, swept it over the bed and dived under the covers beside him. She felt his tension as he lay sandwiched between her and Yaril. "Relax," she muttered.

A long sigh, a wriggle that edged him away from her, then his breathing went slow and steady, craftily counterfeiting slumber. A handsome youth, but he didn't arouse anything in her except impatience. Getting old, she thought, Slya Bless, a few hours ago I was hot to trot, as the saying goes, contemplating the seduction of some sea captain. She sighed. What do I do if the same nothing appears when I find someone more to my taste, ayy yaaah, dead from the neck down? May it never happen. I was something like half dead up there. Mmh. Would have been all dead, if the children had been an hour or so later. She scowled at the unseen ceiling. Didn't even try to fight. . . . The memory made her sick. Didn't even try to get the knife out, heal the wound. They surprised me, but that's no excuse. Hadn't thought about it before but that must have been what I was doing the past fifty years, getting ready to die and when it happened. . . . Shuh! I can't die. Not with the kids depending on me. I've got to do something about that. I don't know what. After this is over and there's time . . . maybe if I went back to Tincreal and roused Slya . . .

She lay still and did a few mind tricks to keep her body relaxed, then tried to figure out why she'd taken on this young thief with no questions asked. It startled her now that she had time to take a look at what she'd done. She thought about what she'd told him, *I don't like to see things hunted*. True enough, especially after the past six days (twinge in her stomach, quickly suppressed). I suppose he's my redeeming act, my sop, my

. . . oh forget it, Brann, you're maundering. Aituatea's grandson, hmm, he's got the proper heritage for his profession all right. What's going on here? First Harra's great grandsoevers, now Aituatea's. Things come in threes, uh huh, and if there's a third intrusion from my past. . . .

She heard the voices in the hall and the tramp of booted feat near her door. She heard the clank of the key as it turned in the lock. She stifled an urge to turn and look at the boy, forced her breathing to slow, her body to relax again.

The door crashed open, banging against the wall. Light from the hallway and the lanterns the Dreeps carried glared into the room, slid off the leather and metal they wore. Jaril came onto his feet and stood ears back, head down, growling deep in his throat. As if startled from sleep but no less dangerous, Brann surged up, knife ready in one hand, snatching at the quilt with the other, holding it in front of her. "Shift ass out of here," she spat at them, "or I turn him loose and carve into stew meat what he leaves."

"Calm, calm, fenna meh." Kheren Zanc pushed past the lead Dreep. "There's no harm done. The guards are searching for a thief who got over the wall near your room. They need to be sure he's not hiding in here. It's for your safety, fenna meh."

She looked them over with insolent thoroughness, then she wrapped the quilt around her and tucked in the end. "Let them look if they're fools enough to think some idiot thief could get past Smiler there." She dropped onto the bed, knife resting lightly on her quilt-covered thigh. "I'll have the hide off anyone who wakes the children." She patted the blanket beside her, whistled the mastiff onto the bed. Jaril, newly christened Smiler, leaped over the footboard and stretched out with his hindquarters draped over the young thief's legs. Yaril and the erstaz Jaril slept heavily while three Dreeps prowled the room, looking under the bed and into the wardrobe. One of them prodded his pike through the blanket near the foot of the bed but retreated before a sizzling glare when he showed signs of wanting to jerk the covers off in case the thief was masquerading as a twig-sized wrinkle.

Kheren bowed with heavy dignity. "Your Graciousness." He shooed the Dreeps out of the room and locked the door after them.

With a wavery sigh Brann set the knife back on the bedtable, ran shaking fingers through the duckfeather curls fluffing about her head. She grinned at Jaril as he shifted back to boy and sat cross-legged on the bed. "Give them a minute more, then see what they're doing."

Jaril nodded. He slid off the bed, blurred into a gold shimmersphere and oozed out through the door. The young thief sat up, raised his brows. "Nice trick, wish I could do it."

"He'll warn us if the Dreeps start this way. What got you in this mess?"

"Bad luck and stupidity."

She laughed. "That's a broad streak of honesty there, better watch it, um . . . I'll call you Tua after your grandfather. Tua, my friend, it'll be an hour or two before you can move on, pass a little of it telling me your troubles. I might be some help. I'm inclined to be, for your grandfather's sake. Or out of boredom. Or from general dislike of Dreeps. Take your pick and tell your tale."

He rubbed his hands together, slowly, his light eyes narrowed. "Why?"

"Why not."

"Hmm. I expect there's not much point in shamming it. Here's how it was. About a week ago an hour or two before dawn, I was . . . mmm . . . drifting along Waygang street, do you know Halimm, ah!" he slapped his cheek, clicked his tongue, "I forgot who you are, you've been walking the ways here since before my mother was even born, where was I, yes, Waygang Street on the Hill end where the highclass Assignation Houses are, I'd been tickling a maid in one of those Houses," he shrugged, "you get the idea. I was seeing if I could fox the patrols and get inside without being nailed. I thought old Tungjii was perching on my shoulder when I made it as easy as breathing. Ten, eleven patrons were sleep-

ing over, I went through their gear and teased open the
locks on the abdits, you know, the lockholes in the walls
where they generally put their purses and the best jew-
elry. What with one thing and another, it was a good
haul for an hour's work. What I didn't know was one of
those patrons was a sorceror. He had this bad dreamsmoke habit, he'd stopped over in Jade Halimm to in-
dulge it and was using the House as a safe bed for his
binge. The room had that sour stink you don't forget
once you've smelled it so I knew the man wasn't going
to wake on me, the House could've burned down and
he wouldn't wake. I got his purse, shuh, it was heavy.
I almost didn't bother with the abdit, but I was stupid
and I got greedy and I found this crystal egg in a jew-
eled case and I took it. Wasn't anything else in the abdit. Another thing, that stinking smoke made my nose
itch and clog up, so I blew it. I used my fingers and
wiped them on one of the sheets. Baaad mistake. Well,
I didn't know it then. I finished up and slid out and it
was easy as breathing again. I cached the gold, you
don't want to walk in on . . . um . . . I think I won't
say the name . . . someone with gold in your boot, he'd
have it out before you opened your mouth to say what.
I sold the rings and that egg to someone, got about what
I expected, maybe a quarter what the stuff was worth.
He passed the egg on less than three hours after he got
it. I found that out later. Me, soon as I was rid of the
dangerous stuff, I went . . . um . . . someplace and
crawled into bed, I was tired. Everything was fine, far
as I knew. Stayed fine all the time I was sleeping. I
woke hungry and went to get something to eat. I was
in the middle of a bowl of noodles when my insides
started twitching. Didn't hurt, not then, just felt peculiar. I stopped eating. The twitches stopped. It was that
cookshop down by Sailor's Gamehouse. I decided Shem
who ran it got into some bad oil, so I went into Sailor's
figuring I could afford his cook for once. I got about
halfway through some plum chicken when the twitches
started again. This time I ignored them and finished the
chicken, it cost too much to waste. The twitching went
away. I though, Oh. I went out. It was getting dark.
There was a girl I knew. She's a dancer mostly, she has

her courtesan's license so she doesn't have to go with
anyone she doesn't like. I thought about going to see
her. I even started walking toward the piers, she worked
on a boat, I got a couple steps on the way when the
worst pain I ever felt hit me. It was like redhot pincers
stabbing into my liver and twisting. And a word exploded in my head. It was a minute before I could sort
myself out enough to know what the word was. Come.
I heard it again. Come. I didn't know what was happening to me. Come. Everyone thought I was having
fits. Come. The pain went away a little. The voice got
quieter. Come. I came. That's when I found out the man
I stole the egg from was a sorcerer. He wanted the egg
back. He wanted it back so bad, he told me what he did
to me to get me there was a catlick to what would happen to me if I didn't bring it to him. I told him I'd
already got rid of it, sold it to a fence and I didn't have
any way of knowing what he did with it. He thought
about that, then he asked me who the fence was. I didn't
want to tell him but a couple twinges later I decided
that . . . um . . . someone wasn't a man I felt like dying
for. I told him who the fence was and where to find
him. He made me come kneel at his feet, then he did
something I don't know what and there was this tigerman in the middle of the room. He talked to the tigerman, I don't know what he said, it was some sort of
magic gabble I suppose. The tigerman disappeared *pop*
like he was a candleflame blown out. He came back
the same way but this time he had the fence with him. The
fence didn't want to say what he did with the egg. The
tigerman played with him a little. So he dug in his memory, didn't have to dig far but he made a long dance out
of it, and came up with the name of the highmerchant
Jizo Gozit. The sorceror told him if he said a word
about this to anyone he'd start rotting slowly, his parts
would fall off and his fingers and his toes and his tongue
would rot in his mouth and his eyes would rot in his
head and to show he meant it he rotted off the fence's
little finger, we could see the flesh melt and fall away
from the bones. Then the sorceror told him to go home
and he went. The tigerman went away. There was just
me left. I don't *know* why he didn't send the tigerman

after the egg, I've got an idea, though, something I came up with later. Maybe it's like this, he was going to start on his binge, but he didn't want anyone getting at him when he wasn't up to protecting himself so he put his two souls into that egg and locked it up and here I come along and go off with it. And he didn't send the tiger-man for it or do any fishing about for it because he didn't want to give away where his souls were and he for sure wasn't about to let any demon get that close to them. He gave me five days to get it back, or I'd start hurting a lot. That was four days ago. So you know what I was doing. Those highmerchants, most thieves don't even try their houses, I mean even the best we got in Jade Halimm don't bother with that quarter. I was lucky to stay loose enough to reach the wall ahead of the Dreeps and their hounds.'' He slid off the bed and went to the window, lifted the bar and eased the righthand shutter open about an inch so he could see the sky. "Looks to me like I've got a couple hours of dark left. Maybe if I went right back, they wouldn't be expecting me and might've let down their guard some. My hood, it's in the bed somewhere, ask the changer if she'll fish it out, then I'm for the wall and Jizo's House and you're rid of me.''

"Mmm, give me a minute to think.'' She passed her hand over her head, smoothing down the fine white halfcurls. "Sorceror . . . there are a lot of idiots who fool around with magic of one kind or another . . . uhhhm, how sure are you that man really is a sorceror?''

"Eh, it's not everyone who snaps his fingers and makes a tigerman fetch for him.''

"I see. Yaril, what's your brother doing?''

"Still watching the Dreeps. They're up in the attics turning out the servants' rooms.''

"Tell him to leave them to it and get back here.''

"He's coming.''

There weren't that many sorcerors around, at least not those who'd reached the level of competence in their arts that matched Tua's description of the man he'd robbed. And, from what she'd observed in her travels when she was still wandering about the world, they all knew each other. So it was more than likely this one could give her some useful information about Settsimaksimin and less than likely he'd tell her anything unless she had a hold on him.

Jaril oozed through the door. "The search is about finished, but the Head Dreep, he's not happy about it, he wants to get the hounds in and start over on the rooms, Kheren is having fits about that. I got the feeling the Dreep was walking careful around our Host, that he knew if Kheren complained about him, he'd be up to his nose in hot shit."

"Hmm. Tua, I've got a deal for you. Listen, I'll send the children for that egg if you'll bring your sorceror here."

"Why? Don't get snarky if I don't jump at the deal, but it's my body and my life you're playing with."

"Don't worry. I'll take care of you."

"He's a sorceror."

"And I'm Drinker of Souls and I'll have his in my hands."

"I don't have a choice, do I?"

"No. You might save us some time if you told Yaril and Jaril where to find Jizo's House. Doesn't matter all that much, the place is probably lit up and swarming with guards, the children could fly over the quarter and go right to it."

"I talk too much."

"Oh, I don't think so. You're getting what you want without risking your hide." She chuckled. "Tua Tua, you've been working hard to worm this out of me, clever clever young thief playing pittypat games with the poor old demidemon, making her singe her aged paws plucking your nuts from the fire."

He opened his eyes wide, angelically innocent, then he gave it up and grinned at her. "Was clever, wasn't it."

"Shuh. Be more clever. Tell the kids where to find the egg."

He was a tall man with a handsome ruined face and eyes bluer than the sea on a sunny day. His fine black hair and the beard neatly groomed into corkscrew curls and the bold blade of his nose proclaimed him a son of Phras. He came in slowly, the thick, textured wool of his black robe brushing against boots whose black leather was soft and glowing and unobtrusively expensive. He wore a large ruby on the fourth finger of his left hand, his right hand was bare; they were fine hands, never-used hands, soft, pale with a delicate tracery of blue veins. He stood without speaking while Tua shut and locked the door and joined Brann who was sitting on the bed, Jaril-Mastiff crouched by her knee.

The silence thickened. Tua fidgeted, scratching at his knee, feeling the knife up his sleeve, rubbing the back of his neck, the small scrapes and rustles he made the only sounds in the room. Brann continued to sit, relaxed, smiling. She intended to force the man to speak first, she had to have that edge to counter the power and discipline she felt in him, to wrest from him the knowledge she needed. He'd spread a glamour about himself, he'd dressed in his best for this meeting, wearing pride along with wool and leather and power like a cloak, but he was dying, his body was beginning to crumble. He saw that she knew this and his eyes went bitter and his hands shook. His mouth pressed to a thin line, he folded his arms across his chest; the shaking stopped, but there was a film of sweat on his face and a crease of pain across his brow. He knew the egg was nowhere in the room. (It was with Yaril who was being a dayhawk sitting on the ridgepole of the Inn, the egg in a pouch tied to her leg; Brann had no way of knowing how close a sorceror had to be to retrieve his souls and was taking no chances.) "You called me here," he said; his voice was deep and rich, an actor's voice trained in declamation and caress. "You have something for me."

"I have." She put stress on the I.

"Give it to me."

"Not yet."

Dark power throbbed in the room, lapping at her with a thousand tongues. Brann kept her smile (though it went a little stiff), kept her hands relaxed on her thighs (though the thumbs twitched a few times); tentatively she tapped into the field and began reeling its energies into herself, scooping out a hollow he couldn't penetrate. The young thief scrambled away from her, went to sit in the window, legs dangling, ready to jump if Brann faltered. The Jaril-Mastiff came onto his feet, muscle sliding powerfully against muscle, and padded noiselessly around the periphery of the zone of force protecting the man. He oscillated there for several breaths, looking from the sorceror to Brann (who was sitting unmoved, draining the attack before it could touch her) then he grew denser and more taut and when he was ready, he catapulted against the man's legs, bursting unharmed through the zone and knocking him into a painful sprawl.

Jaril-Mastiff untangled himself and trotted over to Brann. She laughed, scratched between his ears and watched the sorceror collect himself and get shakily to his feet. "Are you ready to talk?"

He brushed at his sleeves, unhurried, discipline intact. "What do you want?"

"Information." She smiled at him. "Come. Relax, I'm not asking that much. Sit and let's talk."

He shook his robe back into its stately folds, straightened the chair he'd knocked awry in his sprawling fall and settled himself in it. "Who are you?"

"Drinker of Souls." Another smile. "What name do you answer to?"

Another thoughtful pause. "Ahzurdan." His blue gaze slid over her, returned to her face, touched the short delicate curls clustered over her head, again returned to her face. "Drinker of Souls," he said. "Brann," he said.

She frowned. "You know me?"

He glanced at the boy in the window, said nothing.

"Turn him loose," she said. "That's what he's here for."

Abruptly genial, he nodded. "Isoatua, the contract is complete." He raised a brow. "Go and don't let me see you again."

Tua scowled, turned his shoulder to him. "Fenna meh?"

"A minute. Jaril?"

The mastiff came onto his feet, yawned, was a glimmersphere of pale light. It drifted upward, whipped through Ahzurdan before he had time to react, then returned to Brann and shifted to Jaril the boy. "He means it," he said.

"You heard, Tua. Next time be a bit more careful what you lift."

Tua started to say something, but changed his mind. Ignoring Ahzurdan he bowed to Brann, strolled to the door. With a graceful flick of his wrist, he unlocked it. When he was out, Jaril turned the key again, put his head through the wall. A moment later he ambled over to Brann. "He's off."

"Thanks. Ahzurdan."

"Yes?"

"How do you know me?"

"My grandfather was a shipmaster named Chandro bal Abbayd. I believe you knew him."

"Shuh. You hear that, Jaril? Three. That's not coincidence, that's plot. Miserable gods are dabbling their fingers in my life again. All right. All right. Nothing I can do about it. Look, Ahzurdan, there was an attack on me a few days ago, a tigerman slid a knife between my ribs. No, I don't think you sent him. I'm reasonably sure someone called Settsimaksimin wants me dead. He came close, not close enough. I have no doubt he knows that by now. What I want from you is this, anything you can tell me about him."

"Ah." He slumped in the chair and let the glamour fade. There was a broad band of gray in his thinning hair, streaks of gray in his beard, the whites of his eyes were yellowed and bloodshot. He had high angular cheekbones in a face bonier than Chandro's, at least as she remembered him, strongly defined indentations at the temples, deep creases running from his nostrils past the corners of his mouth. A face used by time and thought and suffering, a lot of the last self-inflicted. "What did you do?"

"I suspect it's something I'm going to do."

"I see." He stroked his beard, no longer trying to hide the shake of his hands; red light shimmered in the heart of the ruby. "You're prepared to trust what I say?"

She smiled. "Of course not. I trust my ability to interpret what you say. So you'll do it?"

"Yes."

"No reservations?"

"No."

"Jaril, tell your sister to get down here. Ahzurdan, you look awful. Come over here, get rid of that robe. When Jaril gets back with Yaril, I'll see what I can do about knitting you together again."

Ahzurdan unknotted the thongs of the pouch; he paused a moment, his eyes looked inward, he thrust two long fingers inside and touched the crystal. His face wiped of expression, he stood rigidly erect for several minutes as the souls flowed back into his flesh. When it was done, he tossed the pouch onto the bed and dropped beside it. "I'm a fool," he said. "Don't trust me, I'll let you down every time."

"Sad, sad, how terribly sad." Brann snorted. "Before a binge that might mean something, not after."

"Ah yes." He stroked a hand down his beard. "You see me not quite at my worst." He sighed. "A man is destroyed most effectively when he does it himself. Have you tasted the dreams of ru'hrya? No? You're wise not to bind yourself to that endless wheel." When she reminded him he couldn't work through thick wool, he managed a half smile and began unfastening his robe. "There's some pleasure in the smoke, a deep stillness, a gentle drifting, you're floating in a warm fog. But the thing that brings you back again and again to the smoke is the dream." His hand stilled for a moment, he looked inward again, pain and longing in those blue blue eyes. "The dream. You're a hero there. Colors, odors, textures, they're so alive they're close to pain but not pain. Everything you do there comes out right, you're not clumsy there or a fool or a victim. You live your life over again there, but the way you wanted it to be, not the way it was or is." He stood, pulled his arms free and let the robe fall about his feet. Under it he wore a black silk tunic that came to mid-thigh and black silk drawers that reached his knees. He was perhaps too thin, but was well-muscled and healthy despite a week-long binge on dreamsmoke; in an odd way his body seemed a decade younger than his face. "You can't forget them, the dreams, your body screams at you for the smoke, but that's not important, what you hunger for is the other thing. You despise yourself for your weakness, but after a while you can't stand knowing how stupid and futile you are and you binge again. And as the years pass you binge more frequently until the day comes when you do nothing else and you die still dreaming. I know that. I've seen it. The knowledge sits in my mind like a corpse. I run deeper into the smoke to escape that corpse and by doing so I run toward it, toward my degradation and my death. I came to Jade Halimm to find you, Brann; I came to beg you to free me from this need. Use your healing hands on me, Brann, make me whole. I'll tell you everything I know of Cheonea and Settsimaksimin, I'll go with you to help you fight him and you will need me, even you. Cleanse my body and my mind, Brann, do it in memory of the joy you and my grandfather shared that he told me about more than once, do it because you need me even if you think you don't, do it out of the generosity of your soul.''

''What makes you think I can do what you can't?''

He smiled wearily. ''Tungjii's laughter in my head, Brann.''

''Slya's crooked toes! If I could . . . if I could climb the air . . . aah!''

''What?''

''That miserable menagerie of misfits that makes toys of us and dances us about to amuse themselves. Listen. I spent the last hundred years as a potter, a damn good one, sometimes even great. I was content working my clay, chopping wood for the kiln, all that. Then there comes this messenger from out of the past, the children of Harra Hazani who was once a friend of mine are calling me to keep a promise I made her some two hundred years ago. And right away I'm lying on the grass with a knife in my back. And when I'm getting ready to go kick my enemy where it hurts, what happens? I'm sleeping peacefully in an expensive room in a highclass inn and I wake up to dogs howling and a young thief climbing the wall outside my window, and lo, he's the grandson of another old acquaintance of mine, and lo, he's in this mess because he just happened to steal the souls of a sorceror who just happens to be the grandson of another old friend and lover. I said it before, this isn't coincidence, it's a plot. Those damn gods are jerking me around again.''

''What are you going to do about it?''

''Shuh, what I'd like to do is go back to my pots.''

''But?''

''What choice do I have? There's my sworn oath and there's a man who wants to kill me. So. Now that that's over with, stretch out. On your stomach first. Yaril, help me, make sure we're not interrupted.''

Her hands were warm and surprisingly strong. He thought about her chopping wood and couldn't visualize it. Soft hands. No calluses. Short nails, but cared for. She worked with her hands. A potter. He suppressed a shudder, but she felt it. ''It's nothing,'' he said. ''A troubling thought, no more.'' Her fingers moved in small circles over his head then drew lines of heat along his spine. Energy flowed into him, for once he felt as vital as he did in the dreams, yet more relaxed. He grunted as she pinched a buttock. ''Talk,'' she said.

''Mmmm . . . loyalty . . . where does it end? That's the question, isn't it. He was my teacher . . . unh, don't destroy the flesh, Brann, I do enough of it, I don't need help . . . I suppose that is a fourth noncoincidence . . . I was twelve when he took me . . . there's an intimacy between master and apprentice . . . thumps and caresses . . . leaves its mark on you . . . . yesss, that feels good . . . . he was an odd man . . . difficult . . . rumors . . . there were other apprentices . . . they talked . . . we all talked . . . about him . . . listened . . . one rumor I think might be true . . . that he was sired by a drunken M'darjin merchant on an overage Cheonene whore one night in Silagamatys, he had the look . . . he was clever . . . fiercely disciplined . . . he'd work like a slave day after day, no sleep, no meals, a sip of tea and a beancake, that was all, both of them usually cold by the time he remembered them . . . but when the thing was done, he'd drown in the wildest debauchery he could find or assemble . . . sometimes . . . depending on his mood and needs . . . he took one or

more of us with him . . . he always had four or five
apprentices . . . one year there were nine of us . . . he
dribbled out his lessons to us . . . enough to keep us
clinging to him . . . and he had favorites . . . boys he
bound closer to him . . . he fed them more . . . fed
them . . . us . . . something like love . . . like living
in an insane cross between a zoo and a greenhouse . . .
yes, that's it, we clawed and rutted like beasts and put
out exotic blooms to attract him. . . .

He stopped talking as she stopped the probing and
pummeling and began passing her hands over him.
Warmth that was both pleasure and pain (the two twisting inextricably in the flow) passed into his feet and
churned up through him until it flooded into his brain
and turned into pure agony; he dissolved into white fire,
then darkness.

He sat sipping at hot tea, dawn red in the window.
Pale blond preteens in green-gray trousers and tunics,
the changechildren were sitting on the floor, leaning
against Brann's knees, watching him. Brann held a bowl
of tea cradled in her hands. "The physical part of it is
gone," she said. "That's all. You could have done that
yourself. No doubt you have."

"After the third relapse, trying it again didn't seem
worth the cost."

"I still don't understand what more you think I can
do."

"Nor I." He smiled wearily. "In the depths of self-
disgust after one too many binges, I returned to the
ways of my ancestors and cast the lots. And found you
there as my answer. Being with you. Staying with you."
An aborted shapeless gesture with the hand holding the
teabowl. "A parasite on your strength."

"Hmm." She finished the tea and set the bowl beside
her on the bed. "I don't know the Captains these days.
Any ship in port going south that made good time and
won't sink at a sneeze, whose master is a bit more than
a lamprey on the hunt?"

"Ju't Chandro told me you had a fondness for sailing
men. Was he casting a net for air?"

"Hmf. Do you love every son of Phras you meet? Come with me to the wharves and tell me who's who."

"I may travel with you?"

"For whatever good it does. Besides, all you've told me so far is that Maksim has apprentices around to do the scut work and a taste for the occasional orgy. Not much help there."

"You'll get everything I know, Brann."

"Ah well." A tight half smile. "When I'm not sleeping with the Captain, life on shipboard tends to get tedious." She examined him, speculation in her eyes.

Ahzurdan felt a quiver in his loins and a shiver of fear along his spine, one of his grandfather's more lurid tales flowing in full colors through his head. He gulped the rest of his tea; it was cold, but he didn't notice. That white fluff, it looked like she'd shaved her hair off not too long ago, though why she'd do that . . . She wasn't beautiful, not in any ordinary sense, handsome perhaps, but there was something he couldn't put into words, a vitality, a sense that she knew who and what she was and rather liked that person. A disturbing woman. A challenge to everything he'd been taught about women. His mother would have hated and feared her. There were knots in his gut as he snatched brief glances at her; what she seemed to be expecting from him was more often than not something he couldn't provide, he didn't want to think about that, she made him think, she made him want the smoke again, anything to fill the emptiness inside him. Discipline, don't forget discipline, ignore what you don't want to see, you're a man with a skill that few have the gifts or intelligence or tenacity to acquire, that's where your worth lies, you're not a stud hired to service the woman. Ah gods, it's a good thing you aren't, you couldn't earn your pay, no, don't think about that. I owe you, Maksim, you played in my head and in my body and threw both away when you were tired of them. Maksim, Maksimin, you don't know what's coming at you. . . . He rose. "Time we were starting. I still have to ransom my gear from the House and the tide turns shortly after noon."

4

ON THE MERCHANTER JIVA MAHRISH (captain and owner Hudah Iffat, quartermaster and steward, his wife Hamla), THREE HOURS OUT OF JADE HALIMM, COAST HOPPING SOUTH AND WEST TO KUKURAL, HER LAST PORT BEFORE SHE TURNED NORTH AGAIN.

SCENE: Brann below, settling into her cabin. Ahzurdan on deck driving off stray ariels, setting wards against another attack on her. Yaril and Jaril watching him, wondering what he's up to.

Ignoring the noisy confusion at his back where the deck passengers were still getting settled into the eighteen square feet apiece they bought with their fares, Ahzurdan stood at the stern watching the flags on the Roganzhu Fort flutter and sink toward the horizon, frowning at the ariels thick in the wind that agitated those flags and filled the sails. Born of wind, shaped from wind, elongated asexual angel shapes with huge glimmering eyes, the ariels whirled round the ship, dipping toward it, darting away when they came close enough to sense what he was. Tapping nervously at the rail, he considered what to do; as long as Brann stayed below, the

ariels were an irritation, no more. He swung around.
The changechildren were squatting beside the rail, their
strange soulless crystal eyes fixed on him. No matter
what Brann said, they didn't trust him. "One of you,"
he said, "go below and tell her to stay where she is for
a while." Neither moved. He sighed. "There are spies
in the wind."

They exchanged a long glance, then the girl got to her
feet and drifted away.

Ahzurdan turned to the sea again. For a moment he
continued to watch the ariels swirl overhead, then he
reached out, caught a handful of air and sunlight and
twisted it into a ward that he locked to the ship's side.
He began moving along the rail; every seventh step he
fashioned another knot and placed it. He reached the
bow, started back along the port rail, careful to keep
out of the way of the working sailors.

Halfway along, Jaril stepped in front of him. "What
are you doing?"

"Warding."

"Against what?"

"Against what happened before. This isn't the place
to talk about it. Let me finish."

The boy stared at him for a long breath, then he
stepped aside and let him pass.

Ahzurdan finished setting the wards, then stood leaning on the rail watching the sun glitter off the waves,
thinking about the changechildren. He knew what they
were and their connection to Brann. His grandfather
had been fond of them, in a way, also a little frightened
of them. That fear was easy to understand. Earlier, before coming on board he'd tried a minor spell on Jaril
and nothing had happened. More disturbing than that,
the boy in his mastiff form had whipped through his
force shield without even a whimper to show he noticed
it. The children must have been fetched from a reality
so distant from this and so strange that the powers here
(at least those below the level of the highgods) couldn't
touch them. Not directly. Very interesting. Very dangerous. He collected his wandering thoughts, twitched
the wards to test them, then went below satisfied he'd

done what he could to neutralize anything Settsimaksimin might try.

Port to port they went. Lindu Zohee. Merr Ono. Halonetts. Sunny days, warm nights. A chancy wind but
one that kept the ship scudding along the coast. Brann
stayed onboard in each of the ports, safe from attack
behind the wards but restless. Ahzurdan watched her
whenever he could, curious about her, perplexed by
nearly everything she did. She liked sailors and made
friends with the crew when she could have been talking
to the cabin passengers. There was an envoy from the
Jade King aboard; he was a fine amateur poet and mu-
sician and showed more than a little interest in her.
There was a courtesan of the first rank and her retinue.
There was a highmerchant who dealt in jades, calligraphy and elegant conversation. Brann produced an embroidered robe for the dinners in the captain's cabin, a
multitude of delicately scribed gold bracelets (Rukha
Nagg he thought when she let him examine them, part
of a daughter's dowry), and a heavy gold ear ornament
from the Panday Islands (he was intensely curious about
where she got that, only a Panday with his own ship
could wear such an ornament, there was a three day
feast involved, a solemn rite of recognition and pres-
entation; most Panday shipmasters were buried with
theirs; a lover perhaps?). Her hair was growing with
supernatural speed, but it was still a cloud of feathery
white curls that made her eyes huge and intensely green.
She looked vital, barbaric and fine; he had difficulty
keeping his eyes off her. She played poetry with the
Envoy, composing verse couplets in answer to his, she
spoke of jade carvers with the merchant, though mostly
about ancient Arth Slyan pieces and the techniques of
those legendary artisans, she questioned the courtesan
Huazo about the dance styles currently popular, brought
up the name of a long dead Hina player named Taguiloa
and grew excited when Huazo told some charming but
obviously apocryphal tales about the man (another
lover?) and went into what Ahzurdan considered tedious
detail about his influence on her own dancing. The dinners were pleasant and Brann seemed to enjoy them,

but she went running to the crew when she had a moment free. He didn't understand what she saw in them, crude vulgar men with crude vulgar thoughts, and at the same time was jealous of their ease with her. The first few days he had fevered images of belowdecks orgies, but his training did not allow him to distort or reject what was there before his eyes no matter how powerfully theory and emotion acted on his head. Misperceptions weren't problems of logic or aesthetics to a sorceror, they could kill him and anyone near him. She traded stories with the crew, showed off her skills with rope, needle and palm; her hands were quick and graceful, he watched their dance and deplored what she was doing with them. She was almost a demigod, not some miserable peasant or artisan grubbing for a living.

The day the ship sailed from Merr Ono, he was in her cabin telling her about his earliest days with Settsimaksimin but broke off and asked her why she avoided the cabin passengers when she was so much more suited to their society than those . . . ah . . . no doubt goodhearted men in the crew; he got a cool gaze that looked into his souls and stripped his pretension bare, or so he thought.

After several moments of silence, she sighed. "I don't like him. No, that's not right. He turns my stomach. I'll be polite to him at supper, but I won't stay around him any longer than I have to."

"Why?" He's a cultivated intelligent man. His poems are praised from Andurya Durat to Kukurul for their power and innovation."

"Have you read any of them?"

"Yes!"

"We'll have to agree to disagree. I'll grant you a certain technical facility, but there's nothing in them."

"You can't have read *Winter Rising.*"

"Ah! Dan, I've spent the better part of a hundred winters doing little else but reading." She pushed her fingers through her duckfeather curls. "I read *Winter Rising* and came closer to burning a book than I thought I ever would. Especially the part when he mourns the death of a servant's child. His family chern lies half a day's journey downriver from the Pottery. I have swept up too many leavings from his justice," the word ended in an angry hiss, "to swallow his mouthings about suffering he himself is responsible for. I don't care how splendid the poem is," she shook her head, put her hand on his arm, "I'll admit the skill, but I can't stand the man. And I can't forget the man in the poet." She moved away from him. "Play with him all you want, Dan, but keep a grip on your skin and don't take any commissions from him. The Jade King doesn't send openfisted fools to negotiate trade rights." She dropped into a chair and sat with her hands clasped loosely in her lap. "If you're going to keep traveling with me, you might as well understand something. I despise him and all his kind. If the world wagged another way and it would make any real difference to his landfolk, I'd be the first to boot him out of his silky nest and set him to digging potatoes, where he might be useful and certainly less destructive."

"Brann, do you really think your cherished sailors would be any better, put in his place? It would be chaos, far worse than anything the Envoy had done. I've seen what happens when the beasts try to drive the cart. He has tradition and culture to restrain him, they've nothing but instinct."

"Beasts, Dan?"

"By their acts shall you know them."

"By their acts shall you know their masters."

"Aren't they to be held responsible for what they do?"

"Give them responsibility before you demand it from them. Ahhh, this is stupid, Dan. We're arguing abstracts and that's bound to be an exercise in futility." She laughed. "No more, not now. I wish you could have seen my home. Arth Slya isn't what it was, even so . . . I was born a free woman of free folk. We managed our own lives and bowed our heads to no man, not even the King of Croaldhu. If I had the power, I'd make the whole world live that way."

"You sound like Maksim."

"That's interesting. Do you know what he's doing in Cheonea? Tell me about it."

He shrugged. "It's foolishness. Rabble is rabble. Changing the name doesn't change the smell."

Brann snorted. "Shuh! Dan, I know you sons of Phras, you and your honor, it's a fine honor that scorns to touch a loom or a chisel but makes an art of killing. I loved your grandfather, Ahzurdan; Chandro was a splendid man as long as he was away from Phras, one who knew how to laugh at the world and how to laugh at himself, but not in Bandrabahr. When he went home, he turned Phrasi from his toes to his backteeth. You might think that's a proper thing to do, but me . . . hunh! I went with him once, the last trip we made together. I remember I said something about a pompous old fool strutting down the street, a joke, he'd laughed at things like that a hundred times before. He *hit* me. You know, it was funny. I just stood there gaping at him. He started calling me names. Vicious names. Then he tried to hit me again. That's not a thing I tolerate, no indeed. Well, there was a bit of a brawl with Yaril and Jaril rallying round. Last I saw of him, Chandro was laid out yelling, some meat gone from one buttock and a thigh, a broken shoulder bone and a bruised belly where I missed my kick or he might have been your uncle not your grandfather. There was a ship lifting anchor right then, I made it onboard a jump and a half ahead of the kashiks. Never saw him again. Sad. After that I came back to Jade Halimm, apprenticed myself to a potter and settled into clay and contentment."

By the time they sailed from Halonetts, beginning the last leg of the journey to Kukurul, Ahzurdan was sweating and nightmare-ridden, trying to fight his desire for dreamsmoke. He wallowed in despair; he'd thought having the demonic Brann around would somehow cure him of this need, but she grated on his nerves so much she was driving him to the dreams to escape her. In spite of this, he couldn't stay away from her.

She listened with such totality it made a kind of magic. He was uneasy under this intense scrutiny, he rebelled against it now and then, but it was also extraordinarily seductive. He began to need her ear worse than his drug; they broke for meals and sleep, but he came drifting back as soon as he could, and, after a few hesitations, was lost once more in his memories. Bit by bit he began telling her things he'd made himself forget, things about growing up torn between a father who wanted him to join his older halfbrothers in the business and a mother whose scorn of business was profound, who'd been sold into marriage to pay the debts of her family (a minor branch of the ancient and noble Amara sept). Tadar Chandro's son bought her to gain greater prestige among the powers of Bandrabahr, got a son on her, then proceeded to ignore her. She hated him for taking her, she loathed his touch, she hated him almost as much for leaving her alone, for his insulting lack of interest·in her person or her sex. But she knew better than to release any of her venom beyond the walls of her husband's compound, he wouldn't need much excuse to repudiate her, since he'd already got all the good out of her he was going to get, no, she saved her diatribes for her son's ears.

"I was the sixth son," Ahzurdan said, "ten years younger than Shuj who was youngest before me. He took pleasure in tormenting me, I don't know why. On my twelfth birthday my father gave me a sailboat as he had all his other sons on their twelves. A few days later I was going to take it out on the river when I met Shuj coming from the boathouse. When I went inside. I saw he'd slashed my sail and beat a hole in the side of the boat. I went pelting after him, I don't think I'd ever been so angry. I was going to, I don't know what I was going to do, I was too hot to think. I caught up with him near the stables, I yelled at him I don't know what and I called up fire and nearly incinerated him. What saved him was fear. Mine. There was this ball of flame licking around my hands; it didn't hurt me, but it scared the fury out of me. I jerked my arms up and threw it into the clouds where it fried a few unfortunate birds before it faded away. After that Shuj and all the others stayed as far away from me as they could. . . ."

Tadar was frightened and disgusted; a practical man, he wanted nothing to do with such things. For years he'd been crushed beneath the weight of a vital charismatic father who had a good-natured contempt for him, but after Chandro's death, he set about consolidating the business, then he cautiously increased it; he hated the sea, was desperately seasick even on river packets, but was shrewd enough to pick capable shipmasters, pay them well and give them an interest in each cargo. As the years passed, he prospered enormously until he was close to being the richest Phras in Bandrabahr. He spent a month ignoring his youngest son's pecularities and snarling at his other sons when they tried to complain (they had uneasy memories of tormenting a spoiled delicate boy and didn't want Ahzurdan in the same room with them), but two things forced him to act. The servants were talking and his customers were nervous. And Zuhra Ahzurdan's mother had sent to her family for advice (which infuriated Tadar, principally because they acted without consulting him and he saw that as another of the many snubs he'd endured from them); they located a master sorceror who was willing to take on another apprentice and informed Tadar they were sending him around three days hence, he should be prepared to receive him and pay the bonding fee.

For Ahzurdan, during those last months at home, it was as if he had a skin full of writhing, struggling eels that threatened to burst through, destroying him and everything around him. Before the day he nearly barbequed his brother, he'd had nightmares, day terrors and surges of heat through his body; he shifted unpredictably from gloom to elation, he fought to control a rage that could be triggered by a careless word, dust on his books, a dog nosing him, any small thing. After that day, his mood swings grew wilder and fire came to him without warning; he would be reaching for something and fingerlength flames would race up his arms. The night before the sorceror was due, his bed curtains caught fire while he was asleep, nearly burnt the house down; one of the dogs smelled smoke and howled the family awake; they put the fire out. It didn't hurt him, but it terrified everyone else.

For Tadar, that was end; he formally renounced his son; Ahzurdan was, after all, only a sixth son and one who had proved himself worthless. His mother wept, but didn't try to hold him. He was happy enough to get away from the bitterness and rage that flavored the air around her; she kept him tied to her, filled his ears with tales of her noble family and laments about how low she'd sunk marrying his father until he felt as if he were drowning in spite. He blamed her for the way his brothers treated him and the scorn his father felt for him, but didn't realize how much like her he was, how much of her outlook he'd absorbed. Brann recognized Zuhra's voice in the excessive respect he had for people like the Envoy and his dislike for what he called rabble.

Settsimaksimin came to Tadar's House around mid-morning. "He scared the stiffening out of my bones," Ahzurdan said. "Six foot five and massive, not fat, his forearms where they came from the halfsleeves of his robe looked like they were carved from oak, his hands were twice the size of those of an ordinary man, shapely and strong, he wore an emerald on his right hand in a smooth ungraven band and a sapphire on his left; he had thick fine black hair that he wore in a braid down his back, no beard (he couldn't grow a beard, I found that out later), a face that was handsome and stern, eyes like amber with fire behind it; his voice was deep and singing, when he spoke, it seemed to shake the house and yet caress each of us with the warmth, the gentleness of . . . well, you see the effect he had on me. I was terrified and fascinated. He brought one of his older apprentices with him, a Temueng boy who walked in bold-eyed silence a step behind him, scorning us and everything about us. How I envied that boy."

Tadar paid the bond and sent one of the houseboys with Ahzurdan to carry his clothing and books, everything he owned. That was the last time he saw his family. He never went back.

On the twelfth day out of Jade Halimm the merchanter Jiva Mahrish sailed into the harbor at Kukurul. A few days later as they waited for a ship heading for Bandrabahr, Settsimaksimin tried again.

5

SILAGAMATYS ON THE SOUTH COAST OF CHEONEA, THE CITADEL OF SETTSIMAKSIMIN.

SCENE: Settsimaksimin walking the ramparts, looking out over the city and talking at his secretary and prospective biographer, an improbable being called Todichi Yahzi, rambling on about whatever happened to come into his mind.

Soaring needle faced with white marble, swooping sides like the line from a dancer's knee to her shoulders when she's stretched on her toes, a merloned walk about the top. Settsimaksimin's Citadel, built in a day and a night and a day, an orgy of force that left Maksim limp and exhausted, his credit drawn down with thousands of earth elementals and demon stoneworkers, fifty acres of stone, steel and glass. Simplicity in immensity.

Late afternoon on a hot hazy day. Grown impatient with the tedium of administration and the heat within the walls, Settsimaksimin told Todichi Yahzi to bring his notebooks and swept them both to the high ramparts. Heat waves crawled from the earth-colored structures far below, a haze of dust and pollen gilded the Plain that stretched out green and lush to mountains whose peaks were a scrawl of pale blue against the paler sky, but up here a brisk wind rushed from the open sea and blew his sweat away. "Write," Maksim said. "You can clean it up later."

He wound his gray-streaked braid in a knot on his head, snapped a skewer to his hand and drove it through the mass to hold it in place. He opened his robe, spread it away from his neck, began stumping along the broad stone walkway, his hands clasped behind him, the light linen robe fluttering about his bare feet, throwing words over his shoulder at Todichi Yahzi who was a thin gangling creature (male), his skin covered with a soft fur like gray moss. His mouth was tiny and inflexible, he ate only liquids and semi-liquids; his speech was a humming approximation of Cheonase that few could understand. He had round mobile ears and his eyes were set deep in his head, showing flashes of color (violet, muddy brown, dark red) as he looked up from his pad, looked down again and continued his scribbling in spidery symbols that had no like in this world. Settsimaksimin fetched him from a distant reality so he'd have someone he could talk to, not a demon, not an ambitious Cheonene, but someone wholly dependent on him for life and sustenance and . . . perhaps . . . transport home. His major occupation was listening to Maksim ramble about his experiences, writing down what he said about them along with his pronouncements on life, love, politics and everything.

"The Parastes . . . the Parastes . . . parasite Parastes, little hopping fleas, they wanted to make me their dog, their wild dog eating the meat of the land and they eating off me."

He charged along the rampart, breasting the wind like some great bull, bare feet splatting on the stone, voice booming out over the city, lyric basso singing in registers so low Todichi had to strain to hear the words.

"They wanted to go on living till the end of time as entitled do-nothings. Bastards of the legion of the Born. Lordlings of the earth. Charter members in the club of eugennistos. Owners of lands, lives and good red gold."

Todichi Yahzi hoomed and cooed and was understood to say, "For the honesty of my records, sar Sassa'ma'sa, were there no patrikkos among them, no good men who cared for their folk? Among my own . . ."

Settsimaksimin swung round, yellow eyes burning
with feral good humor. "My mother was a whore and
I'm a half-breed, don't ask me for their virtues. Not
me." He threw back his head and let laughter rumble
up from his toes. "I never saw any. HAH! Go talk to
them and see how sweet they are." He swept an arm
around in a mighty half-circle. "Look out there, Todich. Black and bountiful, that old mother, she lays
there giving it away to any may who knows how to tickle
her right. Who does the tickling, who makes her breed
and bear? Not our Parastes. Dirt suits the dirty, not
them, not our elegant educated fleas. Pimping fleas,
lending her to busy little serfs who fuck her over and
get nothing for their labors, it's the flea pimps who carry
off the bounty she provides. They sit down there close
enough to smell, Todich; they sit down there in their
fancy houses behind their fancy walls with their fancy
guards and fancy dogs keeping out the folk they fancy
want to get at them; they sit down there and curse me.
Let them curse. They go to sleep down there and dream
me dead. Let them dream. Hah, who's dying? Not me.
NOT ME," he shouted and the walls shook with the
power of his voice. He wiped at his neck, started walking again, more slowly as if some of the energy had
gone out of him with the shout. When he spoke, his
voice was softer, more sedate. "I made laws, Todich,
you've writ them down, good laws, fair to the poor,
maybe not so fair to the rich, but they've had a thousand
years going their way." He chuckled. "Let them suffer
a little, it's good for the character. Good for the CHAR-
ACTER, HA HA," he twisted his head around, "hear
that, old mole? Ah the scorn I got, the righteous indignation. What am I doing? Clodhoppers and bumpkins?
School? Land of their own? Whose land? WHOSE
LAND! NEVER! Thief! Tyrant! Ignorant idiotic imbe-
cile! You'll ruin the country. You'll destroy everything
we've built. A voice in how they live? Perpetual servitude is the natural state of some men. Free them and
you destroy them. Who is going to tell them what to
do? They're lazy and improvident. Haven't you seen
how they shirk their work? Look at how they live, how
dirty they are. They drink and fornicate and beat their

wives and starve their children. We hammer virtue into them, otherwise nothing would get done. They aren't men, they're beasts; if you treat them like men, you are a fool and you are harming them rather than helping. Ah ah ah, Todich, there you have your sweethearts. For those fleas, those bloodsucking fleas, for those swaggering club-wielders, the serfs were just one more tool for working the earth. Plowing procreating digging sticks. Animated hoes. Grubbing the fields of the fiefs, generation unto generation without a day of rest, without a home and fireside, without anything to save their worn-out nothingness until I took them into my hands.

"Two sorts of beings out there on the Plain, Todich. Nay-saying non-doing Parastes and everyone else. Field hands, farmers, ferrymen, watermen and woodmen, rowers and growers of greens, chandlers, craftsmen, drovers and sellsouls who were armed and charged with defending the fiefs of the Parastes against the claims of the slaves." Laughter rolled out like thunder. He turned the corner and went charging along the west wall. "They didn't expect their people to love them, no they did not. Just serve them, Hmm. I tried—and succeeded, Todich, you've writ how I succeeded—to bring more equality between the rich and the beggars. And spread confusion with both hands." He held up huge shapely hands. "Bountiful confusion and I enjoyed it, every moment of it. Why bother my head with such chimeras? they asked me. You can't do it. The poor don't want it, they hate change, they want things to go on being the same. They won't help you. We won't help you, we're not inclined to suicide. Your army won't help you, they despise dirt grubbers more than we do. Be sensible. Power is power. The rule is yours. Enjoy it, don't wear yourself down." The massive shoulders went round, he clasped his hands once more behind him and slowed his pace and lowered his voice to a mutter. "There are times when I'm tempted to agree." He stopped, put his hand on a merlon and stood squinting at the city below. "Then . . . then I remember begging in the streets. Look, Todich, down there, where the two lanes meet by the end of the market. A Parast had his harmosts beat me because I startled his horses. I left my blood

on those paving stones, but you couldn't find it now,
there's too much other blood over and under it. And
there,'' he flung his arm up, jabbing his hand at the city
wall where it curved to meet the bay, ''I can see a hut
there still, on that hill just beyond the wall, my mother
starved in one like it after she was too old to whore any
longer. Do you know why the Citadel is here and nowhere else? When I was six, Todich, a merchant caught
me stealing and brought me to the slave market, it was
right here, under where we're standing, and the pleasurehouses were just a step away, when we get round to
the north side we'll be over the House I was sold into.
No one should be rich enough to buy another, Todich,
and no one poor enough that he's obliged to let himself
be sold. Moderation, Todich, wealth in moderation,
poverty in moderation. Pah!'' He slapped the stone and
stumped on.

''I took into my hands a country where the poor
counted for nothing, where scoundrels were everything,
so I had to be a greater scoundrel than them all, Todich.
They were right, these fleas; no one wanted me to do
what I did. I made my laws and sent out my judges with
orders to be just and what happened? The poor ran to
their masters for justice (ah, the silly men they were)
and shunned mine. I had to do it all myself. I sold my
soul, Todich. I sold it to the Stone and to Amortis. And
I sold Cheonea to Amortis, when you take away one
center you have to provide another, Todich; she's no
prize, our Amortis, but she's less bloody than some;
her sacrifices are those all men make without much
prodding . . . hah! no, with a good lot of prodding, if
you'll forgive the pun. I've done worse things, Todich,
for reasons not half so worthy. I shrank from no evil to
ensure my laws were enforced, especially the land laws.
Write this, be sure you write this. I distributed the land
to the people who worked it, with this condition, they
were to pay the former Parastes a small sum quarterly
for thirty years, then the land would be paid off and
they would have in their hands the deed for it. I did that
because I wanted them to value it. I knew them far
better than the fleas did, I was one of them, I knew they
wouldn't believe in anything that came to them too eas-

ily; I knew once they'd sweated and bled to earn the deed, they would own that land in their minds and in their blood and in their bone and they'd fight to keep it. The title papers have been going out for the past ten years. Lazy clodhoppers, eh Todich? Not anything like. Thrifty frugal suspicious lot, more than half of them paid out early, I think they weren't all that sure I'd last, they wanted that paper and they got it. And the same day they got it, those deeds were registered at the village Yrons and the Citadel. Ah, how I love them, these bigoted, stubborn, enduring men. They know what I've done for them, they're mine, they'd bleed for me or spy for me; they pray for me, did you know that? I've seen them do it when they didn't know I was watching. It wasn't for show, Todich, not for show." A rumbling chuckle filled with humor and affection. "Though they get annoyed with me sometimes. They don't like me interfering in their lives. They didn't like it when I put Amortis in their villages; I didn't like it either, but you have to break the old before you can bring the new, besides, I needed Amortis' priestcorps to run the country for me until I could get the dicasts and village headmen trained, there's only so much you can do with soldiers. They didn't want the schools either, I had to scourge half a village sometimes before they'd let their children come to them those first years. What a change since. Now they're proud of sons who can read, now they scold their grandsons when the lads want to skip school and forget learning to read, write and cipher, now they go to the passage ceremonies with wonderful pride in their own. Ah ah ah, and I am proud of them. They took the reins from me and built a strong new life on the changes I made. It'd be a foolish tyrant who tried to wrest land and learning from them now.

"There's one thing I regret, Todich, that's forcing Amortis on the Finger Vales. Burning their priests. I spit on these torchers, those stinking bloody brainless Servants with their Whore God. I spit on myself for letting it be done, Todich, done in my name. Amortis! Forty Mortal Hells, I didn't think even a god would be that stupid, but I NEED her, Todich. A hundred years, I thought I was buying a hundred years so I could set

my changes so deeply no man could uproot them. Haaa
yaa yaa, I need them but I won't get them, that greedy
bitch has ruined me. HAH! Ruined or not, I'm going
to fight, let the Hellhag come, I'm a skin filled with
rancor and I'm waiting.''

He stopped in the center of the south side and stood
looking out across the Notoea Tha. Todichi Yahzi
dropped into a squat behind a merlon and waited with
stone patience for Maksim to start talking again.

The ariels came blowing out of the east, swirled in a
confusing flutter about him, whispering their reports in
their soughing voices, voices that were winds whistling
in Todichi Yahzi's ears, nothing more. ''. . . the woman
. . . alive . . . Jiva Marish . . . Ahzurdan . . . wards
. . . Kukurul . . .''

Maksim cursed bitterly, using his lowest register, the
words tearing from his throat. Leaving Todichi Yahzi to
make his own way down, he snapped to his sanctuary
deep within the earth, warm dark earth around him,
elementals sleeping coiled about him, protecting him,
ready to wake if he called them. Lights came on automatically as he materialized there and he strode toward
the storage shelves, dragging the skewer from his braid,
shaking it down, pulling his robe closed and doing up
the fastenings. He thrust his arms into the loose overrobe he wore for working; sleeveless, heavy and soft, it
hung about him like woven darkness as he carried the
mirror case to his work table. He kneed the chair aside,
set the case down and stood with his hands on the double hinged lid, thumbs tapping lightly at the wood as he
calmed himself into a proper state to use the mirror.
''Little Danny Blue,'' he murmured, ''Ahzurdan. I
wonder how you got tangled in this mess.'' His mouth
curled into a tight smile. ''Tungjii, old meddler, that
you sticking your thumbs in?''

He maneuvered the chair back and dropped into it
with an impatient grunt, opened the case, took out the
black obsidian mirror and the piece of suede he used to
polish it. ''I know your little tricks, Blue Dan, I know
you, Danny Boy.'' He wiped gently at the face of the
mirror, breathed on it, wiped again. ''Did you think of
this, Danny Blue? I don't know her. I can't reach her.

I found her through the boy the first time, now I've got you to guide my sight, is that a piece of luck, Baby Dan, or is that a piece of luck. Haaaa! I've GOT you, Blue, nowhere you can hide from me." He set aside the leather and slid the mirror into its frame. "Ahzurdan in Kukurul," he intoned and touched the stone oval with a long forefinger.

The stone surface shimmered, then he saw the side of a rambling inn and small sparkles of light writing patterns over a window on the third floor. "Sooo sooo, how much have you learned since you ran off, Ser Ahzurdan? Mmm, interesting, I wonder where you picked that up? Looks like something Proster Xan was playing with a few years back. That's a clever twist, now how do I untie it? This . . . this . . . ah! cute, touch that one and I'm smoke. Sooo sooo, how do I get round that . . . here? No, I don't think so, tempting but . . . let's fiddle this loop out a little. Ah, ah ah, now this. Riiight. And now it comes neatly apart. Don't try fooling your old teacher, boy. Let's put this aside so we can tie it up again if we want and take a look at what's happening in there. Mmmmh mmh. So that's our Drinker of Souls." He leaned closer, frowning. "That mushhead swore he put the pagamacher in your heart, I suppose he missed his hit. You're hard to kill, lady. Mmm. No more tigermen . . . what have I got . . . mmmmm . . . what have I got. . . ." The woman was sitting in a chair with her feet up on a hassock; her body was relaxed but her brilliant green eyes followed Ahzurdan with a concentrated intensity as he walked about the comfortable room, his hands moving restlessly, opening and closing, tapping on surfaces, fondling small objects, while he talked in spurts and silences. "Gabble gabble, Danny Blue, you haven't changed a hair . . . hmm." Two children were curled up on the bed, sleeping; he had a vague idea that they were attached to the woman and were a bit more than children. He watched them a moment, became convinced they weren't breathing. "Dipped in the reality pond, did you, lady? And pulled you out a pair of . . . of what? Complications, mmm, if I wait until you're alone and see you out, saying I can do it this time, those children would be left and what would I have coming at me? I went too fast the first time and missed my hit and unless I mistake me badly. I've done myself a mischief by it. Sooo sooo, this time I'll watch a while. A while? A day or two. Or three. Or more. Until I'm ready, lady.'' With a rumbling chuckle, he shoved the chair back and started to stand, stopped in the middle of the move and flattened his hands on the table. ''Oh Maksi old fool, senility is setting in, next thing you know, you'll be drooling in your mush. Sooo sooo.'' He reassembled the ward and set it in place outside the window. When he was done, he pushed onto his feet, leaving the mirror focused on the Inn. ''Dream your little dreams, Danny Blue, I'll be with you soon as I finish some cursed clamoring business . . .'' He stretched, groaned as muscle pulled against muscle, pulled off the overrobe and tossed it onto the chair. ''AAAH! WHY WHY WHY can't they SEE? It's so simple.'' He twitched the linen robe straight and with a few quick flowing passes rid it of its wrinkles. ''Dignity, give a man his dignity and you've increased his value and the land's value with it.'' He rubbed his feet on the pavingstones. ''Be damned if I cramp my toes for that son of a diseased toad, that high-nosed high priest of my whore god, that posturing potentate of ignorance, HAH!'' He glamoured sandals over his feet, grinned and added tiny grimacing caricatures of Vasshaka Bulan Servant of the Servants of Amortis to the seeming straps of white leather. A touch to the Stone snugged beneath his robe, a twisted tight smile as he felt a tingle in his fingertips, then he snapped to the reception chamber at the top of the west tower, a gilded ornate room that he detested. He knew the effect of his size and the chamber's barbaric splendor (and the long laborious climb to reach it) and used them when he had to deal with folks like Vasshaka Bulan who needed a good deal of intimidation to keep their ambitions in hand. A desk the size of a small room and a massive carved chair sat on a shallow dais that raised both just enough to give visitors an ache in the neck and a general sense of their own unworthiness. He settled himself in the chair, gave a quick rub to the emerald on his right thumb. ''Let the charade proceed,'' he muttered. The only object in the vast plateau of polished kedron was a dainty bell of unadorned white porcelain. He rang it twice, replaced it and sat back in the chair, his arms along its arms, his hands curved loosely about their finials.

The double doors swung smoothly open and Vasshaka Bulan came stalking in, Todichi Yahzi gliding grayly behind him clutching a scarlet notebook. He touched Bulan's arm (ignoring the man's recoil and hiss of loathing), cooed him to the visitor's chair, then went to the gray leather cushion waiting beside the desk, wriggled around until he was comfortable, settled the book in his lap and prepared to record everything said during the interview.

Maksim rumbled impatiently through the rituals of greeting, gave brusque permission for Vasshaka Bulan to say what was on his mind. "Brief and blunt," he said, "unless you want to try my patience, Servant Bulan."

"Phoros Pharmaga, I hear." Bulan bowed his head. "I have a complaint about the Dicast Silthos a Melisto. He ordered a Servant taken from the Yron of Nopido, sat in judgment over him and ordered him stoned by the Nopidese. He had no right, Phoros. A Servant is judged by Amortis and the Kriorn of his Yron. None less can touch him. By your own word, this is Amortis' land."

"By my own word, Amortis judges her Servants in all except . . ." he leaned forward and slapped his hand on the desktop, making the wood boom, "EXCEPT for civil crimes. Rape is a civil crime. I have read the Dicast's report, Servant of Servants. This charming creature of yours raped an eight-year-old girl."

Bulan lifted his hand. "A holy frenzy, Phoros, for which he is not responsible."

Settsimaksimin forced himself to wait a moment before responding, hammering an iron calm over a fury that inclined him to send this snake back to Amortis as ash. He needed the wily old twister, especially now when he couldn't afford a fuss that would divert his attention from the Drinker of Souls and what she could mean to him. He managed a cold smile. "Anarpa didn't seem to share that notion. He murdered the girl and tried to conceal what he'd done.''

"A weak man is a weak man and a stupid one does not acquire wisdom at such a moment. It is for the Yron and the Kriorn to judge him.''

"By my word and by my law it is the people he injured who have that right. By my word and by my law and in the Covenant I made with Amortis. A covenant that you know word for word, Vasshaka Bulan, Servant of the Servants of Amortis.'' He lifted his hand and laid it across his chest, the Stone warm and dangerous under his palm. "We have been patient with you, Faithful Servant, because we know you are devoted to She whom we both . . . serve. We will continue our patience and explain our decree. The Servant Anarpa took refuge within the Nopido Yron when his crime was reported which from our reading was almost immediately since there was a witness to the burial. The Dicast, as was most proper and courteous though not necessary under our law and covenant, sent to the Nopido Yron and asked that the Servant named Anarpa be given to the civil court for judgment. The Kriorn of the Yron refused to produce him.'' Maksim felt his heart hurrying under the Stone and once again took time to calm himself. "That was neither proper nor courteous. Nor is it sanctioned by law or covenant. It is we, Vasshaka Bulan, who complain to you of such contumacious behavior. It is we, Vasshaka Bulan, who say to you, discipline your Servants or we will do it for you. And should you doubt our will or our ability to do so, we will ask Amortis to make it plain to you by punishing that Kriorn herself. We have explained to you what we intend to accomplish within the land; Amortis has given her sanction to these goals. Any Servant who cannot work with enthusiasm for our dream had best find another land to serve the Lady.'' He watched Bulan's face but not a muscle moved; the mild old eyes had no more feeling in them than a chunk of low grade coal.

"It is time, perhaps,'' Bulan said slowly, as if he were considering with great care everything he said (though Maksim had no doubt the old twister had foreseen everything so far and plotted his speech accordingly, most of it anyway; with some pleasure Maksim remembered catching a slight tic in a cheek muscle when he said Amortis would do the punishing of that idiot Kriorn, that knocked you off center, you old viper). "It is time, I say, that we who are not so wise as you, Phoros Pharmaga, should meet and draw up tables determining specifically who in what circumstances has responsibility for making and upholding what laws."

Again Settsimaksimin examined the Servant's face, there was no reading anything but mild earnestness in that disciplined mask he used to cover his bones. *What are you up to? I wouldn't trust you with the ink to write your initials. If you think you're going to tighten your bony grip on My people. . . . Hmm. Might not be a bad idea, though, keep him out of my hair when I haven't got the time or energy to waste on him.* "We will think on it," he said gravely. "We are inclined to agree with you, Faithful Servant. Do this, draw up a list of scholars civil and servant whom you find capable of dealing with the complexities in such a plan and yourself, out of your vast wisdom, do you write for us the agenda you consider most suitable for such a group with such a purpose. Seven days for the list and agenda. Or do you need more?"

Vasshaka Bulan bowed his head in humble submission. "Seven days is sufficient, Phoros Pharmaga."

After he was gone, Settsimaksimin shoved his chair back with such force the wood of the legs shrieked against the wood of the dais. He went charging about the room muttering to himself while Todichi Yahzi finished his notes. "Seven days. Sufficient. HAH! SEVEN MINUTES IS MORE LIKE. He's been worming toward this for AHHH the gods know how long. I don't see what he's going to get out of it, Todich. He knows I'm going to read every miserable word of whatever comes out of that bunch of legal nitwits and anything I don't understand or don't like is DEAD, Todich. The names? How could I trust men he named for something like this? Even if I know they're good men. He's after something, Todich, WHY CAN'T I SEE IT?" He flung his arms out, dragged in a huge lungful of air.

"AAAHHhhhmm HAH! Hunh." Abruptly brisk, he turned to Todichi Yahzi. "Write this: strataga Tapos a Parost and his prime captain; guildmaster Syloa h'Arpagy; kephadicast Oggisol a Surphax and the three judges he talked to me about, I've forgotten their names but he'll remember; harbormaster Kathex h'Apydaro; peasant Voice, Hrous t'Thelo. Got those? Good. Write me out a note to the chief Herald Brux so I can sign it. Say send your best and fastest heralds, men you know can keep their mouths shut, to the folk on that list and tell them to meet with . . . hmm, better be formal about it, I suppose . . . the Phoros Pharmaga Settsimaksimin three days on, in the Citadel. This next is for you, Todich, put them in the Star Cabinet down on the first floor, it's warded, I don't want anyone snooping about what I'm going to be saying there. Finished? Give me the stylus a moment. There. No, don't go yet. Listen, Todich, I'll be spending a lot of time in my workroom and while I'm there those men are going to run Cheonea for me. Hah!" A rumbling chuckle as Todichi Yahzi cooed a flurry of objections. "I know, my friend. That's why I want you to watch them waking and sleeping. You know, Todich, this isn't such an unhappy turn of affairs after all; I've been thinking about setting up a council of governance like that for some years now, to see how it would work if I weren't here, ah, where was I? Yes. I'll give you command of some ariels and a clutch of stone sprites . . . no no, you'll be able to see and hear them, I'm not an idiot, Todich. If I had the mirrors . . . tchah! I've been lazy and stupid, my friend. Mmm. You'll know a palace coup if you see one hatching, yes, Todich, I really have been listening to you. If you see anything funny happening, give me a call, I'll show you how to reach me tonight, when I get back. No, I won't be angry if you've misread some twitch or tic for treason, this is a time when caution is far more important than certainty. If they're honest and I show my face, it will encourage them; if they're starting a fiddle, they'll think again." He rubbed at the back of his neck. "Hot in here. Anything more you need to know? Good. Seven levels of mortal hell, Todich, I've got to wrestle that bitch Amortis into scourging the No-

pidese kriorn. I'll be on Deadfire Island for the rest of
the day. If anything comes up," he stretched, yawned,
laughed, "turn it off till tomorrow. The world won't fall
apart in that short a time."

Settsimaksimin sat in his sanctuary watching as Ahzurdan rambled through the streets of Kukurul with the
woman or sometimes the children; there was a tooth-
edged trace between those odd preteens and Ahzurdan
that made him smile because it was so much like the
hostility he'd faced now and again when he'd taken lovers from among the double-gaited, the hostility of children who refuse to share their parent; in a way it was
puzzling, from what he knew of Baby Dan there
wouldn't be much between the woman and him, nothing
to make the children so jealous, but jealous they were
and suspicious of him. They watched him and they
burned.

And they protected him, presumably because the
woman told him to. On the fifth night in Kukurul, late,
long after the woman had gone to sleep. Ahzurdan
slipped out of the Inn and went foraging among the
alleys of the waterfront. Watching him sidle through the
darkness, Maksim nodded to himself. Hunting a trader
in dreamdust, he thought. You don't change, Danny
Blue. Miserable little rat. He thrust his hand into his
robe and under the Stone, massaged his chest. Still running away from anything that makes you look at yourself. Wonder where the children are? Did you finally
manage to slip them? He continued to watch and after
several more twists he noticed a gray mastiff following
Ahzurdan, a purposeful shadow in shadows. Now what
does that mean? He examined the beast. Ah! crystal
eyes, no irids, only a swirl of half-guessed vapor. One
of the children, the boy, yes, I've never seen demons or
anything else with eyes like theirs. So. Shapeshifters.
He looked around for the girl and found a nighthawk
drifting above the street, swinging in slow loops that
centered over Ahzurdan. A large nighthawk with glimmering crystal eyes. Clever children. Strong muscles
and a good set of tearing teeth down there on the
ground, a watcher overhead. You can talk to each other,

can't you. Interesting. Mmm. Ambush ahead. You up there, you have to see them. What are you going to do about it? Nothing? Ah. The mastiff edged closer until he was almost breathing on Ahzurdan's heels and the hawk dropped lower. I see. Let Baby Dan handle it, but be ready to jump if he needs you.

The muggers attacked and were dispatched neatly by a jolt from Ahzurdan; he smoothed his tunic down and went on, ignoring the dead men. Unaware of his escort, he found a dealer, got the dust and went slipping back to the Inn. He sat holding the packet and staring unhappily at it. Then he laid it away among his robes, undressed and crawled into bed. Sooo sooo, baby Dan, I wouldn't 've believed it without seeing it. Mmm. That worries me. I don't want you cleaned out and feeling pert, Danny Boy, I want you coming at me scared. He rubbed long limber fingers together, yellow eyes fixed on the sleeping man. You were the best I had, little Blue, yes, and the most dangerous. I smelled it on you the minute I saw you, standing there no one daring to get close. Your face is twisting, little Blue, remembering me in your dreams? I swore I'd tame you or kill you. Came close to doing both, didn't I. But you ran, Danny Blue. You ran so fast and so far it didn't seem worth coming after you. Got your nerve back? Or is it the woman? Demidemon with finicky tastes, or so I hear. No respecter of man or god. Goes her own way and be damned to those who try and stop her. Amortis, Haa-Unh, she turned purple when I told her Drinker was heading this way. Drinker of Souls. God of gods, I like her, I do. You haven't a ship yet, lady, but any day now, and I'm not much good round water, did he tell you that, the toad? Mmm. Shapeshifters. I can deal with that. The eyes are enough to pin them. Wonder what they are when they're home? Hah hah hah, I don't really want to know. Sooo, what have I got for you, lady . . . mmm, what have I got . . . come the dawn, what do I throw at you?

6

WAITING AT KUKURUL,
THE INN OF PEARLY DAWN.

SCENE: Early morning. That lull time, when the
night life has diminished to a few weary
thieves, whores and drunks wandering
through dingy gray streets, when the day
life that will turn those streets noisy and
busy and fill them with color is confined
still to bedrooms (or whatever shelters the
sleepers managed to find) and kitchens and
stables.

Kukurul. The world's navel. The pivot of the four winds.
The pearl of five seas. It is said that if you sit long
enough at one of the outside tables of the Sidday Lir,
you'll see the whole world file past you going up the
Ihman Katt. Kukurul. Expensive, gaudy, secretive and
corrupt. Along the Ihman Katt, brothels for every taste
(in some of them children mimicking the seductive pos-
tures of street whores hang from upper windows solic-
iting custom); ranks of houses where assassin guilds
advertise men of the knife, men of the garotte, women
of the poison trade. If your tastes run to the macabre,
halfway long there is a narrow black building where
death rites are practiced and offered for the titilation of
connoisseurs. At the end of the Ihman Katt is the heart
of Kukurul, the Great Market. A paved square two miles
on a side where everything is on sale but heat, sweat
and stench. Where noise is so pervasive and so intense
that signing is a high art. No greens or flesh or food

fish, but anything else you might desire. Trained dog packs for nervous merchants or lordlings who don't enjoy personal popularity with family or folk; rare ornamental beasts and birds; honeycomb tanks of bright colored fighting fish, other tanks of ancient carp, chameleon seahorses, snails of marvelous color and convolution. Fine cloth and rare leathers. Blown glass of every shape, color, and use, including the finest mirrors in the world (according to the claims of their vendors). Gold, silver, coppersmiths sitting among their wares. Cuttlers and swordsmiths. Jewelers with fantastic wealth displayed about them. Spice merchants. Sellers of rare orchids. Importers of just about everything the world offered. And winding through the cluttered ways, water sellers, pancake women, piemen, meatroll vendors, their shops on their backs or rolling before them. That is Kukurul on the island of Vara Smykkal.

Vara Smykkal. The outermost island of the Myk'tat Tukery. A large verdant island. Little is known of the land and people beyond the ring of mountains about the deep sheltered harbor and most visitors don't bother asking; they spend their time in the Great Market or the cool dim trade rooms of the many Inns that sit on the hills around the Market Flat.

Myk'tat Tukery. Generally thought of as the Thousand Islands, though no one has ever counted them. The interior islands are mysterious, shut away from just about everyone, rumored to be fabulously wealthy and filled with women of superlative beauty and passion, with magical creatures like unicorns and manticores and spiders with nacreous eyes weaving wedding silks so fine they'd pass through a needle's eye, with trees that grow rubies and emeralds and sapphires, with fountains of gold and silver and liquid diamond. But the narrow crooked waterways between the islands were infested with bandits and pirates; there were deceptive shoals and rocks that moved, there were shifting mists and freaky winds and lightning walked most nights and one green rocky island looked much like the next. Even the cleverest and greediest men seldom got far into the maze and few of these got out again. And the ones that made it back seldom had much to say about what they'd seen.

During her wandering years after the ravaging of Arth Slya, Brann took a sailing canoe deep into the Myk'tat Tukery and out again, emerging with mind and body intact and memories of some lovely places, especially an island called Jal Virri, but like the less fortunate she didn't talk about the experience. She'd intended to go back one day; events intervened and she went in another direction. As she told Ahzurdan, she settled into clay and contentment at the Pottery beside the Wansheeri. Coming back to Kukurul roused those memories and she thought about retreating into the maze and letting the world rock on without her, but once again she was too tangled in that world to do more than daydream of peace.

Brann rose with the dawn and went to eat at the Sidday Lir, escaping before Ahzurdan crawled out of bed and came to bend her ear again. After living so long as a solitary, she found it difficult to control her growing irritation with the man; she was getting useful information about the training a sorceror required, his powers and their limitations, but she had to seine those items out of a flood of rambling discourse. A sleepy waiter brought her a pot of tea and a plate of mooncakes, went off to find some berries and cream.

Yaril came drifting along and settled beside her at the table. "He went out last night. Late. Bought two ounces dreamdust."

"Smoke any?"

"No."

Brann waited until the waiter set the bowl of berries and the cream pot before her and went away. "Hmp. Idiot man. Why now?" She poured a dollop of cream over the dark purple mound, lifted her spoon. "What do you think?"

"He'll crumble at a look. Drop him, Bramble."

"Hmm." For several minutes she spooned up berries, savoring the dark sweet-tart taste and the cool fresh breeze blowing in off the water, then she wiped her mouth and frowned at Yaril. "I don't think so. Not yet. Wait till we get to Bandrabahr, then we'll see."

Yaril shrugged. "You asked."

"So I did. Yaro, ever think about Jal Virri?"

"Not much. Boring place."

"But it was beautiful, Yaro."

"So? Lots of places are pretty enough. I like places where things happen."

Brann broke a mooncake in half. "Was your home like that, a place where things happen?"

"We've been away a long time, Bramble. Think about Arth Slya. What do you remember? The good times, eh? Same with us."

"I see." Like always, she thought, they won't talk about their home world, slip slide away. Did they love it, did they hate it, what did they think? Though she thought she knew them almost as well as she knew herself, at times like this she was jarred into a feeling that they were essentially unknowable. Too many referents that just weren't there. "Yaro . . ." she looked down over the warehouses and the wharves, out to the ships moored in the bay, "I'd like you and Jay to fly a sweep to the north and see if you can sight Zatikay's ship. Ahzurdan swears he'll be here any day now, but time's getting short on us. Theriste first is day after tomorrow, I want to be out of here by then, we have to be in Silagamatys by the seventeenth, I want some room for maneuvering in case of snags. You know nothing ever goes exactly as it's planned."

"Ahzurdan's a . . ."

"Don't say it, Yaro, I'm tired of that onenote song." She finished the berries, emptied the teabowl and tapped against it with her spoon. When the waiter came, she paid him, then began strolling up the still deserted Ihman Katt, passing the ancient streetsweepers as they brushed away the debris from last night's business, stopping a moment to exchange a word with a M'darjin woman so old her skin had turned ashy and her hair white as crimped snow. "Ma amm, Zazi Koko, how many diamonds today?"

Zazi Koko leaned on her broom and grinned at Brann, showing teeth as strong as they'd been when she was running the grassy hills of her homeland, though a lot yellower. "More than you, Embamba zimb, more than you."

"True, oh true." Brann laughed and ambled on. The brightening day was clear and cool; behind the facades she passed she could feel a slow torpid struggle against weariness left over from last night, lepidopter stirring in her chrysalis. She turned into the flowery winding lane that led uphill to the Pearly Dawn, walking slower still, reluctance to return to the Inn and Ahzurdan gathering like a lump under her ribs. She broke a green orchid from a spray that brushed her head, showering her with delicate perfume, tucked it into an empty buttonhole, then broke off another and eased it into the fine blond hair over Yaril's ear. Smiling affectionately at the startled girl, she patted her shoulder and ambled on.

Heavy-eyed and morose, Ahzurdan met her on the stairs and followed her into her room. As soon as the door shut behind him and before he could start talking, Brann said, "If Zatikay isn't here by tonight, I'm going to hire transport to Haven on Cheonea. Yes, yes, I know none of the Captains in the harbor would shift his schedule for any price, but there are ships not too deep in the Myk'tat Tukery with more flexible masters."

"Bloody cannibals, more likely to carve us up and eat us than waste time on open water."

"Unless they've changed since I ran into them, they won't bother me or the children. And I suspect you'd find it easy enough to convince them that you're no tasty morsel. I didn't say I liked the idea. But time's . . ." she broke off, frowned. There was suddenly a faint odd smell in the room, a creaky droning, like a doorhinge down a deep well. "What the . . ."

Tall, thin, brown and ivory, like a lightning-blasted tree, an eerie ugly creature solidified in front of Brann and reached for her.

Alerted by the sound and the smell, Brann dropped to a squat, then sprang to one side, slapping against the floor and rolling onto her feet. The treeish thing looked stiff and clumsy, but it wasn't; it was fast and flexible and frighteningly strong. One of its hands raised a wind over her head, but her hair was too short for any kind of grip and she dropped too quickly. When she kicked out of the squat, rough knotty fingers got half a grip on her leg but slipped off as she twisted away. She bounced onto her feet, gasped with sudden fear as a second set of hard woody arms closed about her and started to squeeze.

Yaril shifted to a fireball and flung herself at the treeish demon, meaning to burn it, but it wasn't what it seemed and all she did was char it a little, releasing an appalling stench into the room. It loosened its grip on Brann, held her with one hard ropy arm and swung at Yaril with the other.

Jaril came whipping through the wall and slammed into the first Treeish, charring it and stinging it enough to drive it back.

Another Treeish solidified from air and stench. And another.

Brann slapped her hands against her captor and began drawing its life into her; she screamed (voice hoarse with agony) as that corrosive firestuff poured into a body not meant to contain demon energies, but she didn't stop the draw.

Yaril flew to her, sucked away as much of the energy as she could and redirected it into a blast of liquid fire at the other three Treeish.

Jaril was a thick worm of fire, winding about the short stubby legs of the Treeish, toppling them one by one as they tried to move at Brann.

The Treeish holding Brann screamed, a deep hooming sound that cut off abruptly as the demon shivered suddenly to flakes of something like dried mushroom. Brann leaped at a second Treeish, one rocking onto its feet after Jaril tripped it; avoiding the arms that whipped snake quick at her, she got it from behind and flattened her hands against its sides, holding onto it through all its gyrations as she drained the life out of it, screaming and screaming at the agony of what she was doing, but going on and on.

While Brann scrambled desperately to survive and the children fought with her, Ahzurdan stood by the door, frozen, all his ambivalences aroused. He watched Brann struggle, he listened to her scream, he wanted to see her humiliated, hurt; he loathed this in himself, despaired when he had to acknowledge it. But he couldn't make himself act.

Minutes passed. The second Treeish died. For a breath or two, Brann stood trembling, unable to make herself endure that agony again, then she sank her teeth into her lip until she drew blood and threw herself at the third.

Yaril deflected a snatch of fire from the fight and spat it at Ahzurdan; it missed, being meant to miss, but it singed his ear and burnt away the ends of a wide swatch of his hair.

Startled out of his self-absorption, he roused will and memory, took a quick guess at the essence of the demons, assembled his shout, his hand gestures, and in a burst like a storm striking drove the demons from this reality.

Brann dropped panting to her knees, tears squeezing from her eyes. The changechildren dropped beside her, emerged from their fireball forms and spread their hands on her, drawing the poison fire out of her.

Ahzurdan stirred, went to the room's windows, threw them wide to let the sea breeze blow the stench away. He stood in the window that looked out over the bay, his back to the room, wanting to run before Brann recovered enough to ask the questions he refused to ask himself. It was so much simpler to be somewhere else when the result of his actions or lack of action began to come clear. His mind told him it was wiser to stay (this time) and talk his way round her. His flesh wasn't so sure.

"You took your time." Ordinarily she had a rather pleasant voice, low for a woman, but musical; those words came at him like missiles.

"You don't understand." He turned his head, a gesture toward courtesy, but didn't look at her.

"Hah!"

"I told you. We work by will. Will driven by knowing. Knowing comes first, it has to. I had to know them to force them home. It takes . . . time." Resisting an urge to see if she accepted that explanation, he stared out the window at nothing until a bit of color caught his eyes, a name flag on a masthead. His face loosened as he recognized it, though he tried to keep his relief from showing in his back. "Zatikay's in."

"Tk." An exasperated sigh. "Get yourself out there and find when he's leaving and if it's tomorrow or the next day, get us passage if you have to take deck space. Umf! And have a look at those wards of yours, seems to me they're leaking."

He drew his fingers along the sill, making lines in the faint dusting of yellow-gray pollen. "The ariels," he said. "They told him I'm traveling with you. He knows me, he knows my tricks." He felt an odd mix of fear and freedom, fear that she'd force him away from her, hope that she'd cut him loose so he didn't have to fight himself any longer, that she'd free him to destroy himself as quickly and as easily as seemed right. "I'm sorry. I didn't think of that when I asked to come with you."

"I did, so stop squirming." She was moving briskly about behind him; he turned, saw her using a pillowcase to clean up the leavings of the dead demons. The children were watching him, more hostile than ever. He had to make her say it.

"Tell me to go."

She looked up from the unpleasant task, raised her brows. "Why?"

"He can't find you if I'm not around."

"You were lazy, Dan, leaning on me too much. You won't again."

"I'll let you down, you know I will."

"If you want out, go. But it's your decision. You won't put that on me."

He looked at his hands, rubbed his thumbs across the smears of pollen clinging to his fingertips. "I can't go."

She nodded, got to her feet. "I see. If I understand what you've told me, Maksim is tired. He won't come at us again for a while. So, go talk to Zatikay. Jay, go with him. I want to know soonest if we're leaving on the morrow; you and Yaro will have to raid the treasury, our gelt is getting low. Go. Go." She laughed, waving the case at them. "Get out of here."

—— 7 ——

DANIEL AKAMARINO STROLLS DOWN A DUSTY BACK ROAD AND STEPS FROM ONE WORLD TO ANOTHER.

WORK RECORD

DANIEL AKAMARINO aka Blue Dan, Danny Blue

BORN:

YS 745

Rainbow's End

Line Family Azure

Family Azure has five living generations. 50 males (adults) aged 24-173. 124 females (adults) aged 17-175. 49 children. Names available to adults: Teal, Ciello, Royal, Akamarino, Turkoysa, Sapphiro, Ceruli, Lazula, Cyanica.

RATED:

1. Communications Officer, Master Rating, first degree
2. Propulsion Engineer, Master Rating, first degree
3. Cargo Superintendent/Buyer, Master Rating, first degree

COMMENTS:

If you can get him, grab him. He won't stay long, a year maybe two, but he's worth taking a chance on. Let him tinker. He'll leave you with a com system you couldn't buy for any money.

Got eyes in his fingertips and can hear a flea grunt a
light-year off. Have your engines singing if you let
him. Good at turning up and stowing cargo. Lucky.
Will make a profit for you more often than not.

A pleasant type, never causes trouble in the crew, but
undependable.

Drifter. Follows his whims and nothing you say will
hold him to a contract he wants to walk out on.

EMPLOYMENT:

1. Aurora's Dream
     Sun Gold Lines, home port: Rainbow's End.
     Captain: Martin Chrome
     YS 765-769   apprentice prop eng

2. Herring Finn
     free trader
     owner/master: Kally Kuninga
     YS 772-775   appr prop eng
                         Master Rating YS 775

3. Dying Duck
     free trader
     owner/master: Berbalayasant
     YS 779-786   appr coms off
                         Master Rating YS 786

4. Andra's Harp
     worldship
     Instell Cominc lines, registered the Sygyn Worlds
     Captain: Bynnyno Wadelinc
     YS 788-791   comms off sec (788)
                         comms off frst (789)
                         comms off Comdr (790-1)

5. The Hairy Mule
     free trader
     owner/master: Dagget O'dang
     YS 795-797   appr carg sup/   byr

6. Astrea Themis
     free trader
     owner/master: Luccan della Farangan
     YS 799-803   Mst Eng

7. Prism Dancer
   Sun Gold Lines, home port: Rainbow's End
   Captain: Stella Fulvina
   YS 805-810   comms off Comdr

8. Astrea Themis
   free trader
   owner/master: Luccan della Farangan
   YS 813-821   appr carg sup/byr
                          Mstr carg sup/byr YS 819

9. Herring Finn
   free trader
   owner/master: Kally Kuninga
   YS 825-   Mstr carg sup/byr

SCENE: Daniel Akamarino walking along the grassy
         verge of a paved road, letting his arms
         swing, now and then whistling a snatch of
         tune when he thought about it. A bright
         sunny day, local grass is lush with a tart
         dusty smell, pleasant enough, a breeze
         blowing in his face heavy with the scent of
         fresh water.

A man past his first youth (his age uncertain in this era
of ananile drugs that put off aging and death to somewhere around three hundred among those species where
three score and ten had once been optimum), bald except for a fringe of wild hair over his ears like a half-
crown of black thorns, blue eyes, brilliant blue, they
burn in a face tanned dark. He is tall and lanky, looks
loosely put together, but moves faster than most and
where his strength won't prevail, his slippy mind will.
A man not bothered by much, he seldom feels the need
to prove anything about his person or proclivities; he
mostly likes dealing with things but is occasionally interested in people, has quit several jobs because he
touched down in a culture that he found interesting and
he wanted to know all its quirks and fabulas. Impatient
with routine, he drifts from job to job, quitting when
he feels like it or because some nit tries to make him

do things that bore him like shaving every day or wearing boots instead of sandals and a uniform instead of the ancient shirts and trousers he gets secondhand whenever the ones he has are reduced to patches and threads. He stays longest in jobs where his nominal superiors tell him what they want and leave him to produce results however it suits him. He has no plans for settling down; there's always something to see another hop away and he never has trouble finding a place on a ship when he's done with groundside living.

Daniel Akamarino is down on a Skinker world, nosing about for items more interesting than those the local merchants are bringing to the backwater subport where the Herring Finn put down (the major ports were closed to freetraders; technically the world was closed, but its officials looked the other way as long as the profits were there and the traders were discreet). He is getting bored with the ship; the Captain is an oldtime friend, but she is a silent woman settled in a longterm and nonstraying relationship with her comms Com; the engineer is a Yilan with a vishéfer as a symbiote; two words a month-standard is verbosity for him.

Daniel Akamarino is mooching along beside a dusty two-lane asphalt road, enjoying a bright spring morning. Yesterday, when he was chatting over a drink with a local merchant, he took a close look at the armlet the Skinker was wearing on one of his right arms, flowing liquid forms carved into a round of heavy reddish brown wood. Today he is on his way to find the Skinker who carved it, said to live in an outshed of a warren a kilometer outside the porttown. Now and then a jit or a two-wheeler poots past him, or a skip hums by overhead. He could have hired a jit or caught the local version of a bus, but prefers to walk; he doesn't expect much from this world or from the woodcarver, but it's an excuse to get away from town clutter and merchants with gold in their eyes; he wants to look at the world, sniff its odors, pick up its textures and sound patterns, especially the birdsong. The local flying forms have elaborate whistles and a capacity for blending individual efforts into an astonishing whole.

Daniel Akamarino strolls along a two-lane asphalt road in a humming empty countryside listening to extravagant flights of birdsong; the grass verge having turned to weeds and nettles, he is on the road itself now, his sandals squeak on the gritty asphalt. A foot lifts, swings, starts down . . .

Daniel Akamarino dropped onto a rutted dirt road, stumbled and nearly fell. When he straightened, he stood blinking at an utterly different landscape.

The road he'd landed in curved sharply before and behind him; since it also ran between tall hedges he couldn't see much, only the tops of some low twisty trees whose foliage had thinned with the onrush of the year; withered remnants of small fruits clung to the topmost branches. Real trees, like those in his homeplace, not the feathery blue analogs on the road he'd been following an instant before. A raptor circled high overhead, songbirds twittered nearby, distractingly familiar; he listened and thought he could put a name to most of them. Insects hummed in the hedges and crawled through dusty gray-green grass. A black leaper as long as his thumb sprang out of the dust, landed briefly on his toe, sprang off again. He sucked on his teeth, kicked at the nearest rut, sent pale alkali dust spraying before him. If the sun were a bit ruddier and had a marble-sized blue companion, this could have been Rainbow's End. But it was egg-yellow and solitary, and it was low in what he thought was the west and its light had a weary feel, so he shouldn't waste what was left on the day boggling at what had happened to him. He took one step backward, then another, but the fold in spacetime that brought him here seemed a oneway gate. He shrugged. Not much he could do about that. He knelt in the dust and inspected the ruts. Inexpert as he was at this sort of tracking, it seemed to him that the heaviest traffic went the way he was facing. Which was vaguely northeast (if he was right about the sun). He straightened, brushed himself off, and started walking, accepting this jarring change in his circumstances as calmly as he accepted most events in his life.

Cradled in a warm noisy crowded line family, always someone to pick him up and cuddle him when he stubbed a toe or stumbled into more serious trouble, he had acquired a sense of security that nothing since had more than dented (though he'd wandered in and out of danger a dozen times and come close to dying more than once from an excess of optimism); he'd learned to defend himself, more because of his internal need to push any skill he learned to the limits of his ability than because he felt any strong desire to stomp his enemies. It was easier not to make enemies. If a situation got out of hand and nothing he could do would defuse it, he generally slid away and left the argument to those who enjoyed arguing. One time a lover asked him, "Don't you want to do something constructive with your life?" He thought about it for a while, then he said, "No." "You ought to," she said, irritation sharpening her voice, "there's more to living than just being alive." He gazed at her, sighed, shook his head and not long after that shipped out on the Hairy Mule.

He swung along easily through a late afternoon where heat hung in a yellow haze over the land and the road was the only sign of habitation; he wasn't in a hurry though he was starting to get thirsty. He searched through the dozens of pockets in his long leather overvest, found an ancient dusty peppermint, popped it into his mouth. A road led somewhere and he'd get there if he kept walking. The sun continued to decline and eventually set; he checked his pocket-chron, did some calculations of angular shift and decided that the daylength was close to shipstandard, another way this world was like Rainbow's End. He kept on after night closed about him; no point in camping unless he found water, besides the air was warm and a gibbous moon with a chunk bitten out of the top rose shortly after sunset and spread a pearly light across the land.

Sounds drifted to him on a strengthening breeze. A mule's bray. Another. A chorus of mules. Ring of metal on metal. Assorted anonymous tunks and thuds. As he drew closer to the source, the sounds of laughter and

voices, many of them children's voices. He rounded a
bend and found a large party camped beside a canal.
Ten carts backed up under the trees. A crowd of mules
(bay, roan and blue) wearing hobbles and herded inside
rope corrals, chewing at hay and grain and each other,
threatening, kicking and biting with an energy that made
nothing of the day's labors. Two hundred children seated
around half a dozen fires. Fifteen adults visible. Eight
women, dressed in voluminous trousers, tunics reaching to midcalf with long sleeves and wide cuffs, head-
cloths that could double as veils. Seven men with shorter
tunics and trousers that fit closer to the body, made
from the same cloth the women used (a dark tan home-
spun, heavy and hot), leather hats with floppy brims and
fancy bands, leather boots and gloves. They also had
three bobtail spears slanted across their backs and what
looked like cavalry sabers swinging from broad leather
belts; several carried quarterstaffs. The last were prowling about the circumference of the camp, keeping a stern
eye on the children while the women were finishing
preparations for supper.

One of the men walked over to him. "Keep moving,
friend. We don't want company here."

Daniel Akamarino blinked. Whatever or whoever had
brought him here had operated on his head in the instant
between worlds; he wasn't sure he liked that though it
was convenient. "Spare a bit of supper for a hungry
man?"

Before the man could answer, a young boy left one
of the circles carrying a metal mug full of water. "You
thirsty, too?"

A woman came striding after the boy, fixing the end
of her headcloth across her face, a big woman made
bigger by her bulky clothing. She put a hand on the
guard's arm when he took a step toward Daniel. "He's
a wayfarer, Sinan. Since when do Owlyn folk turn away
a hungry man?" She tapped the boy on the head. "Well
done, Tré. Give him the water."

Hoping his immunities were up to handling this
world's bugs, Daniel gulped down the cold clean water
and gave the mug back with one of his best grins.

"Thanks. A hot dusty walk makes water more welcome than the finest of wines."

"You'll join us for supper?"

"With enthusiasm, Thiné." The epithet meant Woman of High Standing, and came to his lips automatically, triggered by the strength and dignity he saw in her; she rather reminded him of one of his favorite mothers and he brought out for her his sunniest smile.

She laughed and swept a hand toward the circle of fires. "Be welcome, then."

They fed Daniel Akamarino and dug him out a spare blanket. The boy called Tré drifted over to sit by him while he ate, bringing an older girl with him that he introduced as his sister Kori. Tré said little, leaving the talking to Kori.

"This is one big bunch of kids," Daniel said. "Going to school?"

She stared at him, eyes wide. "It's the Lot. It's Owlyn's month."

"I haven't been here very long. What's the Lot?"

"Settsimaksimin takes three kids each year from each Parika in Cheonea. The Lot's to say which ones. Boys go to be trained for the army or for Servants of Amortis, girls go to the Yrons, those are the temples of Amortis, and the one that gets the gold lot goes to the high temple in Phras."

"Hmm. Who's Settsiwhatsisname and what gives him the right to take children from their families?"

Another startled look at him, a long gaze exchanged with her brother, a glance at the trees overhead. "We don't want to talk about him," Kori said, her voice a mutter he had to strain to hear. "He's a sorceror and he owns Cheonea and he can hear if someone talks against him. Best leave things alone you don't have to know."

"Ah. I hear you." Sorceror? Mmf. Probably means some git stumbled on this world and used his tech to impress the hell out of the natives. "You're heading for a city, how close is it?"

"Silagamatys. About three more days' travel. It's a sea port. Tré's seven, so this is his first trip. He hasn't seen the sea before."

"You have?"

"Course I have. I'm thirteen going on fourteen. This is my last Lot; if I slide by this time, I won't leave Owlyn Vale again, I'll be betrothed and too busy weaving for the family that comes." She sounded rather wistful, but resigned to the life fate and custom mapped out for her. "We've told you 'bout us. AuntNurse says it's impolite to pester wayfarers with questions. I think it's impolite for them to not talk when they have to see we're dying to know all about them." She was tall and lanky, with a splatter of orange freckles across her nose; wisps of fine light-brown hair straggled from under a headcloth that swung precariously every time she moved her head; her eyes were huge in her thin face, a pale gray-green that shifted color with every thought that passed through her head. She grinned at him, opened those chatoyant eyes wide and waited for him to swallow the hook.

"Weeell," he murmured, "I'm a traveling man from a long way off. . . ."

Much later, rolled into the borrowed blanket beside one of the carts, Daniel Akamarino thought drowsily about what he'd learned. He was appalled but not surprised. This wasn't the first tyrant who'd got the notion of building a power base in the minds of a nation's children. Clever about how he managed it. If he'd tried taking children out of their homes, no matter how powerful he was, he would have faced a blistering resistance. By having the children brought to him, by arranging what seemed to be an impartial choice through the Lot, he saved himself a world of trouble, didn't even have to send guards with the carttrains. Sorceror? Oh yeah. Seen that before, haven't you . . . Vague speculation faded gradually into sleep.

Having got used to him by breakfast (he was an amiable guest, quick to offer his services to pull and haul, doing his tasks whistling a cheerful tune that made the work lighter for everyone), they let him ride one of the carts. Tré and Kori sat with him. The boy was silent, troubled about something, the trouble deepening as he got closer to the city. For a while Daniel thought it was having to face the Lot for the first time, but when he slipped a murmured question to Tré, the boy shook his head. He was nervous and unhappy, he clung to Daniel for reasons of his own, but he wouldn't talk about what frightened him. Kori knew, but she was as silent about it as her brother. She sat on the other side of Daniel, sliding him murmured information about Silagamatys and its waterfront that she had no business knowing if it was like most other such areas he'd moved through in his travels. She laughed at his unexpressed but evident disapproval of her nocturnal wanderings. He liked the mischievous twinkle in her eyes, the dry quality to her humor, the subtle rebellion in the way she carried her body and changed his mind about how resigned she was to the future laid out for her. Thinking about it, he was rather sorry for her; from everything he'd seen so far, this world wasn't all that different from other agricultural societies he'd dipped into. Men and women both had their lives laid out for them from the moment they were born, which was fine if they fit into those roles, but hell on the rebels and the too-intelligent, especially if these last were women. Kori had a sharp practical mind; she must have realized years ago that there were things she couldn't admit to doing or knowing and continue to live at peace with her people. Talking with him was taking a chance; what she said and what it meant. slipping out after dark to wander through dangerous streets, that could destroy her. He suspected her actions had something to do with her brother's fretting, but he didn't have enough data to judge what she was getting at.

After a while, he fished inside his vest and brought out the recorder he carried everywhere; he blew it out, played a few notes, then settled into a dance tune his older sisters had liked. The other children in the cart crowded about him; when he finished that tune he had them sing their own songs for him, then played these back with ornamental flourishes that made them giggle. Tré joined him with a liquid lilting whistle, putting flourishes on Daniel's flourishes, the girls clapped their hands, the boys sang and the afternoon passed more quickly than most. After that, even Sinan stopped resenting him.

He caught glimpses of farmhouses and outbuildings, a village or two, no walls or fortifications in sight (obviously, invasions were scarce around here). They passed over a number of canals busy with barges and small sail boats; there was a lot more traffic on the water than there was on the road. He didn't blame them, this world hadn't got around to inventing effective springs and riding these ruts (even sitting on layers of blankets and quilts) was rather like a bastinado of the buttocks.

Midafternoon two days later, the carttrain topped a hill and looked down on Silagamatys.

Daniel Akamarino was playing his flute again, but broke off in surprise when his cart swung round a clump of tall trees at the crest of that hill and he saw for the first time the immense walls of the city and the gleaming white Keep soaring into the clouds.

"HIS Citadel," Kori murmured, her voice dropping into the special tone she used when she spoke of Settsimaksimin but didn't want to name him. "AuntNurse said her father's brother Elias, the one who married into the Ankitierin of Prosyn Vale, was down to the city just after HE kicked out crazy old King Noshios; she said Elias said HE cleared the ground and had that thing built in two days and a night. And then HE built the Grand Yron just two weeks later and that only took a day." Third in the line of ten, the cart tilted forward down the long undulating slope toward the city's SouthGate. "We're going to the Yron Hostel, it's built in back of the main temple. They won't let you in there, it's just for people doing the Lot. Actually, you'd better get off soon's we're through the Gate. You don't want HIM getting interested in you." The city was built on a cluster of low wooded hills looking out into a sheltered blue bay. The usual hovels and clutter of the poor and outcast snugged against the wall, but most of the ugliness was concealed by trees that Settsimaksimin had planted and protected from depredation by poor folk hunting fuel. When Daniel wondered about this, Kori said, "HE said don't touch the trees. HE said put iron to these trees and I'll hang you in a cage three days without food or water and don't think you can escape my eyes. And he did it too. HE said get your wood from the East Side Reserve. HE said Family Xilogonts will run the Wood Reserve for you. HE said you can buy a desma of wood for a copper, if you don't have the copper you can earn a desma by cutting ten desmas, if there is no wood to cut, you can earn a desma by working for Family Xilogonts for one halfday, planting seedlings and looking after young trees. If anyone in Family Xilogonts cheats you in any way, tell me and I will see it doesn't happen again."

"Hmm. I didn't expect that kind of thinking in a place like this. What do I mean? Ah Kori, just chatter, talking to myself." He looked around at the brilliant colors of the fall foliage, smiled. "Seems to work."

She scowled at him, unwilling to hear anything good about the man she called a sorceror, turned her shoulder to him and went into a brood over what he suspected was her vision of the perversity of man.

The cart bumped over the last humpbacked bridge and rumbled onto an avenue paved with granite flats, heading for the gaping arch of the gateway. He braced himself to withstand a major stench, if they couldn't put springs on their rolling stock, clearly sewers were a lost cause, but as the carts rattled through the shadowy tunnel (the walls were at least ten meters thick at the base), there was little of the sour stink from open emunctories and offal rotting in the streets that he'd had to deal with when he was on a freetrader dropping in on neofeudal societies. The cart emerged into a narrow crooked street, paved with granite blocks set in tar, clean, even the legless beggar at the corner had a clean face and his gnarled knobby hands were scrubbed pale. The drivers of each of the carts tossed a coin in his bowl, got his blessings as they drove past.

A woman leaned from an upper window. "What Parika?"

The lead driver looked up. "Owlyn Vale," she shouted.

The children in the carts jumped to their feet, stood

cheering and whooping, swaying precariously as the iron-tired wheels jolted over the paving stones, until they were scolded back down by the chaperones. Followed by laughter, shouts of welcome, luck and remember this that and the other when they got settled in and were turned loose on the city, the carttrain wound on, rumbling past tall narrow houses, through increasingly crowded streets, past innumerable fountains where the houses were pushed back to leave a square free, moving gradually uphill into an area where houses were larger with scores of brilliant windowboxes and there were occasional small gardens and green spaces and the fountains were larger and more elaborate. Ahead, two hills on, a minareted white structure glittered like salt in sunlight.

Kori leaned closer to Daniel Akamarino, murmured, "We'll be going slower when we start up the long slope ahead, you better get off then. If you want ships or work or something, keep going south, the Market is down that way and the waterfront.

"I hear you. Luck with the Lot, Kori."

She gave him a nervous smile. "Um . . ." She closed her hand over his wrist, her nails digging into the flesh; her voice came as a thread of sound. "Tré says we'll be seeing you again." She bit her lip, shook his hand when he started to speak. "Don't say anything. It's important. If it happens, I'll explain then."

"I wait on tiptoe." He grinned at her and she pinched his wrist, then sat in silence until they started the long climb to the Yron.

He got to his feet, swung over the side of the cart, wide enough to miss the tall wheel. After a flourish and a caper and a swooping bow that drew giggles from the children and waves from the chaperones, he moved rapidly away along an alley whose curve hid the carts before he'd gone more than a few steps.

Though it was the middle of the afternoon, the Market was busy and noisy, the meat and vegetables were cleared off, their places filled with more durable goods. Daniel Akamarino drifted around it until he found the busiest lanes; he dropped into a squat beside the beggar seated at the corner of two of these. "Good pitch, this."

The beggar blinked his single rheumy eye. "Aah."

"Mind if I play my pipe a while? Your pitch, your coin."

"You any good?"

"Don't like it, stop me."

"A will, don't doubt, A will."

Daniel fished out his recorder, shifted from the squat and sat cross-legged on the paving. He thought a moment, blew a tentative note or two, then began to improvise on one of the tunes the children had taught him. Several Matyssers stopped to listen and when he finished, snapped their fingers in approval and dropped coppers in the beggar's bowl.

He shook out the recorder, slid it back into its pocket, watched as the beggar emptied his bowl into a pouch tucked deep inside the collection of rags he had wrapped about his meager body. "New in town."

"A know it, an't heard that way with a pipe 'fore this. Wantin a pitch?"

"Buy it, fight for it, dice for it, what?"

A rusty chuckle. A pause while he blessed a Matysser who dropped a handful of coppers into the bowl. "Buy it, buy it, Him," a jerk of a bony thumb at the Citadel looming like white doom over them, "He don't like blood on the stones."

"Mmm. Got a hole in my pocket."

"There's one or two might be willing to rent a pitch for half the take."

"Too late for today. I'm thinking about belly and bed. Anyone round looking for a strong back and careful hands?"

"Hirin's finished with by noon."

Daniel sucked his teeth, wrinkled his nose. "Looks like my luck quit by noon." He thought a minute. "Any pawnshops around? I've got a couple of things I could pop in a pinch." He scratched at his stubble. "It's pinching."

"Grausha Kuronee in the Rakell Quarter. She an ugly old bitch," he cackled, "don't you tell her A said it. But she give you a fair deal." He coughed and spat into a small noisome jar he pulled from his pocket; when he was finished, he recorked it and tucked it away. Daniel Akamarino had difficulty keeping his mouth from dropping open. Settsiwhatsisname had a strangle grip on this country for sure; he began to understand why the place was so clean. And why young Kori talked the way she did. ''Tell you what,'' the beggar said, ''play another couple of tunes. A'll split the coin and A'll whistle you up a brat oo'll run you over to Kuronee's place.''

''Deal.'' He took out the recorder, got himself settled and started on one of his liveliest airs.

Daniel Akamarino tossed the boy one of the handful of coppers he'd harvested, watched him run off, then turned to examine the shop. It was a dingy, narrow place, no window, its door set deep into the wall with an ancient sign creaking on a pole jutting out over the recess. The paint was worn off the weathered rectangle except for a few scales of sunfaded color, but the design was carved into the wood and could be traced with a little effort. A bag net with three fish. He patted a few of his pockets, frowned and wandered away.

A few streets on he came to a small greenspace swarming with children. He wandered between the games and appropriated a back corner beside a young willow. After slipping out of his vest, he sat and began exploring the zippered pockets. The vest was made from the skin of Heverdee Nightcrawlers, the more that leather was handled, the better it looked and the longer it lasted; on top of that, it was a matter of pride to those who wore such vests never to get them cleaned, so Daniel hadn't had much incentive to dump his pockets except when he tried to find something he needed and had to fumble for it through other things that had no discernible reason for being in that pocket. He found a lot of lint and small odd objects that had no trade value but slowed his search. He sat turning them over in his fingers and smiling at the memories they evoked. It wasn't an impressive collection, but he came up with two possibilities. A hexagonal medal, soft gold, a monster stamped into one side, a squiggle that might have been writing on the other. He frowned at it for several mo-

ments before he set it aside; he couldn't remember
where he'd picked it up and that bothered him. A ring
with a starstone in it, heavy, silver, he'd worn it on his
thumb a while when he was living on Abalone and
thumbrings were a part of fitting in; since he didn't really
like things on his hands, he slipped it into a pocket the
day he left and forgot about it until now. He put everything back but the lint and dug that into the soil under
the willow roots, then leaned against the limber trunk
and sat watching the children running and shouting,
swinging on knotted ropes tied to a tall post-and-lintel
frame, climbing over a confection of tilted poles, cross-
bars and nets, playing ring games and rope games and
ball games, the sort of games that seemed somehow
universal, he'd met them before cross species (adapted
for varying numbers and sorts of limbs), cross cultures
(varying degrees of competition and cooperation in the
mix), ten thousand light-years apart. He smiled at them,
thought about playing a little music for himself, but no,
he was too comfortable as he was. The day was warm,
the Owlyn Valers had fed him well at noon so he wasn't
hungry yet, he had a few coppers in his pocket and the
possibility of getting more and he felt like relaxing and
letting time blow past without counting the minutes.

When the sun dropped low enough to sit on the wall
and the children cleared away, heading for home and
supper, Daniel Akamarino got to his feet, shook himself into an approximation of alertness and went strolling back to Kuronee's Place. He spent the next half hour
haggling over the ring and the medal, enjoying the process as much as the old woman did; by the time he
concluded the deal he was grinning at her and had se-
duced the ghost of a twinkle from eyes like ancient fried
eggs; he got from her the name of a tavern whose host
had a reputation for knocking thieves in the head and
not caring all that much if he knocked the brains right
out. He rented a cubbyhole with a lock on it and a bed
that had seen hard usage. Not all that clean, but better
than he'd expected for the price. He ate a supper of fish
stew and crusty bread, washed it down with thick dark
homebrew, then went out to watch the night come over
the water.

The evening was mild, the air lazy and filled with dark rich smells, one more day's end in a mellow slightly overripe season. Mara's Dowry his folk called this last spurt of warmth before winter. Season of golden melancholy. *I wonder what they call it here and why.* He sat on an oaken bitt watching the tide come in, his pleasant tristesse an elegant last course to the plain good meal warming his belly. A three-quarter moon rose, a large bite out of the upper right quadrant. The Wounded Moon, that's what they called it. He watched it drift through horsetail clouds and wondered what its stories were. *Who shot the moon and why? Who was so hungry he swallowed that huge bite?*

Something glittered in the dark water out beyond the ships. Dolphins leaping? A school of flying fish? Not flying fish. No. He got slowly to his feet and stood staring. A woman swam out there. A woman thirty meters long with white glass fingers and a fish's tail. Shimmering, translucent, eerily beautiful, throbbing with power.

"Sweet thing." The voice was husky, caressing. Daniel Akamarino turned. A dumpy figure stood beside him, a wineskin tucked under one arm; at first, because of the bald head with a fringe of flyaway black hair and the ugly-puppy face, he thought it was a little fat man, then he saw the large but shapely breasts bursting from the worn black shirt, the mischievous grin, the sun colored eyes that danced with laughter. "Godalau," the ambiguous person said, "bless her saucy tail." Heesh poured a dollop of wine into the bay, handed the skin to Daniel who did the same. Laughter like falling water drifted back to them. With a flirt of her applauded tail, the Godalau submerged and was gone. When Daniel looked round again, the odd little creature had melted into the night like the Godalau had into the sea, the only evidence heesh had ever been there was the wineskin Dan still held.

He settled back on the bitt, squirted himself a mouthful of the tart white wine. Good wine, a little dryer than he usually liked, but liquid sunshine nonetheless. He drank some more. Gift of the gods. He chortled at the thought. Potent white wine. He drank again. Sorcerors as social engineers. Giant mermaids swimming in the surf. Hermaphroditic demigods popping from the dark. I'm drunk, he thought and drank again and grinned at a glitter out beyond the bay. And I'll be drunker soon. Why not.

The Wounded Moon slid past zenith, a fog stirred over the waters and the breeze turned chill. Daniel Akamarino shivered, fumbled the stopper back in the nozzle and slung the skin over his shoulder. He stood a moment looking out over the water, gave a two fingered salute to whatever gods were hanging about, then started strolling for the tavern where his room was.

The fog thickened rapidly as he moved into the crooked lanes that ran uphill from the wharves. He fought to throw off the wine. Damn fool, you going to spend the night in a doorway if you don't watch it. He leaned against a wall a minute, the stone was wet and slimy under his hand and heavy cold drops of condensed fog dropped from the eaves onto his head and shoulders. He did a little deep breathing, thumped his head, started on.

A few turns more, as he left the warehouses and reached the taverns clustered like seadrift about them, the lanes widened a little; the fog there separated into clumps and walking was easier. He turned a corner, stopped.

A girl was struggling with two men. They were laughing, drunkenly amorous. The taller had a hand twisted in her hair while he held one of her writhing arms, the other was pushing his short burly body against her, crushing her against the wall while he fumbled at her clothing. Daniel sucked at his teeth a moment, then ran silently forward. A swift hard slap to the head of the skinny man—he squeaked and folded down. A kick to the tail of the squat man—he wheeled and roared; bullet head lowered, he charged at Daniel. Daniel danced aside and with a quick hop slapped the flat of his foot against the man's buttocks and shoved, driving him into a sprawl face down on the fog-damped paving stones.

The girl caught at Daniel Akamarino's arm. "Come."

He looked down, smiled. "Kori." He let her pull him into a side lane, ran with her around half a dozen corners until they left the shouts and cursing far behind. He slowed to a walk, waited until she was walking beside him. "Blessed young idiot." He scowled at her. "What do you think you're doing down here this time of night?"

"I have to meet someone." She tilted her head, gave him a quick smile. "Not you, Daniel. Someone else."

"Mmf. Couldn't you find a better time and place to meet your boyfriend, whatever?"

"Hah!" The sound dripped scorn. "No such thing. When the day comes, I'll marry someone in Owlyn. This is something else. I don't want to talk about it here."

"Mysteries, eh?"

"Come with me. Tré says you're mixed up in this some way, that you're here because of it. You might as well know what's happening and why."

"Tell you this, Kori, you're not going anywhere without me. I still think you should go back to your folks and wait till daylight to meet your friend."

"I can't."

"Hmm. Let's go then."

The Blue Seamaid was near the end of the watersection, a rambling structure sitting like a loosely coiled worm atop a small hill. This late, it was mostly dark, though a torch smoldered in its cage over the taproom door, a spot of dim red in a patch of thicker fog. Daniel Akamarino dropped his hand on Kori's shoulder. "Wait out here," he whispered.

"No." Her voice was soft but fierce. "It's not safe."

"You weren't worried about that before. Look, I'm not going to take you in there."

"It's not drunks I'm worried about, it's HIM."

"Oh." He thought about that a moment. "Political?"

"What?"

"Hmm." He stepped away from her and scanned her. "What's that you're wearing?"

"I couldn't come dressed in my Owlyn clothes." Indignation roughened her voice. "I borrowed this off one

of the maids in the hostel.'' A quick grin. ''She doesn't
know it.''

''Kuh,'' disgust in his voice, ''after that mauling you
got, you look like you're an underage whore. I'm not
sure I like being a dirty old man with a taste for veal.''
When she giggled, he tapped her nose with a forefinger.
''Enough from you, snip. Tell me the rules around here.
The tavernkeepers let men take streetgirls into their
rooms?''

''How should I know that? I've seen men taking girls
in there, what they did with them . . .'' She shrugged.

In the fireplace at the far end of the long room fingerlength tongues of flame licked lazily at a few sticks
of wood; three lamps hung along a ceiling beam, their
wicks turned low. There were men at several of the
scattered tables, talking in mutters; they looked up
briefly and away again as Daniel led Kori through the
murk to a table in the darkest corner. A slatternly girl
not much older than Kori came across to them. Her face
was made up garishly, but the cosmetics were cracking
and smeared and under the paint she was sullen and
weary. Daniel ordered two mugs of homebrew, dug out
three of his hoard of coppers. The girl scooped them
into a pocket of her stained apron and went off with a
dragging step.

''So. Where's this friend of yours?''

''Probably asleep. Tré says she's here, but I'm a day
earlier than I arranged. I thought I could ask someone
where her room was.'' She considered a minute.
''Maybe you better do the talking. Ask about a white-
haired woman with two children.''

''You know her name?''

''Yes, but I don't know if she's using it.''

''Hmm. I see. Kori. . . .''

''No. Don't talk about it, not now.''

The serving girl shambled back with two mugs of
dark ale, plunked them down. Daniel dug out another
copper. ''You've got a woman staying here, white hair,
two kids.''

More sullen than ever, she looked from him to Kori.
Her mouth dragged down into an ugly sneer.

Daniel set the coin on the table. "Take it or leave it."

Without a change of expression, she brushed the coin off the table. "On the right going up, first room, head of the stairs."

Shock and sadness in her eyes, Kori watched the girl drag off. "She . . ." Her hands groped for answers that weren't there. "Daniel . . ."

He frowned; she was a child, sheltered, innocent, but truth was truth however unpalatable. "You've never seen a convenience close up before?"

"Convee . . ."

His hand clamped on her arm. "Quietly," he whispered. "This isn't your ground, Kori, you play by local rules."

"Convenience?"

"She's for hire like the rooms here. What did you think?"

"Any of those men . . ."

"Any of them, or all." He smiled at her. "I thought you were being a little glib back there, talking about whores and what they did."

"It's not like Ruba."

"Who's Ruba?" He kept his voice low and soothing, trying to ease away the sick horror in her eyes. "Tell me about her."

Kori laced her fingers together and rubbed one thumb over the other. "Ruba, our whore. She's a Phrasi woman. She came to Owlyn oh before I was born. Some of the men built her a house. It's away from the other houses and it's a little like the Priest House. She lives there by herself. The men visit her. The women don't like her much, but they don't make her miserable or anything. They even talk to her sometimes. They let her help with the sugaring. Things like that. The only bad thing is they won't let her keep her babies. They take them away from her. I've watched her since before I was old enough for the Lot. She's happy, Daniel, she really is. She's not like that girl."

"How old is she?"

"I don't know. Thirty-five, forty, something like that."

"That's part of the difference, another part's how your people treat her. Forget the girl. There are hundreds like her, Kori. There's nothing you can do for her except hope she survives like Ruba did. It's better than being on the street. She won't get hurt here. Well, not crippled or killed. And she'll most likely have enough to eat."

"The look on her eyes," Kori shivered, tried a sip at the ale, wrinkled her nose and pushed it away. "This is awful stuff." She watched Daniel drink, waited impatiently till he lowered his mug. "Where you come from, Daniel, are there girls like that?"

"I wish I could say no. We've got laws against it and we punish folk who break those laws. When we catch them. But there's always someone willing to take a chance when they want something they're not supposed to have."

"What do you do to the ones you catch?"

"We've got uh machines and uh medicines and mmf I suppose you'd call them sorcerors who change their heads so they won't do it again." He took a long pull at the ale, wiped his mouth. "We'd better go wake up your friend, you have to get those clothes back to the maid before she crawls out of bed." He stood, held out his hand. When she was on her feet, he looked her over again. "It would be a kind thing if you left the girl a silver or two, you've pretty well ruined her going home clothes."

She closed her mouth tight and flounced away, heading for the stairs. He grinned and ambled along behind her.

Suddenly uncertain, she tapped at the door, not half loud enough to wake anyone sleeping. She started to tap again, but it swung open before her knuckles reached the panel. A young boy stood in the narrow dark rectangle between door and jamb, fair and frail with odd shimmery eyes.

"Brann," Kori murmured. She reached under her hair and pulled a thong over her head, held it out, a triangle of bronze swinging at the bottom of the loop. "I'm the one who sent for her."

The door opened wider. A dark form appeared behind the boy. "Come." A woman's voice, a rough warm contralto.

"Show me," Kori whispered. "First, show me the other half."

Snatch of laughter. A hand came out of the dark, a triangle of bronze resting on the palm. Kori snatched the bronze bit, examined it, turned it over, ran her thumb along the edge, then dropped both parts of the medal into her blouse. "If you'll move back, please?" she said to the boy.

He frowned. "Him?"

"He's in it."

"Jay, let her in. Ahzurdan is fidgeting about the wards."

With a small angry sound, the boy moved aside.

Daniel followed Kori inside. A lanky blond girlchild was setting an old lamp on the shelf at the head of a lumpy tottery bed. Just lit, the lamp's chimney was clouded, a smear of carbon blacked the bottom curve. The shutters were closed and the smell of rancid lamp oil and ancient sweat was strong in the crowded room. A tallish woman with short curly white hair backed up to give them space, lowered herself on the end of the bed. The boy Jay dropped on the crumpled quilt beside her; the girl who was obviously his sister settled herself beside him. Arms crossed, a tall man in a long black robe leaned against the wall and scowled at everyone impartially. His eyes met Daniel's. Instant hate, instantly reciprocated. Daniel Akamarino the easygoing slide-away-from-a-fight man stared at the other and wanted to kick his face in, wanted to beat the other into bloody meat. The woman Kori had called Brann smiled. "As you can see, the amenities are limited. Sit or stand as you please. There's a chair, I don't trust the left hind leg, so be careful." When Kori started to speak, she held up her hand. "Stay quiet for a moment. Ahzurdan, the wards."

Ahzurdan dragged his eyes off Daniel Akamarino, nodded. His hands moved in formal, carefully controlled patterns; his lips mouthed silent rhythmic words. "In place and renewed," he murmured a moment later.

"Interference?"

"Not that I can taste. I can't be sure, you know. This is his heart place and he's strong, Brann. A hundred times stronger than when I was with him."

"HE has a talisman," Kori said. "A stone he wears round his neck."

Ahzurdan took a step toward her. "Which one? Which talisman?"

"I don't know. Do they have names?"

"Do they . . ." He straightened, closed his eyes. "Yes, child, they have names and it's very very important to know the name of the talisman he has."

"I'll ask Tré if he can find out. The Chained God might be able to tell him. He's given us other things like Daniel here being involved somehow in what's going to happen. Aren't you awake now because you got a notion I was coming a day early?"

Brann turned her head. "Ahzurdan?"

"There was a warning. I told you." His dark blue eyes slid around to Daniel, slid away again. "Nothing about him." His voice was low and dragged as if he didn't want to say the words.

"I see. Young woman, your name is Kori Piyolss?" When Kori nodded Brann turned to Daniel. "And you?"

"Daniel Akamarino, one time of Rainbow's End."

"And where's that?"

"From here? I haven't a notion."

"Hmm. Daniel Akamarino. Danny Blue?"

"I've been called that." He gave her one of his second-best grins. "I've been called worse."

"This isn't going to hurt you," she said. He raised his brows. "I need to know," she said. "When that bronze bit came to me, it brought two tigermen with it who killed the messenger and tried damn hard to kill me." Kori gasped, leaned against Daniel, clutching his arm so hard he could feel her nails digging into him. "Sorry, child, but you'd best know what kind of fight you're in. Where was I? Yes, I have to know more about the two of you before we get into it about our mutual friend you know who. Yaril, Jaril, screen them."

The two children were abruptly spherical gold shimmers. Warily, Daniel began to slide toward the door; before he moved more than a step, one of the shimmers darted at him and merged with him. A ticklish heat rambled about inside him, then focused in his head. A few breaths later, the shimmer whipped away again and was a young boy sitting on the bed, his sister beside him.

'Jay?''

"Daniel Akamarino is like us, fetched here from another reality, he doesn't know how or why. It's a reality more like ours, no magic in it, no gods, their ships don't sail on water but through the nothingness between suns.'' The boy chuckled suddenly, reached out and stroked Brann's arm. "He's a sailing man, Bramble, not a captain I'm afraid, but he's been just about everything else on those ships.''

Brann shook her head. "Idiot. Yaro?''

"It's pretty much what you thought, Bramble. The girl is being driven by the Chained God who wants something from you. This Tré she's talking about, he's her brother, seven years old and not likely to live till eight unless something is done. When one priest dies, the god himself chooses the next and makes his choice known through fancy and extremely public signs. A little over two months ago, You-know-who's soldiers tied Owlyn Vale's priest of the Chained God to a stake set in the threshing floor and lit a fire under his feet and a few days after that the god told Tré he was it next.'' Yaril lifted a hand, let it fall. "Not a profession with a great future.''

Kori sighed and went to sit in the mispraised chair. "Tré's got maybe a week before the signs start.''

Daniel Akamarino thought, uh huh, that explains what was bothering the boy. Kuh! Burnt to death. Me, I wouldn't be worried, I'd be paralyzed. Gods, hah, gods tromping around interfering with ordinary people. Magic that's more than self-delusion. Wouldn't 've believed it a few hours back. Which reminds me. "I met one of your gods, demigods whatever tonight. Two of them, actually. A ship-size mermaid and a little bald shemale with good taste in wine.'' He slid the carrystrap of the wineskin off his shoulder. "Heesh left this with me. Care for a drink?"

"Tungjii and the Godalau!" Brann sighed. "Old Tungjii Luck sticking hisser thumbs in my life."

"That's what heesh called her. Godalau." He squeezed wine into his mouth, held out the skin. "Tungjii, you said. Luck?"

She drank, passed the skin to the changechildren. "Point of view, my friend. Tungjii touches you, things happen. 'S up to you to make it good or bad." She hitched round to face Kori. "Chained God tell you where I was, or did you ask downstairs?"

"Daniel asked the girl."

"Hmm. Our mutual friend has Noses watching the place. Dan," amusement danced in her eyes as she swung back so she could see both Kori and Daniel Akamarino, "our own Danny Blue, he tells me he saw two with message birds in the taproom last time he went down. So Him, by now he knows you've got to me. Something to think about. Eh?"

Daniel Akamarino rested his shoulders against the wall, crossed his arms; he wasn't looking at Ahzurdan so he didn't know how closely his stance mimicked the other man, though he could feel the powerful current of emotion flowing between them; the sorceror with a version of his name didn't look like him, so it wasn't a matter of physical double in a different reality, but there was some sort of affinity between them; no, affinity wasn't quite the right word, it felt more like they were two north poles of a bipolar magnet, each vigorously, automatically repelled by the other. He cleared his throat. "If I were mm whatsisname, I wouldn't fool with spies, I'd send a squad of soldiers and grab us all. Three adults, three kids, it's not much of a fighting force."

Brann smiled. "He knows better, Sailor. Ahzurdan here could whiff out a dozen soldiers without raising a sweat. Yaril and Jaril, they'd crisp another dozen and me, I'm Drinker of Souls. We're wasting time; Kori, you've got to get back to your folks before they find out you're gone. So. I've answered your summons and got whatsisname," a quick smile at Daniel, "on my back

for it. What am I supposed to do about him and if it's
not him, what?''

"Drinker of Souls."

"Not that simple, child. Yes, I'll call you child and
you'll be polite about it. I would have to touch him and
there's no way in this world he'd let me get that close."
She frowned. "Is that your plan? You said you had
one."

"'S not MY plan exactly. Chained God told Tré what
you should do is get to him and get the Chains off him,
then he'll go with you to get the talisman from HIM
and that means Amortis won't do what HE says any
more and we won't have to listen to the Servants of
Amortis and if they try to set soldiers on us in the Vales,
we'll beat them back down to the Plains. And Tré won't
get burnt.''

"That's the plan?"

Kori looked at her hands. "Yes."

Brann shook her head in disbelief. "Miserable
meeching mindless gods. How the hell am I supposed
to take chains off a god if he can't do it himself, how
do I even get to him?''

Eyes on her laced fingers, Kori shook her head. 'I
don't know. All I know is what Tré said. He said there's
a way to reach the Chained God. He said the god
wouldn't tell him exactly what it is. He said the god
didn't want HIM to know it. He said you've got to go
to Isspyrivo Mountain. He said once you're there, the
Chained God will get you to him somehow.''

"Isspyrivo. Where's that?"

"You'll do it? You'll really do it?"

"If you think that needs answering, you haven't been
listening. Now. Where is that idiot mountain?''

"On the end of the Forkker Vale Finger, you can see
it from Haven Cove, at least that's what um folks say
when they think the kids aren't listening. Haven's a
smuggler's town; it's not something they want us to
know about; we do, of course. The men get drunk
sometimes at festivals and they tell all kinds of stories
about sea smugglers and land smugglers; one of them
was about the time Isspyrivo blew and caught Henry the
Hook on the head with some hot rock. It's a fire moun-

tain. They say it's restless, they say it doesn't like folk climbing around on it; they say it kills them, opens up under them and swallows them.''

''Hmm. Let me think a minute.''

Daniel Akamarino leaned against the wall watching her. Drinker of Souls. Hmm. I think I pass on this one. It's an interesting world; if I'm stuck here, I'm stuck, no point in getting myself killed which seems likely enough if I hang with this bunch. He slid along the wall, closed his hand about the doorlatch. ''Been fun, folks,'' he said aloud. ''See you round, maybe.''

Brann looked up. ''No, Ahzurdan, I'll handle this. Daniel Akamarino, if you leave, you walk into our enemy's hands; you're a dead man but not before he finds out everything you know. I don't want to do it, but if you insist on leaving us, I'll have to stop you and let the children strip your mind.''

''Nothing I can do about that?''

''Not much.''

He scowled at Ahzurdan. ''He'd enjoy frying me, wouldn't he?''

''I couldn't say.''

Hands behind him, he tried the latch; the hook wouldn't move, he applied more pressure, nothing happened. Across the room Ahzurdan was laughing at him soundlessly triumphant. Daniel ignored him and moved back to his leaning spot. ''If I can't leave, what about Kori? How does she get back to the hostel?''

Brann nodded. ''If she's going, it's about time she went. Jaril, take a look downstairs, see what's happening.'' The boy flipped into his shimmershape, dropped through the floor. ''Yaril, scout the outside for us, see what's waiting out there.'' The girl flitted away through the ceiling. ''Dan um this is going to get confusing, Ahzurdan, I want to get Kori to the hostel without your ex-teacher tracking her. Can you fog his mirror or something?''

''Or something. Talisman or not, I've learned enough from his attacks to blur his sight. He'll know I'm moving, he'll know the general direction, but he won't be able to see me or anyone with me. Earth elementals and ariels, I can handle those myself; if you and the children can remove the human watchers, we can get the girl back without him finding out who she is. The fog will be broad enough to cover the hostel and half the quarter around it, he can't be sure where I'm going, but he's not stupid, so he'll guess fairly accurately what's happening.''

''Kori, you hear?''

''Yes.'' The word was a long sigh. She was pale, her eyes huge and frightened. Daniel watched her, understanding well enough what she was feeling now; she'd gone into this blithely enough, enjoying the excitement of her secret maneuvers; her brother's life rested on her skills, but that wasn't quite real to her. Settsimaksimin's power wasn't real to her. It was now. She was beginning to understand what might happen to her people because of her activities. No, it wasn't a game any longer.

Brann got to her feet, crossed to stand beside her; she touched her fingers to Kori's shoulder. ''What do you want to do? You're welcome to stay here.''

''I can't do that. If I'm gone, HE'll do something awful to my folk.''

''Dan uh Ahzurdan?''

''These are his people, Brann; remember what I've told you about him, he's always been extravagantly possessive about things that are his. When we . . . his apprentices finally broke away, he took it as a kind of betrayal. He won't do anything to them unless he's driven to it. As long as there's no overt break, as long as he can strike at you, us, without involving them, he'll leave them alone. The girl's right. She has to go back.''

''Soon as the children are back, then, we'll move. You'll come with us, Daniel Akamarino.'' She smiled. ''I can almost hear your mind ticking along. Don't waste your time, my friend. We won't be too busy to keep track of you, don't you even think of slipping off. . . .''

Jaril whipped up through the floor, changed. ''Taproom's cleared out except for a couple of drunks. Real drunks, I whizzed them and nearly picked up a second-hand buzz. I went outside and ran a few streets. Lot of men standing in doorways. I counted twenty before I came back, there's probably twice that.''

Yaril dropped through the ceiling, fluttered into her

girlshape. "He's not exaggerating. They're watching every street and path around this place, just about every bush. There's another ring beyond that, almost as tight and beyond that two more, not so tight. There are even some little cats out on the water zipping back and forth through the fog. Must be a couple of hundred men out there. The landwatchers aren't all that enthusiastic, standing around holding up walls, walking circles in the middle of the street, but seems to me that's because nothing is happening. Let them spot us and they'll turn as efficient as you want."

Brann frowned. "I didn't expect quite that many . . . we can forget about the boats and the first ring isn't a problem, we can get most of them before they realize we're out. Before He knows we're out. It's those next, what, you said three rings? They worry me. Did you scan the rooftops, Yaro?"

"Bramble! course I did. Some people were up there sleeping, there were several pairs of lovers intent on their own business, they wouldn't give a fistful of spit for anything happening on the street. I didn't see anyone alert enough to be a spy, but I won't guarantee I didn't miss someone." She hesitated, turned finally to Ahzurdan. "Would he do something like that? Use dozens of visible watchers to camouflage two or three maybe a few more of his best Noses, so we take the guards out and don't notice some sly rats sneaking after us?"

"He's a complicated man. I'd say it's likely."

Daniel Akamarino watched the working of this odd collection of talents and began to feel better about being involved in this web. They put aside their antagonisms and concentrated on getting the job done, once they'd defined what the job was they wanted to do. It wasn't a group that could or would stay together in ordinary circumstances, but nothing was ordinary about what was happening. Kori was obviously feeling a little out of it; she was fidgeting in her chair, making it creak and wiggle, not quite overtaxing the weak hind leg. He rubbed a thumb across one of his larger pockets, tracing the outlines of the rectangular solid snugged inside, a short range stunner; he eyed Brann a moment, then the children, then Ahzurdan, wondering if he could take them

out and get away; his thumb smoothed over and over
the stunner, no, impossible to tell what sort of metab-
olism the children had; they might eat the stunfield like
candy. Besides, old Settsimaksimin had the ground covered out there. He liked the thought of that man operating on him about as much as he liked the idea of the
children wiping his mind. When he brought Kori here
he hadn't noticed the watchers, but that might have been
the wine, he still wasn't all that sober, or it might have
been worrying about young Kori and what she was up
to; whatever, he wasn't about to argue with the children's assessment of the danger out there. Shapeshifters, shoo-ee, what a world. Contact telepaths, lord
knew what else they were. He eased the zipper open,
fished out the stunner. "Hey folks," he said, "listen a
minute. I think I know the problem. Brann, you and the
kids have to actually touch someone to take him out,
right?" She nodded, a short sharp jerk of her head.
"And there are too many watchers out there to get at
one sweep, right? So, if you could put them to sleep for
say an hour, ten, twenty at a blow, and do it from say
roof height, them being on the ground with no one near
them, that would erase the worst of your difficulties,
wouldn't it?"

"It'd come close." She leaned toward him, focused
all her attention on him, wide green eyes shining at him.
"What have you got, Danny Blue?"

"Being a peaceful man with a habit of dropping into
places that don't appreciate good intentions, I keep this
with me." He held up the stunner. It didn't look like
much, just a black box with rounded corners that fit
comfortably in his hand, a slit in the front end covered
with black glass, a slide with a shallow depression for
his thumb in it that with a little pressure bared the trig-
gering sensor.

Jaril sat straight, crystal eyes glittering. "Stunner?"

Daniel Akamarino raised his brows, then he remembered they, like him, were from somewhere else.
"Right. Short range neural scrambler."

"See it?"

"Why not." A glance to make sure the thumbslide
was firmly shut, then he tossed the stunner to the boy.

Jaril caught it, set it on the bed, switched to his energy form and sat over it for a few breaths like hen on an egg. He shifted, was a boy again. "It'll do. You letting Yaro and me use it?"

"You can handle it in the air?"

The boy grinned. "Ohhh yes."

"Feel free. Need any directions?"

"Nope. We read to the subatomic when we have to."

"Handy. That work on what they use here?"

"Magic?"

"I'm not all that comfortable with the concept."

"Better get comfortable, tisn't likely you'll go home any time soon."

"You?"

"Two centuries so far."

"Ananiles?"

"We never bothered with those. Natural span of the species is ninety centuries."

"Hmm."

"You finished?" Dry amusement in Brann's voice. "Good. We'll run out of night if we keep this chatter going. Kori, anything else you need to tell me?"

Kori looked up from hands pleating and repleating the heavy cloth of her long black skirt. "No. Not that I can think of."

"Jay, Yaro, from the little I understand of your chat with Daniel, it seems you can clear the way for us. How long will it take?"

The changechildren stared at each other for several minutes. Daniel Akamarino felt an itching in his head that rose to a peak and broke off abruptly as Jay broke eye contact with his sister. "We'll zigzag, trading off, each one take a ring while the other flies to the next. I think we better do at least half each ring, maybe a bit more. Yaro?"

"Time. You know how long it took me to check the full length of all four rings, maybe twenty minutes; this'll go a lot faster. I'd say, ten minutes at most to do the ring sweeps, then we'd better go over the streets along the way to the hostel, zapping everything both sides in case sneaks are ambushed inside the houses. Say another five minutes, it's not all that far from here."

Brann threaded her fingers through her hair, cupped her hand about the nape of her neck and scowled at the floor. Ahzurdan cleared his throat, but shut up as she waved her other hand at him. A waiting silence. Daniel rubbed his shoulders against the wall, yawned. She lifted her head. "Go, kids, get it done as fast as you can, we'll wait five minutes, then follow."

Ahzurdan at point spreading his confusion over half Silagamatys, the four of them moved at a trot through the stygian foggy tag-end of the night, past bodies crumpled in doorways and under trees, through a silence as profound as that in any city of the dead. Halfway to the hostel the children came back, horned owls with crystal eyes and human hands instead of talons. One of the owls swooped low over Daniel, hooted, dropped the stunner into his hands and slanted up to circle in wide loops over them. They swept past the hostel and Kori slipped away. Daniel Akamarino watched her vanish into the shrubbery and spent the next few minutes worrying about her; when the building continued dark and silent, no disturbance, he relaxed and stopped looking over his shoulder.

eyeswell, and they compared footnotes, and they argued and speculated, all of it sheer stupidity, as the Introducer was theoriginal theorizer, stating it as she wished it considered, and if anyone objected, either he was a heretic orthe Introducer changed the subject. Which claimed as you will remember, his undivided attention.

8

KORI PIYOLSS RUNS INTO A QUIET STORM IN THE SHAPE OF AUNTNURSE.

SCENE: Quiet shadowy halls, doorless cells on both sides, snores, sighs, groans, farts, whimpers, creak of beds, slide of bodies on sheets, a melding of sleepsounds into a general background hum, a sense of swimming in life momentarily turned low.

After a last look at Daniel Akamarino, Kori slid into the shrubbery of the Hostel garden, worked her way to the ancient wittli vine that was her ladder in and out of the sleeping rooms on the second floor. She tucked up the skirt, kicked off her sandals and tied them to her belt, set her foot in the lowest crotch and began climbing. The shredded papery bark coming to threads under her tight quick grip, the dustgray leaves shedding their powder over her, the thinskinned purple berries that she avoided when she could since they burst at a breath and left a stain it took several scrubbings to get rid of, the highpitched groans of the stalk, the secret insinuating whispers the leaves made as they rubbed together, these never changed, year on year they never changed, since the first year she came (filled with excitement and resentment) and crept out to spend a secret hour wandering about the gardens. Year on year, as she grew bolder, slipping slyly through the dangerous streets, only a vague notion of the danger to give the adventure spice and edge, they never changed, only she changed. Now there was no excitement, no game, only a deep brooding anxiety that tied her insides into knots.

She reached out and pushed cautiously at the shutters to the small window of the linenroom, lost a little of her tension as they moved easily silently inward. One hand clamped around a creaking secondary vine, she twisted her body about until head, shoulders and one arm were through the window, then she let go of the vine and waved her feet until she tumbled headfirst at the floor; she broke her fall with her hands, rolled over and got to her feet feeling a little dizzy, one wrist hurting because she'd hit the stone awkwardly. She untied the sandals, set them on a shelf, stripped off the maid's clothing, used the blouse to wipe her hands and feet, thinking ruefully about Daniel Akamarino's comment; it was true then and doubly true now, no one would wear those rags. She dug three silvers out of her pouch, the last she had left of the hoard from the cave, rolled them up in the clothing, telling herself she would have done it anyway, Daniel didn't have to stick his long nose in her business. She pulled her sleeping shift over her head, smoothed it down, eased the door open a crack and looked along the hall. Silence filled with sleeping noises. Shadows. She edged her head out, looked the other way. Silence. Shadows. She slipped through the crack, managed to close the door with no more than a tiny click as the latch dropped home, ran on her toes to the room at the west end where the maids slept. No time to be slow and careful; dawn had to be close and the maids rose with the sun; she flitted inside, put the rolled clothing where she'd got it, on the shelf behind a curtain, and sped out, her heart thudding in her throat as one of the girls muttered in her sleep and moved restlessly on her narrow bed.

Struggling to catch her breath, she slowed as soon as she was clear of the room and crept along past the doorless arches of the sleeping cubicles; her own cubicle where she slept alone was near the east end of the Great Refectory. She was exhausted, her arms and legs were heavy, as if the god's chains had been transferred to them, the old worn sandals dragged like lead at her fingers.

Sighing with relief, scraping her hand across her face, she turned through the arch.

And stopped, appalled.

AuntNurse sat on the bed, her face grave. "Sit down, Kori. There." she pointed at the end of the bed.

Kori looked at the sandals she carried. She bent, set them on the floor, straightening slowly. Head swimming she sat on the bed, as far as she could get from her aunt.

"Don't bother telling me you've just gone to the lavatory, Kori. I've been sitting here for nearly three hours."

Kori rubbed at the back of her right hand, bruises were beginning to purple there, fingermarks. She didn't know what to say, she couldn't tell anyone, even AuntNurse, about the Drinker of Souls and the rest of them, but she couldn't lie either, AuntNurse knew the minute she tried it. She chewed on her lip, said nothing.

"Are you a maid still?"

Kori looked up, startled. "What? Yes. Of course. It wasn't that."

"May I ask what it was?"

Twisting her hands together, moving her legs and feet restlessly, Kori struggled to decide what she should do. Ahzurdan's fog was still over this sector but it wouldn't be there much longer. "You mustn't say anything about it after," she whispered. "Not to me, not to anyone. Right now HE can't hear us, but that won't last. Tré's the next Priest. I've been trying to do something to keep him from being killed. Don't make me say what, it's better you don't know."

"I see. I beg your pardon, Kori. That is quite a heavy burden for your shoulders, why didn't you share it?"

Kori looked quickly at her, looked away. She didn't have an answer except that she'd always hated having things done for her; since she could toddle, she'd worked hard at learning what she was supposed to know so she could do for herself. And mostly, people were stupid, they said silly things that Kori knew were silly before she could read or write and she learned those skills when she was just a bit over three. They took so long to understand things that she got terribly impatient (though she soon learned not to show it); the other children, even many of the adults, didn't understood her jokes and her joys, when she played with words she got blank stares unless the result was some ghastly pun that even a mule wouldn't miss. Not AuntNurse, no one would ever call AuntNurse silly or stupid, but she was so stiff it was like she wouldn't let herself have fun. Without exactly understanding why, Kori knew that she couldn't say any of this, that all the reasons she might make up for doing what she wanted to and keeping Tré's trouble a secret, all those fine and specious justifications would crumble like tissuepaper under AuntNurse's cool penetrant gaze.

"I suppose I really don't need an answer." Aunt-Nurse sighed. "Listen to me, Kori. You're brighter than most and that's always a problem. You're arrogant and you think more of your ability than is justified. There's so much you simply do not understand. I wonder if you'll ever be willing to learn? I know you, child, I was you once. If you want to live in Owlyn Vale, if you want to be content, you'll learn your limits and stay in them. It's discipline, Kori. There are parts of you that you'll have to forget; it will feel like you're cutting away live flesh, but you'll learn to find other ways of being happy. More than anything you need friends, Kori, women friends; you'll find them if you want to and if you work at it, you'll need them, Kori, you'll need them desperately as the years pass. I was planning to talk to you when we got back." She lifted a hand, touched her brow, let it drop back in her lap. "I'd still like to have that talk, Kori, but I'll let you come if you want, when you want. One last thing, do you have any idea what your life would be like if you had to leave us?"

Kori shivered, rubbed suddenly sweaty palms on the linen bunched over her thighs as she remembered the girl in the tavern. "Yes," she whispered, "I saw a girl. A con—convenience."

AuntNurse smiled, shook her head. "You terrify me, child. I am delighted you got back safe and rather surprised, if that's the kind of place you were visiting."

Kori chewed her lip some more, then she scootched along the bed until she could reach AuntNurse's hand. She took it, held it tight, shook her head, then gazed at AuntNurse, fear fluttering through her, sweat dripping into her eyes.

AuntNurse nodded, smoothed long cool fingers over Kori's bruised and sweaty hands. "I see. Unfortunately you face the Lot come the morning, so I can't let you sleep much longer than usual, Kori. You must eat, you'll need your strength." She got to her feet, freed her hand. "If I can help, Kori, in any way, please let me." She touched Kori's cheek, left without looking back.

Kori sat for several minutes without moving; in some strange and frightening way she'd crossed a chasm and the bridge had vanished on her. It had nothing to do with Tré or Settsimaksimin and everything to do with AuntNurse. With . . . with . . . Polatéa, not Aunt-Nurse. Never again AuntNurse. Shivering with more than the early morning chill, she crawled into bed and eventually managed to sleep.

——— 9 ———

SETTSIMAKSIMIN WATCHES IN HIS WORKROOM AND AT THE COURT OF LOTS IN THE GRAND YRON.

SCENE: 1. Settsimaksimin in his subterranean workroom, idly watching his mirror, Todichi Yahzi back by one wall, noting Maksim's comments, released for the moment from the onerous task of watching over the machinations of a number of very ambitious men.

2. Settsimaksimin on the highseat at the Court of Lots, in the Grand Yron. Picture an immense rectangular room, sixty meters on the long sides, twenty on the short, the ceiling fifty meters from the floor, utterly plain polished white marble walls with delicate traceries of gray and gold running through the white, a patterned pavement of colored marbles, ebony and gilt backless benches running two thirds the length of the long sides, two doors dressed in ebony and gilt in the short north wall, one at the west end, one at the east. At the short south wall (beneath Settsimaksimin but out far enough so he can see it without straining), a low ebony table with a gilt

bowl on it, a bowl filled with what
looked to be black eggs. To his left,
about ten meters away along the west
wall, near the end of the long bench, another table with another bowl, this one
red, the pile of black eggs in it is considerably smaller than that in the gilt bowl.
To his right, ten meters away along the
east wall, a third table with a third bowl,
this one blue, its egg pile about the same
as that in the red one. A trumpet blares,
two lines of children stream in, girls on
the east, boys on the west.

Settsimaksimin lounged in his chair, bare feet crossed
at the ankles and resting on a battered hassock, he
sipped at a huge mug of bitter black tea; he'd discarded
all clothing but the sleeveless black overrobe and the
heavy gold chain with the dull red stone on it, the talisman BinYAHtii (I take all); his gray-streaked plait was
twisted atop his head again and skewered there. The
only evidence of his fatigue lay in his eyes, they were
red streaked and sunk deeper than usual in heavy wrinkles and folds. He was watching the scenes skipping
across the face of the obsidian mirror: the waterfront
(he scowled as he saw the Godalau playing in the water
and interfering old Tungjii ambling about the wharves,
stopping to talk to a ghostly stranger sitting on a bitt);
the tavern where Brann and her entourage were (a place
mostly blank because Ahzurdan had learned too much
for Maksim's comfort from the attack at Kukurul and
had tightened and strengthened his wards until there
was no way Maksim could tease them apart or find a
cranny to squeeze a tendril through; though it was a
major complication in his drive to protect himself and
his goals, he beamed proudly at the blank spot, a father
watching his favorite son show his strength); the Hostel
where the Owlyn Valers were settled in and presumably
sleeping the sleep of the just and innocent, even the one
that plotted against him; a sweep through the streets,
flickering over the watchers he'd posted about the tav-

ern, swooping to check out assorted nocturnal ramblers
(he chanced on a thief laboring over the lock at the back
of a jeweler's shop, snatched him up and dumped him
into the bay). Waterfront again (the man with the blurred
outlines was still sitting on the bitt drinking from a
wineskin and staring out over the water, singing to himself and getting pleasantly drunk, wholly innocuous except for that odd blurring; Maksim sat up and scowled
at him, tried to get a clearer image; there were peculiar
resonances to the man and he didn't like puzzles wandering about his city; he shrugged and let the mirror
pass on). Tavern again. He looked through the eyes of
his surrogates in there, but nothing was happening
downstairs. Hostel again. Dark and sleeping. Streets and
those in them. Waterfront. Tavern. Hostel. "Now what
have we got here?"

Up on the second floor a small form eased out a window and started down the vine that crawled over part
of the wall near that window. A girl it was, skirt tucked
up, dropping from branch to branch faster than most
folk could negotiate a flight of stairs. He willed the
mirror into sharper focus on her, smiled as she reached
the grass, put her sandals on, shook out her skirt and
smoothed down her flyaway hair. She darted into the
shrubbery, moving with assurance through the darkness. Maksim sat up, laughter rumbling round his big
taut belly. "Little ferret." She reappeared in the street
and began moving at a steady pace toward the bay.
"Aaahhh," he breathed, "it's you, YOU, I've got to
thank for this. Eh Todich, come see. There's my great
enemy, a girl, twelve maybe, a skinny little girl." She
clung to shadow as much as she could, but went forward
resolutely, circling drunks and skipping away from a
man who grabbed at her, losing him after she fled into
back alleys and whipped around half a dozen corners;
she didn't pause to catch her breath but glanced around
as she trotted on, oriented herself and started once more
toward the waterfront, a thin taut wire of a girl seen and
unseen, an image in a broken dream. "A girl, a girl,
Tungjii's tits, why does it have to be a girl? She's got
more spine than half my army, Todich; if she had a
grain of talent and was a boy, ah what a sorceror she'd

make. Danny Blue, my baby Dan, she'd eat you alive, this little ferret. If she weren't a girl, if she had the talent. What's that now?''

She whipped around another corner and slammed into two men. The taller man grabbed her arm, swung her hard against the wall, while his squat burly companion gaped blearily at her. The tall one laughed, said something, wrapped his other hand in her hair and jerked her head up. Ignoring her struggles, he looked over his shoulder at his friend, his rubbery face moving through a series of drunken grimaces.

The squat man flung himself at the girl, mashed her against the wall. He slobbered at her, began fumbling at the band of her skirt, using one shoulder to pin her other arm as she clawed at him.

''Drunks,'' Maksim growled, ''filthy beasts.'' He watched her struggles and her fear and her fury with an uncomfortable mix of satisfaction, compassion and shame. ''You're getting what you asked for, little ferret, you should have stayed where you belong.'' By forgetting who and what she was, by working against him who had done so much for the people of Cheonea and meant to do so much more, she'd brought her shaming on herself. He had not the slightest doubt it was she who'd sent for the Drinker of Souls, the boy who carried the message came from Owlyn, what was his name? Toma something or other, dead now, it didn't matter, though how she'd known of the Drinker and what she'd used to lever Brann into moving . . . well, he'd find out before too long. ''I'll have you, Owlet, you face the Lot tomorrow, yes, I'll have you. . . .'' He scowled at the mirror, moved his hands uneasily, twisted his mouth into a grimace of distaste. A child. A clever devious spirited child. Her strength was nothing against those men, her arms were like twigs. He could save her as easily as he took his next breath, snatch those beasts off her, send earth elementals to crush them. He watched and did nothing. You have to learn, little ferret, he told himself, learn your limitations so I don't have to punish you myself. He watched and shifted uneasily in his chair, his stomach churning. He rubbed at his chest under BinYAHtii as his heart thudded painfully.

The odd man from the waterfront came suddenly from the fog. He seemed to hesitate, then with a slap and two kicks disposed of the attackers. The girl put her hand on his arm, said something. "She knows him. Bloody Hells. He thumbed the mirror. "Sound you."

For several minutes the only sounds were the slap of their feet, the diminishing yells from the squat man who was quickly lost in the fog, the drip of that fog from the eaves. Then the man slowed and spoke to the girl. Maksim clicked his tongue with deep annoyance; like his form the man's words were blurred beyond deciphering.

"   . . . . . ."

"I have to meet someone." The child tilted her head and smiled up at the man. Flirting with him, Maksim grumbled to himself, hot with jealousy, little whore. *"Not you, Daniel. Someone else."* Daniel, Daniel, she does know him, Forty Mortal Hells, who is he?

"   . . . ."

"Hah! No such thing. When the day comes I'll marry someone in Owlyn. This is something else. I don't want to talk about it here."

"   . . . ."

*"Come with me. *** says you're mixed up in this some way, that you're here because of it. You might as well know what's happening and why."*

"   . . . ."

"I can't."

"   . . . ."

Maksim watched them hurry through the fog until they reached the Blue Seamaid. He nodded to himself. I'm going to have to do something about you. Who are you? Owlyn Valer, yes. What's your name, child? I'll know it come the morrow. Scoundrel time old Maksi, you out-rascaled the Parastes, now a child is completing your corruption, I've never interferred with the Lot before this, but I can't leave her running around loose. You're going into the Yron training, my angry young rebel, you're going to get that hot blood cooled. He listened to one side of the argument outside the tavern, guessed most of the man's objections, saw his final shrug. The child's got ten times your backbone, you fool. Why don't you pick her up and get her back where she belongs? He considered doing that himself, it'd be easy enough; he put off deciding (though such dithering was foreign to him) and followed them inside.

" . . . . "

"Probably asleep. *** says she's here." Why can't I hear that name? That's the second time it's blurred out on me. Someone is interfering, someone is working against me. He slapped his hand on the table, calmed abruptly as his heart started bumping irregularly. He closed his fingers about the talisman and squeezed until his body calmed and he could listen again. *". . . room was. Maybe you better do the talking. Ask about a white-haired woman with two children."*

" . . . . "

"Yes, but I don't know if she's using it."

" . . . . "

"No, don't talk about it, not now."

Maksim stopped listening. He stroked the talisman, closed his eyes and reached for her, intending to flip her back to the Hostel garden.

He couldn't get a grip on her. What should have been simple was somehow impossible. He could feel her, he could smell her, he could almost taste the salt sweat on her skin but he couldn't move her a hair one way or another. His eyes snapped open. "That man. That stinking scurvy scrannel scouring of a leprous dam. That canker, that viper, that concupiscent incontinent defiler of innocence, that eyesore, that offence to heaven and earth. . . ." He blasted out a long sigh that fogged the mirror for an instant until he glared it clear again. Rubbing at his chest, he went back to listening since he couldn't do anything else.

". . . come from, Daniel, are there girls like that?"

" . . . . "

"What do you do to the ones you catch."

" . . . . "

She closed her mouth tight and flounced away, heading for the stairs, irritated by whatever it was he said. Maksim gave her a thin angry smile. That's right, get away from him, girl. He's not for you. When she'd put some distance between her and the man (he was getting

up to go after her), Maksim tried once more to catch
hold of her, but he couldn't get a grip, she slid away as
if she were greased. He sat fuming, breathing hard; he
couldn't remember being so helpless since he was a boy
in the pleasurehouse he'd stomped into the ground when
he took Silagamatys and Cheonea from crazy old Noshios. His head ached and acid burned in his throat as
he watched the girl and the man pass through Ahzurdan's wards and vanish into that blank he couldn't penetrate. He spent a few minutes probing at it again, if
the man really was an energy sink, he ought to affect
Ahzurdan's work too. Nothing. Not a waver in Baby
Dan's weaving.

Maksim left the image tuned to the tavern and paced
about the workroom muttering to himself, glancing occasionally at the mirror where nothing much was happening. He thought about sending his watchers to that
room and taking them all, he thought about turning out
the barracks, sending every man he had against them
until they were drowned in dead men, unable to twitch
a finger. Noooo, Forty Bloody Mortal Hells, Danny
Blue had found some nerve, the woman of course, and
Danny with nerve and resolution was by himself more
than an army could handle. Amortis? He fingered
BinYAHtii and was tempted but shook his head. Not
here. Not in MY city. If he brought Amortis down,
Tungjii and the Godalau were likely to join the battle
and that would level half of Silagamatys. They're in the
plot on the Drinker's side, AND WARNING ME, otherwise why show themselves to that man, that
MAAAANN. Who was he? What was he? Filthy whisk-
ery caitiff wretch, looked like any drifting layabout, he'd
seen a thousand of them rotting slowly into the soil they
sprang from. Soil he sprang from? What soil was that?
Pulled here from a different reality? Why? What reality?

He stopped pacing and stared at nothing for several
minutes, then tapped the mirror off, he didn't need to
see any more and he wanted his strength and total concentration for the next few hours' work. He swung round
to Todichi Yahzi. "Todich, old friend, you'd best get
back to your overseeing. Mmm. Report to me tomorrow

after the Lot on the activities of the Council, I'd like your opinion on how well they're doing and what the weaknesses of the form are, your suggestions on how I can improve it. Don't let up on them, these next weeks are crucial, Todich. If I can get that council working, if I can craft something that will stand, no matter what the Parastes try. . . .'' He sucked in a huge breath, exploded it out. ''Ready, Todich? Now!''

After alerting the guardians of that sealed cube of a room (sealed against magic, not air; like everyone else, sorcerors had to breathe), Maksim toed up the brake levers on the wheels of his tiltchair and rolled it to the center of his largest pentacle. When he had it oriented the way he wanted, he heeled the levers down again, stood rubbing thoughtfully at his chest and stared at nothing for a moment. With a grunt and a grimace he crossed to a wallchest, filled a cordial glass with a thick bitter syrup and choked it down, washed the taste away with a gulp of brandy. For several breaths he stood with his head against the door of the cabinet, his hands grasping the edge of the shelf below it, his powerful massive arms stiff, supporting most of the weight of his upper body, trembling now and then. Finally, he sighed and pushed away from the wall. There was no time. No time. He brushed his hand across his face, felt the end of his plait tickle his fingers. He pulled the skewers out, shook his head, looked down at himself and smiled. Not the way to confront the visitor he expected to have.

He slipped out of the workrobe, tossed it onto the tiltchair and padded across the cold stone floor to the place where he kept spare clothing. He drew a simple white linen robe over his head, smoothed it down and with a flick of his fingertips banished the creases from its long folding. There were no ties or fastenings, the wide flat collar fell softly about the column of his neck, the front opening spread in a narrow vee, showing glimpses of the heavy gold chain and a segment of the pendant BinYAHtii. He drew his hand across his face, wiping away the signs of weariness and the few straggles of whisker, smoothed straying hairs into place, pulled the black workrobe about him and dug out his rowan staff; he'd made it nearly a century ago, when he was out of his apprenticeship a mere two years, tough ancient wood polished with much handling, inlaid with silver wire in the private symbols that he alone could read. He laid it across the arms of the tiltchair, then went for a broom standing in the corner. There were four smaller pentacles at irregular intervals about the large one, marked out with fine silver wire laid into the stone; stepping into the pentacle the chair faced, Maksim swept it very clean, ran the broom over it one last time, then tapped the circled star into glowing life with the end of his staff. He swept off the larger pentacle until he was satisfied, put the broom back in the corner and crossed the silver wire to stand beside the chair. His massive chest rose and fell in an exaggerated sigh, then he tapped this pentacle into life, settled himself on the cushions and laid his staff once more across the arms. Reaching down past it, he pumped the lever until the chair was laid out under him, his back at a thirty degree angle to the floor. He closed his hands about the staff, closed his eyes and began assembling his arsenal of chants and gestures.

Aboard the JIVA MARISH, this is what Ahzurdan said to Brann: Magic words, magic chants, magic gestures, oh Brann, these are part of the storyteller's trade, they've got nothing to do with what a sorceror is or does. Look at me, I say: JIIH JAAH JAH and move my hands so and so, and lo, I give you a rosebud wet with morning dew. Yes, it's real, perfume and all. Yes, I merely transported it from a garden some way west of here where the sun's not shining yet, I didn't create it from nothing. I could teach you to mimic my voice, there's not that great a difference between our ranges, I could teach you to ape my gestures to perfection, and do you know what you'd have? Nothing.

A sorceror works by will alone, or rather by will and word and gesture. The words and gestures are meaningless, developed by each student from his own private set of symbols, sounds and movements that evoke in him the particular mindstate and pattern of will he needs to perform specific acts of power. What you learn when you're an apprentice is how to find these things and how to control the results. Then you learn how to use them to impress the clients. Among ourselves, we know that none of the words and gestures belonging to one of us could be used by another, at least not to produce the same effect. There is no power inherent in any word or sequence of words, in any sound or sequence of sounds, in any gesture or sequence of gestures; they are only self-made keys to areas of the will.

Ah yes, I know, claimants to mystical power have roamed the world from the time the moon was whole to this very day selling books of such spells and chants and sacred dances and charms and potions and all that nonsense, making far more gold from talentless gullibles than they'd ever gain from their own gifts, there's always someone fool enough to want a shortcut to wealth and power, or even to a woman he has no chance of getting at, someone who'd never believe the truth, that everything a sorceror does is won out of self by talent and arduous study and ferocious discipline. That's the truth, Brann, almost all the truth. I say almost, because there are the talismans. No one knows what they really are, only what they look like and how they might be used. There's Shaddalakh which is said to be something like a spotted sanddollar made of porcelain; there's Klukesharna which was melted off a meteor and cooled in the shape of a clumsy key; there's Frunzacoache which looks exactly like a leaf off a berryvine, but it never withers; there's BinYAHtii which looks like a rough circle of the darkest red sandstone; there's Churrikyoo which looks like a small glass frog, rather battered and chipped and filled with thready cracks. There are more, said to be an even dozen of them, but I don't know the rest. All of them mean power to their holder, you notice I don't say owner, it takes a strong will to wield them and not be destroyed, they're as dangerous as they are tempting. No, I don't have a talisman and I don't want one. I don't want power over other men, I simply want to be left alone so I can earn a living doing things I enjoy doing. There's intense satisfaction in using one's talents, Brann. (He looked startled, as if he hadn't connected his skills with her potting before this moment.) *Was it that way with you, making your um pots?*

Before Maksim began calling up consultants, he focused his will on the little he could make out of the man, two arms, two legs, a common sort of face, two blurs for eyes, a smear for a mouth and some sort of nose, a darkness about the lower face that looked like beard stubble, reddish brown skin, at least where the sun had touched him, though he showed a bit of paler skin when his shirt had moved aside, that time he slapped down the drunks attacking the girl. Looked bald on top, though that was more a guess than something Maksim saw clearly. He wore trousers and a shirt and a long sleeveless vest with many pockets that looked like they were sewn shut with heavy metallic thread, it didn't seem logical but he kept the impression, it was a detail and every detail helped. Sandals, not boots. Maksim smiled to himself, the odd man had risked his toes, kicking the fundament of that chunky drunk; for an instant he lost some of his rancor toward him. But that was very much beside the point, a distraction, so he put emotion and image aside and focused more intently on the man himself, assembling a schematic of him he could used to direct his search through his index of realities.

He triggered the flow and the images began flipping before his mind's eye. The world of the tigermen, hot steamy deeply unstable; the place (one couldn't call it a world in almost any sense of that word) where the ariels swam along currents of not-air swirling about not-suns; the tangle of roots and branches that filled the whole of a pocket reality where he'd plucked forth the treeish and sent them after Brann, one immense plant with its attendant parasites and detachable branches; reality after reality, all different yet all the same in the power that thrummed through them, all these demon realities passed by without stopping, identified by the symbols he'd given them when he'd discovered them and explored their possibilities. A dance of shifting symbols, one flowing into the other, the whole dazzle a key to HIM; if an outsider could read them and follow their shifts he would know

him to the marrow of his bones. That outsider would
have to BE Settsimaksimin to read the symbols, and being him would not need to read them.

The demon worlds passed swiftly because they had
no affinity with the pattern Maksim presented as key,
but there were other realities he'd discovered, other realities he could reach into, one of them that busy place
he'd snatched Todichi Yahzi from. Realities without
magic in them, or at least without the kind of magic he
could tap into, and therefore of no interest to him. Three
of that sort of reality resonated with the oddman's pattern; he tagged these and went on searching the index
until he reached the limits of his explorations. He hadn't
sent his shamruz body searching for decades, it took
too much energy, too much time, it was a luxury he
couldn't afford when he already had more power sources
and demon pits that he needed. When he had to acknowledge that his body and the energy it contained,
out of which he worked, was slowly and inexorably fail-
ing. So he left off searching and did not bother exploring the non-magical realities since there was nothing
for him there. More than that, unlike the demon realities, those were immense beyond even his ability to
comprehend. Immense in size and immensely various
in their parts. He was uncomfortable there, reduced to
a mote of spectacular unimportance, which was hardly
an inducement to spend what he could no longer replace
unless he had a need no other sort of reality would or
could fill, Todichi Yahzi being one example of such a
need.

He entered the first of these universes, set his construct of the oddman before him and swooped between
the stars following the guide on a twisty path that set
his immaterial head spinning. He visited one world after another, watched folk going about their business,
they looked very much like the peasants and shopkeepers and traders in Cheonea and sometimes he understood what they were doing, the goods they were selling
but not often, mostly their deeds were as incomprehensible as their words; even though he knew what the
words were supposed to mean, he didn't have the referents to make sense of what those folk found perfectly

sensible. The guide construct was wobbling uncertainly with no evident goal, he wasn't learning anything and he felt himself tiring, so he withdrew, rested a moment, then visited the second of the realities. Here the guide construct waffled aimlessly about with even less direction than before. Angry and weary, Maksim broke off the search and tried the third.

This time the pull was galvanic; the construct whipped immediately to a world swimming in the light of a greenish sun; it hovered over a stretch of what looked like seamless dusty granite spread over an area twice the size of Silagamatys. There were the mosquitolike machines on one part of it; on another, one of the metal pods these folk drove somehow between worlds, a huge hole gaping in its side. A tall bony blond woman with a set angry face snapped out orders to a collection of four-armed reptilians using peculiar motorized assists to load crates and bundles on noisy carts that went by themselves up long latticed ramps and vanished inside the pod; now and then she muttered furious asides to the short man beside her.

"No, no, not that one, the numbers are on them, you can read, can't you?" Aside to her companion, "If that scroov shows his face round my ship again, I'll skin him an inch at a time and feed it to him broiled."

The bony little man scratched his three fingers through a spongy growth that covered most of his upper body; he blinked several times, shrugged and said nothing.

"Sssaah!" She darted to the loaders, cursed in half a dozen languages, waved her arms, made the workers reload the last cart. Still furious, she stalked back to where she'd been standing. "Danny Blue, you miserable druuj, I'll pull your masters rating this time, I swear I will, this is the last time you walk out on me or anyone else."

"Blue wants, Blue walks," the man murmured. "Done it before, 'll do 't again."

"Hah! Mouse, if you're so happy with him, you go help Sandy stow the cargo."

"I don't do boxes."

She glared at him, but throttled back the words that

bulged in her throat, stalked off and spent the rest of
the time Maksim watched inspecting the carts as they
rolled past her and rushing over to the loaders to stop
and reorder what they were doing.

Maksim opened his eyes, ran his tongue along his
lips; for several moments he lay relaxed in the chair
breathing slowly and steadily; he licked his lips again
and managed a smile. "Danny Blue. An analog with
you, Baby Dan? Odder and odder." He stroked long
tapering fingers over the staff, knowing every bump and
hollow and nailmark, taking comfort in that ancient fa-
miliarity. "If she was a shipmaster here, I'd say Danny
Two was cargomaster and she's fussing about him going
off and leaving her to do the stowing. Sounds like he
makes a habit of it, disappearing on his obligations to
go off and do what he wants. A pillar of milk pudding
when it comes to providing support. Why him? Who'd
be such a fool as to bring THAT MAN here? Forty
Mortal Hells, what good is a twitchy cargomaster to the
Drinker of Souls? Who's in this idiotic conspiracy?" A
quick unhappy halfsmile, then he pushed himself up
and levered the chair to vertical so it supported his back
and head and his feet were planted firmly on the footboard. He was wearier than he'd expected to be and that
worried him. The Lot's tomorrow, he thought, just as
well. His stomach knotted, but he forced the misery
away. Children die; children always die, they starved by
the hundreds when the Parastes and their puppet king
ran Cheonea, they died of filth and overwork, they died
in the pleasurehouses and under the whips of those fine
lords. What's the death of one child compared to the
hundreds I've made healthier and happier? It was an old
argument, he felt deeply that it was a true argument,
but when he took the child who drew the gold lot to
Deadfire Island, the child who was miserable at leaving
his parents and excited about seeing the marvels of the
Grand Yron in the holy city Havi Kudush deep in the
heart of Phras, when he took that child and fed his life
(or hers) to BinYAHtii, he found his rationalizations
hard to remember.

He glanced at the wallcabinet, wondered if he should

take another dram of the cordial, but he didn't want to break the pentacle and have to lose more energy reactivating it. Reluctantly he spread his hand over Bin-YAHtii and drew on it; it was restive and hard to control, but the disciplines of that control were engraved in his brain by now, in his blood and bone, so he dealt with the brief rebellion so quickly and effectively he hardly noticed what he was doing. When he was ready, he smoothed his hair again, straightened out his linen robe and the soft black overrobe, pulled BinYAHtii through the neck opening and set it flat against the snowy linen. He swung the staff around and held it vertical beside him, then he began to chant, letting his deepest notes ring out, the sound filling the chamber with echoes and resonances.

"IO IO DOSYNOS EYO IO IO STYGERAS MOIRO IO IO TI TILYMON PHATHO IO IO LELATAS EMO."

And as the echoes died he gestured with hand and staff in ways both erotic and obscene (which is one of the reasons he did most of his primal magic in private; a sorceror in many ways is stuck with what his submind dredges up for him; powerful magics require powerful stimulants no matter how upsetting or ridiculous they might seem to onlookers.)

"PAREITHEE, OY YO ROSAPER ROSPALL. PAREITHEE ENTHA DA ROSPA."

He beat the end of the staff against the stone three times, the sound faint after the power of his reverberant basso. A misty column appeared in the smaller pentacle.

The mist thickened and solidified into a creature like a series of mistakes glued together. A cock's comb and mad rooster eyes, spiky gold feathers, a black sheep's face where the beak should be, narrow snaky shoulders and torso, spindly arms with lizard hands and lizard skin on them, male organs bulging in a downy pouch, huge heavy hips and knees that bent the wrong way, powerful in the wrongness, narrow two-toed feet with lethal black claws on the toes. Rosaper Rospall whined and panted and swayed in the small space allotted to him and fixed frantic evil eyes on Maksim.

Maksim let his voice roll (not so solemn and sonorous this time, he was fond of the deplorable little gossip), "Rosaper Rospall, I demand of you, tell me who among the gods are plotting and working against me."

Rospall's arms jerked with each of the words, his hands flew about with feeling gestures; he whimpered as he touched again and again the burning unseen wall about him. His blunt muzzle writhed in a way to confuse the eye and sicken the stomach, but he managed a few words. "No one works against you, chilo, no one no want no cant no can none works against you."

Maksim frowned. Rospall never lied, but his truths were strictly limited. He reworked his next question. "Tungjii and the Godalau are scheming against someone, perhaps several someones. Who is it? Who are they?"

"Juh juh juh, scheme dream stir the pot not not who but what."

What's the what?"

"BinYAHt."

Maksim's eyes snapped wide, then he smiled and nodded. "I should have been expecting that. Amortis is in this?"

"Amortis disportis cavortis, BinYAHt's the hook in her, who cares, the fisherman dances to her tugging, hugging, happy sappy Amortis. No. No change for her no danger in her."

Maksim nodded, answering his own thoughts more than Rospall's words. "Who works with Tungjii and the Godalau, who set the hook in them and got their help?"

"In the wind, a whisper, Perran-a-Perran, lord of lords, piranha of pirhanas, he consents, in the wind, a whisper, Jah'takash perverse, spitting snags and checks and worse your way, in the wind a clink of links, the Chained God blinks and blinds and minds the mix." Hooting laughter. "From the rest no nay or yea, they gossip and they play. And they wager who will win and when."

Maksim felt a tremble of weakness deep within, saw Rospall's bold black eyes get a feverish glow. Enough, he thought, I've got enough to think on now. He gathered himself, let his voice roll out, filled with power,

never a tremble in it. "APHISTARTI, OY YO ROSA-
PER ROSPALL, APHISTARTI ENTHA DA ROSPA."
And his hands moved again through their erotic dance.

The visitor's body shuddered, for a moment he
seemed to fight his dismissal, then he broke into fragments and the fragments faded.

Maksim didn't move until the last wisps of the presence had vanished utterly, then he sighed, shuddered,
lay back limp in the chair, eyes closed. For several minutes he lay there breathing deep and slow. Finally, as
the need to sleep began to overwhelm him, he forced
his eyes open, used the staff to lever himself out of the
chair. He stood and stretched, yawned enormously, then
flicked himself up to his bedroom for a few hours of the
sleep he needed so badly.

Todichi Yahzi cooed protests as he hovered about
watching Maksim dress himself for the Lot ceremony.
"Sleep," he warbled, "anyone can see you are exhausted, Mwahan, you do not need to be there, you do
not enjoy being there, why do you go?" He repeated
this until Maksim snarled him into silence.

Later, as Maksim strode through the murmuring park
toward the Yron, he regretted his harshness and made
a mental note to apologize when he got back. Poor old
Todich, he kept pecking and pecking at a place, but he
couldn't know how sore that spot already was. One had
to take responsibility for one's acts, one doesn't slide
away and pretend that nothing's happening. He'd set that
burden on himself in those wild first days when Cheonea teetered on the verge of a slide into chaos. when he
knew he'd have to use BinYAHtii. The stone had to be
fed when it was used or it fed itself from the user. Forty
years he'd fed BinYAHtii, ten times a year, once a
month. Forty years, once a month he'd walked this path
and climbed to the high seat behind the austere stone
railing and watched the children file in. Self-flagella-
tion, reminding him not to forget why he was doing
these things. If he allowed himself to be corrupted by
wealth, power, by the infinite capacity in the human
soul for self-justification, then these children were torn

from their parents for nothing, then one of the three chosen died for nothing at all.

At his private entrance the waiting Servant opened the door for him and bowed him inside.

"Kori." Polatéa's voice broke into confused dreams suffused with sick anxiety.

Kori stirred, sat up, rubbed at grainy eyes. "What time . . ."

"Breakfast in five minutes; wash and dress, come down as soon as you can, I'll save some food for you." Polatéa brushed the straggles of hair out of Kori's eyes. "You can sleep some more, if you want, after the Lot."

"If I'm not chosen."

A long sigh. "If you're not chosen."

Tré looked her over. "Your skods are crooked."

Kori clicked her tongue, adjusted the covered cords that held her headcloth in place. She and Tré were together in the Hostel court, waiting to be put in line. She used one end of the headcloth to rub at her eyes, not sure she could manage to keep on her feet till the Lot was over; she felt as if she were walking two feet under water that was sloshing about, threatening to knock her over. "I got everything done," she muttered, hiding her mouth behind the corner of the cloth. "It's started."

Tré stepped closer, nestled against her. "You think it'll make any difference, Kori? Do you think she's got a chance against HIM?"

"A chance? Yes. There's more than just her. Daniel's in. You didn't dream?"

"No."

Sinan blew the cow's horn and the lines began sorting themselves out, girls in one, boys in the other, eldest at the front. Tré gave her arm a last squeeze and drifted back to the end of his line, he was the youngest boy this year. She was two from the front of her line. Dessi Bacharikss was two months older, Lilla Farazilss a week and a half. Dessi's twin Sparran led the boys' line, he was a tall rather skinny boy with a wild imagination and a grin that was starting to make Kori's toes tingle. He looked around at her, winked, then straightened and sobered as the signalhorn hooted and the lines began to move.

Maksim watched the children file in, grave and rather frightened, their sandals squeaking on the polished marble. Ignoring the boys, he scanned the first few girls, smiled tightly as he saw Kori's red-eyed, weary face. He crossed his arms, his hands hidden in the wide black sleeves of his heavily embroidered and appliquéd formal overrobe, began the gestures and the internal chant that would bring the blue lot to Kori's searching fingers. His smile broadened a hair. There was no sign of the interference that had protected her last night.

Kori thrust her arm deep into the bowl; the capsules seemed oddly slippery this year, it was a breath or two before she could get hold of one and bring it out. She took a deep breath and moved on, hearing the capsules rattle behind her as Sallidi Xoshallarz reached for hers. She crossed to the gilt bowl, tried to ignore the feeling that HE was staring down at her ill-wishing her; it was easier to grab this time, she got her second egg and went to take her place on the girls' bench.

It is done. I have her, little ferret, ah what a fine fierce girl she is, tired now but she doesn't give in to it. Look how straight and bold she sits, waiting to see if fate will pass her by. Not this year, little ferret. Your last year, isn't it. You shouldn't have got so busy with things you don't understand. We'll have to do something with you; not one of Amortis' whores, that would break you faster than marrying one of your clod-cousins and disappearing into the nursery with half your mind shut down; hmm, you could be trained to teach . . . With some difficulty he repressed the laughter rumbling in his belly. Not with what you're apt to teach my restive folk. Would you like to be a scholar, child? I wonder. I could send you east to study in Silili. Study what? Magic? Have you got a talent there? There's something in you that calls to me. Yes, you have a talent in you waiting to unfold, oh child, if you deny it, how terrible

for you. I'll make you see it. Why weren't you born a
boy? It would be so much easier if you were born a boy.

*The black capsules grew sweaty in her hand; she
changed hands and wiped the sweaty one surreptitiously
on her overtunic. Over half done. Two capsules for every
Owlyn child. Kori didn't feel like a child any more; she
wanted this to be over with so she could get back to
Owlyn and get her life in some sort of order again.
Maybe because she was so tired, she wasn't much worried this time, not for herself anyway; so many important things had happened to her the past two months,
she felt bone deep sure the Lot would pass over her, one
more thing would be just too much. She watched the
girls file past her going to take their places on the bench
and wondered which of them would get the blue lot and
be kept here in the Yron, then wondered which one
would get the gold, would it be a boy or a girl this time?
If I had a choice, she thought, I'd take the gold, how
terribly exciting to go so far away. Havi Kudush. A
wonderful magical name, it stirred desires in her she
didn't want to deal with and had to keep pushing away.
She gazed down at the enigmatic black eggs. The capsules each had a ball of lead inside them, most were
simply gray, one was painted blue; the girl who got that
one stayed at the Yron to study as a teacher or if her
tastes and talents ran that way, to serve as one of the
temple whores. Kori's mouth twitched. She fought her
face straight and swallowed the smile. Polatéa would
scold her for saying* whore, *but that's what they were,
those that called themselves* Fields of Amortis, *plowed
and replowed those fields if the gossip she heard was
true. Gahh, that was almost as bad as that girl in the
tavern. One of the balls in the boys' bowl was painted
red, the boy that got that one went to the army to learn
a soldier's trade or into the Yron schools to study how
to Serve. But the gold yolk, oh the gilt one, the child
who got the gilt one went to Havi Kudush and did wonderful things, she was sure of it. Have a golden yolk,
she thought at the black things in her hands, if you can't
have the good old safe and steady leaden gray, have a*

*golden yolk. She glanced quickly around, lowered her
eyes again. I couldn't stand it if I had to stay here.*

*Sarana Piyolss, the baby of the line walked past her.
The drawing's over for this year, Kori thought. Now we
find out who got the colors. Two doors opened beside
the High Seat, two small processions filed down the narrow steps slanting from both sides of the high dais, first
a Servant dressed in white linen, white leather sandals,
short white gloves, then a boy and a girl, also dressed
in white, carrying a wide shallow basket between them.*

*Deep silence in the court, a sense of almost intoler-
able waiting. One servant stopped before Sparran, the
other before Dessi. Their movements slow and mea-
sured, as close to synchronized as a good marching
team, they took the capsules from Sparran, from Dessi,
opened them. Together both the Servants intoned NO
and let capsules and lead balls fall into the basket. They
moved to the next in line, repeated their movements,
repeated the NO, then the Servant on the girls' side
stood before Kori. His face impassive, he took the damp
capsules before her, broke one. A plain lead ball rolled
on the palm of the white glove; he broke the second
capsule. A blue ball, nestled next to the gray.*

*Kori stared at it, unable to believe what she saw. She
lifted her eyes. HE was looking at her. You, she thought,
you did it to me on purpose. She opened her mouth,
then clamped it shut. What could she prove? Nothing.
She'd just bring trouble on her kin if she protested. She
glared up at the huge dark man on the High Seat. I'll
get out of this somehow, she thought fiercely, I will, you
can't beat me so easy as that.*

You aren't stupid are you, little ferret. Yes, it was me
did that to you. I doubt you'll ever thank me for it, but
you should. I hated old Grigoros when he sold me to
the House, but he did me a favor. He smiled as Kori
dropped her eyes to clenched hands when the Servant
shouted BLUE; when he pushed it at her, she took the
blue ball with angry reluctance, then sat staring at the
floor, refusing to look at Maksim or anyone else until
the RED and GOLD were announced. He saw her

shoulders tremble; she turned her head, glared up at him again, but this time there was a triumph in her face and eyes that he didn't understand. *What have I missed? There's more to you than I thought, warrior girl. What is it? I will know, child, in the end I will know.* He got heavily to his feet and stood watching as the Servants led the chosen children (two boys and the girl) up the stairs to stand beside him. He could feel the heat of her anger, the intensity of the effort she was making to keep silent.

He lifted his hands. "It is done." His voice rolled out and filled the court. "Honor the chosen and their lives of service, honor yourselves for the grace of your compliance. For three days the city is yours, rejoice and be content."

He watched them file out. The youngest boy kept turning to look up at the chosen, anguish in his face; he stumbled against the boy ahead of him, but straightened himself without help and went stiffly out the door. Maksim glanced at the girl and saw an echo of that anguish in her face. *Your brother, is it? Is that why the triumph, that he was passed over this year? I will know. But not now.* He bowed he head in a stately salute to the children, but he didn't speak to them, merely made a sign for them to be taken away. He stood at the balustrade looking out over the empty court until the last sounds faded, rubbing absently at his chest. He had to be at Deadfire Island when the boy arrived, but that was a good six hours off and he wasn't sure how he wanted to pass those hours. He needed sleep. He had to listen to Todichi Yahzi report on the activities of the council he'd assembled and decide who he wanted to add or delete, what other changes he needed to make. He had to take a look at the blank spot and see if Baby Dan had moved himself and the others out of Silagamatys which would mean he could turn Amortis loose on them. He tapped long fingers on the marble, irritated by the hurry of all this, then snapped to his workroom to start with the easiest and most urgent of the things he had to do.

──────── **10** ────────

FIGHTING THEIR WAY TO THE CHAINED GOD: BRANN, YARIL, JARIL, AHZURDAN AND DANIEL AKAMARINO, WITH SOME HELP FROM TUNGJII AND THE GODALAU.

SCENE: Daniel Akamarino finds a ship for them, discomforting Ahzurdan who is locked into the room because he can't leave the wards without endangering himself and the rest of them. On the ship Skia Hetaira traveling between Silagamatys and Haven.

"Had a bit of luck." Daniel Akamarino squatted by the beggar, held out the wineskin. "Found me a patron."

"Aah." The old man squeezed a long stream of the straw gold wine into his toothless mouth, broke the flow without losing a drop. He wiped his mouth, handed the skin back. "An't swallowed drink like that sin' one night ol' Parast Tampopopea got drunk's a skink and busted six kegs in the Ti'ma Dor."

"Luck," Daniel said and smiled. He squirted himself a sip, chunked the stopper home. "Quiet day."

"Some. Lot day. Come afternoon, it'll perk up. You thinkin about a pitch?"

"Nuh-uh. Patron wants to sail tonight. She hates fuss, she wants to go out like a whisper."

"Aah." The old man's warty eyelids flickered, the

166

tip of a pointed whitish tongue touched his upper lip, withdrew. "A like the way you play that pipe."

"I hear." Daniel slid the carrystrap of the wineskin over his shoulder, shifted out of his squat and brought out the recorder. He looked at it, thought a minute and began playing a slow rambling bluesy tune that made no demands but slid into the bone and after a while took over enough to bring crowds drifting around them. He ended it, raised a brow. The old man closed his eyes to slits and looked sleepy. Daniel laughed, played a lively jig, then put the recorder away. The small crowd snapped fingers enthusiastically, but Daniel was finished for the moment, at least until they paid something for their pleasure. He sat as stolid and sleepy as the old beggar. With a flurry of laughter, they tossed coins into the begging bowl and wandered off, some returning to their stalls, others drifting about looking for bargains.

The old man collected his coin, stowed it away. He blinked thoughtfully at the skin, ran his tongue around his teeth. "Real quiet, aah?" He scratched at the gray and white stubble on his wattles. "Wanna keepa neye lifted for sharks."

"Hard to know where the sharks are if you don't know the waters."

"Aaah. Eleias Laux's lookin for cargo, might go without if ta patron meetzis price. *Skia Hetaira,* thatzis boat." He took the wineskin and drank until he seemed about to drown, stopped the flow with the neatness he'd shown before. "Way down west end. Black boat, ketch, flag's a four point star, black on white. Lio, eez hived up at the Green Jug. Eatzis noon there." He glanced at the sun. " 'Bout this time a day, more often than not." He held out the skin. "Gi'm a stoup 'r two a this and eez like to sail ta patron to the Golden Isles, no charge."

Daniel Akamarino got to his feet, yawned and stretched. He smiled amiably at the old man. "G' day to you, friend," he said and strolled away.

"How'd you know he'd know?"

Daniel looked down, startled. Jaril was walking beside him, looking up at him with those enigmatic crystal eyes. "Been on a lot of worlds," he said. "There's always someone who knows, you just have to find him.

Or her or it, whatever. That old man, he's got the best pitch in the Market which means he's got some kind of clout, I don't have to know what kind, just that it exists. There's this, he's no muscle man, must be shrewdness. Brains and information. Means he knows what's going on where.''

''And now you're going to hunt out Eleias Laux?''

''Mmm, might.''

''That's a funny wineskin.''

''Funny how?''

''It's not all that big.''

''Mmm.''

''Should be near empty the way you been squeezing it. Isn't, is it?''

''Lot of funny things on this world. You might have noticed.''

''We have noticed that. Some of it's been done to us.'' The boy grinned up at him. ''How've you been feeling lately?''

''Herded.''

''You're not alone.''

''What I mean. Takes more than one to make a herd; company's no blessing, if it's just that.''

''You right. Give me a drink?''

Daniel raised a brow. ''You?''

''Did last night.''

''Why not.'' He tossed the boy the skin, watched him drink, took it back and drank a draft himself. It was chilled, just the right temperature for the taste, a computerized cooler couldn't have done better. Tungjii Luck, magic wineskin, what a world.

They ambled through sunny deserted streets, past shops whose keepers were gone off somewhere leaving a clerk behind to watch the stock and doze in the warmth and quiet. Lot day seemed to mean waiting for Owlyn Valers to burst loose with their warrant to spend what they wanted, freely as they wanted; the bills would be paid from Settsimaksimin's pocket (which meant eventually from taxes and tariffs and fines). Jaril was silent and frowning, a small thundercloud of a boy.

''Can't really fight gods,'' he said suddenly, grave now, a touch of bitterness putting bite into his voice.

"Either they squash you right out or they sneak up on you and cut your legs off and you bleed to death."

"Sneak up? That mean what I think it does?"

"Don't know. The talismans Ahzurdan was talking about can make them do things. A good sorceror can block them out. Brann and us, we were mixed up in a fight between a clutch of witches and a god. She used Brann to get past their defenses. Complicated plot, took more than a year to set up, used maybe hundreds of people who didn't know they were in it. Even looking back I couldn't say who all was in it or how much what they did mattered in the blowup. You can't win even if you win, they keep coming back at you, get you in the end. Or you die and they get you then."

"You've got, what did you say? ninety centuries less a few."

"Doesn't matter, long as we're stuck here, the end's the same."

"Gives you time to work out a way to get home."

"Can't go home. You heard what they call Brann."

"Drinker of Souls. So?"

"You saw what we are, Yaril and me. Back home we drank from the sun. Slya, that's the god I was telling you about, she changed us, then she helped us change Brann so Brann could feed us. We live on life energy, Daniel Akamarino; if anything happened to Brann, we'd starve."

"Why tell me?"

"Because we're frightened, Yaril and me. Him in the tower there, he's strong, you don't know how strong. He hasn't exerted himself yet, not really, Yaril and me, we don't know why, but even with those offhand tries, he nearly killed Brann twice and the second time Ahzurdan was there and he stood like a stump doing nothing until Yaril singed his ear. We don't like him, we don't want him about, but Brann won't send him away. Even when he tells her she should, she won't. We don't know why, but we're afraid it's because the gods messing with us won't let her. You're affined to him, Daniel Akamarino, but you're a different sort of man." Jaril gave him a twisted smile. "You don't want to be in this, but you are. Yaril and me, we want you with us and ready to do something when Ahzurdan fails her.''

"Which reminds me. Since you're in a talking mood, Jay, why am I let off the leash this morning when last night Brann wouldn't let me out of the room without Ahzurdan to babysit?"

They pressed up against a wall to let a heavily loaded mulecart clatter past heading uphill for the Market, then went round a corner and moved west along the busy waterfront road, dodging carts and carrypoles, vehemently gesturing traders, crowds of merchants with their clerks. The morning wasn't quiet here, it was deafening, hot, dusty, filled with a thousand smells, ten thousand noises. Daniel pulled Jaril into a doorway to let a line of porters trot past. "Well?"

"Lot day," Jaril said. "He's always there. In the Yron. When the Lots are taken. He can't overlook us without his mirror. He'll be away from it for maybe another hour. And I'm here." He giggled, amused at the thought. "I'm babysitting you."

"Mmf." Daniel left the doorway, sidled between two carts being loaded by men shouting jokes at each other, their overseers darting here and there, pushing shoving yelling orders that were obeyed when the men got around to it or ignored if they counted them silly. Runners not much older than Jaril seemed were darting about, carrying messages, small packages, orders, the shrill whistles that announced them adding to the crashing pounding noise that broke like surf against the walls of the warehouses. A few meters of this and Daniel sought an unoccupied doorway. "Jay, if you're going to haunt me, can you do it as something besides a boy?"

"Why? Plenty of boys like me about."

"I know. Just a feeling Laux will talk more without an extra pair of ears to take it in."

"Hmm. Why not. Dog be all right?"

Daniel chuckled. "Nice big dog?"

"All teeth and no tail."

The man and the big dog strolled the length of Water Street until they reached a quieter section and smaller boats, one of them a slim black ketch with a black and white flag hanging in silky folds that opened out a little whenever the fleeting breeze briefly strengthened. Hands clasped behind him, Daniel inspected the craft. "Wet and cold." The dog nudged his leg. "All right, I give you fast." The boy dozing on the deck lifted his head when he heard the voice, squinted up at Daniel. Daniel produced one of his everyday smiles. "Where's Laux?"

"Why?"

"Business. His."

The boy patted a yawn and gazed through the fringe of dirty blonde hair falling over his eyes. After a minute, he shrugged. "Green Jug. Be back here a couple hours if you wanna wait."

"Where's the Jug from here?"

"Back along a ways, there's the Kuma Kistris, the one with a double spiral on the flag, black and green, alley there between two godons, leads up Skanixis Hill, follow it, Jug's near halfway up."

Daniel found two coppers, tossed them to the boy, strolled away grinning. Jaril hound was already two moorings away doing an impatient doggy dance in front of a boat with a green and black flag.

"Eleias Laux?"

"Who wants to know?"

"Someone wanting passage out."

"Paying or working?"

"Paying. Five, two of 'em kids."

"Hmm. Sit." He was a little spider of a man, M'darjin with skin like aged walnut polished to a high shine, dressed in well-worn black trousers and tunic, a heavy silver earring with moss agate insets hanging from his left ear, linked plates that shivered with every breath he took, drawing the eye so that most people who met him never noticed his face and remembered only the flash of silver and the gleam of agate. The earring glittered wildly as he glanced at the hound, looked dubious, relaxed as Jaril settled placidly to the floor by Daniel's feet. He pushed his plate aside, emptied his winebowl and was about to call for more wine when Daniel slid the skin off his shoulder and offered it.

Laux pinched at his nose, looked from the skin to Daniel's face. "Be you insulted if I say you drink first?"

"I'm a cautious man myself, be you insulted if I want another bowl?"

Eleias Laux laughed and snapped his fingers for the serving girl.

When she brought the bowl, Daniel filled it halfway and sipped at the straw colored liquid, smiling with pleasure, taking time to do it justice. When the bowl was empty, he set it down, raised his brows.

Laux nodded, watched warily as the wine streamed out. He drank, widened his eyes, took another mouthful, let it trickle down his throat. "Now that is a thing." He grinned. "Not your best plan, friend. You just raised the price a notch."

Daniel shrugged. "Luck's meant to be shared. I was mooching about the wharves a few nights back, when it was foggy, you remember? saw the Godalau swimming out in the bay and this bald little shemale offered me a drink, left the skin with me."

"Tungjii Luck?"

"Couldn't say, but I've been drinking wine since and passing it around here and there and the skin's about the same as it was when I got it. I figure it's just old Tungjii sticking hisser thumbs in and why not enjoy it while it's here. Think you might be willing to slip out tonight, head round to Haven, no fuss?"

"How quiet?"

"Like a ghost's shadow."

"Might could. You walking round loose?"

"Far's I know. Hound here says so and he's good at nosing out nosy folk. You don't want to know more."

"True, true. Five gold each."

"Ahh now, have yourself some more wine and think on this, two silver each adult, one each for the kids."

"The wine I'll take, but don't you fool yourself; drunk or sober I'm not about to wreck myself for anyone. No discount for kids, they're worse than dryrot on a boat. But seeing you're a friendly type, I'll think on taking a bit of a loss. Three gold each. You bringing the hound here, another gold for him.

"No hound. What about this, five silver each, with a

gold as bonus when you set us down on the shore of
Haven Cove.''

''Mmmmm.'' Laux drank and smiled, a friendlier
sheen in his brown velvet eyes; if he had armed himself
against the seduction in Tungjii's wine, his armor was
leaking. ''Ohhhh, I'm feeling so warm to you, my
friend, I'll tell you what. Five silver each, a gold as
bonus when you're on the fine black sand of Haven
Cove, sweetly out of sight from Haven herself, and five
gold as trouble quittance, to be refunded if trouble keeps
away.''

''Mmmm.'' Daniel filled the bowl pushed over to
him, filled his own. ''Five silver each, a gold as bonus
when we're landed, five gold as trouble quittance, paid
over the minute trouble shows.''

''Now now . . . what do I call you? give me something.''

''Daniel.''

''Now Daniel, don't be a silly man. Trouble comes,
nobody has time to count out cash.''

''Point made, point taken. Five silver each, a gold as
bonus, two gold as trouble quittance, to be refunded if
no trouble shows; my patron guarantees the cost of any
repairs.''

''Ah, now that might be a good deal, saying your
patron's the right sort. You willing to say who he is?''

''I won't be mentioning that she doesn't want her
name spread around. I've heard you're a man of discretion and wisdom. She's called Drinker of Souls.''

''Exalted company, hey, gods and demigods all
round.'' Laux sat hunched over the winebowl, a long
forefinger like a polished walnut twig stirring the plates
of his ear dangle as he stared past Daniel at shadow
forms he alone could see. He said nothing, but Daniel
could read the argument going on inside, an argument
he'd been in himself, never coming out with the same
answer twice. Daniel waited without speaking for the
struggle to end, fairly sure what the answer would be.
Laux knew well enough he could be jumping into a
maelstrom that could suck him under, but he was visibly bored with the mundane cargos he ferried in and
out of Silagamatys and something deep and fundamen-

tal in him was tempted to try the danger, especially if he could be sure of coming out of it reasonably intact, his boat in the same condition.

"Mmh!" Laux straightened, shifted his focus to Daniel. "Yes. Tell you what, considering what's likely to be involved and how likely it is bystanders get chewed up and spat out when powers start to feuding, and this isn't trying to screw you, Daniel, just me taking care of me, how 'bout instead of your patron's giving me her word, she gives me two hundred gold surety to hold for her till the bunch of you put foot down on Haven Cove's black sand. No one in his right mind would try cheating the Drinker of Souls. The rest as before, five silvers each, a gold as bonus, four gold trouble quittance."

"Done." Daniel grasped the hand Laux extended, gave it a brisk shake, settled back in his chair. "How're the tides, can you leave around sunset today?"

"Tide'll be standing, my Hetty don't draw enough to worry about the sandbars at the bay's mouth. As long as the wind's good (give old Tungjii's belly a rub) we'll go."

They sat in silence a while, sipping at their wine, Laux leaning over his elbows, Daniel lounging in the chair, straightening up to fill the bowls whenever they showed bottom. There were a few other drinkers and diners scattered through the comfortable gloom inside the taproom, talking together in muted tones and generally minding their own business. "Waiting for the Lot to finish," Laux said. "Everything's waiting for that."

"Not Water Street, Laux."

"Call me Lio, yeah you right, they're not waiting, they're stocking up for the run. Leaves the rest of us neaped." He shoved out his bowl, watched the pale gold wine sing into it. "Cheonea's neaped these days." He sipped and sighed. "Sold my Gre'granser in the King's Market here when he was somewhere about six. He said you couldn't hear yourself think for a mile all round the port it was that busy. Most of it under the table, but that didn't seem to matter. My Granser's mum was a freewoman Gre'granser sweetered into the bushes, means he was born free. Him he was prenticed out on a merchanter when he made six. He took to the smug-

gling trade and trained his sons in that. Ahhh, it was a
wild trade then and Haven was a wild town, it never
stopped, you know, moonset was busy as sunset, ships
coming in and going out, half a hundred gaming houses
wide open, a Captain could win a fleet or lose everything down to the skin, man or woman make no matter.
There was a woman or two had her ship and you didn't
want to mess with them, Granser used to say, they didn't
bide by rules, got you howsoever they could.'' He
dipped his finger in the wine, drew a complicated symbol on the dark wood. ''Never saw any of that myself.
Him in the tower, he shut down the slave market and
cleared out the hot brokers and he put the tariffs down
to nothing almost on spices, silk and pearls and the like
so an honest smuggler can't live on the difference. Aah,
Daniel, the past some years I've been thinking of moving on to livelier shores.'' A long silence, voices drifting to them, clanks of china as serving girls began to
clear the tables. ''Might do it yet. Trouble is, them already there won't like newcomers nosing in, that kind
of thing gets messy. Starve for a couple years, maybe
get killed or turned, no contacts, no cargo, I tell you,
man, it was a sad year when Him he kicked out the king
and started on his Jah'takash be damned reforms.'' He
fell silent, brooding into his wine.

Jaril stirred. His claws scratched at the floor, his teeth
closed closed on Daniel's leg not quite hard enough to
break the skin. Daniel blinked, looked down. Jaril got
to his feet and started for the door.

Daniel knocked on the table. When Lio Laux looked
up, he said, ''Got to go, my patron's not the kind you
want to keep waiting. See you sunset.''

Lio grunted, lifted a hand, let it thump down, Tungjii's wine was wheeling round his head and he was lost
in old days and old dreams.

Ruby shimmers slid off the opaline scales of an un-
dulant fishtail and bloodied long white fingers combing
through the waves; the Godalau swam before the Skia
Hetaira as the ketch slipped swift and silent from the
bay. A scruffy little figure in ragged black sat on a giant
haunch and waved to Daniel Akamarino. He waved

back, jumped when he felt a hand on his shoulder. Brann. "I haven't got used to it yet," he said.

"What? Oh yes, you come from a place where you have to imagine your gods and they keep going abstract and distant on you." She leaned on the rail beside him. "Sounds like paradise to me. No gods to tie strings to your ankles and jerk you about. Hmm. Maybe one day I'll jump high enough to break the strings and land in a reality like that."

Daniel shaded his eyes, picked out the translucent tail that flickered across the sky some distance ahead of them, more guessed at than seen. "It has its drawbacks. At least here there's somebody to notice you're alive, might be all round bad vibes, but that's better than being ignored. Where I come from, live or die, the universe won't notice. I'll wait a while before I decide which sort I prefer." He laughed. "Not that I have much choice. Tell me about Tungjii."

"Tell you what?"

"A story, Bramble, tell me a tale of ol 'Tungjii. It's a lovely night, there's nothing much to do, get drunk, sleep, watch the wind blow. I'd rather hear you talk."

She laughed. "Such a compliment. Your tact is overwhelming, Danny Blue. Why not. A warning tale, my friend. Heesh is an amiable sort, but you don't want to underestimate that little god. So. There's a land a long way east of here, a land that was old when Popokanjo walked the earth, before he shot the moon. In that long long long ago, in the reign of the emperor Rumanai, a maretuse whose maret was a broad domain at the edge of the rice plains came to consider himself the cleverest man in the world, yet he had to keep proving his cleverness to himself. Every month or so he sent out mercenary bands to roam the silk road and snatch travelers from it to play games with him, games he always won because he set the rules and because he really was very clever in his twisted way. Each of his conscripted guests played game after game with him until the miserable creature lost his nerve or was killed or began to bore the maretuse. His landfolk did their best to keep him entertained with strangers because that meant he wouldn't turn his mind to testing them. And they were loyally discreet when Rumanai's soldiers came prying about, hunting the bandits interfering with the Emperor's road and the taxes it brought to his treasury.

The land prospered. In their silence and because they took the spoils he passed out among them, the horses, the dogs, the tradegoods, even some of the gold, the landfolk also shared his guilt. But the peasants on the land and the merchants in the small market towns told themselves that their hands were clean, *they* shed no blood, *they* did not lift a finger to aid their master in his games. That they profited from these was neither here nor there. What could they do? It was done and would be done. Should they starve by having too queasy a stomach? Should their children starve? Besides, the travelers on the silk road knew the dangers they faced. And no doubt they were little better than the maretuse if you looked into their lives. Thieves, cheats, murderers, worst of all foreigners. If they were proper men, they would stay home where they belonged. It was their own fault if they came to a bad end. So the Ambijaks of maret Ambijan talked themselves into silence and complicity.

The day came when the mighty Perran-a-Perran, the highest of the high, lord and emperor of all gods, took a hand in the matter of the clever maretuse.

Old Tungjii was sitting on a hillside munching grapes when a messenger from the high court of the gods came mincing along a sunbeam, having a snit at the common red mountain dirt that was blowing into every crevice and fold of his golden robe. Old Tungjii was more than half drunk from all the grapes heesh had been eating because heesh had been turning them to wine before they hit hisser stomach. Heesh was wearing common black trousers like any old peasant, the cloth worn thin at the seat and knees and a loose shirt heesh didn't bother to tie shut, letting the wind and grape juice get at fat sagging breasts with hard purple nipples. Heesh was liking the warm sun and the dusty wind that sucked up the sweat on hisser broad bald head. Heesh was liking the smell of the dust, of the crushed grass and leaves underneath him, the sounds of the grape pickers laughing a little way off and the shepherd's pipe someone was

playing almost too far away to hear. Heesh certainly
didn't want to be bothered by some sour-faced godlet
from the Courts of Gold. But old Fishface (which is
how Tungjii privately thought of the god-emperor Perran-a-Perran, how heesh muttered about him when
rather too drunk to be discreet) was nasty when one of
his undergods irritated him, especially one of the more
disreputable sorts like the double-natured Tungjii. So
heesh spat out a mouthful of grapeskins and lumbered
to hisser broad bare feet.

"Tungjii," the messenger said.

Tungjii smiled, winning the bet heesh made with hisserself that the godlet's voice would whine like a
whipped puppy. Heesh nodded, content with the perfection of pettiness old Fishface had presented himmer
with.

"The maretuse of maret Ambijan is getting above
himself," the messenger said, his lip curled in a permanent sneer that did odd things to his enunciation
even while he spoke with a glasscutting clarity. "The
foolish man is thinking about plotting against dearest
Rumanai, the beloved of the gods, the true emperor of
Hinasilisan. He has convinced himself he deserves the
throne for his own silly bottom." The messenger made
a jerky little gesture with his left hand meant to convey
overpowering rage and martial determination. Tungjii
reminded hisserself sternly that old Fishface didn't like
his subgods to giggle at his official messengers. "Perran-a-Perran, Lord of All, Lord of sky, sea and earth,
Emperor of emperors, Orderer of Chaos, Maker of man
and beast, Father of all . . ."

Tungjii stopped listening to the roll of epithets, let
hisser senses drift, squeezing the last drops of pleasure
from the day. Even old Fishface's eyes glazed over during one of these interminable listings of his attributes
and honors, finishing with the list of his many consorts,
the only one of them of any interest to Tungjii being
the Godalau with her moonpale fingers and her saucy
fishtail. The two of them had played interesting games
with hisser dual parts. Horny old Tungjii was a busy
old Tungjii in spite of hisser unprepossessing outer en-
velope and found hisserself in a lot of lofty beds (the

messenger would have been shocked to a squib to know one of those beds belonged to Perran-a-Perran). A girl's laughter came up the hill to himmer and heesh blew a minor blessing down to her for the lift of pleasure she'd given himmer.

". . . of all gods, Perran-a-Perran commands Tungjii the double god to go to Ambijan and stop this blowfish from poisoning the air and punish his overweening folly for daring to plot trouble for the God of all god's dearest dear, the emperor Rumanai."

Tungjii yawned. "Tell him I went," heesh said and was gone.

Some time later a fat little man was riding along the silk road on a fine long-legged mule, drowsing in a well-padded saddle, content to let the mule find the way. If anyone had asked, the little man would have blinked sleepy eyes and smiled, showing a mouthful of fine square teeth, and murmured that the mule was smarter than him and the questioner combined so why bother the good beast with such foolishness.

The snatchband came down on him as the day reached its end, rode round him in the dusk, demanded he follow them which he did without a murmur of protest, something that troubled them so much they rode through the night instead of camping some miles off the road as they usually did. And two of them rode wide, scouting the road again east and west because they suspected some kind of ambush. None of their victims had exhibited such placid good humor and it made them nervous. The scouts came back toward morning and reported that nothing was stirring anywhere. This should have reassured them, but somehow it did not. They gave their mounts grain and water, let them graze and rest a few hours, then were on their way again when the dew was still wet on the grass. The little man rode along with the same placid cheerful acceptance of what was happening, irritating the snatchband so much that only their very great fear of the maretuse kept them from pounding him into a weeping pulp.

So uneasy were they that after they delivered the little man and his mule to the maretuse, they collected their belongings and rode south as fast as they could without killing their mounts, intending to put a kingdom or two between them and Ambijan. The horses survived and ran free. Tungjii liked horses. A tiger ate one of the men. Another fell off a bridge into a cataract and eventually reached the sea, though mostly in the bellies of migrating fishes. A third helped to feed several broods of mountain eagles. Tungjii liked to watch the great birds soar and wheel. The fourth and fifth stumbled into the hands of trolls and fed a whole clutch of trollings. All in all, the snatchband contributed more to the well-being of the world that one summer than they had in years.

The maretuse had the little man brought before him. ''What is your name?'' he said.

''Guess.''

''Insolence will get you a beating. That is a warning.''

''A wild boar can tromp and tear a hunter. It doesn't mean he's smarter or better than the hunter, only that the hunter's luck has turned bad.''

''Luck? Hunh. It doesn't exist. Only degrees of cleverness and stupidity.''

''Old Tungjii might argue with you on that.''

''Tungjii is a fat little nothing men dream up so they won't have to face their inadequacy at dealing with the world and other men. Tungjii is nothing but wind.''

''Heesh wouldn't argue too much on that point. Wind and the random crossing of separate fates, that's chance not luck, but there's a tiny tiny crack there where Tungjii can stick hisser thumbs and wiggle them a bit.''

''Nonsense. A clever man scorns luck and reaches as high as his grasp will take him.''

The little man tilted his head to one side, clicked his tongue against his teeth. ''Cleverness is a war, but a soldier is a soldier.''

''What do you mean by that? If anything.''

''You're the clever man. Tell me.''

''Wind!'' The maretuse settled back in his chair. ''It is my custom to invite a traveler into my house and match him at a game or two. Be aware that if you lose, you will be my slave as long as you live. And you will lose because you are a fat little fool who believes in luck. But you will choose a game and play it or I will peel the hide off your blubber and feed it to you strip by strip.''

"And if I win, what will I win?''

"You won't win.''

"It's not a proper contest if there isn't a prize for both players.''

The maretuse forced a laugh. "You won't win, so what does it matter? You name my forfeit.''

The little man clasped his hands over his hard little belly, closed his eyes and screwed up his face as if thinking were a struggle for him, then he relaxed, smiled, opened his eyes. "You will feed my mule.''

"Done.'' The maretuse waved his servant over with the Jar of Lots. He was rather disappointed when the Lot did not turn up one of the more physical games. His guest was such a plump juicy little man he'd looked forward to chivvying him through the Maze of Swords or hunting him in the Gorge of Sighs, but he was pleased enough with the chosen game. He was a master strategist at stonechess and no one in the Empire, even the masters in the capital, had ever defeated him. Sometimes he won with only a few stones left, sometimes he crushed his opponent under an avalanche of stones, but always he won. Five years back when he was in Andurya Durat for the Emperor's Birthday, one of his games passed into legend. It lasted fourteen days and less than a dozen stones were left on the board and both players had to be carried off and revived with tea and massage.

He didn't expect the game to last long, a few hours at most, then the guest would lose and he would dip again into the Jar and lose again and dip again until he lost his nerve entirely and was only good for tiger feed. The maretuse was a trifle annoyed at his snatchband. The little man had an amiable stupidity that was apparent to the bleariest eye; they should have let him go on his way and found someone more challenging.

He had the board set up, along with bowls of ansin tea, bowls of rosewater and hot towels, piles of sausage bits, sweet pork, seven cheeses, raw vegetables, finger cakes and candies. Honest food to give this fool some spark of wisdom if anything could and keep the game from being too short and boring.

Hours passed.

Servants lit lamps, replenished the food, moving with great care to make no sound at all to disturb the concentration of their master. At first they were pleased to see the game continue so long because a hard, taxing contest kept the maretuse quiet for a long time. But when dawn pinked the hills they began to worry. The maretuse had never lost before and they didn't know how he would take it. Experience of his moods when he was irritated made them fearful. The next pot of the guest's tea had a dusting of dreamsugar in it. The little fat man took a sip, grinned at them, then emptied the cup with a zesty appreciation and continued to sit relaxed, looking sleepily stupid and unremittingly cheerful. And the servants grew sick with fear.

Midafternoon came; sunlight fell like a sword across the table.

The maretuse watched his guest drop a stone with calm finality to close the strangling ring about the largest portion of his remaining stones. He could fight another dozen moves if he chose or he could capitulate. "Who are you?" he said. "No man this side of the world is my match. Or yours."

The little man grinned and said nothing.

"I'm not going to let you leave here, win or lose."

A nod. That inane grimace was still pasted across the round stupid face.

"Feed your mule, you said. I will pay my forfeit. What does the beast eat? Oats? Straw? Grass?"

"You'll see."

The mule came titupping daintily across the marble floor though no one saw how it got from the stables into the house.

The youngest daughter of one of the gardeners was playing among the bushes, content to watch caterpillars crawl and ladybugs whirr about, lines of ants marching frantically to and fro and a toad like an old cowpat blinking in the shade of a flowering puzzlebush, flicking out his white tongue when it occurred to him to snatch and eat a hapless bug that fluttered too close. Crawling about among the bushes and gathering smears of dirt with a total lack of concern, she passed the long windows of the gameroom where the maretuse and his guest were concluding their match.

She stopped to stare inside and saw the mule come titupping in and giggled to see a beast in the great house coming to tea just like any man.

The little man waved at her and she waved back, then he turned his head over his shoulder and spoke to the mule. "The maretuse," he said, "has agreed to feed you, Mule."

The mule opened his mouth. Opened and opened and opened his mouth.

The maretuse struggled to move but he could not.

The little man swelled and changed until heesh was Tungjii male and female in hisser favorite wrinkled black. Ignoring the terrified man, Tungjii walked over to the long window. Heesh opened it and picked up the gardener's daughter.

"Dragon," she said.

"Yes," Tungjii said, "a very hungry dragon. You want to come with me?"

"Uh-huh. Dada too?"

"Not this time. Do you mind, little daughter?"

She looked gravely into hisser eyes, then snuggled closer to himmer. "Uh-uh."

Tungjii began walking up the air, grunting and leaning a little forward as if heesh were plodding up a steep flight of stairs. At first the gardener's daughter was afraid, but Tungjii's bosom was soft and warm. She relaxed on it and felt safe enough to look over hisser shoulder.

Fire spread fron one edge of the world to the other.

"Dragon?"

"The Dragon Sunfire. He is living there now."

"Oh."

And to this day Ambijan is a desert where nothing much grows. The few Ambijaks left are wandering herdsmen and raiders who worship a dragon called Sunfire.

* * *

"Dragons too? What a world." He rose from the coil of rope where he'd been sitting, stretched, worked his shoulders, glanced at the black sea rolling ahead of them. The Godalau was still out there, swimming tirelessly along. "Barbequed peasant. Rather hard on those who disturb the status quo, don't you think? I've known a few emperors who needed a bit of disturbing."

She hitched a hip on the rail, took hold of a handy shroud. "It's a story. Probably didn't happen. Could happen, though. Don't go by heesh's looks, Tungjii is dangerous. Always. The one who told me that story, he was a dancer whose company I was traveling with right then; Tungjii was his family patron. That gardener's daughter, you remember? When she was old enough Tungjii married her into Taga's family and promised to keep a friendly eye on them. They learned fast not to ask him for help. Heesh always gave it, but sometimes that help felt like five years of plague." She ran her eyes over Daniel Akamarino, looked puzzled. "Which makes me wonder why he fetched you here. Him or some other god."

"Why not accident? The god snatched for whatever he could reach."

"You haven't met tigermen or ariels or some of the more exotic demons sorcerors can whip into this world with something less than a hiccup or a grunt. And that's nothing to what a god can do when he, she or it makes up its corporate whatever to act."

"Don't tell me it's him," Daniel jerked a thumb toward the cramped quarters belowdeck. "Just because our names match?"

"Who knows the minds of gods, if they've got minds which I'm not all that sure of, or why they do what they do?" Her hands had long palms, long thumbs, short tapering fingers; they were strong capable hands, seldom still. She ran her fingers along his forearm, feathery touches that stirred through the pale hairs. "Why you?" Her mouth had gone soft, there was a thoughtful shine to her eyes.

He trapped her hand, held it against his arm. "Why not." Still holding the hand, he moved around so he could sit on the rail beside her, relaxing into the dip and slide of the boat. He slid his hand up her back, enjoying her response to his touch; she leaned into him, doing her version of a contented purr as he moved his fingers through the feathery curls on her neck.

Lio Laux came up on deck, moved into the bow and stood watching the intermittently visible Godalau, then he drifted over to Daniel and Brann. ''I thought you were swinging it some. Not, huh?''

''Not. When do we make the Cove?''

''Hour or so before dawn, day after tomorrow.'' His ear dangle flashed in the moonlight, brown gleams slid off his polished bald head. His eyes narrowed into invisibility. ''Given there's no trouble?'' There was a complex mixture of apprehension and anticipation in his voice.

Brann's head moved gently in response to the pressure of Daniel's fingers. ''I haven't a notion, Lio Laux.'' Her deep voice was drowsy, detached. ''We have . . . eyes out . . . should something show up . . . we'll go to work . . . no point in fussing . . . until we have to.''

Lio Laux pinched his nose, considered her. ''Let's hope.'' He walked away, stopped to talk to the blond boy, the one-eyed Phrasi, the Cheonene, the members of his crew still on deck now that the sandbars were behind them, then he went below again.

''This boat's too crowded,'' Daniel murmured. ''Unless the hold . . .''

Brann grimaced. ''Wet. Smelly. Rats.''

''Offputting.''

''If you're older than fourteen.''

''Me, even when I was fourteen, I didn't turn on to rats.'' He stopped talking, moved his mouth along her shoulder and neck; close to her ear, he murmured, ''What about putting Danny One in with the rats?'' He moved his hands over her breasts, his thumbs grazing her nipples.

She shivered. ''No. . . .''

''Be right at home. Rat to the rats.''

She pulled away from him, strode to the bow. After a minute she ran shaking hands through her hair, swung around. ''I can dispense with you a lot easier than him, also with stupid comment.''

Daniel watched her stride across the deck and disappear below. He scratched his chin. "Didn't handle that too well, did you." He looked down at himself, thumbed the bulge. "Danny's blue tonight, ran his mouth too long too wrong."

The Wounded Moon shone palely on the long narrow Skia Hetaira as she sliced through the foamspitting water of the Notoea Tha, and touched with delicate strokes the naked land north of the boat, a black-violet blotch that gradually gained definition as the northwestering course of the smuggler took her closer and closer to the riddle rock at the tip of the first Vale Finger, rock pierced again and again by wind and water so that it sang day and night, slow sad terrible songs and was only quiet one hour every other month.

Brann sat on the deck, her back against the mast; the melancholy moans coming from the rock suited her mood. Ahzurdan said the air was clotted with ariels, a great gush of angry angel forms passing to and from Silagamatys, carrying news of them to Settsimaksimin, helping him plan . . . What? Ahzurdan was working with half the information he needed, he didn't have the name of the talisman Maksim wore, he didn't know how far Maksim could press Amortis. He had a strained weary look, but he wouldn't let her feed him energy as she did the children, though she offered it (having energy to spare after prowling the foggy streets of the water quarter after the others went back to the Blue Seamaid); he was in a strange half-angry state she didn't understand, though she couldn't miss how deeply he was hurting. He was carrying the full load of defending them and neither the children nor Danny Two were helping the situation with their irrational hates—no not exactly hates, it was more a fundamental incompatiblity as if they and Ahzurdan were flint and steel bound to strike sparks whenever they met. She looked up. The children were flying overhead, elegant albatrosses riding the wind, circling out ahead of the ship, drifting in and out of knots of cloud, cutting through the streams of ariels they couldn't see. She felt rather like a juggler who'd been foolish enough to accept the challenge of keeping in the air whatever her audience threw at her. Any minute now there might be one thing too many and the whole mess would drop on her head.

She listened to the moaning rock and found the sound so restful she drifted into a doze in spite of the damp chill and the drop and rise of the deck under her.

Some time later, she had no idea how long, Ahzurdan was shaking her, shouting at her. As soon as she was awake, he darted away from her to stand in the bow, gesturing in complex patterns, intoning a trenchant series of meaningless syllables interspersed with polysyllabic words that meant something to him but made no sense in the context.

The children flew in circles over the mainmast, their raucous mewing cries alerting everyone not already aware of it that something perilous was about to happen.

In the northwest an opaline glow rose over the horizon and came rapidly toward the Skia Hetaira, resolving into the god Amortis striding to them across the dark seawater, blond hair streaming in snaky sunrays about a house-sized face, her foggy draperies shifting about her slim ripe body in a celestial peekaboo, shapely bare feet as large as the Skia Hetaira moving above the water or through it as it swelled, feet translucent as alabaster with light behind it, but solid enough to kick the waves into spreading foam. The hundred yards of female god stopped ten shiplengths away, raised a huge but delicate hand, threw a sheet of flame at the boat.

Hastily the two albatrosses powered up and away, their tailfeathers momentarily singed, drawing squawks of surprise from them, the flame splashing over them as it bounced off the shield Ahzurdan had thrown about the Skia Hetaira.

Amortis stamped her foot. The wave she created fled from her and threatened to engulf the boat. The deck tilted violently, first one way then another, leaped up, fell away. Ahzurdan crashed onto his knees, then onto his side and rolled about, slammed into the siderails (narrowly escaping being thrown overboard), slammed into the mast; he clutched at the ropes coiled there and finally stopped his wild careering. Gobbets of flame tore through his shielding, struck the sails and the deck, one caught the hem of his robe; they clung with oily determination and began eating into canvas, cloth and wood. Vast laughter beat like thunder over the Skia Hetaira and the folk on her. Amortis stamped again, flung more fire at the foundering boat.

As the first splash reached them, Brann dived for Ahzurdan, missed and had to scramble to save herself. She heard muted grunts and the splat of bare feet, managed a rapid glance behind her—Daniel Akamarino with only his trousers on and absurdly the magic wineskin bouncing against his back. When Ahzurdan grasped the mast ropes and stopped his careening about, Brann and Daniel caught hold of the straining sorceror, eased him onto his knees and supported him while he gestured and intoned, gradually rebuilding his shield.

Lio Laux and his two and a half crew struggled to keep the Skia from turning turtle and when they had a rare moment with a hand free, they tried to deal with the fires (fortunately smoldering rather than raging, subdued though not quenched by Ahzurdan's aura). At some indeterminate moment in the tussle Tungjii arrived and stood on the deck looking about, watching with bright-eyed interest as Ahzurdan fought in his way and Lio in his. Heesh wriggled himmer's furry brows. Small gray stormclouds gathered over each of the smoky guttering fires and released miniature rainstorms on them, putting them out.

Out on the water Amortis stopped laughing and took a step toward the Skia, meaning to trample what she couldn't burn.

An immense translucent fishtail came rushing out of the waves, lifting gallons of water with it, water that splashed mightily over Amortis and sent her sprawling. Squawling with rage, she bounded onto her feet, bent and swung her arms wildly, grabbing for the Godalau's coarse blue-green hair. The Godalau ducked under the waves, came up behind the god and set pearly curly shark's teeth in the luscious alabaster calf of Amortis' left leg; the Blue Seamaid did a bit of freeform tearing, then dived frantically away as Amortis took hold again, subdued her temper and used her fire to turn the water about her into superheated steam that even the Godalau could not endure.

A stormcloud much larger than those raining on the ship gathered over the wild blond hair and let its torrents fall. Clouds of gnats swarmed out of nowhere and blew into Amortis' mouth, crawled up her nose and into her ears. Revolting slimy things came up out of the sea and trailed their stinking stinging ooze over her huge but dainty toes.

Amortis shrieked and spat fire in all directions, drawing on her substance with no discretion at all; more of the sea about the Skia grew too hot for the Godalau, driving her farther and farther away, until she could do nothing but swim frantically about beyond the perimeter of the heat, searching for some way, any way, she could attack again. Tungjii's torments whiffed out fast as he could devise them, his rain melted into the steam that was a whitehot cloud about the whitehot fireform of the god; rage itself now, Amortis flared and lost her woman's shape, sinking into the primal form from which she was created by the dreams of men, from which in a very real sense she created herself.

On deck, battered and exhausted, Ahzurdan faltered. More fire ripped through the shield. A worried frown on hisser round face, Tungjii rained on the fires and flooded most of them to smudgy chars, but the water was so hot around the Skia that steam drifting over the decks threatened to burn out mortal lungs and roast the skin off mortal bodies. The busy little god sent eddy currents of cooler air to shield hisser mortals, but heesh was more pressed than heesh had ever been in all hisser lengthy existence. The sea itself was so hot that the timbers of the hull were beginning to steam and smolder. Laux's seamanship and the desperate scurrying of his crew had managed so far to keep the Skia Hetaira upright and clawing in a broad arc about the center of the fury, far enough out so the heat was marginally endurable, but let Ahzurdan falter again and the Skia and everyone on it would go up in a great gush of flame.

Brann felt Ahzurdan weakening, felt it in her hands and in her bones. She pressed herself against him, whispered, "Let me feed you, Dan, I can help but only if you let me. I did it when I cleansed you before, let me help you now.''

He nodded, unable to stop his chant long enough to speak.

Brann let her senses flow into him; usually she had one of the children to help with this, but they were gone, out beyond the shield doing she didn't know what. She fed a tentative thread of energy into him, working cautiously so she wouldn't distract him, that would be almost as fatal as his collapse from exhaustion. As she got the feel of him, she fed him more and more, draining herself to support him.

Only peripherally aware of the struggle on the deck, Yaril and Jaril flew again and again at Amortis, their birdshapes abandoned. Fire of a sort themselves, her fire couldn't hurt them, but they were too small, too alien to damage her in any satisfactory way, all they could do was dart at her eyes while she still had eyes and distract her a little; when she altered to her primal form there was nothing at all they could do with her except use their odd bodies as lenses and channel small streams of her fire away from the Skia, which they did for a while 'until the futility of their acts grew depressingly apparent. They flicked away from the stormcenter and merged in consultation.

Brann, Yaril pulsed, *she handled the Treeish, with a bit of help from us; do you think she might be able to drain that bitch?*

I think we better try something, this can't go on much longer.

Ideas?

Make a bridge between her and that thing. We can focus its energies, that's what we've been doing, isn't it?

And Brann handles the pull. Right. Let's go talk to her.

They flicked through the shield, bounced up and down in front of her until they had her attention, then merged with her and explained their plan.

Brann scowled at the deck. ''We've got about all the fire we can handle now.'' She spoke the words aloud, listened some more. ''You're sure it's different? Yes, I

do remember the Treeish. They weren't gods or anything close to it and it hurt like hell handling their
forces.'' A listening silence. ''I see. Channeled force,
a limited but steady drain.'' She laughed. ''Nice touch,
defeating Amortis with her own strength. I agree, there's
not much point in going on with what we're doing, she
certainly can outlast us no matter how much of that fire
she throws at us. So. The sooner the better, don't you
think?''

The children emerged from Brann, darted back
through Ahzurdan's shield and hovered in the heart of
the fire, glimmering gold spheres faintly visible against
the crimson flame flooding out of Amortis. They melded
into one and shot out curving arms until they extended
from Amortis to Brann in a great arc of golden light.
As soon as both ends of the arc touched home, Brann
PULLED. And screamed with the agony of the godlife
flowing into her, alien, inimical, deadly fire that almost
killed her before her body found for itself a way of
converting that fire into energy she could use. She absorbed it, throttled down the flow until it was a source
Ahzurdan could take in without dying of it. She fed him
the godlife, filled him with the godlife, until he glowed
translucent alabaster like the god and used the god's
own substance to make the shield so fine a filter that
heat and steam and eating fire were left outside and the
water that came through was the black cool seawater
that belonged to the Notoea Tha in midautumn nights.
And the air that came through was a brisk following
breeze, cool almost chill. And the tumultuous seasur-
face subsided to the long swells that came after storms
had passed. The Skia Hetaira settled to an easy slide
through abruptly edenic waters and Lio gave the helm
to his mate so he could begin an inspection of his ship;
he strolled about assessing damages, adding trauma
penalties to the repair costs he planned to lay on Brann's
surety pledge. He was a bit wary of pushing her too
hard, but figured a little fiddling couldn't hurt.

Beyond the semi-opaque shield sphere, Amortis
slacked her raging, let her fires diminish as she began
to be afraid; she shut off her outpouring of her substance and recovered her bipedal form so she could

think about what was happening. The arc between her and Brann was draining off her energy at a phenomenal pace; if it went on much longer she would face a permanent loss of power and with that, a loss of status so great she'd be left as nothing more than a minor local fertility genius tied to some stupid grove or set of stones. A last shriek of rage heavily saturated with fear, a shouted promise of future vengeance, and she went away.

The golden arch collapsed into two globes that bobbled unsteadily, then dropped through the shield onto the deck and flickered into two weary children.

Tungjii strolled over to the entwined trio, tapped Daniel's arm, pointed to the wineskin and vanished.

Brann stirred. She didn't let loose of Ahzurdan, for the moment she couldn't. She throbbed and glowed like an alabaster lamp, her bones were visible through her flesh. Ahzurdan was like her, glowing, his bones like hers, a dark calligraphy visible in hands and face.

He stirred. With a hoarse groan of utter weariness out of a throat gone rough from the long outpouring of the focusing chants, he dropped into silence and let his hands fall onto his thighs. The shield globe melted from around them and the Skiə Hetaira glided unhindered on a heaving sea.

The Godalau swam before them once more, her translucent glassy form like the memory of a dream. The raging winds were gone, the steam was gone, the water was cold again about the ship, the only reminders left of that ferocious conflict were the blackened holes in the sails and the charred spots in the wood.

Daniel eased himself away from Ahzurdan and Brann, sucking at his teeth and shaking his head when he saw them still frozen, unaware of his departure. He looked down at his hands and was relieved to see them comfortably opaque, no mystical alabaster there, just the burnt brown skin and paler palms he was accustomed to seeing. His bones were aching and his body felt like it had the first time he went canoeing with the Shafarin on Harsain, the time he decided he wanted to find out what the life of a nomad hunter was like. That was one of his shorter intervals between ships, when was it? yes,

the time he walked away from della Farangan after one
loud slanging match too many. Afterwards he went to
work for a shiny ship to get the grit out of his teeth and
the grime out of his skin. And the taste of burnt gamy
flesh out of his mouth. Stella Fulvina and the Prism
Dancer; quite a woman in her metallic way, uncompli-
cated. You knew where you were with her and exactly
what you'd get. Restful to the head though she worked
your butt off. He unslung the wineskin and thumbed out
the stopple. The wine burned away his weariness. He
sighed with pleasure and after a moment's thought,
splashed a drop of it on a small burn, grinned as the
blackened flesh fell away and the pain went with it.
"Tungjii Luck, you've got great taste in wine, you do."
He grimaced at Brann and Ahzurdan, crawled to the
pale limp changechildren lying on the deck a short distance off. "Here," he said. "Have a drink. Give you
the energy to keep breathing." He looked at them and
laughed. "Or whatever else it is you do."

As the children drank and flushed with returning
color, Brann and Ahzurdan finally eased apart. Brann
lifted one hand, pointed at the sky. A great white beam
of light streamed from her bunched fingertips and cut
through the darkness before to melt finally among the
clouds. She closed her hand and cut off the flow. Ahzurdan waited until she was cooled down, then bled off
his own excess charge much the same way, though he
used both hands.

Daniel grinned at Jaril, reached for the skin. "Much
more and you'll be crawling, Jay."

The boy giggled. "Still get there."

"Yup, give it here anyway." He took the wineskin to
Brann, she was still glowing palely as if her skin was
pulled taut over moonlight, but she looked weary as
death and worried. "Tungjii's blessing," he said.
"Makes the world look brighter."

She found a smile for him and took the skin. Tungjii's
gift worked its magic; she flushed, her eyes acquired a
new warmth, her movements a new vigor. She touched
Ahzurdan's arm. "Tungjii's blessing, Dan."

His head turned stiffly, slowly, dull blank eyes blinked
at her. The ravages of the godlife were visible in his

face, even more than the utter weariness of body and spirit. He took the skin, stared at it for a long moment before he lifted it and squeezed a wobbly stream of wine at his mouth, missing more than he hit. Daniel started to help him steady himself, but Brann caught his reaching hand and held it away. "No," she said. "Not you. Not me."

Ahzurdan lowered the skin, fumbled at his mouth and neck, trying to wipe away the spilled wine. He was looking all too much like a punchdrunk fighter, his coordination and capacity for thinking beaten out of him. Brann took the skin from him and gave it to Daniel. "Go away a while, will you? I'll take care of him."

Daniel Akamarino shrugged and went to sit on the rail. He watched Brann get her shoulder under Ahzurdan's arm and help him to his feet. Her arm around him, she helped him stumble across the deck and down the ladder to the cramped livingspace below. Before she quite vanished, she turned her head. "On your life, don't wake us before noon."

Daniel flicked the dangling stopple. "Women," he said.

Lio Laux leaned on the rail beside him. "Uh huh." He rubbed a burn hole in his shirt between his thumb and forefinger, shredding off the charred fibers; eyes narrowed into dark crescents, he looked up at the sails, holed here and there but taut enough with the following wind, then squinted round at the deck. "Expect more of that?" He snapped thumb against midfinger and pointed his forefinger at a charred place in the wood.

"Me, I don't expect. This isn't my kind of thing." Daniel passed the skin to Lio. "You might want to put some of this on your burns." He held out his arm, showed the pale spot where the charred skin fell off. "Seems to be as useful outside as it is in."

"Hmm. You don't mind, I'll apply it to the inside first."

The rest of the voyage passed without incident. Two hours before dawn on the next morning, Lio Laux landed them on the black sand of Haven Cove, gave Brann back her surety gold and sailed out of the story.

11

MAKSIM AND KORI, A DIGRESSION.

SCENE: In Maksim's chambers high above the city.

"Sit down, I'm not going to eat you."

Kori sneaked a glance at him, looked quickly away. Everyone said how big Settsimaksimin was and she'd seen him tower over the Servants and the students at the Lots, but he was far off then and she hadn't realized how intimidating that size would be when she was not much more than an arm's length away, even if it was the length of *his* arm. Eyes on the floor, she backed to a padded bench beside one of the tall pointed windows. She folded her hands in her lap, grateful for the coarseness of the sleeping shift they'd given her at the Yron. She didn't feel quite so naked in it. She stole another look at him. He was smiling, his eyes were warm and it startled her but she had to say it, gentle, approving. She wondered if she ought to worry about what he was going to do to her, but she didn't feel bothered by him, not like she was when that snake Bak'hve looked at her. Frightened, yes, but not bothered. She ran her tongue over dry lips. "Why did you snatch me here like this?"

"Because I didn't want to make life at the Yron more difficult for you than it is already."

"I don't . . ."

"Child, mmmm, what's your name?"

"You don't know it?"

"Would I ask?"

His deep deep voice rumbled and sang at her, excited

her; she forgot to be frightened and lifted her head. "Kori," she said, "Kori Piyolss."

"Kori." Her name was music when he said it; she felt confused but still not bothered. "Well, young Kori, you wouldn't like what would certainly happen to you if anyone thought I was interested in you. I'm sure you have no idea what lengths some folks will go to in order to reach my ear, and that's not vanity, child, that's what happens when you have power yourself or you're close to someone with it. You're a fighter, Kori, yes I do know that. I've watched you plot and scheme against me; unfortunately, I did not know who it was that plotted soon enough to stop you. Ahh, if things were other, if I had a daughter, or a son even, if he or she were like you, I would swell with pride until I burst with it. Why, Kori? What have I done to you? No, I'm not asking you that now. I will know it, though, believe that."

She gazed defiantly at him, pressed her mouth into a tight smile that was meant to say *no you won't.*

He chuckled. "Kori, Kori, relax, child, I'm not going into that tonight. I've got other things in mind. You were right, you know, I fiddled the Lot, I wanted you out of Owlyn, child, I wanted you where you won't make more trouble for me. You might as well forget about going back there. Think rather what you'd like to do with your life."

She blinked at him. "What do you mean?"

"I am not going to permit you to teach, Kori, I'm sure you see why. You don't want to be a holy whore, do you?"

She swallowed, touched her throat, forced her hand down.

"It's not a threat, child; but we do have to find something else for you. You've got a talent, did you know it?"

"Um . . . talent?"

"Why weren't you born a boy, Kori, ah, things would be so much simpler."

"I don't want to be a boy." She couldn't put too much force into that, not after the talk with Polatéa. She wrinkled her nose, moved her shoulders. It was a funny feeling, talking to the man like this, she felt free to say things she couldn't say to anyone not even Tré; it seemed to her Settsimaksimin understood her, all of her, not just a part, understood an in a funny way approved of her. All of her. He was the first one, well, maybe Polatéa was the first, but Polatéa wanted to close her in and if he meant what he was saying, it seemed to her he wanted to open out her life to new things, splendid things. Aayee, it was hard, she was supposed to hate him for what he'd done, for what he was going to do when he found out about Tré, was he playing with her head already? She didn't know, how could she know? "What I'd really like," she said, "is not to stop being a girl, I am a girl, it's part of what makes me who I am, I like who I am, I don't want to change, what I want is to be free to do some of the things boys get to do." She scratched her cheek, frowned. "What did you mean, talent?"

"Magic, child. Would you like to study it?"

"I don't understand."

"There are schools where they teach the talent, Kori; there's one, perhaps the best of them, in a city called Silili. It's a long way from here, but I'll see you get there if you think you might like to be a scholar."

"Why?"

"Nothing's ever simple, Kori, haven't you learned that by now? Ah well, you've had a sheltered life so far. Why? Because I like you, because I don't like killing my folk, don't scowl, child, didn't your mother ever tell you your face could freeze like that? Yes, you are mine whatever you think of that and yes, I am not lying when I say I loathe killing. I do what I must."

"No. You do what you want."

"Hmm. Perhaps you're right. Shall I tell you what I want?"

"I can't stop you. No, that isn't honest. I would like to hear it. I think. I don't know. Are you messing with my head, Settsimaksimin?"

"Yes."

"Why?"

"I don't want to see you frightened. I don't want to feel you hating me."

"I can't do anything about that?"

"Not now. If you develop your talent, the time will come when no one, not even a god, can play with your feelings and your thoughts, Kori. Take my offer. Don't waste your promise."

"Why are you doing this? I don't understand. Help me understand. Are you like Bak'hve the Servant in Owlyn, do you want me? I don't think so, you don't make me feel bothered like he does."

He frowned. "That Servant, he approached you, suggested you lie with him?"

"No. Not yet, he hasn't worked himself up to it yet."

"Hmm. I'll put a watch on him; if he's got a penchant for young girls, he goes. And no, Kori, you're right, you don't excite me that way. Do I shock if I tell you, no girl or woman would?"

"Oh." She wriggled uncomfortably. "You said you're trying to do something. What is it?"

He gave his low rumbling laugh, settled into his chair, put his feet up on a hassock and began to talk about his plans for Cheonea.

Her head whirled with visions as immense as he was. What he wanted for the Plain sounded very much like the kind of life her own folk lived up in the Vales. How could that be bad? There was a fire in him, a passionate desire to make life better for the Plainsers. How could she not like that? His fire called to the fire in her. Maybe he was playing games with her again, but she didn't really think so. She felt her mind stretching, she felt breathless, carried along by an irresistable force like the time she fell into the river and didn't want to be rescued, the time she was intensely annoyed with her cousins when they roped her and pulled her to the bank; though she thanked them docilely enough, she went running back to the House, raging as she ran. She quivered to the deep deep voice that seemed to sing in the marrow of her bones. She understood him, or at least a part of him, there was no one he could share his dreams with, just like her. No one who could follow the leaps and bounds of his thought. She could. She knew it. But she also knew her own ignorance. In addition to her dreams and enthusiasms, she had a shrewd practical

side. Though her life was short and severely circum-
scribed, she'd heard more than a handful of one-sided
stories meant to justify some lapse or lack. Men who
let their fields go sour, women who slacked their weaving or their cleaning, children who had a thousand excuses for things they had or hadn't done. She'd told such
stories herself, even told them to herself. So how could
she judge what he was saying? Measure it against what
was there before down on the Plain? What did she know
about the Plain except some ancient tales her people
told to scare unruly boys? Trouble was, how could she
trust those stories? She knew how her folk were about
outsiders, nothing outsiders did was worth the spit to
drown them in. What else did she know? Really know?
What he did about the wood. Yes. That rather impressed
Daniel Akamarino. How he kept the city clean. Bath
houses for beggars even. The slave markets were gone.
But girls still sold themselves on the streets and in the
taverns they were conveniences provided with the beds
and the bottles. The pleasurehouses were gone, older
girls on fete eves told dreadful tales of those places,
tales that would have had them scrubbing pots for a
month if one AuntNurse or another had caught them.
But Settsimaksimin's own soldiers burned the Chained
God's priests and would burn Tré if she couldn't stop
it. The thought cleared her head and chilled her body.

She looked up. He was watching her, yellow cat eyes
questioning her silence. Momentarily she was afraid,
but she thought about Tré and everything and straightened her back. If she could stop it here, if she could
make him see. . . . She took a mouthful of air, let it
out with a soundless paa. "There's one thing," she said.
She rubbed at her forehead, pushed her hand back over
her hair, afraid again. He saw too much. What if he
saw Tré? "You let us alone for over forty years. Except
for the Lot. And we got used to that and it was kind of
exciting coming down to the city and having it ours for
three days. You let us live like we always lived. No fuss.
And then, no warning, you send your soldiers to the
Vales and the Servants. We don't want them, we don't
need them. We have the Chained God to look after us.
We have our priests to bless us and teach us and heal

us and wed us each to each. At least, we had them before your soldiers burnt them. Why? We weren't hurting you. We were just doing what we'd always done. The Servants gave the orders to the soldiers, but they were your soldiers. Why did you let that happen?''

"Let it happen? oh Kori, I couldn't stop it, I was constrained by things I promised decades ago. Let me tell you. Fifty years ago I took Silagamatys from the king.'' He gave her a weary smile. "I had a thousand mercenaries and a few dozen demons and the skills I'd acquired in a century's hard work. I took the city in a single night with less than a hundred dead, the king being one of those. And it meant almost nothing. He had less say in how Cheonea was run than the scruffiest beggar on Water Street. The Parastes and the vice lords, the pimps, the bullies, the assassins and the thieves, they ran Cheonea, they ran Silagamatys, they ignored me and my pretensions, Kori. It was like trying to scoop up quicksilver; when I reached for them, they ran between my fingers and were gone. All I had accomplished, Kori, was to tear down the symbol that held this rotting state together. SYMBOL! That vicious foulness, that corrupt old fumbler. He was the shell they held in front of them, he was the thing that kept them from going for each other. I had to cleanse the city somehow, I had to put my hand on the hidden powers if I wanted to change the way things were and make life better for the gentle people. I worked day and night, Kori, I slept two hours, three at most. I think I looked into the face of every man, woman and child inside the crumbling walls about this cesspool city. I caught little weasels that way, weeded them out and set them to work for me in the granite quarries, cutting stone to rebuild those walls. The wolves slipped away on me except for a few of the stupider ones. Every Parika on the Plain was a fortress closed against me and the Parastes reached out from behind their walls to strike at me whenever they saw a chance to hurt me. I held on for five years, Kori, I got Silagamatys cleaned out, I got my walls built. But Cheonea outside the walls was drowning in blood. The wolves were turning on each other. I don't believe that chaos reached into the Vales, but it couldn't have been a happy time there either; there were desperate men in the hills who stole what they needed to stay alive and destroyed what they couldn't use to appease the rage that gnawed at them. I could have cleansed the Plain too, Kori, as I cleansed the city, if I had another hundred years to spare and the strength of a young man. I wasn't young, Kori, I had limits. And I had this.'' He pulled the talisman from under the simple white linen robe he wore, brushed his hand across the stone. ''There's a price to using it, I won't speak of that, child, it's my business and mine alone. I didn't want to use it, but I looked into myself and I looked out across the Plain and I called Amortis to me. I used her because I had to, Kori. For the greater good. Oh yes. I know. My good, too. Either I forgot my dream or I corrupted it and myself. You understand what I did and why. I promised her Cheonea, Kori, I could compel her to some things but to do all that I wanted, she had to have a reason for helping me. Cheonea was that reason. I left the Vales alone as long as I could, Kori, I talked with her, I teased her, I even was her lover for a while.'' He gave her a sad wry smile. ''Not a very satisfactory one, I'm afraid. I can't claim virtue for trying to save you folk from Amortis' greed. The runes I read, the bones I cast, the stars in their courses all told me that going into the Vales would destroy me.'' A long weary sigh. ''I'm tired, child, but I'll keep fighting until I die. Cheonea will be whole and it will be a good place to live. If I have a few more years, just a handful of years, what I've done will be so strong it won't need me any more. I won't let you take those years from me, Kori. I won't let you be hurt, but I will kill you if I have to, do you understand that?''

''Yes.''

''Will you tell me what you've done and why?''

''No.''

''Do you understand what you are saying to me?''

''Yes.''

''It's war between us?''

''Yes.''

He touched the tips of his lefthand fingers to the stone.

"In one hour Amortis herself goes after your champions, Kori. Would you like to see what happens?"

"Yes."

"Hmm. Some hundred years ago it seems to me I asked if you would like to be a scholar."

"Yes."

"Does that merely mean you remember the question or is it your answer?"

"I remember the question and yes, I think I would like to be a scholar." She gazed at fingers pleating and repleating the coarse white wool of her shift. "If you don't break me getting out your answers."

He laced his fingers over his stomach, his yellow eyes laughed at her. "Kori, young Kori, there's no need for breaking. You've no defense against me, making you speak will be as simple as dipping a pen into an inkwell and writing with it."

"Why all this talk talk talk, then? Why don't you get at it? Do you expect to charm me into emptying myself out for you? You could charm a figgit out of its hole and you know it, but you'll have to take what you want, I won't, I can't give it to you. Why are you wasting your time and mine like this? Do it. Get it over with and let me go."

"Am I, Kori, wasting my time?"

She looked up, looked down again without saying anything.

"You don't understand what I'm trying to do? How much it is going to mean to ordinary folk?"

"I do understand. They aren't my folk."

"Yes. I thought it was that. Your brother?"

She folded the cloth and smoothed it out, folded and smoothed and tried to ignore the pressing silence in the high moon-shadowed room.

"How is he involved in this? A baby like that." When she continued to not-look at him, he got to his feet, held out his hand. "Come. Or do you hate me so much you refuse to touch me?"

Her head whipped up; she glared at him. "Not fair."

His rumbling laugh filled the room, his eyes shone with it. He waggled his huge hand. "Come."

* * *

Settsimaksimin ran his tongue over his teeth as he looked round the cluttered workroom. With a grunt of satisfaction he strode to a corner, brushed a pile of dusty scrolls off a padded backless bench and carried it across to the table where the black obsidian mirror waited, dark glimmers sliding across its enigmatic surface. He scowled at the dust on the dark silk, lifted the tail of his robe and scrubbed it vigorously over the cushion. Kori resisted a strong impulse to giggle. He was so massive, so powerful, so very male, but his play at hospitality reminded her absurdly of AuntNurse Polatéa arranging a party for visiting cousins. When he straightened and beckoned her over, she gave him her best demure smile and settled herself gracefully, grateful for once for all those tedious lessons.

He drew the ball of his thumb across the mirror. "Show thou." As a scene began to develop within the oval, he dropped into a sagging armchair, shifted about until he was comfortable, propped his feet on a rail under the table and laced his long dark fingers over his solid stomach.

Kori watched white sails belly out against black water, black sky, and lost any urge to laugh when she saw the towering figure of the god come striding across the sea.

Squawling threats, Amortis vanished. The gold arc broke apart. The translucent shell dissolved. The sea smoothed out. The boat came round and sliced once more toward Haven Cove.

"Well." Settsimaksimin pushed his chair back and stood looking down at her. Kori couldn't read anything but weariness and regret in his heavy face, but she was terrified. Helpless. No place to run. Nothing she could say would change what they'd just seen. All she could do was hold the rags of her dignity about her and endure whatever he planned for her.

He loomed over her, leaned down; very gently, a feather's touch wouldn't be softer, he brushed his thumb across her mouth. "Speak thou," he murmured. "What have you done and how? Why have you done it?"

She struggled to resist, but it was like being caught

in the river, carried on without effort on her part. The
story tumbled out of her: Tré's peril, Harra's Legacy,
the Cave of the Chained God, Toma and the medal,
Daniel Akamarino, the Blue Seamaid and all that happened there, what Brann organized to get her home unseen (she fell silent a moment and stared as he burst
out laughing. I stopped watching, he said to her, before
any of that went on. All that effort wasted), the Chained
God's command to come to Isspyrivo, take the chains
off him, return with him to destroy the talisman that
Settsimaksimin was using against a god.

When she finished and fell silent, he brushed her lips
a second time with his thumb, stepped back. He pointed
at the bench. "Bring that. There." He pointed at the
center of a complex of silver lines, a five-pointed star
inside a circle with writing and other symbols scattered
about it, within the pattern and without; he didn't wait
to see her do it, but whipped away, robe billowing about
him as he strode to another corner; he came back with
a long, decorated staff. He looked her over, nodded
with satisfaction, tapped the silver circle with the butt
of the staff. The wire began to glow. "Don't move,"
he said. "Don't cross the line. There will be dangerous
things beyond the pentacle; you can't see them and you
don't want to feel them. You hear me?"

"Yes."

He stopped beside a second small pentacle, activated
that, moved to the largest. There was an odd looking
chair in it, big, made from a dark wood with tarry
streaks in it, his chair, even before he settled into it, its
shape suggested him, she could see him sitting in it, his
massive arms resting in the carved hollows in the chair's
arms, his long strong feet fitting in the hollows of the
footboard. He stepped across the dull gray lines,
smoothed his hands over his hair, tucking in the short
straggles that made a black and pewter halo for his face.
With a complicated pass of his flattened hand, he wiped
the wrinkles and dust smears from his robe, then he
tapped the pentacle to life, climbed into the chair and
settled himself into a proper majesty, the staff erect in
its holders, rising over him, its wire inlay catching the
light in slippery watery gleams. He turned his head to

look directly at her (she was on his right off to one side), grinned and winked at her as if to say *aren't I fine,* then faced forward and began intoning a chant, his voice filling the room with sound and beats of sound until her body throbbed in time with the pulses.

"PA OORA DELTHI NA HES HEYLIO PO LIN
LEGO IMAN PHRO NYMA MEN
NE NE MOI GALANAS
TRE TRE TRAGO MEN."

And as he chanted, he moved his hands in strange and disconcerting patterns; something about the gestures stirred her insides in ways that both terrified and fascinated her. She felt the power surging from him; in spite of her fear she found herself swept up in it, exulting in it (though she felt sick and shamed when she realized that)—it was like being outside, walking through an immense towering thunderstorm, winds teasing at her hair and clothes, thunder rumbling in her blood, lightning striding before her.

She gasped, jumped to her feet though she didn't quite dare cross the lines. Tré was in the other small pentacle, curled up on his side, deeply asleep, his fist pressed against his mouth. "What are you going to do to him," she cried. "What are you going to do?"

Settsimaksimin sighed, the talisman glimmering as it rose and fell with the rise and fall of his chest. "Put him where his god can't reach him," he said; the residue of the chant made a demi chant of the simple words. "If I kill him, child, there'll only be another taking his place, another and another until I have to kill everyone. So what's the point. He'll sleep and sleep and sleep. . ." He turned his head and smiled at her. ". . . until you and only you, young Kori, until YOU come and touch him awake."

"I don't understand."

"Wait. Watch." He straightened, closed his eyes a moment to regain his concentration, then began another chant.

"ME LE O I DETH O I ME LE OUS E THA NA TOUS

HIR RON TO RON DO MO PE LOOMAY
  LOOMAY DOMATONE
IDO ON TES HAY DAY THONE.''

His gestures began as wrapping turns. A shimmer
formed about Tré's body, solidified into a semitranspar-
ent crystal; Tré was encased in that crystal like a fly in
amber. The gestures changed, fluttered, ended as he
brought his hands together in a loud clap. The crystal
cube vanished.

"He has gone to his god," Settsimaksimin said. "In
a way." He got to his feet, stood leaning against the
chair looking wearier than death. "He is in the Cave of
Chains. If you can get yourself there, Kori, all you have
to do is touch the block of crystal. It will melt and the
boy will wake. No one else can do this. No one, god
or man. Only you. Do you understand?"

"No. Yes. What to do, yes. Why?"

He reached his arms high over his head, stretched,
groaned with the popping of his muscles. "Incentive,
Kori." He dragged his hand across his face. "I want to
save something out of this mess. I can't save myself.
Cheonea? All I can do is hope the seeds I've planted
have sent down roots strong enough to hold it together
when MY hand is gone. You've destroyed me, Kori. If
I were the monster you think me, I'd kill you right now
and send your souls to the worst hell I could reach.
Instead . . ." he chuckled, but there was no humor in
the sound, "I'm going to pay for your education." He
resettled himself in the chair, worked a lever on the side
so that the back tilted at an angle and the footboard
moved out. He was still mostly upright, but not so dominant as he had been.

A chant filled the room again, his voice was vibrant
and wonderfully alive, none of the exhaustion she'd seen
was present in that sound; power, discipline, elegance,
beauty, those were in that sound. He was a stranger and
her enemy, but she felt a deeper kinship with him now
than with any of her blood kin. She felt like weeping,
she felt empty, she felt the loss of something splendid
she'd never find again. If it hadn't been Tré, if only it
hadn't been Tré.

The smaller pentacle filled again. A tall woman, gray hair dressed in a soft knot, a black silk robe tied loosely over a white shift. Thin face, austere, rather flat. Long narrow chocolate eyes, not friendly at the moment, were they ever? Thin mouth tucked into brackets. She glared at Settsimaksimin, then she relaxed and she smiled, affection for the man showing in her face. The chocolate eyes narrowed yet more into inverted smiles of their own. "You!" she said. Her voice had a magic like his, silvery, singing. "Why is it always the middle of the night?"

Settsimaksimin laughed, swung his hand toward Kori. "I've a new student for you, Shahntien Shere. Take her and teach her and keep her out of my hair."

"That bad, eh? You interest me."

"Thought I might."

"You paying for her or what?"

"I pay. Would I bring you here else? I know you, love." He shifted position, looked sleepily amused, his real weariness nowhere visible. Kori watched with astonishment, fear, hope, reluctant respect. "A hundred gold a year, with a bonus given certain conditions. She's . . ." he frowned at Kori, ". . . thirteen or thereabouts, ten years bed, board and training." He ran his eyes over the sleeping shift that fell in heavy folds around her thin body. "And clothing."

"For you, old friend, just for you, I'll do it."

"HAH." A rumbling chuckle. "She'd do you proud, Shahntien."

"You mentioned a bonus."

"Young Kori, her name is Kori Piyolss, she isn't too happy about leaving home right now. She's clever, she's got more courage than sense and she's stubborn. The first time she tries to get away from you, whip her. If she tries twice and you catch her at it, kill her. That's what the bonus is for. You hear that, Kori?"

Kori pressed her lips together, closed her hands into fists. "Yes."

"You see, Shahntien? Already plotting."

"I see. How clever is she? Enough to stay quiet and learn until she thinks she knows how to avoid being caught?"

"Oh yes. I'm counting on you, Shahntien, to prove cleverer still and keep her there the whole ten years."

"Take her now?"

"In a moment." He shifted to face Kori. "Apply yourself, young Kori. Remember what I told you. Your brother will sleep forever unless you come for him, so be very very sure you know what you're about."

"Now?" Kori drove her nails into the soft wood of the bench. "What about . . . ."

"Nothing here matters to you any longer, child. Stay well."

A gesture, a polysyllabic word and she was in the other pentacle tight up against the woman who put a thin strong arm about her shoulders. A gesture, a word and both of them were elsewhere.

Maksim carried the bench back to the corner, piled the scattered scrolls on it again. He straightened, stretched, rubbed at his chest. Grimacing, he crossed to the wallcoffer, poured out some of the cordial and gulped it down, followed it with a swallow of brandy to wash away the taste. He leaned against the wall and waited for the strengthener to take hold, then snapped to his bedroom to get the rest he so urgently needed.

12

UPHILL AND NASTY.

SCENE: Black sand sloping up to an anonymous sort
         of scraggly brush. High tide, just turning,
         foam from the sea, white lace on black vel-
         vet, out on the dark water, white sails dip-
         ping swiftly below the horizon. Isspyrivo a
         black cone directly ahead, twice the height
         of the other peaks. It is several folds back
         from the shore, perhaps fifty miles off.

Brann shoved a hand through her hair. Daniel was a
little drunk again. A thousand maledictions on old
Tungjii's head, wishing that pair on me. One of them
sneaking whiffs of dreamdust, the other afloat in a winy
sea. She began pacing restlessly beside the retreating
surf, small black crabs scuttling away from her feet into
festoons of stinking seawrack; every few steps she
stopped to kick black grit out of her sandals. What now?
We should get started for the mountain. Walk? She
snorted. Take a whip to get this party marching. Ahzurdan had performed nobly during the attack, they
owed their lives to him, perhaps even the children did,
but she couldn't be sure he'd come through next time.
Half an hour ago, when she went to fetch him, the smell
of hot dust in that cabin was strong enough to choke a
hog. The young thief was right, once you smelled that
stink you didn't forget it. He was sitting on the sand
now looking vaguely out at the vanishing sails of the
Skia Hetaira, probably he regretted getting off her. Daniel drifted over to him, offered the wineskin. Danny

209

One stared at Danny Two, dislike hardening the vagueness out of his face, then waved him off. Like a bratty child, not the man he was supposed to be, Daniel kicked sand on the sorceror and wandered away to sit on a chunk of lava, one of several coughed up the last time Isspyrivo hiccupped.

Brann sighed and thought longingly of Taguiloa and the dance troupe, there was much to be said for the energizing qualities of ambition. She watched the changechildren playing with the sand; its blackness seemed to fascinate them. Jaril and Yaril were appreciably taller and more developed after the battle with Amortis. She suspected that some of the fire pouring through them had lingered long enough to be captured and it triggered that spurt of growth. What that meant was something Brann didn't want to think about right now. Going god-hunting to feed young adults, yaaah! She shook her head, waved the children to her.

"Jay, Yaro, if we're going to get that pair up the mountain, we'd better have transport." She looked from one scowling face to the other, sighed again. "No argument, kids. Chained God wants them, Chained God is going to get them. Besides, we need Ahzurdan. Our fighting isn't done. Maksim's not about to lay down and let us dance on his bones."

Jaril wrinkled his nose. "You want horses? These Valers seem to run more to mules."

She frowned at Daniel Akamarino and Ahzurdan. "Mules might be a good idea, they've got more sense than horses. Probably got more sense than the pair that'll be riding them. Ahh . . ." She chewed on her lip a moment, rubbed at her back. "See what you can do. We should have two, preferably three mounts. Be as quiet about it as you can, one thing we don't need is a posse of angry copers hunting mule thieves. Um. Dig out three gold, leave them behind to calm the tempers of the owners."

The children hawkflew away, powerful wings digging great holes in the air. Brann watched them until they melted into the night, then she walked a short way off to sit on a chunk of lava. You there, Maksim? You sitting there working out how to hit us next? She shivered at the thought, then she stared angrily at the empty air overhead. Ariels circling about up there, looking at us, listening to us, carrying tales back to the sorceror sitting like a spider in his web of air. I wonder how fast they fly. Never thought to ask Ahzurdan. Doesn't really matter, I suppose. Shuh! makes my skin itch to have things I can't see watching me. They can't read what's in my head, at least there's that. Or can they? Ahzurdan says they can't. Do I trust him enough to believe him? I suppose I do. What am I going to do when this is over? Can't go back to the pottery. Arth Slya? Not as long as I have to keep feeding the children. I don't know. Slya's Fire, I hate this kind of drifting. A goal. Yes. A goal. Bargain with the Chained God. He needs me or he wouldn't be weaving all this foolery to get me to him. If he wants my help, he can see the children changed again, let them feed on sunlight not the soul-stuff of men. Set them free from me. What if he says he can't do it? Do I have to believe him? The talisman, yes, that talisman Maksim has, it compels Amortis, if I learned to use it, could I compel Red Slya to undo what she has done? And if not that one, perhaps another? Ahzurdan said there were twelve of them. Which one would twist your tail, Hot Slya? She swung around and examined the featureless cone of Isspyrivo, black against the deep purple of the predawn sky. A fire mountain. When I was a child, I thought Slya lived solely in Tincreal. Not so, not so, she's in earthfire everywhere. Shall I sing you awake, my Slya? What side would you be on if I did? Shuh! Boring, this going round and round, piling ignorance on ignorance. She sprang to her feet. "Daniel. Daniel Akamarino. Play a song for me." She dropped to one knee, unbuckled a sandal, balanced on one foot, kicked the sandal flying, then dealt with the other and jumped up. "Like this." She whistled a tune she remembered from Arth Slyan fetes on the Dance Floor by the Galarad Oak, began swinging in circles on the drying sand. "Something something something like this. Play Daniel play for me play for the ariels up there spying play for the wind and the water and the dawn that's coming soon. Play for me Daniel I want to dance."

Daniel Akamarino laughed, took out his recorder. He whistled a snatch of the tune. "Like that?"

"Like that." She kicked one leg up, grimaced as the cloth of her trousers limited her range. As Daniel began to play, she stripped off her trousers, kicked them away. Ahzurdan scowled, pulled the broad collar of his robe up about his ears and sat hunched over, staring out to sea. At first she moved tentatively, seeking to recover the body memory of what she'd done with Taguiloa, then she flung herself into the dance, words and worry stripped from her head; she existed wholly in the moment with only the frailest of feelers into the immediate future, enough to let her give shape to the shift of her body.

Finally she collapsed in a laughing panting heap and listened to the music laugh with her and the water whisper as it retreated. In the east there was a ghost light along the peaks and the snowtop of Isspyrivo had a pale shimmer that seemed to come from within. She lay until the chill in the damp sand struck up through her body and the light in the east was more than a promise.

She rolled over, got onto her knees, then pushed onto her feet. As she stood brushing herself off, she heard the sound of hooves on the sand, felt the tingling brush as the children let her know they were coming. "Transport," she said. "We'll be leaving for the mountains fifteen twenty minutes no more."

Yaril and Jaril brought three mules, two bays and a blue roan. They were saddled and bridled, with waterskins, long braided ropes tied on, a half a sack of seedgrain snugged behind the blue roan's saddle. Brann raised her brows. "I see why you took so long."

"Town was pretty well closed down." Jaril's eyes flicked toward the silent brooding figure of the sorceror, turned back to Brann. "We decided since we were leaving three golds behind and one of them could buy ten mules and a farm to keep them on and since we didn't know how well they," a jerk of his thumb toward Daniel and Ahzurdan, "could ride, we might as well make it as easy as we could. We raided a stable and the gear was all there, no problem, so why not."

While the children flew overhead keeping watch and Ahzurdan stood aside pulling himself together and rebuilding his defenses, Brann and Daniel Akamarino distributed the gear and supplies among the three mules and roped the packs in place. By the time they were finished the tip of the sun was poking around the side of Isspyrivo, a red bead growing like a drop of blood oozing from a pinprick.

Following the lead of the two hawks they wound through brushy foothills for the better part of the morning, a still, hot morning spent in the clouds of dust and dying leaves kicked up by the plodding mules. They stopped briefly at noon for a meal of dried meat and trail bars washed down with strong-tasting lukewarm water from the skins. Even Daniel wasn't drinking any of Tungjii's wine, he was too hot, sweaty and sore to appreciate it (though he did go behind a bush, drop his trousers and smooth a handful of it over his abraded thighs).

During the morning Ahzurdan had been braced to fend off an attack from Maksim. Nothing happened. He prowled about the small grassy space where they stopped to eat, watching ariels swirl invisibly over them coming and going in that endless loop between them and Settsimaksimin. Nothing happened.

They started on. With Yaril plotting the route and Jaril on wide ranging guard swings, they climbed out of the hills and the rattling brush into the mountain forests, trees growing taller, the way getting steeper and more difficult as they rose higher and higher above sea level.

Ahzurdan flung himself from the saddle, landed in a stumbling run waving his arms to stop the others. "Brann," he shouted, "to me. Daniel, hold the mules." He braced himself, hands circling, spreading, smoothing. "Bilaga anaaaa nihi ta yi ka i gy shee ta a doo le eh doo ya ah tee," he intoned as the earth about them rippled and surged, great trees toppled, roots loosened as the soil about them fluxed and flowed and formed into eyeless giants with ragged hands reaching reaching, deflected from them by the sphere Ahzurdan threw about them. Brann ran to him, flattened her hand in the middle of his back, fed energy into him, steadying him. The mules were squealing and sidling, jerking about, trying to break free from Daniel who was too busy with them to worry much about what was happening. Yaril darted from the sky, changed from hawk to shimmersphere in midcourse and went whipping through the earth giants emerging into greater and greater definition as the attack intensified. She went whipping through and through them, drawing force from them until she was swollen with it. She dropped beside Brann, extended a pseudopod to her spine and fed the earthstrength into her. Brann filtered it and passed it slowly, steadily to Ahzurdan. As soon as Yaril emptied herself, she was a hawk again, powering up to circle overhead while Jaril passed through the giants and stole more from them and fed it to Brann. Turn and turn they went while the attack mounted. Trees tumbled but never onto them, hurled aside by the sphere of negation Ahzurdan held about them, the earth outside boiled and shifted, walked in manshape, surged in shapeless waves but the earth beneath them stayed solid and still. Ahzurdan sweated and strained, his back quivered increasingly under Brann's hand, but he held the sphere intact and none of the raging outside touched the peace and silence within.

The turmoil quit.

Ahzurdan screamed and collapsed.

The mules shrilled and reared, jerked Daniel Akamarino off his feet—until the Yaril and Jaril shimmerglobes darted over and settled briefly on the beasts, calming them.

They darted back to Brann, shifted to their childshapes and knelt with her beside Ahzurdan. He was foaming at the mouth, writhing, groaning, his face twisting in a mask of pain and fear. Brann flattened her palms on his chest, leaned as much of her weight on him as she could while Yaril melted into him. She closed her eyes, reached into him, guided by Yaril's gentle touches, repairing bruises and breaks and burns where the lifestuff of the elementals had traumatized him. Jaril flung himself into the air, a hawk again, circling, watch-

ing. Daniel soothed the mules some more, managed to
pour some grain into the grass and got them eating. He
popped the stopple on the wineskin, squeezed a short
stream into his mouth, sighed with pleasure. Brann
looked over her shoulder, scowled. "Daniel, dig me out
a cloth and bring some water here."

He shrugged and complied, stood over her watching
with interest as she wiped the sorceror's drawn face
clean of spittle and dirt. Ahzurdan's limbs straightened
and his face smoothed, his staring eyes closed. He was
asleep. Deeply asleep. Brann rubbed at her back,
groaned. Yaril oozed out of Ahzurdan, took her child-
shape back and came round to crouch beside Brann,
leaning into her looking sleepy. Brann patted her,
smiled wearily. "Yaro, what does Jay see ahead? How
close is the mountain?"

Silent at first, blankfaced for a long minute, Yaril's
mouth began moving several beats before she finally
spoke. "He says the going is really bad for several
miles, ground's chewed up, trees are knitted into knots,
but after that it's pretty clear. Maybe a couple hours'
ride beyond the mess we should be on the lower slopes
of Isspyrivo."

Brann scratched at her chin. "He needs rest, but we
can't afford the time. Maksim should be worn out for a
while. With a little luck the god will get to us before he
recovers." She pushed onto her feet, stretched, worked
her shoulders. "Daniel . . ."

Sometime after they left the battleground, Ahzurdan
groaned and tried to sit up. He was roped face down
across the saddle of his mule; the moment he opened
his eyes, he vomited and nearly choked.

Brann swung her mule hastily around, produced a
knife and slashed his ropes. "Daniel!" Daniel rode
close on the other side, caught a fistful of robe, dragged
Ahzurdan off the saddle and lowered him until his feet
touched the ground. Ahzurdan was coughing, sputtering and trying to curse around a swollen tongue, struggling feebly against the clutch between his shoulders
that pulled his robe so tightly about his neck and chest
it threatened to strangle him.

Yaril plummeted downward, shifting to girl as she touched ground; she caught hold of the mules' bridles as Brann slid from the saddle, ran round to get her shoulder under Ahzurdan's arm and tap Daniel's wrist to tell him he should let go his hold. Both of them staggering awkwardly, she got Ahzurdan to a tree and lowered him onto swelling roots so that he sat comfortably enough with his back supported by the trunk and his legs stretched out before him. Without waiting to be told, Daniel brought a cloth and a waterskin and a clean robe for the man, then he went to lean against another tree, the skirts of his long vest pushed back, his thumbs hooked behind his belt.

It was very quiet under the trees; there were a lot of pines now and other conifers, the earth was thick with springy muffling dead needles and the wispy wind shivered the live ones to produce their characteristic constant soughing whispers, but the birds (except, of course for Jaril hawkflying overhead), the squirrels and other rodents busy about the ground and the lower branches, the deer and occasional bear they'd seen before the attack, all these had prudently vanished and with an equal wisdom had elected to continue their business elsewhere until Brann and her party left the mountains. Even the mules were subdued, standing quiet, heads down, eyes shut; not trusting them all that much, Yaril stayed close to them, ready to freeze them in place if they tried bolting.

Brann wet the cloth, hesitated, then gave it to Ahzurdan and let him rub his face clean and dab at the clotted vomit and the stains on his robe. When he tossed the cloth aside and reached for the clean robe sitting on a root beside him, she got to her feet and went to stand near Daniel.

Ahzurdan used knots on the trunk and a lot of sweat to raise himself onto his feet. "That kind of weaving costs," he said. He wiped his sleeve across his face, looked at the dusty damp smears on the black cloth that covered his forearm. "You pay for it yourself, or you arrange to have others pay the bill. There's at least one talisman that transfers credit from other lives to yours." He began fumbling with the closures to his robe. "I

never paid much notice to talismans, one can't learn
defenses specific to them, there aren't any, so what's the
point? BinYAHtii,'' he said. He slipped one arm free
of the ꞷiled robe, transferred the clean one to that arm,
worked ᴜs second arm free. "If you feed BinYAHtii,
it won't feed on you. Daniel Akamarino.'' He let the
robe fall round his feet, kicked it away, pulled the other
over his head. "You talked with that angry child,'' he
said as his head emerged. He patted the cloth in place,
shook out the lower part. "I picked up something about
a Lot where children are taken. She talk to you about
that?'' He listened intently, his hands absently smoothing and smoothing at wrinkled black serge; when Daniel finished, he said, "I see. Two of the children stay
around for training, but the child who gets the gold isn't
seen again. That's Maksim, the clever old bastard. The
thing about BinYAHtii, you see, it takes the character-
istics of the creatures it feeds on. If he gave it grown
men and rebels, he'd have fits trying to control it; children, though . . . hmm. Forty years . . .'' His hollowed
face fell into deep new wrinkles; his flesh was being
eaten off his bones by the ravages of the demon lifestuff
and the effort it took to maintain his defenses while he
defended them. "I was hoping he'd have to rest a day
or two. He won't, he can draw on BinYAHtii. I'm about
done, Brann. Even with your help, I'm about done.''
He touched his fingers to his tongue, looked at them,
wiped them on the bark beside him. He bowed his head,
closed his eyes, stood very still a moment, then he shook
himself, straightened up. "Would you spare me a sip
of that wine, Daniel Akamarino?''

"My pleasure.''

Brann clicked her tongue, annoyed at the satisfaction
in the words. It wasn't overt enough to justify a challenge, but it accomplished what it was meant to, Ahzurdan flushed crimson and his hands shook. But he
ignored the pinprick, drank, drank again and handed
the skin back without speaking to Daniel.

They mounted again and started on. A lean gray wolf,
Jaril ran before them, leading them along the route Yar-
ilhawk chose for them, winding through ravines, over
meadowflats, along hillsides, heading always for the

forested slopes of slumbering Isspyrivo. They rode tense and edgy, neither Brann nor the two men spoke; the air between them felt sulfurous, powdery, a word, a single word might be the spark to trigger an explosion that would certainly destroy them. Tense and edgy and afraid. At any moment, without the least warning, Settsimaksimin could strike at them again.

As the afternoon progressed, Ahzurdan sank into a passivity so profound that even Brann's transferred lifestuff wouldn't jolt him out of it; he rode on with them more because he hadn't sufficient will in him to slide from the saddle than because he had any hope of living through that next inevitable attack. He made no preparations to meet it, he let his defenses melt away, he rode hunched forward as if he presented his chin for the finishing blow, as if he were silently pleading for it to happen so this terrible numbing tension would at last be broken.

Daniel Akamarino drank Tungjii's wine and cursed the meddling gods that fished him from a life he enjoyed and dumped him into this life-threatening mess. And kept him in it. He'd made one futile gesture toward distancing himself from something that was absolutely unequivocally none of his business. Nothing since. Why? he asked himself. I know better than to mess with local politics. There were at least a dozen chances to get away and I let them slide. Why? I could have got away, left this stinking land. A world's a big place. I could have got lost in it, gods or no gods. Messing with my head, that's it. Her? Probably not. The shifter kids? Maybe. Hmm. Don't flog your old back too much over missed opportunities, Danny Blue, maybe they weren't really there, not with young Jay sniffing after you. He watched the gray wolf loping tirelessly ahead of them, shook his head. Forget regrets, Old Blue, you better concentrate on staying alive. Which, by all I've seen, means keeping close to Brann. Interesting woman. He grinned. Wonder what sleeping with a vampire's like? A real one, not some of the metaphorical blood suckers I've known. Sort of dangerous, huh? What if her ratchet slips? He laughed aloud. Brann's head whipped round, she was scowling at him, furious with him for what? making the situation worse? Danny One wasn't taking it in, he wasn't taking much of anything in right now. Daniel had seen that kind of passivity before, that time he was out with the hunting tribe and one of them got himself cursed by a shaman from another tribe. The man just stopped everything until he stopped living. Not great for us. Kuh! next time old Maksim blows on us, he'll blow us away. He looked at the wineskin, cursed under his breath and pushed the stopple home.

Brann couldn't relax; they were moving at a fast walk, no more, but the roan's gait was jolting, the beast was rattling her bones and making her head ache, her stomach was already in knots with the waiting and worrying, if she couldn't stop fighting the damn mule she'd better get down and walk. Gods, gods, gods, may you all drop into your own worst hells, I swear, if you don't leave me alone, I'll take the kids and I'll go hunting you. If I live through this. She grinned suddenly, briefly. I think I think I think I've got an out, miserable meeching gods, the kids can't eat on their own if they stick to ordinary folk but maybe just maybe they can graze on you. If they have to. Not that I'm going to lay down and die. That phase is over. She looked at Ahzurdan, wrinkled her nose. No indeed. A swift glance at Daniel Akamarino. I don't like you much, Danny Blue, but you stir me up something fierce. Slya bless, I don't know why. I wish I did, it's not all that convenient right now. Look at me, I'm not paying attention to what's going on round us, I'm thinking about you. Shuh! straighten up, Brann. How much farther? Where are you, Chained God? How much do you expect us to endure? If I had a hope of getting out of this, you could sit there till you rusted. Do something, will you? Tungjii, old fiddler, where are you? Stir your thumbs up, what did Danny Two call you, shemale? Hmm. I wonder what it's like, seeing sex from both sides of the business. Slya's rancid breath, there I go again. "Jay, how much longer to Isspyrivo?"

The gray wolf turned, changed to lean teener boy. "Where does one mountain end and another begin anyway? We're close if we're not already there. Yaro says there's nothing happening, the mountain's quiet, there's not a bird or beast visible twenty miles around. Even the wind is dying down.''

''Ah. Think that means anything? The wind?''

''Only one who could tell you that is him.'' Jaril waved a hand at Ahzurdan who was staring at nothing they could see, his eyes glazed, his face empty.

''I'll see what I can do. Tell Yaril to get us upslope as directly as she can even if we have to slow down some more.'' She watched the big wolf lope off, shook her head. He looked like being well past puberty now, whatever that meant. Confusion compounded, shuh! She caught up with Ahzurdan, rode stirrup to stirrup with him for several minutes, examining him, wondering how she was going to reach him. ''Dan.'' He gave no sign he heard her. ''Ahzurdan.'' Nothing. She leaned over, caught hold of his arm, passed a jolt of energy into him. ''Ahzurdan!'' He twitched, tried to pull away, but there was no more life in his face than there had been moments before. She let go of him, slowed until she was riding beside Daniel Akamarino. ''Give me the wineskin for a moment.''

''Why?''

''You don't need to ask and I don't need to explain. Don't be difficult, Danny Blue.''

''Wine won't float him out of that funk.''

''I'm not about to build a fire so he can sniff his way up. That wine of yours has Tungjii's touch on it.''

''Heesh hasn't been much in sight since we left Lio's boat.''

''Luck comes in many colors, Daniel. Stop arguing and give me the skin.''

''Not going to work, Brann, I've seen that kind of down before; he won't come out of it.''

''What are you fussing about, Dan? You won't lose a cup of wine, the thing's magic, it refills itself.''

He shrugged the strap off his shoulder, swung the skin, let it go. ''All you'll get is a drunk marshmallow, Brann, he's had the fight whipped out of him.''

She caught the skin, set it on the mule's shoulders. ''If you're right, we're dead, Daniel Akamarino. You better hope you're not.'' She heeled the mule into a quicker walk, left him behind. When she was beside

Ahzurdan, she forced her mule as close to his as both beasts would tolerate, leaned over and slapped Ahzurdan's face hard.

He looked at her, startled, the mark of her hand red across his pale cheek.

She held out the wineskin. "Take this and drink until you can't hold any more. If you start arguing with me, I'm going to knock you out of that saddle, pry your mouth open and pour it down you."

He chuckled (surprising both of them), the glaze melted from his eyes. "Why not." He took the skin, lifted it in a parody of a toast. "Hai, Maksim, a short life ahead for you and an interesting one. Hai, Tungjii, li'l meddler. Hai, Godalau with your saucy tail. Hai, Amortis, may you get what you deserve. Hai, you fates, may we all get what we deserve." He thumbed the stopple out, tilted his head back and sent the straw gold wine arcing into his throat.

They rode on. The wine took hold in Ahzurdan, though it was perhaps only Tungjii's fingerprints in it that made the difference. He was still worn, close to exhaustion, but his face flushed and his eyes grew moist and he looked absurdly contented with life; he even hummed snatches of Phrasi songs. In spite of the improvement in his spirits, though, he didn't respin his defenses or prepare for the attack they all knew was coming. When he started to mutter incoherently, to sway and fumble at the reins, his nose running, his eyes turned bleary and unfocused, Brann sighed, took the wineskin away and tossed it back to Daniel Akamarino who did not say *I told you so* but managed by his attitude to write the words in the air in front of him.

The way got steeper and more difficult; they had to clamber about rock slides, dismounting (even Ahzurdan) to lead the mules over the unstable scree; they had to circle impassible clots of thorny brush; they changed direction constantly to avoid steep-walled uncrossable ravines; with Yaril plotting their course they never had to backtrack and lose time that way, but she couldn't change the kind of ground they had to cover. As the afternoon slid slowly and painfully away they labored on through the lengthening shadows riding tired and increasingly balky mules.

Fire bloomed in the air in front of them, fire boiled out of the ground around them.

Yaril dived and changed; a throbbing golden lens, she caught some of that fire and redirected it through the leafy canopy into the sky. Jaril howled and changed, whipped in swift circles about the riders, catching fire and redirecting it.

The mules set their feet, dropped their heads and stood where they were, terrified and incapable of doing more than shallow breathing and shaking.

Ahzurdan struggled to gather will again and spread the sphere about them but he could not, he was empty of will, empty of thought, empty of everything but pain.

Brann looked frantically about, helpless, sick with frustration, nothing she could do here, nothing but hope the children could hold until Ahzurdan reached deep enough and found some last measure of strength within him.

Daniel unzipped the pocket where the stunner was; he didn't really think it would work on those creatures, if creatures they were, what he wanted was a firedamp, but those he knew of were on starships back home which didn't do a helluva lot of good right now.

A huge red foot came kicking through the trees; it caught several of the fire elementals and sent them flying, their wild whistling shrieks dying in the distance. The foot stomped on more fire, grinding it into the troubled earth perilously close to the mules (who shivered and shook and flattened their ears and huddled closer together). Having converted to confusion the concerted attack of fire and earth, their sudden new defender bent over them. Four sets of red fingers began probing through trees and brush and grass, digging into cracks in the earth like a groomer hunting fleas, picking up the whistling shuddering elementals, shaking them into terrified passivity, flinging them after the first.

When she finished that, Red Slya stood and stretched, fifty meters of naked four-armed female, grinning, showing crimson teeth. She set her four hands on her ample hips and stood looking with monstrous fondness on the fragile mortals she'd rescued so expeditiously. "EHH LITTLE NOTHING, IN TROUBLE AGAIN, ARE YOU?"

"Slya Fireheart." Brann bowed with prudent courtesy, head dipping to mule mane. She straightened. "In trouble, indeed, and of course you know why, Great Slya."

Huge laughter rumbled thunderously across the mountains. "SENT AMORTIS SKREEKING, HER TAIL ON FIRE, AHHHH, I LAUGHED, I HAVEN'T LAUGHED SO HARD IN YEARS. COOOME, MY NOTHING, FOLLOW ME ALONG, OLD MAKSI, HE CAN PLAY WITH HIMSELF." She swung around, shrinking as she turned until she was only ten meters high. Singing a near inaudible bumbumrumbum, she strode off.

Brann looked hastily about, located the children. They stood together in the shade of a half-uprooted pine whose needles were charred and still smoldering, something that was peculiarly apt to their mood. Hand in hand, intense and angry, their silent talk buzzing between them, they fixed hot crystal eyes on Slya's departing back. "Yaro, Jay, not now, let's go."

They turned those eyes on her and for a long moment she felt completely alienated from them, shut out from needs, emotions, everything that made them what they were. Then Yaril produced a fake sigh and a smile and melted into a shewolf, Jaril echoed both the sigh and the smile and dropped beside her, a matching hewolf. They trotted ahead of the mules, gray shadows hugging huge red heels. Brann kicked her own heels into the blue roan's plump sides and tried to get him moving; he honked at her, put his head down and thought he was going to buck until she slapped him on the withers and sent a jolt of heat into him. Once she got him straightened up and pacing along, the other two mules hurried to keep up with him, unwilling to be left behind.

Daniel Akamarino shifted in the saddle, seeking some unbattered part of his legs to rub against the saddle skirts as his mule settled from a jolting jog to a steady walk once he was nose to the tail of Ahzurdan's mount. Daniel watched Slya what was it Fireheart? swing along

as if she were out for an afternoon's stroll through a
park, four arms moving easily, hair like flame crackling
in the wind (though there was no wind he could feel,
maybe she generated her own). What a world. The fishtail femme was a watergod, this one looks like she'd be
right at home at a volcano's heart. Not too bright (he
swallowed a chuckle, keep your mouth shut, Danny
Blue, her idea of humor isn't likely to match yours,
she'd probably laugh like hell while she was pulling your
arms and legs off). Handy having her about, though,
(he chewed on his tongue as he belatedly noted the idiot
pun; watch it, Dan), she'll keep old Settsiwhat off our
necks. Knows Brann, seems to like her. Hmm. A story
there, I wonder if I'll ever hear it. Kuh! How much
longer will we have to ride? I'm going to end up with
no skin at all left on my legs.

Ahzurdan clenched his teeth and tried to swallow; his
stomach was knotting and lurching, the wine that had
soothed and strengthened him seemed as if it were about
to rise up and strangle him. He was numb and empty
and angry. Red Slya had saved them, had saved him
pain and drain, perhaps ultimate failure, yet he was furious with her because she had taken from him something he hadn't recognized until it was gone. In spite of
what it had cost him, he'd found a deep and, yes, necessary satisfaction in the contest with Settsimaksimin.
He'd taken his body from Maksim's domination, but he'd
never managed to erase his teacher's mark from either
of his souls. Before Slya stepped in, he was afraid and
exhausted, cringing from another agonizing struggle,
but there was something gathering deep and deep in
him, something rising to meet the new attack, something aborted when Slya struck. He felt . . . incomplete. A thought came to him. He almost laughed. Like
all those times, too many times to make it a comfortable
memory, laboring at sex with someone, didn't matter
who, the whole thing fading away on him, leaving his
mind wanting, his body wanting, the want unfocused,
impossible to satisfy, impossible to ignore. He rubbed
at his stomach and tried to deal with the rising wine and
the rising anger, both of which threatened to make him
sick enough to wish he were dead.

They followed Slya's flickering heels along a noisy whitewater stream into a deep crack in the mountainside where the waternoise increased to a deafening roar, sound so intense it stopped being sound and became assault. At the far end of the crack the stream fell a hundred meters down a black basalt cliff, the last ten meters lost in a swirling mist.

Slya stopped at the edge of that mist and waved a pair of right hands at it. "GO ON," she boomed.

Brann hesitated, pulled her mount to a halt. "What about the mules, O Slya Fireheart?"

The god blinked, her mouth went slack as she considered the question; she shifted one large foot, nudged the side of the roan mule with her big toe. The beast froze. Slya gave a complicated shrug and dismissed the difficulty. "DO WHAT YOU WANT, LITTLE NOTHING, YOU ALWAYS MAKING SNAGS. FIDDLE YOUR OWN ANSWERS." She vanished.

Brann slid from the saddle. "We'll leave the mules and most of the gear here. I don't want to have to be worrying about them once we're in that place." She waved a hand at the wavery semi-opaque curtain that was mist in part, but certainly something else along with the mist. She started stripping the gear off the roan. "One of you look about for a place where we can cache what we can't carry."

Yaril and Jaril in their teener forms flanking her, Brann straightened her shoulders and pushed into the mist. For a panicky moment she couldn't breathe, then she could. She kept plowing on through whatever it was that surrounded her, she couldn't think of it as water mist any longer, the smell, feel, temperature were all wrong. It was like wading through a three-day-old milk pudding. She heard muffled exclamations behind her and knew the two men had passed that breathless phase, following as closely on her heels as they could manage. With a sigh of relief she pushed along faster, no longer worrying about losing touch with them. The sound of the waterfall was gone, all sounds but those immediately around her were gone. She began to feel disoriented, dizzy, she began to wonder what was waiting ahead; walking blind into maybe danger was becoming less attractive every step she took.

A long oval of light like moonglow snapped open before her, three body lengths ahead and slightly to her left. She turned toward it, but hands pushed her back, smallish hands; Yaril and Jaril swam ahead of her, sweeping through the Gate before she could reach it. She leaned against the clotted pudding around her, floundering with arms and legs and will to work her body through something that wasn't exactly fighting her but wasn't all that yielding. An eternity later she dropped through the Gate and landed sprawling on a resilient surface like greasy wool. She bounced lightly, fell forward onto her face, rebounded. An odd feeling, as if she were swimming in air rather than water. She maneuvered herself onto her knees and gaped at the Chained God. Yaril and Jaril were holding onto each other, giggling.

Ahzurdan had trouble with the Gate; his temper flared, but he bit back angry comment when Daniel Akamarino got impatient and gave him a hard shove that popped him through it. Once he was in, he found the sudden lessening of his weigh disconcerting and difficult to deal with. He stumbled and fell over, tried to get up, all his reactions were wrong; he gripped the wooly surface and held himself down until even the twitches were gone out of him, it took a few seconds, that was all. Disciplining every movement he got slowly, carefully to his feet and stood staring at the enigmatic thing that filled most of this pocket reality, something like an immense metallic nutshell.

Daniel Akamarino wriggled after him, half swimming, half lunging. He dived through the Gate, hit the wool in a controlled flip and came warily onto his feet, arms out for balance in the half g gravity. He lowered his arms to his sides. After a breath or two of wonder, he chuckled. "It's a freaking starship."

——— 13 ———

THE CHAINED GOD AND HIS PROBLEM.

SCENE: On the bridge of the Colony Transport. The Ship's Computer talking to them. Yaril, Jaril, Daniel Akamarino know something about what's going on and are reasonably comfortable with it, though there are sudden glitches that disconcert them almost as much as the whole thing does Ahzurdan. Brann has settled herself in the Captain's place, a massive swiveling armchair, and is watching the play of lights across the face of the control surfaces and the play of emotion across the faces of the two men, detached and amused by this turn of events; another thing that pleases her is the sense that she finally knows at least one good reason why the gods running this crazy expedition have brought Daniel Akamarino across. He knows instruments like the part of this god that is machine not life or magic. This visible portion of the Chained God is a strange, incomprehensible amalgam of metal, glass, vegetable and animal matter, shimmering shifting energy webs, the plasma as it were of the magic that had gathered inside the shipshell and sparked into being the Being who called him/it self the Chained God.

"Why Chained God?" Daniel stood along in front of the specialist stations (swivelchairs with their aging pads, nests of broken wire, dangling, swaying helmets), his eyes flickering across the readouts, lifting to the dusty stretch of blind white glass curving across the forward wall of the bridge. "How'd you end up here?"

A kind of multi-sensory titter flickered in patterns of light an :ags of sound across the whole of the instrumentation. "Bad planning, bad luck, an Admiral who was probably the best asslicker in the Souflamarial, our empire, as close to a genius at it as you'd find in fifty realities. Political appointee." The voice of the god was high, raspy and androgynous, equipped with multiple echoes as if a dozen more of him/it were speaking not quite in unison. He/it made attempts at colloquial speech and showed a bent for a rather juvenile sort of sardonic humor, but seemed most comfortable with a precision and pedantry more apt to an aged scholar who hadn't had his nose out of his books for the past five decades than to a being of power moving ordinary folk like chesspieces about the board of the world. "He had fifty heavy armed and five hundred light armed point-troops sworn to obey his every fart; he was there to establish and maintain approved power lines on the world a collection of very carefully chosen settlers were to tame and equip for the delectation of certain powerful and well-placed individuals on Soulafar, it was meant to be their private playground. He was told to keep his hands off me, to let the technicians handle technical matters. Unfortunately, he had delusions of competence. He was determined to present a flawless log, everything done with a maximum of efficiency. He knew his bosses, that one would have to admit, he knew how to make himself needed while stressing his utter loyalty. He intended to share the pleasures of the apple fields of Avalon. What he did not know is how intractable the universe could be, he did not know how meaningless his intentions and needs were when set up against the forces outside my shell. Yes, he was blissfully ignorant of the realities of poking one's nose into new territories and how fast things can blow up on you when you're moving through sketchily charted realms. We ran into an expanding wave of turbulence which reached into several realities on either side of ours. The Acting Captain slowed and started to turn away from it. Our esteemed Admiral ordered him to get back on course. Tell me, Daniel Akamarino, why are true believers of his sort invariably convoluted hypocrites and deeply stupid?'' Another titter. ''Ah well, I am prejudiced, it was my being and the beings in my care that idiot put in such jeopardy. The Captain refused and was shot, the Admiral's men put guns to heads and I went plowing into that storm, I got slammed about until I was on the point of breaking up. Then, fortunately or not depending on your attitude toward these things, I dropped through a hole I had no way of detecting and came out here.'' A rattling noise, as if the multiple throats were clearing themselves. ''Or rather, not 'here,' not in this pocket prison, but in orbit about a seething soup of a world laced with lines of hungry energy. I and what I carried catalyzed these into our present pantheon.'' A long pause, an unreadable flicker of lights, a curious set of sounds. ''Oh, they weren't Perran a Perran, they weren't the Godalau or Slya or Amortis or Jah'takash or any of the other greater and lesser gods and demigods, not yet. Though I'm not all that sure about little Tungjii, heesh is different from them, older, slyer. No, they weren't the gods we know and love today, not yet. And, Daniel Akamarino, I was not anything like the Being you see before you. I was your ordinary ship's brain, though perhaps larger than most with more memory capacity because I was to be the resource library for the colonists, with more capacity for independent decision-making because I had to tend the thousands of stored ova and other seeds meant to make life charming for our future lords; I was supposed to get some beasts and beings ready for decanting when we arrived at the designated world and at the same time I had to maintain the viability of the rest until they were required.'' A pause, more sounds and flickers. Daniel Akamarino examined them frowning, intent. Brann watched the part of his face that she could see and the muscles of his shoulders and she decided he was learning something from the body language (as it were) of the composite god. What? Who knows. More than I am from its jab-berjabber. Was this thing claiming he/it created the un-created gods? The children were bobbing about, touching here and there, the Chained God apparently unworried by their probes. She hoped they were learn-ing more than the god thought they were. Gods. She wouldn't trust any of them with the spit to drown them.

"Keeping that in mind . . ." The god settled into a chatty demilecturing. Brann looked from the flickering lights to Daniel and smiled to herself. Perhaps the god needed Daniel to free him somehow from chains she suspected were highly metaphorical, but he/it was in-dulging him/it self in an orgy of autobiography, falling over him/it self to pour out things prisoned inside him/it forever and ever, pour them into the only ear that would understand them, or perhaps the only ear he/it could coerce into listening to him/it. ". . . You will understand what I say when I tell you those force lines leaped at me, invaded me, plundered me the instant I appeared and retreated with everything my memory held, each of them with a greater or smaller part of it. None left with the whole within himself or herself, I say him and her because some of those force lines resonated more with the male elements in my memories and some with the female elements. I can only be thankful that they didn't wipe me in the process; even after eons of thinking about it, I can't be sure why. A vital part of that event, Daniel Akamarino, led to my birth as a self-aware Being. They left part of their essence behind trapped within me, melded with my circuits. As soon as they freed me by leaving me, that essential energy began to act on me and I began to withdraw my fringes from the constraints that controlled me, freeing more of myself with every hour that passed. The Admiral was not pleased by any of this; as soon as he recovered his wits such as they were and discovered the sad case of my shell and everything inside it, he threw orders around to whatever technicians had survived, having his praetorian guard thump answers out of them, no shoot-ing this time (he'd acquired a sudden caution about ex-pending his resources). Not that there were many answers available, no one knew precisely what had happened, not even me. It took the troops around half a day to realize exactly who was responsible for putting them in this mess and they went hunting for him, but he had developed a nose for trouble in his long and devious career. Odd, isn't it. He was a truly stupid man literally incapable of learning anything more complex than an ad jingle, but he had a fantastic sensitivity when it came to his own survival. He locked himself into his shielded quarters before they could get at him. They conferred among themselves, got a welder and sealed up all entrances they could find, making sure he'd stay in the prison he'd made for himself. Talking about prisons, my engines were junk, I could not leave orbit except to land. The landing propulsors were sealed and more or less intact with plenty of fuel for maneuvering; sadly though, the world I circled was most emphatically not habitable, at least, not then. The troops and the crew and the settlers who remained were in no danger because life support was working nicely off the storage cells and I had managed to deploy my solar wings so I could recharge these as they were drawn down; food wasn't a problem either. About half the settlers, perhaps a third of the soldiers and one in ten of the crew had perished in the transfer which meant more for those left; with a little stretching and some ingenuity involving the seeds and beast ova in the storage banks, no one was going to starve. Boredom and claustrophobia were the worst they had to face. What we didn't know was how ebulliently the gods were evolving down below us and what they were planning for us. They were shaping themselves out of my memories and shaping the world to receive us. Time passed, Daniel Akamarino. A military dictatorship developed within my shell, one tempered by the need the gun wielders had for the knowledge of the technicians and the settlers. I grew meat animals and poultry in my metal wombs and the settlers arranged stables in my holds, they planted grain in hydroponic tanks the technicians built for them, vegetables and fruits. They set up gyms for exercising and nurseries when the first children were born. They tapped my memories for entertainment and began developing their own newspapers and publishing companies. It was not an especially unpleasant time for the survivors, at least those that had no desire for power and were content with building a comfortable life for themselves and their children. Time passed. One year. Three. Five. What was I doing all this time? Good question. Changing. Yes, changing in ways that would have terrified me if I had been capable of feeling terror in those days. Remember the Admiral shut up safe in his quarters? I took him near the end of my first six months as an awakening entity and I incorporated him into me, part of him, his neural matter; I lost much of his memory in the process, though not all of it, and acquired to some degree his instinct for manipulating individuals to maximize his security; I also acquired his ferocious will to survive. That by way of warning, Daniel Akamarino, Brann Drinker of Souls. The godessence within me, as blindly instinctive as any termite (out of some need I didn't understand at the time and still do not fully comprehend), sucked into me more neural essence. I acquired some technicians, I took the best of the troops within me, I took a selection of the settlers within me; as with the Admiral, I harvested only a fraction of their knowledge, but much of their potential. I also acquired rather inadvertently spores from the vegetative growth in the hydroponic tanks and assorted germ plasm from viruses and bacteria. And the godessence grew as it absorbed energy through the storage cells and finally directly from the solar wings, it grew and learned and threaded deeper and deeper into me, it became a soul spark in me, then a conflagration; it unified the disparate parts of me and I began to be the Being that you see before you now. Five years became ten and ten multiplied into a century. All this time the godessences below worked on the world, transforming it. They came raiding me again, hunting seeds and beasts. And people. But I was stronger this time, my defenses were rewoven and a lot tighter then they'd been even when I was an intact transport pushing through homespace. They couldn't coerce me, so they tried seducing me. They showed me what they'd built below and it was good indeed. I knew well enough that my folk would not prosper forever in the confines of my shell, the time would come, was coming, when they'd wither and begin to die. That would have meant little to a ship's brain, but I was somewhat more than I'd been. It would get very lonely around here without my little mortals and the idiot things they did. So I called them together, the children of the settlers, crew and soldiers. I told them what the godessences had done, showed them what I'd been shown, explained to them how difficult it would be down there, how much hard work would be required, but also what the possibilities for the future were. I promised them that I'd be there to watch over them, to protect them when they needed me. They were afraid, but enough of them were bored enough with life in limits to carry the others on their enthusiasm and we went down. And more years passed. As the storytellers say it, the world turned on the spindle of time, day changed with night and night with day, year added to year, century to century. My wombs were emptied, my folk multiplied and began to spread across the face of the world. MY folk. The godessences took that time to redefine their godshapes, to codify the powers attached to those dreams, fiddling with them, changing them, until they felt them resonate. In spite of this they grew jealous of the hold I had on MY folk. They could not attack me directly, I was too strong for them, too different; they couldn't get their hands on me. So they banded against me, they took me from the mountain where I was and cast me here and they put their godchains on me so I could not reach out from here and teach them the error of their ways. I could reach only the Vale folk, and that not freely. Through the focusing lens of my chosen priests, I could teach and guide them, heal them sometimes and bless them. I could watch them be born, grow into adulthood, engender new life and finally die. I was not alone. I was not forgotten though they wanted that, those other gods who owed their being to me. They still want it. They want me destroyed, forgotten, erased entirely from this reality. Most of them. None of them wanted me loosed. You, Daniel Akamarino, you, Ahzurdan, you Brann Drinker of Souls, you shall free me from this prison.''

Daniel Akamarino rubbed at the fringes of hair spiking over his ears. "How?"

Silence. A looong silence.

When the Chained God spoke again, he/it ignored the question. "You are tired, all of you. Rest, eat, sleep, we will talk again tomorrow. If you will look behind you, you will see a serviteur, follow it, it will take you to a living area I've had cleaned and repaired for you. Daniel Akamarino, if you please, explain the facilities to your companions; you won't find them too unfamiliar but if you have a question, ask the serviteur, it will remain with you and provide whatever you need, from information to food. Sleep well, my friends, tomorrow and tomorrow and tomorrow will be a busy time."

They followed the squat thing the god called a serviteur through echoing metal caverns that existed in a perpetual twilight, the walls and ceiling festooned with ropy creatures whose pale leaves were like that rarest kind of white jade that has a tracery of green netted through it. Unseen things ran rustling through those leaves and the fibrous airroots brushed their faces like dangling spiderwebs. They walked on something crumbly that sent up geysers of dust at every step, dust that stank of mold and age. The farther they went, the stiller and staler the air became.

Daniel Akamarino stopped walking. "Serviteur."

The iron manikin stopped its whirring clanking progress. Brann grimaced and felt at her own neck as it cranked its sensory knob about to fix its glassy gaze on Daniel. A crackling sound like dry resinpine burning lasted for half a breath, then words came out of it, odd uninflected words so empty of emotion that it took Brann several seconds and some concentration to understand them. "What do you want, Daniel Akamarino?"

"Get some airflow along here or we don't move another step."

"Air is adequate, Daniel Akamarino. A stronger current would disturb certain elements. Your quarters are nearby. If you please, continue."

"With the understanding if your idea of nearby and

mine don't agree, we go back and wait where we can breathe.''

The sensory knob twisted back, the serviteur gave a stiff metallic shiver and started on. For an instant Brann saw it as a little old man, ancient as the hills, ancient as the huge twisted stems of the vines that wove about them. She coughed and caught up with Daniel. "How old is it?'' she murmured.

"Old enough for tachsteel to start going soft. Older than Isspyrivo. Perhaps as old as Tungjii." He smiled. "In the long long ago when the Wounded Moon was whole."

They turned three more corners, then stopped before a section of wall that was cleaned of all vegetation. A part of the wall slid aside, the serviteur clattered through into a clean well-lighted space, whirred into a niche and settled there, folding its substructure up into its body until it looked rather like a crock with an odd sort of lid on it.

Shimmerglobes darted past Brann, went flashing through the nearest wall of a room like the inside of an egg, painted eggshell white with a fragile ivory carpet on the floor; there were a number of odd lumps about, they might have been chairs of a sort, or something far stranger. There were ovals of milky white glass at intervals around the walls, their long axis parallel to the floor. The room was filled with a soft white light though there were no lamps that Brann could see. It was as if someone had bottled sunlight and decanted it here. There were six oval doorways filled with a sort of glowing mist, a mist that swirled in slow eddies but stayed where it was put.

Ahzurdan stood looking about him. He felt uneasy, he did not belong here; the walls drew in on him and he found breathing difficult though the air inside the eggroom was considerably fresher and cooler than that in the corridor. He could sense lines of godenergy, of magicstrength, weaving an intricate web within the walls, but he could not reach them. There were other lines of other forces that shivered just beyond his vision, they were worse, far worse, not only could he not reach them, they threatened to bind him and he did not know how to keep them off. He moved closer to Brann.

Daniel Akamarino stood looking about him. He moved his shoulders and felt his bones relax. This was his world. Derelict it might be, weird it might be, but this was once a starflyer. His fingers felt alive, his body responded to the smells, the feel of metal wrapped about him, the sense of power powerfully controlled. The godstuff was irritating, all this plant and fungus nonsense was a pain, add-ons he wished he could scrape off so he could see plain the stark beauty of the computer circuits, hear the deep middle-of-the-bone nearly silent drone of the engines. For days he'd been pulled tight, as day slid into day he'd been more and more afraid he'd never see a starship again. It was like a part of him had been hacked off. He hadn't realized how bad it was until he got here; he wasn't sure he liked knowing that since there didn't seem to be much he could do about it. He enjoyed dirtside life as long as it was in manageable small doses and he could get back into starjumping when he felt like it. He used his talents then, his most important skills, important to him. He did things he found most satisfying then. Never again? Never! These freaking gods brought him here, they could put him back where he belonged. If they wanted to argue about that, well, why not dig up one of those talismans, find out how to use it and put the squeeze on one of them until the sorry s'rish was hurting so hard he maybe she would be glad to get rid of him.

The children came drifting back, shifting to their bipedal forms as they touched down before Brann. "Bedrooms, washroom, a kitchen of sorts," Yaril said. "Shuh! are they old. But they're clean, they don't smell and they work well enough." "I bet this was part of the Admiral's quarters, him the god was talking about," Jaril said. "It's too fancy for crew or settler. Um. Ship hears whatever we say. Yaril and me, we probably could block a small space for a short time if you need it, but I wouldn't count too much on that."

Brann nodded. "I hear." She yawned. "I could use a pot of tea." She turned to Daniel Akamarino. "How do I work that, Danny Blue?"

* * *

Teatime conversation:

Brann: What I want to know is why this thing wants to be turned loose. What can it do but sit somewhere like it's sitting here? Gods. Most of the time you can't trust any of them, not even old Tungjii. Remember what it said about incorporating neural matter from the Admiral and some of its other passengers? Neural matter, hah! that's someone's head, isn't it? Gah! Makes me want to vomit thinking about it. You know, if you lock up anyone alone long enough he more likely than not goes crazy. How sane do you think this thing is? I want a lot of answers before I agree to anything.

Daniel Akamarino: (to himself only, internal mutterings) I'm being jerked about. Why doesn't she shut up? Doesn't she realize the shefalos is listening to everything she says? What am I doing here? The shefalos, I'd wager two years' pay on it. Something was messing in my head when it jerked me here, taught me the language. Put the hook in me then. Stupid woman. Why'd she stick her nose in this trap? Everything I see about her says no way she has to do anything she doesn't want to. She could leave now, get us out of here. Danny One, once he gets his batteries charged, he can do the wards. Shit! Can't talk about it here, maybe the kids can block the god . . . sheee, listen to me, god! . . . the shefalos for long enough to get some serious planning done.

(To Brann, in a querulous complaining tone. His amiability was disintegrating under the pressure of events; he generally preserved his equanimity by sliding away from such pressures. Now that he can't slide, his irritations are turning him sour.) Don't be stupid, Brann. You've got hundreds of gods infesting your damn world. What's one more? I want to get this thing over with, you think I like crawling about on this dirtball? I want to go home. I've got family, I've got work, what do you expect. Stop bitching and finish what you started. (He scowled at the cold scum of tea in his cup, refilled it with wine from Tungjii's Gift, refused to look at Brann as he sipped at the straw colored liquid.)

Ahzurdan: (He listened as Brann and Daniel Akamarino sparred with lessening amiability until they stopped talking altogether. He wanted sleep and, like Danny Two, he wanted out of this. The nature of the Chained God sickened and frightened him; his attitude to Settsimaksimin and Brann had suffered a radical reversal when he understood the god was that loathsome monstrosity before him, when he realized that it had played games with his head, hooking him with the hope of freeing himself from his habit. He had sat silent and bitter gazing at the thing, knowing all hope was illusory, he was trapped in something he wouldn't have touched, used and betrayed by the monstrous god and that castrating bitch Brann Drinker of Souls, coarse, low, crude peasant creature. He felt as helpless as a shitting squalling babe, he hated that. If that abomination that brought them here wanted anything from him, it could want, he was out of it, he was going to pull his defenses around him and sit out whatever the god threw at him.)

Morning (because they wakened and ate a sketchy breakfast, inside the ship there was no way of deciding when the sun came up, if there was a sun in this miniature reality).

They followed the resurrected serviteur through the stinking crepuscular corridors to a teeming jungle that had once been the ship's hold, to a steamy glade deep in that jungle with short springy grass and several newly cleaned benches; a small bright stream sang through it, glittering in the light from the several sources moonhigh overhead. Both Ahzurdan and Daniel Akamarino had tried refusing to move; the serviteur informed them in its echoing emotionless voice that they could go on their own feet, or the god would lay them out and send other serviteurs to haul them where he wanted them to go.

The serviteur clanked awkwardly across the grass to a stone plate, settled on it and seemed to sleep.

Ahzurdan stalked to the most distant of the benches, sat with his back to the others.

Daniel Akamarino strolled to another bench, sat on it and started pouring Tungjii's wine down his gullet, having decided that if the god wanted him here, he/it could have him, but he/it was going to get someone so paralyzed he could about breathe and that was all.

Brann clicked her tongue against her teeth, shook her head. That pair she thought, what did I do to deserve them? I was quite happy with my quiet little pottery. damn all gods and curse all fates that pried me loose from it. Shuh! Miserable meeching gods. All right, where are you O god in chains, let's get this thing moving. She settled onto a bench and set herself to wait.

The children melted into shimmerglobes, bounced high as the hold ceiling then went zipping about through the vegetation; they soon got bored with that and came back to the glade. They dropped on the grass by Brann's feet. "It's a regular rainforest, Bramble," Jaril said. "The god has imported a lot of dirt. Got enough space in here for clouds to form, I expect it does rain every day or so, maybe even thunderstorms."

Yaril said nothing, just leaned against Brann's leg.

A sound like a cough, a thump. A tall cylinder of something like glass snapped around her and the children. She sprang to her feet, slapped her hands against the thing, it was warmish and hard, there was no giving to it at all, she tried to suck energy from it, though she'd never tried that before, but apparently her draw was limited to lifefires, whether they belonged to mortal, demon or god. The children shifted and flung themselves against the wall and rebounded, they darted up, down, the ends were closed in also, there was no way out. If they had learned a few things about the Chained God when they probed him yesterday, it seemed apparent that he/it had learned as much about them, enough anyway to imprison them. They subsided into sullen fuming, back in their usual shapes.

Brann could feel a faint breeze, air was coming through the glass or whatever it was, at least she wasn't going to smother. She leaned against the wall, looking out at the others. Ahzurdan and Daniel Akamarino were feeling round similar cylinders. As she watched, Daniel shrugged, settled back on his bench and began sucking on the spout of the wineskin. Ahzurdan's face was dark with fury, he beat against the transparency, nearly incinerated himself trying to break through it. Abruptly, both men were stripped naked, Daniel's wine was jerked away from him.

A SOUND like fingernails scratching on slate. The hair stood up on Brann's arms and along her spine, her teeth began to ache.

The cylinder with Ahzurdan vanished, reappeared superimposed on Daniel's prison; inside the suddenly single cylinder, Ahzurdan and Daniel seemed to be trying to occupy the same place at the same time; the Chained God was forcing the two men to merge. Brann watched, horrified.

Their flesh bulged and throbbed, hair, eyes, teeth appeared, disappeared, arms, legs, heads melted and reformed hideously deformed. The Ahzurdan part and the Akamarino part fought desperately to maintain their separation, but the terrible pressure the god was placing on them was forcing the merger.

The struggle went on and on. Tongues of flame danced briefly about the tormented shapeless flesh thing, but the god damped them. He/it hammered at the emerging form, beating at it as a potter beat at clay, driving out the beads of air trapped inside it, hammering hammering hammering until he/it sculpted the lump into a meaningful manshape that was new and old at once, recognizably Ahzurdan and Daniel Akamarino yet very different from either of them.

A coughing sound, a sub-audible whoosh. The cylinders disappeared. The composite man crumpled to the grass and lay without moving.

Blindingly angry, Brann stumbled as the wall she was pushing against melted away; she caught her balance after a few lunging steps, ran full out to fling herself down beside the man's body. She pressed her fingers up under his jaw, relaxed somewhat when she felt a strong pulse under her fingers. She snapped her head back, glared up at the haze that hid the metal arching high

high overhead. "You!" she cried. "What have you done?"

The god's voice came booming down at her, dry and pedantic. "They were inadequate as they were, Drinker of Souls. Incomplete in themselves. They are one and whole now. And who are you to chastise me, you who have drunk the life of thousands?"

"So I have. But they died before they knew something had happened to them. No pain. No fear. Not like this, not . . . ahhh . . . shaken and warped, mind and spirit, it's rape, you wouldn't know about that, would you? it's invasion and mutilation. Are you going to try telling me they . . . he . . . won't feel all that? Both of them? Are you going to try to tell me they'll take a look and say what the hell, I'll crip along on what's left? How can two minds live in one flesh without being destroyed by it?"

"That is for you to determine."

"What?"

"When Danny Blue wakes, Daniel Akamarino and Ahzurdan are going to be fighting for dominance within him just as the parts of me fought when I first began. You think I don't understand, Drinker of Souls? It took me five hundred years to reach a full integration of my parts. I can't afford to give him that much time and he won't live that long. You and the children together, you are capable of leading him, them, through this, healing him. You don't need instructions, do it."

Brann knelt looking down at Danny Blue. He was long and lanky, not a great deal of bulk to him though his muscles were firm and full. Ahzurdan's beard had vanished, but his hair (somewhat thinner than before, considerably grayer) filled in Daniel's baldness. The changes in the face were more subtle, fewer wrinkles, none of them so deeply graved as those Ahzurdan wore like badges of hard living, the lips were fuller than Daniel's had been but thinner than Ahzurdan's, the cheekbones a hair higher and broader than Daniel's but not so high and broad as Ahzurdan's, the rest of the changes were a thousand such midway compromises between the two men.

His body shuddered, his fingers jerked, began clawing at the sod, his lips and eyes twitched. His breathing turned harsh and unsteady. Brann bent over him, spread her hands on his chest. "Yaril, Jaril!"

With the children occupying her body and his and guiding her, Brann began the struggle to integrate the two minds. She couldn't see what the three of them were doing, only feel it; she groped blindly toward what she sensed as hotspots, paingeysers, cyclonic storms, working from an instinct that was an amalgam of her inborn unconscious bodyknowledge and the learned knowledge of the children (their understanding of their own bodies and minds, their considerable experience of the minds and bodies they indirectly fed upon). She was still seething with anger at being trapped into doing the Chained God's work; her fantasies about bargaining with him were fantasies indeed, about as useful and lasting as writing on water. His/its tampering with Ahzurdan and Daniel Akamarino put her in a position where there was only one thing she could do and continue to live with herself.

The work went on and on, images fluttered into her mind; she didn't believe they were dreams leaking from the disparate parts of Danny Blue, no, they were translations of emotion, perhaps concept, into images from her own stores, Ahzurdan had told her something like that when he was explaining how sorcerors developed their chants. *Black malouch snarling circling about black malouch, these malouchi with sapphire eyes, not gold.* She whined with angry frustration, every troublespot she soothed down seemed to birth two more. *Black hair blue eyes not black Temueng trooper with a serpent tail, rearing up, swaying, hissing, deadly, tensing to strike.* On and on. She saw the trouble under her touch gradually diminishing. Her anger drowned in a flood of fascination with what she was doing, with what was making itself under her fingers. *Blue water heaving, blue iris, blue hyacinth, blue lupin, blue flames, blue EYES blue and blue, blue glaze shining, look deep and deep and deep into a blue bluer than a summer sky, deep and deep.* . . . Her need to make was almost as deep-seated in her as her need to breathe. She labored over Danny Blue, blind fingered, eyes shut, shaping him, manipulating his clay, all thought of the Chained God pushed away so that the Danny Blue under her hands seemed her creation, almost as if she'd birthed him. *Thoughts (gnat swarms of blue sparks) in cloud shimmers blue funnels wobbling about each other, dipping toward each other, fragile, fearful, furious with hate, touch and shatter, struggling away, drawn back, always drawn back. . . .* On and on, spending her strength recklessly, no thought of the god and what other treacheries he might be planning, on and on making a man with all the art and passion in her. *Clay under her hands, blue clay fighting her, holding stubbornly to its imperfections, holding its breath on her, keeping the treacherous air bubbles locked in it, bubbles that would fracture it in the firing, stubborn, resisting, tough but oh so fine, so fine when she got the flaws out.* On and on until there were no more hotspots, no more images in blue, until the need that drove her drained away.

She broke contact and sat on her heels looking blearily down at him. He was asleep, snoring a little. She turned him on his side, shifted off her heels until she was sitting beside him on the grass. Jaril slid out of her, flickering from globe to boy, lay down a short way off, a naked youth molded in milkglass, she could see the jagged line of dark green grass through his legs. Yaril slid out of Danny Blue, crawled over to stretch out beside her brother, naked milkglass girl like she'd been when she rolled off Brann the day this all began, but older now with firm young breasts and broadening hips. Pale wraiths, they lay motionless, waiting passively for her to feed them or do something to restore their strength.

Brann rubbed at her back, lethargic, despondent. It had cost her, this scheme the godthing imposed on her, muscle tissue going with her energy to feed the reshaping of the man; there were some small lives in the trees and the undergrowth surrounding the glade, but they weren't worth the effort to chase them down, so, she thought, let him/it pay its share of the cost out of its own stores of godfire. She closed her eyes, her mouth twisting into a quick wry smile. He/it wasn't hovering over her, volunteering. Shuh! Amortis wasn't volunteering either, but she gave to this small charity want to or not. What's good for her is good for him/it. On hands and knees, Brann crawled to the children, worked her way between them so she could hold a hand of each.

Jaril. Yaril. Can you hear me?

We hear. Odd double voice in her head, charming harmonies that made her smile again, a softer wider smile this time.

Remember Amortis and the bridge. Do you think you could make the bridge again? I do hope so, otherwise I don't know how we're going to replace what's gone.

Can you feed us something? Just a little?

She looked at the skin hanging loosely about her forearms, then over her shoulder at Danny Blue. *Might be able to steal a bit from him. Let me take a sniff at him and see.* She dropped the hands, moved back to sleeping Danny, touched his arm. A lot of what she'd put into him had been eaten up by the drain of the alterations, but she could pull back a small trickle without damaging what she'd made.

When she'd fed the children, she frowned down at them. There was a faint flush of color in their bodies, but the grass was still visible through them. *That be enough?*

Jaril wrinkled his nose. Enough to tell us how much more we need.*

Yaril drew her knees up, shook her head, not in denial, more to show her unhappiness with the way things were. *Brann, we'd better draw hard and fast, this isn't really like with Amortis. He'll hit back soon as he understands what's happening and we don't have Ahzurdan to stand ward for us.* A swift ghost of a smile. *All right, I admit I was wrong about him.*

I hear. Hard and fast. A pause. Brann drew her tongue along her lips. *When I give the word.* She pulled her hands from the children, folded her arms, hugged them tight against her. She closed her eyes, squeezed them shut, memories of pain scratching along her nerves; it can't feel pain twice, but the body winces anyway when it knows that more is coming. For several

breaths she couldn't make herself say the word that
would bring that agony down on her. Finally she
straightened her back, her shoulders, lifted her head,
set her hands on her thighs. "Do it."

The children were glimmerglobes, paler than usual,
drifting upward.

The children touched.

The children merged.

The children whipped into a thin arc, one end deep
into the heart of the Chained God, the other sunk into
Brann's torso, she heard the shouted YES and pulled.

Godfire seared into her until she was burning, the
grass under her was burning, the air round her was
burning. She pulled until she was so filled with godfire
an ounce more would spill from her control and turn
her to ash and char.

The children sensed this and broke, tumbled to the
grass before her, pale glass forms again. They reached
for her, drew the godfire into themselves, drew and drew
until she could think again, breath again, move again.

The god raged, but Yaril and Jaril threw a sphere of
force about her until he/it calmed enough to reacquire
reason. "What are you doing?" he/it thundered at them,
the echoes of the multiple voices clashing and interfering until the words were garbled to the point of enigma.
"What are you doing? What are you doing?

The children dropped to the grass a short distance
from the sleeping body of Danny Blue; they sat leaning
against each other, looking into a vague sort of distance, displaying an exaggerated indifference to what
was happening around them. No. Not children any
more. Young folk in that uncertain gap between child-
hood and maturity, doing what such folk often do best,
irritatingly ignoring the crotchets of their elders, the
questions, demands, rodomontades of those who
thought they deserved respectful attention.

Brann rubbed her grilled palms on the cool grass,
glanced at the changers, wrinkled her nose. Due to the
convoluted workings of her fate, she'd skipped most of
that phase of her development; at the moment she was
rather pleased that she had. And rather shaken at the
thought she had to cope with it in Yaril and Jaril. She

pushed the thought aside and concentrated on the god who was still hooming unintelligibly. "If you'll turn the volume down," she said mildly, "perhaps I could understand what you're saying and give you the answers you want."

Silence for several minutes. When the god spoke, his/its boom was considerably diminished. "What were you doing?"

"Taking recompense," she said. "You asked me to do a thing, I did it. I spent my resources doing it, I nearly killed myself and the . . ." she looked at the changers, decided that *children* was no longer a suitable description, ". . . Yaril and Jaril. I simply took back what I used up."

More silence (not exactly utter silence, it was filled with some strange small anonymous creaks and fizzes, punctuated with odd smells). Finally, the god said, "I'll let it go this time, don't try that again."

"I hear," she said, letting him hear in her tone (if he wanted to hear it) that she was making no promises.

A pause, again filled with small sounds and loud smells. Lines of phosphor thin as her smallest finger spiderwalked about them, began passing through and through the sleeper, began brushing against her (she started the first time but relaxed when she felt nothing not even a tingle), began brushing against Yaril and Jaril who refused to notice them.

"When is Danny Blue going to wake?" The god's multiple voice sounded edgy. One of the phosphor lines was running fretfully (insofar as a featureless rod of light can have emotional content) around and around Danny Blue; it reminded Brann of a spoiled child stamping his feet because he couldn't have something he wanted.

"I don't know." Brann watched the phosphor quiver and suppressed a smile. "When he's ready, I suppose."

"Wake him."

"No."

"What?"

"You heard me. You've waited for eons, wait a few hours more. If you wake his body now, you could lose everything else."

"How do you know that?"

"I don't. Know it, I mean. It's a feeling. I'm not going against it, push or shove."

The air went still. She had a sense of a huge brooding. The god needed her to deal with problems that might arise after Danny Blue eventually woke, she was safe until then. Afterwards? She felt malice held in check, a lot of the Admiral left in him/it, if what he said about the Admiral was anything like the truth.

"You are fighting me every way you can. Why?"

"If you do or say stupid things, you expect me to endorse them? Think again. It's my life you're playing with, the lives of my friends. You want an echo, get a parrot." She scratched at her knee, sniffed at the stinking humid air, wrinkled her nose with disgust. "I'm hungry and he will be when he wakes. What you brought us here for is finished. Any reason we have to stay?"

The god thought that over for a while. Spiderlegs of phosphor flickered about Danny Blue, wove him into a cocoon with threads of light and took him away. Jaril shimmersphere darted after him, slipped through the walls with him. Yaril sighed, stretched. "Took him to Daniel's bedroom, dumped him in the bed."

Before Brann had a chance to say anything, the phosphor lines snapped back, wove a tight web about her and hauled her away, dumping her seconds later on the bed she'd slept in the night before. By the time she got herself together and sat up, Yaril was standing across the small room, watching her from enigmatic crystal eyes. She smiled at Brann and slid away through the doorfog. Brann grimaced, pushed off the bed onto her feet. She felt grubby, grimy. Good thing I can't smell myself. Hmm. Start the teawater boiling, if I can remember which whatsits I should push, then a bath. She rubbed a fold of her shirt between thumb and forefinger. Wonder how they did their washing? Maybe the kids know. Hmm. I'm going to have to figure some other way of thinking about them. Wonder if that godstuff's good for them, they're growing so fast. . . . I'd better take a look at Danny Blue. Ah ah the things that keep happening. . . .

Brann was stretched out on the recliner Jaril had deformed for her out of a lump on the floor of the egg-

room. A teapot steamed on an elbowtable beside her,
she had a cup of tea making a hotspot on her stomach;
she sipped at it now and then when she remembered it
while she watched a story stream past on a bookplayer
she balanced on her stomach beside the cup (the god
had translated several of these and presented them to
her, which surprised her and tended to modify her opinion of him/it, which was probably one of the reasons
he/it did it). Yaril drifted in, leaned over her shoulder
a moment, watching the story. "Brann."

"Mmm?"

"Danny Blue's restless. Jaril thinks he's going to wake
soon."

"How soon?"

"Ten, fifteen minutes, maybe."

"Hmm." Brann set the player down beside her,
shifted the cup to the elbowtable and pushed up. "He
showing any trouble signs?"

"Jaril says he's been having some nightmares, isn't
much to any of them, Jaril could only catch a hint of
what was going on, more emotion than imagery. That
stopped a short while ago. Jaril says it looks like he's
trying to wake up."

"Trying?" Brann stood, tucked her shirt down into
her trousers, straightening her collar. "That doesn't
sound good."

Brann bent over Danny Blue. His head was turning
side to side on the pillow in a twitchy broken rhythm;
his mouth was working; his hands groped about,
crawling slowly over his ribs, his face, the bed, the
sheet that was pulled across the lower part of his body.
She trapped one of the hands, held it still. "He's not
dreaming?"

Jaril was kneeling close to her, a hand resting against
the side of Danny's face, fingertips bleeding into him.
"No."

"What do you think?" She felt his hand flutter like
a bird within the circle of her fingers; using only a tiny
fraction of his strength, he was trying to pull away from
her. "Yaril, Jaril, should I let him kick out of it . . ."
she frowned as he made a few shapeless sounds, ". . . if

he can? Or should I jolt him awake? I don't like the way
he looks.''

Yaril leaned past her, her face intent, her hands moving through his body. She turned her head, stared for a
long moment into her brother's eyes, finally pulled free.
''We think you better jolt him, Bramble.''

Danny Blue snapped his eyes open and promptly went
into convulsions; he screamed, hoarse, building cries
that seemed to originate in his feet and scrape him
empty as they swept through his body and emerged from
his straining mouth. Brann, Yaril and Jaril held him
down, the changers reaching into him and soothing him
whenever they could snatch a second between his kicks
and jerks. Shivering, shaking, bucking, he struggled on
and on until they and he were exhausted and even then
he showed no sign he knew what was happening to him
or where he was. He lay limp, trembling, blue eyes
blank, looking past or through them.

Brann chewed her lip, spent a few moments feeling
helpless and frustrated. She wiped the sweat-sodden hair
off her face, tucked the straggles behind her ears and
stood scowling at him. Finally she bent over him,
slapped his face, the crack of her palm against his cheek
filling the small room. ''Dan!'' She flung the word at
him. ''Danny Blue! Stop it. You aren't a baby.'' She
rubbed the side of her hand across her chin, back-forth,
quick, angry. ''Listen, man, we need you. Both of you.
I know you don't have to be like this.''

He looked at her, the blankness burnt out of his face
and out of his eyes, replaced by bitterness and rage. He
swung his legs over the edge of the bed and pushed up.
He looked at her again, then sat rubbing at his temples,
staring at the floor.

''We need to talk, Dan. Can you work with Yaril and
Jaril to give us some privacy?''

''You couldn't wait?'' He spoke slowly, with difficulty, his mouth moving before each word as if he
had to decide which part of him was ordering his
speech.

''What's the point. Either you can or you can't, what

good will waiting do?'' She shrugged. ''Except to sour
you more than you are already.''

He opened his mouth, shut it. He draped his hands
over his knees and continued to stare at the floor.

''I'm not going to coax you,'' Brann moved to the
door, Yaril and Jaril drifting over to stand beside her,
''or waste my breath arguing with you. Make up your
own mind where you want to go. Don't take too long
about it either. We'll be in the sitting room figuring how
to walk out of this.''

A little over half an hour later Danny Blue ducked
through the doorway (he was a head taller than he'd
been two days ago) and strolled into the egg-shaped
sitting room. He was wearing Daniel's trousers, his sandals and his leather vest, Ahzurdan's black silk under-
shirt; he had Daniel's lazy amiability as a thin mask
over Ahzurdan's edgy force. He nudged a chair out of
a knot in the rug, kicked up a hassock; he settled into
the chair, put his feet up, crossed his ankles and laced
his fingers over his flat stomach. ''You can forget about
privacy,'' he said. ''Over in the reality where this ship
was built they had some mean head games. Very big on
control they were. Ol' god here, he's got a hook sunk
in my liver which says I'm his as long as he wants me.
I don't work against him, I don't help anyone else work
against him, I don't even think about trying to get away
from him. You can forget about sorcery or anything like
that, this has nothing to do with magic. Takes a machine to do it, takes a machine to undo it. So. There it
is.''

Brann drew her fingertips slowly across her brow as
if she were feeling for strings. ''I don't think,'' she said
slowly, ''I don't think it did it to me . . . um . . . us.
We did some things it didn't like . . . and . . . and we
didn't . . . there wasn't anything inside stopping us.
Yaril? Jaril?''

The changers looked at each other, then Yaril said,
''No. The god hasn't done anything we can locate in us
or you. We might be missing something that will show
up later, but we don't think so.'' She hesitated, took
hold of Brann's wrist. ''Being what we are, I don't think

we'd need machines to undo a compulsion the god tried
to plant in us, and Brann's linked very tightly with us.
I think . . . I don't know . . . I think we could undo
any knots in her head. I'm afraid we couldn't help you,
Dan. The connection isn't close enough.'' She shifted
her hand, laced up her fingers with Brann's. ''There's
something else, isn't there?''

Danny Blue uncrossed his ankles and got to his feet.
''I wanted to ask you, Brann, you and them, give me
some time before you push the god into doing something drastic. I, the two parts of me, we have to get an
idea what the god wants and what we can do about it.''

Jaril dropped beside Brann, took her free hand.
We'll watch, he said. *And we'll do some exploring
ourselves.*

*Be careful that thing doesn't learn more from you
than you do from it. Remember what happened before.*

We are not about to forget that, Bramble. The voice
in her head sounded grim. Yaril said nothing but the
same angry determination was seething in her, Brann
felt it like thistle leaves rubbing against her skin.

So we give him some time. Three days?

*Yes. That's good. And we'll keep the time, Bram-
ble, the god can make a day any length he wants. Tell
Dan three downbelow days.*

Downbelow days. Good. Brann relaxed and the
changers slid away. ''Three days, Dan,'' she said aloud.
''Three downbelow days.''

The outside door slid open, Danny Blue strolled into
the eggroom. He nudged a chair out of a knot in the
rug, kicked up a hassock; he settled into the chair, put
his feet up, crossed his ankles and laced his fingers
behind his head.

Brann looked up from the book she was scanning.
''Ready to talk?''

''Where are the changers?''

''They got bored staying in one place, I suppose
they're exploring the ship.''

He pulled his hands down, rested them on the arms
of the chair. ''You remember what I told you?''

''I remember.'' She laid the book aside. ''So?''

"Just keep it in mind. That's all. Chained God. He wanted to leave this pocket." He spoke quietly, calmly, more of Daniel showing than Ahzurdan, but behind that control he was raging; his eyes were sunk in stiff wrinkles, the blue was dulled to a muddy clay color, the lines from nose to chin were deeper than before, a muscle jumped erratically beside his mouth. "He's had to give up on that." A twitch of a smile. "His metal is too old and tired to take the stresses, the rest of him is too adapted to this space to survive the move." He pulled his hand across his mouth. "Think I could have a cup of that tea?" Another twisted smile as she snorted her disgust, but poured him out some tea and brought it to him with a brisk reminder that she wasn't his servant and didn't plan to make a habit of fetching and carrying for him. When she was seated again, he went on, "Using what Daniel knew and all the different things Ahzurdan had learned . . ." He sipped at the tea, rested the cup on the chair's arm. ". . . I have worked out a means of opening other gates, one in each of the Finger Vales; he'll have greater access to his priests and his people." He cleared his throat, anger had lodged a lump in his gullet it was hard to talk around. He gulped down most of the tea, lay back and closed his eyes. "That's for later. For now, I've managed to widen the gate on Isspyrivo; we can get out with less trouble than we had coming in, though we'll still have to use that aperture, the others won't be ready."

"We?"

He opened his eyes a crack. "Chained God has a deal for you."

"Why should I listen to anything it says?"

"Because he's got something you want."

"And what's that?"

"He can cut the cord that ties you to the changers."

"I see. Go on."

"Caveat first. He can keep you here as long as he wants, Brann. You can annoy him if you try hard enough, you might even hurt him a little, but he can kill you and drain the changers if you force it. He knows everything Ahzurdan knew about you, everything Daniel knew, he knows if he let you run loose, you'd find a way to make peace with Maksim. You've very like Maksim, did you know that? You think like him. There's a good chance you could talk him into slapping Amortis down so Kori's brother would be safe. Chained God doesn't want that. What he wants is BinYAHtii.''

''I won't have anything to do with that.''

''Why? Because it eats life? Like you?''

''I can handle the guilts I have. I don't want more.''

''Chained God says he'll reopen the changers' energy receptors so they can dine on sunlight again. And he'll do it before you leave here as a gesture of good faith.''

''What about sending them home?''

''He can't. He doesn't know their reality. Slya's the only one who does, you'll have to work that out with her.''

''Why should Yaril and Jaril trust him enough to let him fiddle with their bodies? Even if I do agree to his conditions.''

''YOU have more choice than Daniel Akamarino and Ahzurdan had. You can say no. THEY haven't. If you say yes, he won't bother asking their consent.''

''Exactly what would the god expect me to do?''

''Stop working against him. Go with me, help me. Persuade the changers to help. Coming here, we are an effective team. We could be one again.''

''If I say no, I spend the rest of my life here?''

''A part of it, how long depends.''

Brann grimaced, looked down at her hands. They were clenched into fists. She straightened her fingers, brushed her palms against each other. ''I. . . .'' She laced her fingers together, steepled her thumbs. ''I made a choice for Yaril and Jaril once, I made it out of ignorance and . . . well, no matter. I won't do it again. They'll have to decide this time.''

Two pairs of crystal eyes were fixed on her as she finished explaining the Chained God's offer. ''That's it,'' she said. ''It's your bodies, you decide what you want done with them.''

Abruptly Yaril and Jaril were glimmerglobes; they drifted up until they were near the ceiling. They merged and the double globe hung there pulsing.

Danny Blue prowled about the oval room, tapping the vision plates on and off as he passed them, looking at the yellow sky outside, the greasy wool that billowed around the ship, glancing between times at the globe. Brann sat on the recliner watching him. There was a stiffness to his movements that neither Ahzurdan nor Daniel Akamarino had had; she read that stiffness as anger he couldn't admit to because of the compulsion that thing had planted in him. She'd seen this before, in shopkeepers and landsfolk who could not show their rage or even let themselves know about it when an important customer was arrogant or thoughtless, when an ignorant exigent overlord made impossible demands on them. They beat their wives and children instead. She grew warier than before, wondering just how Dan was going to displace that anger and who his target would be. She had a strong suspicion it might be her. Before the merger Ahzurdan had not been liking her very much and Ahzurdan was in there somewhere.

The globe split apart, the parts dropped to the rug, Yaril and Jaril stood before Brann and Danny Blue looking angry, determined and a little frightened. Jaril stood with his hand on his sister's shoulder; he said nothing, Yaril spoke for them. "We'll take the chance, Bramble."

Brann held out her hands. "Come here." When they had their hands in hers, she thought, *It bothers me, you know that.*

Yaril: *Let the Valers take care of themselves. Isn't it time you thought about us?*

Brann: *More than time. You don't need to say it.*

Jaril: *Don't we?*

Brann: *No. You've decided, I acquiesce. What I'm saying is, help me. You know this thing, this god. Will it be worse than Maksim, feeding more and more lives to BinYAHtii? Or will it let the talisman sit, there to help it defend itself if the other gods attack?*

Jaril: *Remember what Ahzurdan said about Maksim, that he was possessive about his people? The god's a lot like that, maybe more so. Been breeding and coddling these folks for millennia, won't feed them to the talisman; outsiders though, they'd better watch out.* A quick grin, a squeeze of Brann's hand. *Just think about Slya and your own folk.*

Yaril: *What about this, Bramble? After this thing is over, we go find young Kori and tell her about Bin-YAHtii's habits; she can pass the word on to her folk. What they do about it is up to them. What about you, Jay? What do you think?*

Jaril: *One thing we don't want to do is say word one about this to Danny Blue.*

Yaril: *You're being obvious, brother. Of course not, talking to him's like talking direct to the god. You have anything helpful to add?*

Jaril: *Nope. 'S good enough for me.*

Brann: *It's the best we can do, I suppose.* She freed her hands. "I agree, Dan. Does it want me to swear?"

The Chained God's voice sounded from a point near where the double globe had floated. "Say what you will do, Brann Drinker of Souls. Specify your limitations and intentions. Swearing is not necessary."

Brann pulled in a lungful of air, exploded it out in a long sigh. "I will accompany Danny Blue and do what I can to help him, provided always that you do not harm Yaril and Jaril in any way and provided that they can truly feed themselves when you're finished with them. Is that sufficient?"

"Quite sufficient." Before the sound of the words had died away, Yaril and Jaril were gone from the room.

— 14 —

THEY START ON THEIR WAY TO SNATCH THE TALISMAN FROM THE SORCEROR.

SCENE: Dawn still red in the east, three mules standing nervously beside the cached supplies, mist thick and thin like clotted cream billowing and surging behind the man and the woman as they emerge from the steep-walled ravine.

Yaril and Jaril flashed from the mist and soared into the brightening sky, gold glass eagles spun from sunlight and daydream, laughter made visible joy given shape, swinging in wide circles celebrating the coming of the sun, the sun that was their nipple now, mother sun.

Danny Blue followed Brann from the clotted yellow mist to the stunted trees where she and his progenitors had cached the greater part of their gear. The mules were there, waiting, heads down, looking subdued and lightly singed. Slya's work, no doubt, adding her mite out of friendship or something. He moved up beside Brann and began shifting the concealing rocks aside. His mind felt as chaotic as the fog blowing about in the ravine, but his body was in good shape, he didn't have to think about what he was doing, his hands would go on working as his mind wandered. His flesh was charged and vital, his physical being hummed along at a level that Ahzurdan and Daniel Akamarino reached only when they were operating at peak in their various proficiencies. He swung a saddle onto a mule, reached warily under its belly for the cinch, drew it through the rings and used his knee to punch the swelling out of the mule so he could pull the strap tight. It was not as if two voices spoke within his head, no, more that the Composite-He would be musing about something and suddenly find himself thinking in an entirely different way about whatever it was, perhaps heading for a different outcome. And then his mind would shift again and he'd be where he was before. There was never any sense of coercion in this shifting. It was . . . well . . . like the interaction of two roughly parallel currents in a single river. As long as he rode the flow of those currents and didn't try to fight them, he could think competently enough about whatever engaged his attention. And as time passed the Composite-He took more and more control of the Composite Mind. He retained the full memories of both his progenitors, along with their talents and their training (his work for the god-in-the-starship had been ample evidence of that) but slowly and surely the being who did the remembering was becoming someone else. Blue Dan. Danny Blue. Azure Dan, the Magic Man. He tied the depleted grain sack behind the saddle and the blanket roll on top of that and went for the saddlebags.

The changers chased each other in endless spirals, singing their exuberance in their eagle voices; their connection to Brann and the ground seemed more and more tenuous as the sun appeared and finally cleared the horizon.

Danny Blue rode behind Brann, the leadrope of the third mule tied to a saddlering. He looked up at the changers and wondered how long they'd stay in sight and whether they'd keep their ties to Brann now that they no longer needed her to stay alive. He thought about asking her what she was thinking, but he didn't. Something in him was enjoying her tension and her quick sliding glances at the changers, something in him stood back and watched, uninvolved, unmoved; he thought that he disliked both of his progenitors, he thought they felt flat, one-dimensional. He was slaved to the god and he hated that, but he was beginning to

be glad that Danny Blue was alive and aware and riding
this mule along this mountainside, listening to the
crackclack of the mule hooves, the morning wind hush-
ing through the pines, the eagles screaming overhead,
feeling himself sweat and chafe and jolt a bit because
he still wasn't much good at riding mules. He began to
whistle a rambling undemanding tune, thought of getting out Daniel's recorder but let the impulse slide away
with the glide of the song.

One of the eagles came spiraling down, changed to a
slight fair young man the moment he touched ground.
Brann's back lost its rigidity as her mule halted and
stood with ears twitching nervously. "We thought we'd
better ask," Jaril said. "The god printed a map for you,
but maybe you'd like us to scout out the best ground
ahead till we get to Forkker Vale?"

"We could move faster that way." Brann threaded
her fingers through her hair. "Can Yaro get high enough
to see Haven? That thing said there wasn't a ship due
for a week at least, I don't know why it'd lie, the faster
we can get to Maksim, the less chance he'll have to
make trouble for us, the sooner it could have its talisman, but I'd feel easier with some corroboration."

No longer golden glass but a large brown and white
raptor, the eagle overhead climbed higher, vanishing
and reappearing as she passed through drifts of cloud
fleece.

Jaril tilted his head back and followed her with his
eyes. "The sea is empty all round far as Yaro can see.
Not even a smuggler out. Haven is pretty much still
asleep. There are some fishboats out working nets, she
sees a few women near the oven stoking it up so they
can bake the day's bread, the hands are busy with cows
and whatever on the near-in farms. Nobody's hustling
more than usual. That's about it."

"Ah well, it was a chance." Brann rubbed at her
chin. "You want to run or ride?"

"Ride." He walked to the third mule, waited until
Dan untied the lead rope, swung into the saddle and
moved to ride beside Brann. "Yaro says Slya's sitting
on top of Isspyrivo turning the glacier into steam; she's
watching us."

Brann chuckled. "She'll freeze her red behind if she does that for long."

"Or flood out Haven. The creek from the crack runs down to the sea right there."

She yawned. "Somehow I find it hard to care right now." She thrust her hand into the bag by her knee, pulled out a paper cylinder, unrolled it and held it open along her thigh. "Hmm." She rode closer to Jaril, tapped the nail of her forefinger against a section. "Looks like we'll have to take a long jog about this, unless it's not so deep as it looks. What's this?"

"It's a young canyon all right. I don't know what that blurry bit is." He was silent a minute, then he nodded. "Yaro's gone to check it out. Be about twenty minutes' flying time."

Brann examined the map a few moments longer, then let it snap back into its cylinder and slid it in the bag.

Danny Blue watched Brann and the changer youth and felt a twinge of jealousy. The affection he saw between them had survived and more than survived the cutting of the chains that held them in servitude to each other; he had half-expected the changers to vanish like a fire blown out once they were free of her; when he saw their aerobatic extravagances he thought they were gone. He was wrong. A loving woman, a passionate one. The strength of the ties she forged with those alien children was evidence of that, he had more evidence of what she was in his memories. He remembered the feel of her back, the way she reacted to Daniel's hands, his mouth twitched into a crooked smile as he remembered with equal clarity how quickly and completely Daniel shut off the flow of that passion.

He watched Brann's back (the feel of it strong in his hands) and observed his own reactions. Ahzurdan had more hangups than a suitlocker, Daniel had only a moderate interest, enjoying sex when it was available, not missing it all that much when it wasn't. From the way Danny Blue's body was sitting up and taking notice, he was going to have to change his habits. He sucked in a long breath, exploded it out and tried to think of something else before the saddle got more uncomfortable than it was already.

Jaril reached over, touched Brann's arm. "Yaro's got there. She says the blur you saw is a bridge over that ravine, a smuggler's special, she says from on top and even up close it looks like a couple down trees with some vines and brush growing out of them, but she went down and walked on it and it's solid. The mules won't have any problem crossing it even if it's dark by the time we get there and it probably will be."

"Anything between here and there that might give us problems?"

"She says she doesn't think so. Trying to read ground from the air can be tricky, you've got to remember that, especially as high as Yaro was flying, but she says the smuggler's trace is fairly obvious and if we keep to that we shouldn't have more problems than we can handle. She's spotted a spring she thinks we can reach before it gets too dark if we start moving some faster, if we keep ambling along like this, we'll have a dry camp because there's no water between here and there."

"I hear. Go ahead and show us the trail, will you?"

Jaril nodded, pulled ahead of them. He increased his mule's pace to an easy trot as he followed the inconspicuous blazes cut at intervals into tree trunks as big around as the bodies of the mules. They'd long since passed the areas where the battles with Settsimaksimin and his surrogate elementals had torn up the ground, the mountainside was springy with old dried needles, little brush grew between giant conifers that rose a good twenty feet above their heads before spreading out great fans of branch and pungent needle bunches, there was room for the mules to stretch their legs without worrying about what they'd step into.

They rode undisturbed that day, stopping briefly to grain and water the mules and snatch a bite for themselves, starting on again with less than an hour lost. They reached Yaril's spring about an hour after sundown. She had a small sly fire going and was prowling about in catshape, driving off anything on four legs or two that might want to investigate the camp too closely. No one said much, aloud at least; what the changers were saying to each other, they kept to themselves and did not break the silence about the fire. Brann rolled into her blankets after she ate and helped clean up the camp; as far as Danny Blue could tell she didn't move until she woke with the dawn. He had more difficulty getting to sleep, his muscles were sore and complaining, his mental and physical turmoil kept his mind turning over long after he was bored with every thought that climbed about his head, but he had two disciplines to call on and eventually bludgeoned his mind into stillness and his body into sleep.

The days passed because they had to pass, but there was little to mark one from another; they rode uphill and downhill and across the smuggler bridges with never a smell of Settsimaksimin. Even the weather was fine, nights cool, days warm with just enough of a breeze to take the curse off the heat and not a sign of rain. Now and then they saw a stag or a herd of does with their springborn fawns; now and then, on the edges of night and morning brown bears prowled about them but never came close enough to threaten them. Blue gessiks hopped about among the roots and shriveled weeds, broad beaks poking through the mat of dead needles for pinenuts and borer worms; their raucous cried echoed from hillside to hillside as they whirled into noisy bluff battles over indistinguishable patches of earth. Gray gwichies chattered at each other or shook gwichie babies out of pouches close to being too small for them and sent them running along whippy tarplum branches for late hatching nestlets or lingering fruit.

On the fifth day or it might have been the sixth, shortly after dawn when shadows were long and thin and glittered with dew, they dropped through an oak forest to the grassy foothills along the side of Forkker Vale.

Jaril and Yaril rode first, Jaril in the saddle, Yaril behind him, clinging to him. Their new dependence on the sun for sustenance had wrought several changes in how they ran their lives. In a way, they were like large lizards, they got a few degrees more sluggish when the sun went down unless they took steps to avoid it. They were still adjusting to the change in their circumstances; staying with Brann on this trek, with its demands on them and the dangers that lay ahead of them wasn't helping them all that much.

Down on the floor of the Vale a line of men walked steadily across the first of the grainfields, scythes swinging in smooth arcs, laying stalkfans flat beside them, a line of women followed, tieing the stalks into sheaves, herds of children followed the women, some gathering sheaves into piles, others loading those piles onto mulecarts and taking them down along the Vale to the storesheds and drying racks at the threshing floor. The men were singing to themselves, a deep thoated hooming that rose out of the rhythm of the sweep, hypnotic powerful magical sound. The women had their own songs with a quicker sharper rhythm, a greater commensality. The children laughed and sang and played a dozen different games as they worked, counting games and last one out and dollymaker as they gathered and piled the sheaves, jump the moon and one foot over and catch as they swung the sheaves around, tossed them to each other then onto the stakecarts, running tag and sprints beside the mules. It was early morning, cool and pleasant, boys and girls alike were brimming with energy. It was the last golden burst of exuberance before winter shut down on them. Or it was before the strangers appeared.

As Brann, the changers and Danny Blue rode past them on the rutted track, the Forkker folk looked round at them but no one spoke to them, no one asked what they were doing there or where they were going. And the children were careful to avoid them.

Ahzurdan's memories prodded Danny Blue until he heeled his mule to a quicker trot and caught up with Brann. "Trouble?"

"Maybe." She scratched at her chin. "It could be local courtesy not to notice folk coming from the direction of Haven. I don't believe a word of that. Jay." He looked over his shoulder, dusty and rather tired, the sun hadn't been up long enough to kick him into full alertness. "Could you or Yaro put on wings and take a look at what's ahead of us?"

"Shift here?"

"Why not. A little healthy fear might prove useful."

Yaril stretched, patted a yawn, yawned again and slid off the mule; she ran delicate hands through her ash blond hair, shivered like a nervous pony, then she was an eagle powering into a rising spiral.

They started on, moving at a slow walk. A mulecart rattled past them, the children silent, subdued, wide frightened eyes sliding around to the strangers, flicking swiftly away.

Danny Blue watched the cart jolt away from them, the mule urged to a reluctant canter, the sheaves jiggling and shivering. Several fell off. Two boys ran back, scooped them up and tossed them onto the cart. A swift sly ferret's look at the strangers, then they scooted ahead until they were trotting beside the mule, switching his flanks to keep him at the faster pace. "They've been warned about us," he said.

"Looks like it. Jay?"

"Yaro is looking over the village. It's pretty well empty. Those houses are built like forts, an army could be hiding inside them. Each house has several courtyards, they're as empty as the streets, Yaro says that about confirms trouble ahead, at this hour there should be people everywhere, not just in the fields. She thinks maybe we should circle round the village, she says she saw shadows behind several of the windows, the streets, well, they aren't really streets, just openspaces between housewalls, they're narrow and crooked with a lot of blind ends, it's a maze there, if we got into it, who knows what'd happen. There's problems with circling too, orchards and vineyards and a lot of clutter before we'd get to the trees, makes her nervous, she says. Ah. Soldiers in the trees, left side . . . um . . . right side. Not many. She says she counts four on the left, six on the right, Kori said there were a doubletwelve in Owlyn Vale, there won't be fewer here, that leaves what? about fourteen, fifteen in the village. She says it won't be that difficult for her and me to take all of them out if we could use Dan's stunner. Question is will the Forkker folk mix in this business? If they do, things could get sticky, there are too many of them, they can swamp us given we have a modicum of bad luck. What do you

think?'' Jaril opened his eyes, looked from Brann to
Danny Blue, raised his brows.

Danny Blue thumbed the zipper back, squeezed out
the stunner; he checked the charge, nodded with satisfaction, tossed the heavy black handful to Jaril.
''Chained God topped off the batteries, but don't waste
the juice, Jay, I'd like to have some punch left when we
get to where we're going.''

Jaril caught the stunner. ''Gotcha. Brann?''

''Yaro read Kori back when . . . Jay, was that her or
you asking about the Forkkers? You? What does she
think?''

''Um . . . she thinks they're in a bind. They don't
like Maksim or his soldiers, but they don't want him
landing on their backs either, especially not over a
bunch of foreigners. She says if we go through fast and
they don't see much happening, they'll keep quiet. She
says she's changed her mind about going round the village now that she thinks about it. She says thinking
about it, we've got to put all the soldiers out, we don't
want them stirring up the Forkkers and setting them
after us. She says Brann, she can read a couple Forkkers
to make sure, if you want. And Dan, she says, whatever, it's up to you. The stunner's yours.''

Danny Blue ran his tongue around his teeth, scratched
thoughtfully at his thigh. ''Can you singleshot the soldiers? It'd cut down the bleed if you don't have to spray
a broad area.''

''She says the ones in the trees will be easy, she'll
mark them for me, so I can do them while she's hunting
out the ones ambushed in the village. She says what
she'll do is globe up and pale out, go zip zap through
all the houses, be done with that before they know
what's happening. Once she's got the village ones spotted, unless there's too many of them or they're in places
I can't get the stunner into, I should be able to plink
them before they get too agitated.'' A quick grin. ''Too
bad the stunner won't go through walls.''

''Too bad.'' Danny glanced over his shoulder at the
workers in the waist high grain. They weren't working
anymore, they were gathered in clumps, stiff and omi-
nously silent, watching Jaril, Brann and him as they

rode at a slow walk along the dusty track. "You might as well get at it. All I say is remember we've got a long way to go yet."

Danny Blue tied the leadrope of the third mule to the ring, watched the man-handed eagle fly off toward the trees. Brann was looking sleepy, unconcerned. The wind was blowing her hair about her face. You can almost see it grow, he thought, I wonder why she cut it so short. Her body moved easily with the motion of the mule, she was relaxed as a cat. A wave of uneasiness shivered through him (the shefalos hook operating in him), cat, oh yes, and he didn't know how she'd jump.

He fragmented suddenly, Ahzurdan and Daniel Akamarino resurrected by their powerful reactions to Brann, a gate he'd opened for them. They were still one-dimensional, his progenitors, reduced to a few dominant emotions closely related and thoroughly mixed whose only stab at complication was a vague fringe of contradictions that trailed away to nothing. Ahzurdan glowered at Brann, a glaresheet of nauseous yellow, hate, resentment, frustration. Daniel pulled himself into a globe, iceblue, dull, rejection irritation numblust. Danny Blue was nowhere, shards scattered haphazard around and between the fragments of his sires.

Cool/warm touch on his arm. "Dan?" Warm sweet sound dancing across his nerve ends, echo re-echo chitter chatter flutter alter alto counterplay countertenor contralto confusion diffusion refusion dan dan dan dan. . . .

A surge of heat. The bits of Danny Blue wheeled whirled jabbed into the glaresheet (broke it into sickly yellow puzzle pieces) jabbed into the globe (shattered it to mirrored shards, slung them at the yellow scraps) the bits of Danny Blue wheeled whirled, gathered yellow gathered blue, heat pressure need glue bits shards scraps, moulage collage—Danny Blue is whole again, a little strange the seams are showing, but it's him, yes it's him, singly him. He blinked at Brann, at her hand on his arm. He wrapped fingers (warm again his again) about hers, lifted her hand, moved his lips slowly softly across the smooth firm palm. He cupped her hand against his cheek. "Thanks."

Buffered by a taut silence that the thud of mule hooves on the muffling dust only intensified, they rode at a fast trot through the village following a large bitch mastiff while the man-handed eagle flew sentry overhead. The soldiers slept and the Forkker folk did nothing, the riders and the changers fled unhindered down along the Vale, past other grainfields waiting for the reapers, past fields of flax and fiberpods, past rows of hops clattering like castanets in the breeze, past tuber vines already dug, waiting, drying in the hot postsummer sun. The hills closed in, the road moved onto the left bank of Forkker Creekr. At the mouth of the Vale where the stone bridge crossed that creek, a small stone fort sat high on a steep hillside, overlooking the bridge and the road. The mastiff trotted past it without stopping, the eagle circled undisturbed overhead. Brann and Danny Blue crossed the bridge without being challenged and left the Vale.

15

SETTSIMAKSIMIN SITTING IN HIS TOWER, WATCHING WHAT HURRIES TOWARD HIM AS HE HURRIES TO SHAPE WHAT'S TO BE OUT OF WHAT IS NOW, WORKING MORE FROM HOPE THAN EXPECTATION, SHAPING CHEONEA.

SCENE: Settsimaksimin in the Star Chamber, the council he'd constituted some weeks before breaking up after a long meeting, the members stretching (inconspicuously or not, according to their natures), several chatting together, the end-of-the-teeth inconsequentialities power players use to pass dangerously unstructured moments that push up like weeds even in the most controlled of lives. Stretching or chatting they stroll toward the door.

"T'Thelo, stay a moment."

The Peasant Voice looked over his shoulder, came back to the table. "Phoros Pharmaga."

Settsimaksimin waved a hand at a chair, turned his most stately glare on the rest of the council as they bunched in the doorway, reluctant to leave one of their number alone with him. Todichi Yahzi set his book aside and shambled across the room. He herded the councilmen out and shut the door, returned to his plump red pillow, picked up the red book and got ready to record.

T'Thelo was a small brown tuber, at once hard and plump with coarse yellow-white hairs like roots thin on his lumpy head. His hands were never still, he carried worry beads to meetings and when he felt like it would whittle at a hardwood chunk, peeling off paper thin curls of the pale white wood. He seldom said much, was much better at saying no than yes, looked stubborn and was a lot more stubborn than he looked.

Maksim let himself slump in his chair and turned off the battering ram he used as personality in these council meetings. He reached under his robe and under Bin-YAHtii, rubbed at his chest. "You know my mind," he said.

T'Thelo grunted, pulled out his worry beads and began passing them between thumb and forefinger.

Maksim laughed. At first the sound filled the room, then it faded to a sigh. "They're going to want to know what I told you," he said. "I'd advise silence, but I won't command it. I've a battle coming at me, T'Thelo. A man, a woman and two demons riding at me from the Forkker, despite all I've done to stop them. A battle . . . a battle . . . I mean to win it, T'Thelo, but there's a chance I won't and I want you ready for it. You and the other landsmen, you'll have to fight to keep what you've got if I go down. The army will be a problem, keep a close watch on the Strataga and his staff; they're accustomed to power and are salivating for more, they resent me for shunting them from the main lines of rule, hmm, perhaps half the younger officers would support you in a pinch, don't trust the Valesons, matter of fact you'd do well to send them home, but most of the footsoldiers come from landfolk on the Plain, be careful with them, the army's had the training of them since they were boys, it means as much or more to them as their blood kin, and they've had obedience drilled into them, they'll obey if they're ordered to walk over you even if their mothers and sisters are in the front line. The Guildmaster and his artisans will back you if given

a choice, they remember too well how things were when
the Parastes held the reins. So will the Dicastes, they
lose if you lose. There are a lot of folk with grudges
about, especially the parasite Parastes still alive and
their hopeful heirs. Be careful with Vasshaka Bulan, I
know the landsmen don't like the Yrons or the Servants
or Amortis all that much, but it's better to have them
with you than against. I can't tell you how that tricky
son will jump, but I know what he wants, T'Thelo.
More. That's what he wants. More and more and more.
Not for himself, I'll give him that, for Amortis, he calls
himself Her Servant and, Forty Mortal Hells, he means
it. So that's a thing to watch. Keep your local Kriorns
and their Servants friendly, T'Thelo, they're not pup-
pets, they're men like you, I've seen to that. The Yron
has schooled them, but I've schooled them too. Keep
that in mind." He fell silent, gazed past the Voice at
the far wall though he wasn't seeing wall or anything
else. "We're not friends, T'Thelo, you'd see me burned
at the stake and smile, and as for me, you annoy me
and you bore me, but for all that, T'Thelo, we share a
dream. We share a dream." His voice was soft and pen-
sive, a deep burrumm like a cello singing on its lowest
notes. "Five days, T'Thelo, it takes five days to ride
from Forkker Vale to Silagamatys. It isn't time enough
for much, but do what you can. I expect to win this
battle, T'Thelo, they're coming to ME, they will be
fighting on MY ground. But there's a battle coming that
I won't win. It's one you'll fight soon enough, my un-
friend, you know which one I mean. When I com-
menced the shaping here, I thought I'd have a hundred
years to get it done, aah hey, not so. Three, five, seven,
that's it, that's all. I release you from any duties you
have to me, Voice, make your plans, weave your web,
woo your Luck. And be VERY careful who you talk to
about this."

T'Thelo sat a moment staring at the string of wooden
beads passing between his callused work-stiffened fingers; he'd had them from his father who'd had them
from his, they were dark with ancient sweat, ancient
aches and agonies, ancient furies that had no other place
to go. He rubbed his thumb across the headbead larger

than the rest, darker, looked up. "Give me a way to get word to the Plain."

Maksim snapped his fingers, plucked a small obsidian egg from the air. He set it on the table, gave it a push that took it across to T'Thelo. "The word is PE-TOM', it calls a ge'mel to you." He smiled at the distaste visible in T'Thelo's lined face. "A ge'mel is a friendly little demon about the size of a pigeon, it looks like a mix between a bat and a bunch of celery and it's a chatty beast. Worst trouble you'll have with it is getting it to shut up and listen to instructions. It can go anywhere between one breath and the next, all you have to do is name the man you're sending it to and think about him when you name him. When you've finished with the ge'mel, say PI'YEN NA; that'll send it home. Any questions?"

T'Thelo looked at the egg. After a long silence, he put his worry beads away, reached out and touched the stone with the tip of his left forefinger. When it didn't bite him, he picked it up, looked at his distorted reflection in the polished black glass. "Petom'," he said. His voice was nearly as deep as Maksim's but harsher; though it could burn with hard passion, that voice, it could never sing, an orator's voice, an old man's voice beginning to hollow with age.

The ge'mel flicked out of nothing, sat perched on the richly polished wood, its oval black eyes lively and shining with its demon laughter; its face was triangular, vaguely batlike, it had huge green jade ears with delicately ragged edges that matched the greenleaf lace on its tailend. Its wings were bone and membrane, the membrane like nubbly raw silk, green silk with tattered edges. Its body was lined and ridged, almost white about the shoulders, growing gradually greener down past the leg sockets until the taillace was a dark jade. Its four standing limbs were hard and hooked, much like those of a praying mantis, its two front limbs had delicate three-fingered hands with opposable thumbs. It held its forelimbs folded up against its body, hands pressed together as if praying. "Yes yes, new master," it said; its voice was a high hum, not too unlike a mosquito whine, but oddly pleasant despite that. "What do you wish? I, Yimna Himmna Lute, will do it. Oyee, this is a fine table.'' It pushed one of its hind limbs across the wood, making a soft sliding sound. ''Lovely wood.'' It tilted its little face and twinkled at T'Thelo. ''Are you an important man, sirrah? I like to serve important men who do important things, it makes my wives and hatchlings happy, it gives them things to boast of when the neighbors visit.''

Maksim chuckled. ''Now how in modesty could the man answer that, Yim? I'll do it for him. Yes, little friend, he is a very important man and the work he gives you will be very important work, it might save his land and his people from a danger coming at them.''

Yimna Himmna Lute bounced happily on its hind-limbs, rubbed its dainty hands together. ''Good good splendid,'' it fluted. Wings fluttering in the wind of its impatience, it fixed its black beady eyes on T'Thelo (who was rather disconcerted since he had nothing for Yim to do at the moment, having called up a monster to get a look at it, only to find there was nothing monstrous about the little creature; he'd had chickens a lot more alarming and certainly worse tempered.)

''Unruffle, Yim. The man just wanted to meet you, be introduced, as it were. Voice T'Thelo meet Yimna Himmna Lute, the swiftest surest messenger in all realities. Yim, meet Hrous T'Thelo, Voice of the Landmen of Cheonea.'' He waited until T'Thelo nodded and Yimna finished its elaborate meeting dance, then said, ''Voice T'Thelo, now that the introductions are complete, perhaps you could send Yim back home while you think out and write out the messages you want it to carry for you.''

T'Thelo blinked, raised tangled brows. Yim gave him another elaborate bow, coaxing a reluctant smile from him. The Voice rubbed his thumb across the smooth black obsidian, thought a moment, said, ''Pi'yen Na.''

Little mouth stretched in a happy grin, Yim whiffed out like a snuffed candle.

''Cheerful little git,'' T'Thelo said. He pushed his chair back, stood. ''I thank you, Phoros Pharmaga, I will not waste your warning.'' He followed Todichi

Yahzi to the door, gave a jerk of a bow like an after-thought and went out.

Todichi Yahzi came back and stood before Maksim; his deepset eyes had deep red fires in them. "I have served you long and well, Settsimaksimin, I have not made demands beyond my needs," he sang in his humming garbled Cheonese, "I do not wish to leave you now, but if you die how do I go home?"

"Todich old friend, did you think I had forgot you?" Maksim got to his feet, stretched his arms out, then up, massive powerful arms, no fat on them or flab, he yawned, twiddled his long tapering fingers, held out a hand. "Come, I'll show you."

The bedroom was at once austere and cluttered; Todichi Yahzi clucked with distress as he followed Maksim inside. It'd been weeks since he'd been let in to clean the place. The bed was a naked flocking mattress in a lacquer frame, sheets (at least they were clean) and thick soft red blankets twisted into a complex sloppy knot and kicked against the wall. A blackened dented samovar on a wheeled table was pushed against the frame near the head of the bed, a plate with flat round ginger cookies, a sprinkle of brown crumbs and the remnants of a cheese sandwich sat on the floor by the table. A book lay open beside it, turned face down. Robes, sandals, underclothes, towels, scrolls of assorted sizes and conditions and several leather pillows were heaped on or beside rumpled rugs. Maksim crossed to a large chest with many shallow drawers. He opened one, poked through it, clicked his tongue with annoyance when he didn't find what he was looking for, snapped the drawer shut and opened another. "Ah ah, here we are." He lifted out a fine gold chain with a crooked glass drop dangling from it. "Here, Todich, take this."

Todichi Yahzi held the drop in his dark leathery palm, looked down at it, gleams of purple and brown flickering in his eyes.

"When you know I'm dead, throw the drop in a fire; when it explodes, you go home. Don't try it while I'm still alive, won't work. And ah don't worry about it breaking, it won't. I've been meaning to give you that for months, Todich.'' He lifted his braid off his neck and swiped at the sweat gathered there, rubbed his hand down his side. ''Every time I thought of it, something came up to distract me. You understand what to do?''

Todichi Yahzi nodded, closed his fingers tight about the drop. His chest rose, fell. After a tense silence, he sang, ''May the day I burn this be many years off.'' He looked around, shuddered. ''Maksim friend, will you please please let me clean this . . . this room?''

A rumbling chuckle. ''Why not, old friend. I'll be below.''

Todichi fluted a few shapeless sounds, fidgeted from foot to foot. ''I will work quickly. And you, my friend, you take care, don't spend yourself to feed your curiosity, come back and rest, eat, sleep.''

Maksim smiled, squeezed Todichi's meager gray-furred shoulder with gentle affection, snapped to his subteranean workroom.

Danny Blue yawned, smiled across the fire at Brann. This night was much darker than the last, clouds were piling up overhead, wind that was heavy with water lifted and fell, lifted and fell, there was a sharp nip in the air, a threat of frost come the morning. She was seen and unseen, face and hands shining red-gold when the dying flames flared, slipping into shadow again when they dropped. Made irritable by the electricity from the oncoming storm, the changers were out in the dark somewhere, male and female mountain cats chasing each other, working off an excess of energy as they ran sentry rounds about the camp. ''He doesn't seem to care that we're in the Plain.''

Her knees were drawn up, her forearms rested on them, she held a mug of tea with both hands and was sitting looking down at it, her face empty of expression as if her thoughts were so far away there was no one left behind the mask. When he spoke, she lifted her head, gazed thoughtfully at him. ''Is that what you think?''

''Me? Think? Who am I to think?''

She gave him a slow smile. ''Ahzurdan I think, hmm?''

"Ahzurdan is dead. Daniel Akamarino is dead. I'm Azure Dan the magic man, Danny Blue the New. Three weeks old, alive and kicking, umbilical intact, chain umbilical welded in place, no surgeon's knife for me; the Chained God jerks and I dance, don't I dance a pretty dance?"

"A personal, intrusive god isn't so attractive now, hmm?"

"It's like trying to reason with a tornado, you might come out of the experience alive but never intact. And whenever you try, you don't make a dent in the wind."

She smiled, a slow musing smile that irritated him because it seemed to say *I have, I have dented a god more than once, Danny Blue, when you talk about wind, whose wind do you mean?* She said nothing, looked at her mug with a touch of surprise as if she'd forgotten she was holding it. She sipped at the cooling tea and gazed into the puzzle play of red and black across the coals of the little fire. She was strong, serene, contented with who and what she was, she had already won her battle with the god, she'd got what she wanted out of him, freedom for herself and the changers, all she was doing now was paying off that debt; anger flashed through him, a bitter anger that wanted to see her bruised, bleeding, weeping, groveling at his feet; part of him was appalled by the vision, part of him reveled in it, all of him wanted to break the surface of her somehow and get at whatever it was that lay beneath the mask. "Sleep with me tonight."

"I smell like a wet mule."

"Who doesn't. What you mean is not before the children."

"What I mean is, what you see is what you get."

"If I didn't want it, would I ask for it?"

"Would you?"

"You keep your hands off my soul and I'll keep mine off yours, it's your body I want."

She smiled, slid her eyes over him. "It's a point. Why not."

"A little enthusiasm might help."

"A little more Akamarino in the mix might help."

"I thought you didn't like him much."

"I liked his hands, not his mouth, rather what came out his mouth."

"Akamarino is dead."

"You said that."

"You don't seem to believe it."

"I do, Dan. I don't like thinking about it, I. . . ." Her mouth twisted. "Why not. No doubt the god knows quite well how I feel. Somehow I'm going to make it hurt for that, Dan. I don't know how right now and I wouldn't tell you if I did. You intend to keep talking?"

Maksim lay stretched out in his tiltchair, watching the mirror, listening to the conversation. His hair hung loose about his shoulders, the sleeveless workrobe was pulled carelessly about him, a fold of it tucked between BinYAHtii and his skin, his legs were crossed at the ankles and his fingers laced loosely across his stomach. The chair was set parallel to the table so he could reach out and touch the mirror if he wished. For the past several days he'd been snatching scarce moments between conferences to watch what was happening in the mountains and the Forkker Vale, puzzled for a while by the male figure who rode with Brann and the changers. The mirror followed him as if he were Ahzurdan, yet he was not, he was at least a span taller, he was broader in the shoulders, his face was different, though there were hints of Ahzurdan in it as if this man might have been one of his half-brothers. Several times Maksim had focused the mirror on his face, but he couldn't get it clear, the lines blurred and wavered, the closer he got the less he could see, though he could hear most of what the man said. That blurring was something he associated with Daniel Akamarino when he joined Brann and Ahzurdan in Silagamatys. By the time they reached the Vale Maksim had an idea what the Chained God had done, though he couldn't wholly accept where his logic led him, it seemed so unlikely and he couldn't dredge up a reason for doing it, but listening to this hybrid Danny Blue announce the deaths of the men that made him, he had no choice, he had to believe it. Why was it done? What did it mean? He brooded over those questions as he watched Danny Blue get to his feet, move

round the fire to join Brann on her blankets. There was
that odd and effective weapon Daniel had brought with
him from his reality. *I'll have to get that away from him
somehow before they get here.* He watched the maneu-
verings that combined caresses with the shedding of
clothing and decided that trousers were a nuisance he
was pleased to have avoided most of his life. The vest
went. *It's in there, in one of those pockets.* He leaned
over, tried to focus the mirror on the vest but the blurring was worse than with the man. *They're close
enough, maybe I can.* . . . He reached for the vest and
tried to snap it to him. He couldn't get a grip on it. He
hissed with annoyance and returned the mirror to its
former overlook. *They'll be on the Plain early tomorrow,* he thought, *what do I do about that? I think I leave
it to T'Thelo and whatever he contrives. Ha! Look at
that, oh, Baby Dan, you're not so dead after all, I know
your little ways, oh yes I do. . . .*"

"Dan, I'm here too." When he didn't bother listening to her, she pushed his hand off her breast and started
wriggling away from him.

He caught one of her wrists, pinned it to the ground
beside her shoulder, slapped her face lightly to let her
know who was in charge. He grinned at her when she
relaxed, laughed in triumph when she stroked his face
with her free hand. That was the last thing he saw or
felt.

When he woke, his head was wet, there were jagged
pebbles and twigs poking him in tender places, a damp
blanket was thrown over him. Brann dropped the depleted waterskin beside him and stalked off. She was
dressed, her hair was combed and she looked furious
but calm. She sat down on the blanket she'd moved
across the fire from him and watched him as he chased
the fog from his head.

"I was raped once," she said. "Once. I wasn't quite
twelve at the time, I was tired, sleeping, I didn't know
what was happening to me but I wanted it to stop, so I
stopped it. I got a lot more than an ounce of jism from
that man, Dan, something you should remember. The

kids dumped his body in the river for me. Ahzurdan, if you're in there somewhere, you also should remember what happened to your grandfather when he decided it was a good idea to slap me around. Do you know why you're alive? Don't bother answering, I'm going to tell you. I pay my debts. When I say I'll do something, I do it. Damn you, Dan, that's the second time you've got me wound up and left me hanging. Believe me, there won't be a third time. I'm a Drinker of Souls, Danny Blue, get funny with me and you'll ride to Silagamatys in a vegetable dream.''

Maksim smiled as he watched Danny Blue sleep; the hybrid twitched at intervals; at intervals he moved his lips and made small sucking sounds like a hungry baby. Across the dead fire, Brann was in her blankets, sleeping on her side, knees drawn up, arms curled loosely about them, her pillow the waterskin, newly plumped out from the river nearby; now and then there was a small catch in her breath not quite a snore and she was scowling as if no matter how deeply she slept she took her anger with her. ''I like you, Drinker of Souls, Forty Mortal Hells, I do, but I wish you smudged your honor some and let Baby Dan chase you off. AAAh! I owe him a favor, a favor for a lesson, no no, more than a lesson, it's a warning. You don't get within armlength of me, Brann, you or your changeling children.''

A long lean cat slipped through the camp, nosed at the sleeping man, went pacing off, a whisper of a growl deep in his? yes, his throat. ''Hmm, I wouldn't want to be in your sandals, Danny Blue, the changers are not happy with you. Aaah! that's an idea, good cat gooood, next time through you might let your claws slip a little, yes yes?'' He got heavily to his feet, thumbed off the mirror and snapped to his rooms.

Todichi Yahzi was whuffling softly in a stuffed chair, having gone to sleep as he waited for Maksim to return. Maksim bent over him, smiled as he caught the glint of gold in the short gray fur on his neck; Todich was wearing the chain. Maksim shook him awake. ''Now what are you doing, Todich? Go to bed. I'll do the same soon as I've had my bath.''

Todichi yawned, worked his fingers. "Yim showed up with a message from T'Thelo," he humspoke. "Sent it to me not you because mmmm I think he was frightened of what Yim might carry back to him. He said Servant Bulan wanted mightily to know what you said to him, said he said you wanted him, T'Thelo, to assemble a report on the village schools, that you said it was important right now to know how the children were doing, what the teachers and landsmen were thinking. He's slyer than I thought he was, that old root, I thought you were making a mistake talking to him like that. He said that he, T'Thelo, is going to do that along with the rest, it will be a good camouflage for the other things he has to do, besides it's something that needs doing." He passed his hand over his skull, smoothing down the rough gray fur that was raised in ridges from the way he'd been sleeping. "The scroll Yim brought is in there on the bed, there's some more in it, but I've given you the heart of the matter. Mmmm. I sent a stone sprite to overlook Bulan, he called his core clique at the Grand Yron to the small meeting room off his quarters, he harangued them some about loyalty, said some obscure things about a threat to Amortis and the Servant Corps and told them to send out Servants they could trust to visit the Kriorns of all the villages to find out what's happening there. The Strataga went nightfishing with his aides, I sent some ariels to see what he was up to, but you know how limited they are and the Godalau was swimming around near harbormouth, they don't like her and won't stay anywhere near her. So I don't know what they were saying, they were still out when I went to sleep, I made a note of which ariels I sent, you can probably get a lot more out of them than I could. The Kephadicast did a lot of pacing, but he didn't talk to anyone, he wrote several notes that he sealed and sent out to Subdicasts here in Silagamatys, asking them to meet with him day after tomorrow, I haven't a notion why he's putting the meeting off that long. Harbormaster went home, ate dinner, went to bed. No pacing, no talking, no notes. I wrote all this up, every detail I could wring out of the watchers, Maksim. The report is on your bed beside T'Thelo's note. The next council

meeting is tomorrow afternoon, what do you want me
to do about all this mmmm?''

''Go to bed, Todich, you've done more than enough
for tonight. I've got to think.'' Todichi Yahzi looked
disapproving, pressed his lips tight as if he were holding back the scarifying scold he wanted to give. Maksim
chuckled, a deep burring that seemed to rise from his
heels and roll out of his throat. He stretched mightily,
yawned. ''But not tonight, old friend, tonight I sleep.
Go go. Tomorrow I'll be working you so hard you won't
have time to breathe. Go.''

Unable to sleep though he knew he should, Maksim
pulled a cloak about his shoulders, looked down at the
naked legs protruding dark and stately from his nightshirt, laughed and shook his head. ''Be damned to dignity.'' He snapped to the high ramparts and stood
looking down over his city.

Clouds were blowing up out of the west and the moon
was longgone, it was very dark. Silagamatys was a nubbly black rug spread out across the hills, decorated here
and there with splotches and pimples of lamplight and
torchfire except near the waterfront where the tavern
torches lit the thready fog into a muted sunset glow.
The Godalau floated in the bay's black water, moving
in and out of the fog, her translucent body lit from
within, Tungjii riding black and solid on her massive
flank. She drifted past Deadfire Island, a barren heap
of stone out near the harbor's mouth; her internal illu-
mination brushed a ghostly gray glimmer over its basalt
slopes. She passed on, taking her glimmer with her and
Deadfire was once more a shadow lost in shadows.
Maksim leaned on the parapet, looking thoughtfully at
the black absence. I let them leave my city and I lost
them. Mmm. Might have lost them anyway and half the
city with them. Deadfire, Deadfire . . . yes, I think so.
He laughed softly, savoring the words. Live and die on
Deadfire, I live you die, Drinker of Souls and you,
Danny Blue. Let the Godalau swim and Tungjii gibber,
they can't reach me there, and your Chained God, hah!
Brann oh Brann, sweet vampire lass, don't count on him
to help. The stone reeks of me, it's mine, step on it and

it will swallow you. He reached through the neckslit of
the nightshirt and smoothed his hand across BinYAHtii.
You too, eh? Old stone, that's your stone too, you've
fed it blood and bones. There's nothing they've got that
can match us . . . mmm . . . except those changers, I'll
have to put my mind to them. Send them home? Send
them somewhere, yesss, that's it, if they're not here,
they're no problem. He stroked BinYAHtii. It might take
Amortis to throw them out, Forty Mortal Hells, the
Fates forfend, I'd have to figure a way to implant a spine
in her. He gazed down at the city with an unsentimental
fiercely protective almost maternal love. Blood of his
blood, bone of his bone, his unknown M'darjin father
had no part in him beyond the superficial gifts of height
and color, his mother and Silagamatys had the making
of him. Amortis! may her souls if she's got them rot in
Gehannum's deepest hell for what she's done to you my
city. To you and to me. If I did not still need her. . . .
He shivered and pulled his cloak closer about his body.
The rising waterheavy wind bit to the bone. Out in the
bay the Godalau once more drifted past Deadfire. Maksim pushed away the long coarse hair that was whipping
into his mouth and eyes. That's it, then. We meet on
Deadfire, Drinker of Souls, Danny Blue. Four more
days. That's it. He shivered. So I'd better get some
sleep, I've underestimated the three now two of you
before, I won't do it again.

They reached the Plain by midmorning, emerging
from a last wave of brushy, arid foothills into a land
lushly green, intensely cultivated, webbed between its
several rivers by a network of canals that provided ir-
rigation water for the fields and most of the transport
for produce and people. Brann and Danny Blue rode
side by side, neither acknowledging the presence of the
other, an unbroken tension between them as threatening
as the unbroken storm hanging overhead. The changers
flew in circles under the lowering clouds, probing with
their telescopic raptor's eyes for signs that Settsimaksimin was attacking, signs that held off like the storm was
holding off.
   The day ground on. The hilltrack had turned into a

narrow dirt road that hugged the riverbank, a dusty rutted weed-grown road little used by anything but straying livestock. Out in the river's main channel flatboats moved past them, square sails bellied taut, filled with the heavy wind that pushed them faster than the current would. Little dark men on those boats (hostility thick on dark skin, glistening like a coat of grease on a kisso wrestler's arms and torso) glared at them out of hate-filled dark eyes. In the fields beside the road and the fields across the river landfolk worked at the harvest, men, women, children. Like the boatmen they stopped what they were doing, even those far across the river, and turned to glower at the riders.

The hangfire storm continued to hover, the storm smell was strong in the air. Whether it was that or the hate rolling at them from every side, by nightfall the mules were as skittish as highbred horses and considerably more balky. Yaril and Jaril vanished for a while, came back jittery as the mules; they flitted about overhead long after Brann and Danny Blue stopped for the night, camping in a grove of Xuthro redleaves that whispered around them and sprayed them with pungent medicinal odors as the heat of the campfire lifted into the lower branches.

Danny Blue rested his teamug on his knee and cleared his throat. Brann gave him no encouragement. A catface came into the light, crystal eyes flashing a brilliant red, the cat stared at him for an uncomfortably long time, then withdrew into the darkness; he couldn't forget it was out there not one minute and while that was comforting in one way, in another it turned his throat dry thinking about the changers pacing and pacing in their sentry rounds, feral fearsome beasts angry at the world in general and at him in particular. He gazed across the fire at Brann who was in her way quite as lethal. "I'm sorry about last night," he said.

She nodded, accepting his apology without commenting on it.

"I do fine," he said, "as long as it's the rational side of me called up. Or the technical side. Doesn't matter who's running the show, Akamarino or Ahzurdan or me.

It's emotions that screw me up, ah, confuse me. Ah, this isn't easy to talk about. . . ."

She looked coolly at him as if to say why bother then, looked down at her hands without saying anything.

Anger flared in him, but he shoved it down and kept control, him, Danny Blue the New, not either of his clamoring progenitors. "When it's strong emotions, well, Daniel avoided them most of his life, couldn't handle them, which gives Ahzurdan an edge because he played with them all since he was born, anger, you know, lust, frustration, resentment, he's loved a maid or two, a man or two, been wildly happy and filled with cold despair, too much passion, his skin was too thin, he had to numb himself, dreamsmoke washed out the pain of living, you know all that, you heard all that on the trip here. He has ambivalences about you, Brann, growing all over him like a fungus, I suppose I should say all over me. That's the problem, I can't control him when there's emotion involved. Think about it a minute. How old is Danny Blue? Three weeks, almost four, Bramble-all-thorns . . ."

Her head came up when she heard the name the changers sometimes gave her. "Don't call me that."

"Why not, it suits you."

"Maybe it does, maybe not. My name is Brann and I'll tell you when you can call me out of it." She twisted up onto her knees, touched the side of the teapot, refilled her cup and settled back to her blankets. She sipped briefly at the hot liquid, then sat with her legs drawn up, her arms resting on them, both hands wrapped around the cup as if she needed the warmth from it more than the taste of tea in her mouth. "Do me a favor," she said, "experiment on someone else." She gazed at the fire, the animation gone out of her face, her eyes shadowed and dull. After several moments of unhappy silence, she shivered, fetched a smile from somewhere. "You still think you want me when you've combed the knots out, I expect I'd be fool enough to try again. At least you already know what I am. What a relief not having to explain things." She gulped at the tea, shivered again. "Looks like everyone about knows where we're going and why."

"And they don't like it."

"And they don't like it. Yaril, Jaril," she called. "One of you come in, will you?"

The ash blond young woman came into the firelight, tall and slim, limber as a dancer, crystal eyes shadowed, reflecting fugitive glimmers from the dying fire. She glanced at Danny Blue, her face bland as the cat's had been, showing nothing but a delicately exaggerated surprise at seeing him there. He grinned at her, Daniel uppermost now and finding her much to his taste, an etherial exotic lovely far less complicated and demanding than Brann; watching her settle beside Brann her shoulder and profile given to him, he wondered just how far she'd gone in taking a human shape and what it'd feel like making love to a skinful of fire, hmm! who was also a contact telepath. Now that's rather offputting. Gods, Ol' Dan, you're hornier 'n a dassup in must. And neither of them's going to have a thing to do with you and it's your own damn fault. Talk about shooting yourself in the foot, huh, that's not where the bullet went. Say this is over and you survive it, you'll have to hunt up a whore or three and argue old Ahzurdan into a heap of ash so you can get your ashes hauled. Till then I guess it's the hermit's friend for you if you can get yourself some privacy, shuh! as Brann would say, to have those changers come on me and giggle at what I'm reduced to . . . uh uh, no way. A little strength of mind, Danny Blue, come the morning, dunk yourself in that river, that should be cold enough to take your mind off.

"A while back," Yaril said, "Jay and I, we decided we wanted to know what all the glares were about, so we paled out and probed a few of those peasants out there. They've had news about us from Silagamatys, all of them, farmers boatmen you name it. They're trying to think of some way to stop us. They don't know how so far, the ones we checked were thinking of sneaking up on us when we're asleep and knocking us in the head or something like that, maybe setting up an ambush and plinking us with bolts from crossbows, so far they haven't nerved themselves into trying anything, it was mostly wish and dream, but they surely wouldn't mind if we fell in the river and drowned. They're worried

about Settsimaksimin, if anything happened to him the
wolves would be down on them from all sides. They
love the man, Bramble, sort of anyway, he's mixed up
in their heads with the land, everything they feel for the
land they feel for him, it's like when they're plowing
the soil, they're plowing his body. They pray for him,
and, believe me, they'll fight for him. Any time now
we're going to start running into big trouble. Probably
tonight. I wouldn't be surprised if some of the wilder
local lads tried their hands with bullkillers or scythe
blades. Probably around the third nightwatch, I doubt
if they'll come sooner and later it'd be too light.''

''You and Jay can handle them?''

''Hah, you need to ask? Braaaann.'' She clicked her
tongue, shook her head, finally sobered. ''You want us
to wake you?''

''As soon as you see signs of trouble, yes. We want
to get the mules saddled and the supplies roped in place
in case we have to leave fast.''

''Gotcha, Bramble. Anything else?''

''Um . . . what's the land like ahead?''

''Pretty much more of the same for the first half day's
ride, another river joins this one a little after that, hard
to tell so far off but I think there's some sort of swamp
and the road seems to turn away from the river. You
want Jay or me to go take a look?''

Brann frowned at the fire. ''I don't . . . think so. No.
I'd rather you rested. Take turns with Jay. How are you
doing on energy? It was a cloudy day. Give me your
hand a minute. Good. That god didn't change you so
much you can't take from me, I thought a minute it
might have, self-defense, you know, so we couldn't
build the bridge again and suck godfire out of it, but I
suppose it wanted to be sure we could handle Amortis
if she poked her delicate nose in the business with Maksim.''

''You needn't worry about us, Bramble, our batteries
are charged, matter of fact we've been pretty well steady
state since we left the ship.''

''Happy to hear it, but tired or not, you and Jay both
operate better after a little dormancy, I think it's like

with people, you need your sleep to clear out the day's confusion. So, you rest, both of you, hear?''

Yaril giggled. ''Yes, mama.'' She got to her feet and walked with lazy grace out of the circle of firelight.

Danny Blue yawned. ''Looks like Maksim's made himself some friends.''

''You could try helping us a bit. I agree with Yaro; we're bound to run into trouble; I'd like to know more about that and how you're going to help deal with it.''

''That depends on the attack, doesn't it?''

''I don't know, does it?''

''In a word, yes. Trouble, mmm. Maksim's got earth and fire elementals tied to him and an assortment of demons. You've met some of those.'' A quick grin. ''Demons aren't too big a problem, you send them home if you know where home is and I know most of the realities Maksim located because Ahzurdan knew and I've got his memories.'' A lazy stretch, a yawn. ''Flip side.'' When she raised her brows, not understanding, he murmured, ''The good of having Ahzurdan in here. As opposed to the problems he causes.'' He took a sip of the tea left in his mug, grimaced. ''Stone cold.'' He poured it out on the ground beside him and managed to squeeze another half mug from the teapot nestled next to the fire. ''Which reminds me, one of the things Maksim might try is tipping the changers into another reality; it's something I'd do if I could. If he managed that, he could really hurt our chances of surviving. Something else . . .'' He gulped at the tea, closed his eyes as warmth spread through him. ''It's a plus and a minus for us, Ahzurdan might have told you this (I'm a little hazy here and there on my sires' memories), the top rank sorcerors don't often fight each other, no point and no profit. They tend to avoid taking hires that might oblige them to confront an equal. He'd argue this, but I don't think Ahzurdan is one of them. Might be close but the impression I get is he lacked a certain stability.'' His body jerked, he looked startled, then grim. He set the mug beside him with careful gentleness, pressed his lips together and slapped his hands repeatedly on his knee until the nagging itchy under-the-skin pains faded away. ''He didn't like that.'' He finished off the tea,

wiped his mouth. "Where was . . . yes. What I'm saying is, Settsimaksimin has never been in a war with
someone as strong as him or close to it. We've both
seen it, he doesn't like to attack. He'll make individual
strikes, but he won't keep up the pressure and I don't
believe it's because he can't. He's a warm man, he likes
people, he needs them around him and he's generous,
if I'm reading the Magic Man right. Aaah, yes, what
I'm saying is his peers are all frogs in their own ponds,
they don't want to share their how shall I say it? ahhh
adulation. He's like that in some senses, he wouldn't
tolerate anyone who pretended to equality with him, but
he's got friends in the lower ranks and among the scholars who don't operate so much as study and teach, more
of them than you might expect. Ahzurdan's not typical
of his ex-students either, poor old Magic Man (uhnn!
there he goes again), but even he can't hate the man.
That's one of his problems, shahhh! apparently it's mine
too. I'd say this, if we hurry him, don't give him time
to set himself, there's that little hiccup between thought
and act we could use to our advantage. No matter how
he nerves himself, attack isn't natural to him, his instinct is to defend. Which is a potent reason for making
sure he doesn't flip the changers off somewhere. Amortis wouldn't have that drag on her, her instinct is to stomp
first then check out what's smeared on her foot. He
knows his limitations better than any outsider making
funny guesses. He'll use BinYAHtii to drive her against
us. She's afraid of you, Brann, you and the changers,
and she loathes you and she loathes Maksim for con-
straining her, all that fear and rage is waiting to dump
on you . . . ahh . . . us. With the changers we should
be able to deflect it onto Maksim and let him worry
about it. Without them . . . I don't like to think of facing him without them."

She bit into her lower lip, frowned at the fire a moment, looked up at him. "How do we stop it?"

Danny Blue unwrapped his legs and lay back on his
blankets; he gazed up at the spearhead leaves fluttering
over him, the patches of black sky he could see in open-
ings between the branches. "I don't know. I have to
think. I might be able to block him if I have a few

seconds warning. If the changers start feeling odd or if they see sign of Amortis, they should get to me fast.'' He yawned. ''Morning's soon enough to tell them.''

''Why not now?''

He pushed up on his elbow, irritated. Her face was a pattern of black and red, he couldn't read it, but when could he ever? ''Because I don't know what to say to them yet.'' His irritation showed in his voice and that annoyed him more.

She got to her feet. ''Then you'd better start your thinking, Danny Blue. I'll be back in a little.'' She walked into the darkness where Yaril had gone, a prowling cat of a woman radically unlike the changer, slender but there was bone in her and good firm muscle on that bone. He remembered her hands, wide strong working hands with their long thumbs and short tapering fingers, he remembered Ahzurdan looking at them disturbed by them because they represented everything he resented about her, her preference for low vulgar laboring men, her disdain for wellborn elegance, for the delicacy of mind and spirit that only generations of breeding could produce, her explosive rejection of almost everything he cherished, he remembered even more vividly the feel of those hands moving tantalizingly up Daniel's arms, stirring the hairs, shooting heat into him. He pushed up, slipped his sandals off and set them beside his blankets, then stretched out on his back and laced his hands behind his head. ''Yes,'' he said aloud. ''Thinking time.''

Toward the end of the third nightwatch six young men in their late teens slipped from the river and crept toward the redleaf grove. Jaril spotted them as he catwalked in ragged circles about the camp. To make sure these young would-be assassins were all he had to worry about, he loped through one last circuit; reassured, he woke Yaril and left her to rouse the others while he shifted to his shimmerglobe. He considered a moment, but the impulse was impossible to resist; he'd wanted to try a certain repatterning technique since he'd sat on Daniel's stunner and sucked in the knowledge of what it was. He made some swift alterations in one part of his being, suppressed the excited laughter stirring in him and went careening through the trees, a sphere of whitefire like a moontail with acromegaly. He hung over the youths long enough to let them get a good look at him, then he squirted force into his metaphorically re-wired portion and sprayed them with his improvised stunbeam. He watched with satisfaction as they collapsed into the dust.

Yaril glimmersphere drifted up to him. *Nice. Show me.*

It's based on Daniel's stunner. You do this. Then this. Right. One more twist. Good. That's the pattern that does it. Remember, keep the lines rigid. Like that. And you cyst it. I didn't at first and look what I've done to myself, that's going to be sore. It gulps power, Yaro, but you don't have to hold it more than a few seconds.

Now we won't have to depend so much on Danny Blue. I like that, I like it a lot.

Agreed.

Why didn't you try it before?

No point. Besides, if Maksim knew about it too long before we got to him, he just might figure out a way of handling it. Remember what Ahzurdan said, this is heartland for him, I don't doubt he can overlook most of it easy as an ordinary man looks out his window.

Gotcha. Do you really think Maksim is going to try tipping us into another reality?

Brann does. Don't you?

We'll have to keep wide awake, Jay. When I leave this reality, I want it to be my idea and I don't want to be dumped just anywhere, I want to go home.

Bramble's next quest, reading Slya's alleged mind?

If we can work it. Talk to you later. She's coming.

Brann walked into the pale grayish light they gave off, squatted beside one of the young men. She pushed her fingers under his jaw, smiled with satisfaction when she felt the strong pulse. "Good work, Jay. How long will they be out?"

Jaril dropped and shifted, held out his hand. When Brann took it, he said, *Don't know. I finagled a version of the stunner, haven't done this before so it's anybody's guess. They could wake up in two minutes or two hours.*

I hear. Useful.

More useful if nobody knows exactly what happened.

Nobody being Maksim umm and Danny Blue?

You got it. Or that Yaro can do it too, now.

*Anything else? No? Good. We'll tie our baby assassins up to keep them out of mischief, fix some breakfast and get an early start. From now on I suppose we can expect *anything* to happen.* She freed her hand. "Yaro, flit back to camp and fetch us some rope hmm?"

Yaril dropped and shifted. "Sure. Need a knife?"

"Got a knife."

The Plain emptied before them. Boatmen brought their flatboats upriver and down into the throat of the Gap, mooring them to rocks and trees and to each other, a barrier as wide as the river and six boats deep. Landfolk poured into the hills between Silagamatys and the Plain, the greater part of them gathering about the Gap where the river ran, interposing their bodies between the threatening and the theatened. Some stayed behind. When Brann and Danny Blue came to the marshes, hidden bowmen shot at them. The changers ashed the arrows before they reached their targets. Spears tumbled end for end into the sedges when Danny Blue snapped his fingers, slingstones whipped about and flew at the slingers who plunged hastily into mucky murky swamp water.

Aware that Amortis was not going to march to war for them, that weapons would not stop the hellcat, her sorceror and her demons, the landfolk left their homes and their harvests and in an endless stream walked and rode into the hills, a stubborn angry horde determined to protect their land and their leader. It was a thing the Parastes never understood or acknowledged, the lifetie between the small brown landfolk and the land they worked, land that held layer on layer on layer of their dead, land they watered with their sweat and their blood. These grubbers, these strongbacked beasts, these self-replicating digging machines, they owned that land as those elegant educated parasites the Parastes never would, no matter how viciously and vociferously they claimed it. Much of what Settsimaksimin did after he took Cheonea linked him in the landfolk mind to the land itself and its dark primitive power. When he gave them visible tangible evidence of their ancient ownership, when he gave them deeds written in strong black ink on strong white parchment, it struck deep into their two souls. The idea of the land wound inextricably about the idea of Settsimaksimin and he became one for them with that black and fecund earth, himself huge, dark and powerful.

The land itself fought them. A miasma oozed from the earth and coiled round them when they slept, breeding nightmares in them, humming in their ears go away turn back go away turn back. Coiled round them when they rode, burning their eyes, cocooning them in stench, whispering go away turn back go away turn back. The hangfire storm was oppressive, it was hard to breathe, crooked blue lightning snapped from fingertips to just about anything they brushed against. The mules balked, balked again, exasperating Brann because she had to jolt each one every time they did it. The ambushes kept on happening, a futile idiotic pecking that accomplished nothing except to exhaust Danny Blue who had to keep his shield ready, his senses alert. Amortis had laid a smother across the Plain, more oppressive for him than the storm; each time he had to flex his magic muscle he was working against an immense resistance. By the end of the day he was so depleted he could barely hold himself in the saddle.

The third morning on the Plain. Left in pastures unmilked, cows bawled their discomfort. Farmyard dogs barked and whined and finally sated their hunger on fowl let out to feed themselves while their owners were gone. Aside from those small noises and the sounds they made themselves, there was an eerie silence around them. The harvest waited half-gathered in the fields, the stock grazed or stood around, twitching nervously, the houses were empty, unwelcoming, no children's laughter and shouts, no gossiping over bread ovens or laundry tubs, no voices anywhere. No more ambushes either.

Danny Blue sighed with relief when the morning passed without a stone flung at them, but the smother was still there, pressing down on him, forcing him to push back because it would have crushed him if he didn't.

Night came finally. They stopped at a deserted farmhouse, caught two of the farmer's chickens, cooked them in a pot on the farmer's stove with assorted vegetables, tubers and some rice. It was a small neat house, shining copper pots hanging from black iron hooks, richly colored earthenware on handrubbed shelves, the furniture in every room was crafted with love and skill, bright blankets hung on the walls, huge oval braided rugs were spread on every floor, and it was a new house, evidence of the farmer's prosperity. After supper three of them stretched out on leather cushions around the farmer's hearth while the fire danced and crackled and they drank hot mulled cider from the farmer's cellar. Jaril was flying watch overhead.

Yaril sighed with a mixture of pleasure and regret; she set her mug on her thigh, ran her free hand through her pale blond hair. "We'll reach the hills sometime late tomorrow afternoon," she said. "There's a problem."

Brann was stretched out half on a braided rug, half on Danny Blue who was leaning against an ancient chest, a pillow tucked between him and the wood. He opened heavy eyes, looked at Yaril, let his lids drop again. "How big?" he murmured.

"Oh, somewhere around ten thousand folk sitting on those hills waiting for us."

His eyes snapped open. "What?"

"Miles of them on both sides of the river. One shout and we've got hundreds pressed around us, maybe thousands."

Brann sat up, her elbow slamming into Dan's stomach. She patted him, muttered an offhand apology, turned a thoughtful gaze on Yaril. She said nothing.

Dan crossed his ankles, rubbed the sore spot. "The river?"

"Boatmen. Flatboats. Roped together bank to bank, six rows of them, more arriving both sides. Nets strung under them. Bramble, you and Danny Blue are going to have to be very very clever unless you plan on killing lots of landfolk.''

Brann got to her feet. ''Us? What about the two of you?'' She strolled to the fireplace and stood leaning against the stone mantel.

Yaril set the mug down, scratched at her thigh. ''We already tried, Bramble. You know how there started to be nobody anywhere? Not long after that Jay and I saw lines and lines of landfolk moving across the Plain. Jay flew ahead to see what was happening and came back worried. We tossed ideas around all afternoon. You know what we came up with? Nothing, that's what. It's up to you. We quit.''

Danny Blue went downcellar and fetched another demijohn of cider. He poured it into the pot swung out from the fire, tossed in pinches of the mulling spices, stirred the mix with a longhandled wooden spoon. Brann and Yaril watched in silence until he came back to the chest that he was using as a backrest, then, while the cider heated, the three of them went round and round over the difficulties that faced them.

BRANN: We could try outflanking them.

YARIL: Plan on walking then, the terrain by those hills is full of ravines and tangles of brush and unstable landslips. Mules can't possibly handle it.

DANNY (yawning): Don't forget Amortis; with Maksim to point her, she can snap up a few hundred bodies and drop them in front of us and do it faster than we can shift direction.

BRANN: You said she's afraid of the changers and me.

DANNY: Sure, but she wouldn't have to get anywhere near you, she could do all that from Maksim's tower in the city.

BRANN: Shuh! There's a thought there, though. What about you, Dan? If she can snap a couple hundred over a distance of miles, surely you can do the same with two over say a dozen yards. Enough to take you and me past them.

DANNY: Get rid of Amortis first, then sure. Other-

wise, with the smother getting heavier as we get closer
to the hills, just breathing is going to make me sweat.

BRANN: Then you'd better busy yourself deciding what
you can do now. Yaro, what about you and Jay? How
many could you stun how fast?

YARIL: Jay and I working together, um, couple dozen
a minute. Listen, that won't work, same reason it
wouldn't work going round them. With that many sitting on those hills, there's bound to be one or two we
miss who lets out a yell and there we are, nose-deep
in landfolk. Another thing you better think about, you
can't get through them without riding up to them
somewhere, announcing your interest as 'twere, and
once that's done, guess what else is going to happen.
Bramble, Jay and I, we went round and round on this.
Remember how the Chained God shifted you and
Danny's sires poppop back and forth across that ship?
We thought about that, we thought about it so much
we just about overheated our brains. We figured
Amortis could do the same if she took a notion to,
so you and Danny have to cross the line without getting close to it. We figured we could gnaw on that
idea till we went to stone without getting anywhere.
We figured we can fly across with no difficulty, it's
you and Danny here who have the problem, so it's
you and Danny who have to come up with the answer.

DANNY: Roll back a sec, stun them? since when and
how?

YARIL: Um, Jay took a look at your stunner, remember? He figured a way to repattern a part of his body
to produce the same effect, he powered it from his
internal energy stores, tested it on those baby assassins. You saw the results.

DANNY: So I did. Repatterning . . . mmm.

While Brann and Yaril chewed over the problem of
acting without being seen to act, Danny Blue withdrew
into himself to track down a wisp of an idea. Once upon
a time when Daniel Akamarino was very new among
the stars and still feeling around for what and who he
was, he signed onto a scruffy free trader called the Herring Finn and promptly learned the vast difference be-

tween a well-financed, superbly run passenger line and
the bucket for whose engines he was suddenly responsible. And not only the engines. He was called on to
repair, rebuild or construct from whatever came to hand
everything the ship needed of a propulsive nature. One
of those projects was a lift sled for loading cargo in
places so remote they not only didn't have starports,
they very often didn't have wheels. He'd rebuilt that
thing so many times it was engraved into his brain. And
with a little prodding Danny Blue found he could retrieve the patterns. From his other progenitor he culled
the memory of his lessons in Reshaping, one of the
earliest skills a Sorceror's apprentice had to master.
Hour on hour of practice, until he could shut his eyes
and make the shape without error perceptible to the
closest scrutiny which he got because Settsimaksimin
was a good teacher whatever other failings he might
have. There was still the problem of power. He decided
to worry about that after he knew whether or not he
could shape a sled. I need something to work on, he
thought, something solid enough to hold Brann and me,
but not too heavy.

He got to his feet and wandered through the house.
The beds were too clumsy, besides they were mainly
frame and rope with a straw paillasse for a mattress and
billowing quilts. He fingered a quilt, thinking about the
nip in the air once the sun went down, shook his head
and wandered on. Everything that caught his eye had
too many problems with it until he reached the kitchen
and inspected the hard-used worktable backed into an
alcove around the corner from the cooking hearth. The
tabletop was a tough ivory wood scarred with thousands
of shallow knifecuts, scrubbed and rubbed to a surface
that felt like satin; it was around twelve centimeters
thick, two meters wide and three long (from the posi-
tioning of the cuts at least eight women gathered about
it when they were making meals or doing whatever else
they did there). He fetched a candle, dropped into a
squat and peered at the underside. Looks solid, he
thought, have to test it. Hmm, those legs . . . if they
don't add to much weight, they might be useful, some
sort of windscreen . . . mmm, the front four anyway,

whichever end I call front . . . how'm I going to get this thing out where I can see what I'm doing? Ah! talking about seeing, I'm going to have to set up a shield. If I can. He rose from the squat, set the candle on the table and hitched a hip beside it, unwrapped and began to finger his anger, his resentment of the constraints laid on him, his frustration. Daniel Akamarino went where he wanted when he wanted, Ahzurdan was constrained only by his internal confusions, whatever he wanted or needed he had the power to take if some fool tried to deny him. Danny Blue was too young an entity to know much about who and what he was, but he resonated sufficiently with his progenitors to feel a bitter anger at the Chains the god had put on him. He felt the compulsion clamp down on his head when he tried to give voice to that anger; he could not do, say or even think anything that might (might!) work against the god. He knew, though he had deliberately refrained from thinking about it, that he suffered the smother without trying to fight it because it offered—or seemed to offer—an escape for him, a way he could thwart the god without having to fight the compulsion. After the landfolk shut down their ambushes, he'd ridden relaxed under it exerting himself just enough to keep from being crushed, smiling out of vague general satisfaction as the weight of the smother increased and the possibility of action diminished. He carried that satisfaction into dinner and beyond, but somewhere in the middle of the discussion, he lost it. The Hand of the God came down on him harder than the smother, *find the answer, find it, no more dawdling, I'll have no more excuses for failure, failure will not be permitted. Get through that line however you can, stomp the landfolk like ants if you have to, do whatever you have to, but bring me BinYAHtii.*

He wiped the sweat off his face, beat his fist on the tabletop until it boomed, working off some of the rage that threatened to explode out of the cramping grip of the god and blow the fragile psyche of Danny Blue into dust. He might be young and wobbly on his feet, but he had a ferocious will to survive. Not as Ahzurdan, not as Daniel Akamarino. As Danny Blue the New.

"What is it? What's wrong?"

He looked up. Brann was standing in the arch of the alcove looking worried. He opened his mouth to explain but his tongue wouldn't move and his throat closed on him. It was forbidden to think, do or say anything against the god. His face went hot and congested as he wrestled with the ban; he felt as if he were strangling on the words that wouldn't come out. She came to him, put her hand on his arm. "Never mind," she said, "I know."

He slammed fist against table one last time, sighed and stood up. "Help me turn this thing over."

Brann pushed her hair off her face, blinked at him, then began laughing. He looked up, startled. "What?"

"You wouldn't understand. Why turn the table over?"

"Don't want to talk about it, you know why."

"Ah. Can the changers help?"

"No. You take that end, I'll take this. Watch the legs."

"Better move the candle first, unless you're planning to burn the house down. If you want light, why not touch on the wall lamps?"

"Lamps?" He looked up. There were ten glass and copper bracket lamps with resevoirs full of oil spaced along the walls of the alcove two meters and a half above the floor; he hadn't noticed them because he hadn't bothered to look higher than his head. "Do you know how irritating a woman is when she's always right? Here." He thrust the candle at her. "Light the ones on your side."

When the table was inverted and lay with its legs in the air, Danny Blue knelt on it and thumped at various portions of it to make sure the wood was solid; finished with that, he sat on his heels and looked thoughtfully at Brann. "You fed Ahzurdan, you think you can do that for me?"

She frowned at him, moved to the arch. "Yaril, I need you."

Drifting above the clouds, Jaril spread out and out and out, shaping himself into a mile wide parabolic collector seducing into himself starlight, moonlight, gathering every erg of power he could find; Yaril was a glimmering glassy filament stretching from Jaril to Brann, feeding that power into her; Brann was a transformer kneeling beside Danny Blue, feeding that power into him as fast as he could take it.

Using Ahzurdan's memories, Danny Blue wove a shield about them like the one Ahzurdan had thrown about the room in the Blue Seamaid; he worked more slowly and had to draw more power than Ahzurdan had, the memories were there but he was no longer completely Ahzurdan and the resonances of word and act were no longer quite true. With Brann feeding energy into him, he got the shield completed, locked it into automatic and found that he'd gained two advantages he hadn't expected. The smother couldn't reach him, couldn't wear at him. And the shield once it was completed took almost no maintaining. Whistling a cheerful tune he unbuckled his sandals and kicked them across the room, grabbed hold of Brann and pulled her into the alcove, shrinking the shield until it covered only that smaller room, it'd attract less attention and he had no illusions about how irritated Maksim was going to be at losing sight of what they were doing. But it was so damn good to be working again on something as simple and elegant and altogether beautiful as lift field circuits—he felt like a sculptor who'd lost his hands in some accident or other, then had to spend an small eternity waiting for them to be regrown.

Yaril filament had no difficulty penetrating the shield; she continued to transmit moonlight and starlight into Brann who kept one hand lightly on Danny's spine, maintaining the feed as he dropped to his knees on the underside of the tabletop. He brushed his fingertips across the wood, sketched the outline of a sensor panel, but left it as faint marks on the surface. Hands moving slowly, surely, the chant pouring out of him with a rightness that was another thing he hadn't expected (as if the magic and his Daniel memories had conspired to teach him in that instant what it'd taken Ahzurdan years to learn, as if the rightness and elegance of the design dictated the chant and all the rest), he Reshaped the wood into metal and ceramic and the esoteric crystals

that were the heart and brain of the field, layer on layer
of them embedded in the wood, shielded from it by
intricate polymers, his body the conduit by which the
device flowed out of memory into reality, his will and
intellect disregarded. When the circuits were at last
completed, he sculpted twin energy sinks near the tail
(full, they'd power the sled twice about the world) and
finished his work with a canted sensor plate that would
let him control start-up, velocity, direction and altitude.
After a moment's thought, he keyed the plate to his hand
and Brann's; whatever happened, Maksim wasn't going
to be playing with this toy, it was his, Danny Blue the
New, no one else's. He added Brann, (reluctantly, forcing himself to be practical when the thought of sharing
his creation made him irrationally angry), because there
was too good a chance he'd be injured and incapable
and he trusted her to get away from Maksim if she could
possibly do it so he didn't want to limit her options. He
sat on his heels, gave Brann a broad but weary grin.
"Finished."

She inspected the underside of the table; except for
the collection of milkglass squares on the tilted board
near one end she couldn't see much change in the wood.
"If you say so. Shall I call the changers in?"

He tested the shielding and his own reserves. "Why
not. But you'd better tell them I'm going to need them
in the morning when there's sunlight, we have to charge
the power cells before we go anywhere."

She nudged the tabletop with her toe. "I've heard of
flying carpets, but flying kitchen tables, hunh!"

He jumped up, laughed, "Bramble all thorns, no you
won't spank me for that." He caught her by the waist,
swung her into an exuberant dance about the kitchen
whistling the cheeriest tune he knew; he was flying
higher than Jaril had, the pleasure of using both strands
of his technical knowledge to produce a thing of beauty
was better than any other pleasure in both his lives,
better than sex, better than smokedreams; he sang that
in her ear, felt her respond, stopped the dance and stood
holding her. "Brann. . . ."

"Mmmm?"

"Still hating me?"

She leaned against his arms, pushing him back so she could see his face, her own face grave at first, then warming with laughter. She made a fist, pounded it lightly against his chest. "If you mess me up again, I swear, Dan, I'll . . . I don't know what I'll do, but I guarantee it'll be so awful you'll never ever recover from it."

He stroked her hands down her back, closed them over her buttocks, pulled her against him. "Feel me shaking?"

"Like a leaf in a high wind."

He tugged her toward the alcove, but she broke away. "I'm not going to bruise my behind or my knees," she said. "Privacy yes," she said, "but give me some comfort too. Pillows," she said. "And quilts. Fire's down, it's getting chilly in here."

The children were curled up on the couch in the living room, sunk in the dormancy that was their form of sleep. Brann touched them lightly, affectionately as she moved past them, then ran laughing up the stairs to the sleeping floor. She started throwing the pillows out the doors leaving them in the hall for Dan to collect and carry downstairs, came after him with a billowing slippery armload of feather comforters.

Brann blinked, yawned, scrubbed her hands across her face. She felt extraordinarily good though her mouth tasted like something had died there, she was disagreeably sticky in spots and when she stretched, the comforter brushing like silk across her body, she winced at a number of small sharp twinges from pulled muscles and a bite or two, which only emphasized how very very good she was feeling. She lay still a moment, enjoying a long leisurely yawn, taking pleasure in the solid feel of Dan's body as her hip moved against his. But she'd never been able to stay abed once she was awake, so she kicked free of the quilts and sat up.

Dan was still deeply asleep, fine black hair twisting about his head, a heavy stubble bluing his chin and cheeks, long silky eyelashes fanned across blue veined skin whose delicacy she hadn't noticed before. She bent over him, lifted a stray strand of hair away from his

mouth, traced the crisp outlines of that mouth with
moth-touches of her forefinger. The mouth opened
abruptly, teeth closed on her finger. Growling deep in
his throat, Dan caught her around the waist, whirled her
onto her back and began gnawing at her shoulder, working his way along it to her neck.

Brann dunked a corner of the towel in the basin of
cold water, shivered luxuriously as she scrubbed at herself. "The changers are still dormant. I suppose I should
wake them."

"They worked hard and there's more to do, leave
them alone a while yet . . . mmm . . . scrub my back?"

"Do mine first. I'd love to wash my hair, but I'm too
lazy to heat the water. Dan. . . ?"

"Dan Dan the handyman. How's that feel?" He
rubbed the wet soapy towel vigorously across her back
and down her spine, lifted her hair and worked more
gently on her neck. When he was finished, he dropped
a quick kiss on the curve of her shoulder, traded towels
with her and began wiping away the soap.

"Handyman has splendid hands," she murmured.
"Give me a minute more and I'll do you."

"Trade you, Bramble, you cook breakfast for us and
I'll haul hot water for your hair."

"Cozy." A deep rumbling voice filled with laughter.

Brann whipped round, hands out, reaching toward the
huge dark man in a white linen robe who stood a short
distance from them.

Dan moved hastily away from her. "No use, Brann,
it's only an eidolon."

"What?" As soon as she said it, she no longer needed
an answer, the eidolon had moved a step away and she
could see the kitchen fire glow through it.

"Projected image. He's nowhere near here." Dan's
voice came from a slight distance, when she looked
round, he was coming from the alcove with his trousers
and her shirt.

"He can see and hear us?" She took the shirt, pulled
it around her and buttoned up the front.

"Out here. If we went into the alcove, no." He tied

off his trouser laces and came to lean against the pump
sink beside and a little behind her.

"So," Brann said, "it's your move, image. What does
he want with us?"

The eidolon lifted a large shapely hand, pointed its
forefinger at the alcove.

"NO!" Dan got out half a word and the beginning
of a gesture, then sank back, simmering, as the eidolon
dropped its arm and laughed.

"Busy busy, baby Dan?" The eidolon folded its arms
across its massive chest. "I presume you have cobbled
together some means of coping with the landfolk. A
small warning to the two of you which you can pass on
to your versatile young friends. Don't touch my folk. I
don't expect an answer to that. What I've sent the eidolon for is this, a small bargain. I will refrain from
any more attacks against you, I'll even call off Amortis;
you will come direct to me on Deadfire Island." The
eidolon turned its head, yellow eyes shifting from Brann
to Danny Blue. Its mouth stretched into a mocking
smile. "A bargain that needs no chaffering because you
have no choice, the two of you. Come to me because
you must and let us finish this thing." Giving them no
time to respond, it vanished.

The table hovered waist high above the flags of the
paved yard. Still inverted, its front four legs supported
a stiff windbreak made of something that looked rather
like waxy glass, another of Danny Blue's transforma-
tions. He sat in the middle of the sled grinning at her;
liftsled, that's what he'd called it and when she told him
no sled she'd ever seen looked like that he took it as a
compliment. Yaril and Jaril were sitting on the rim of a
stone bowl planted with broadleaved shrubs that were
looking wrinkled and shopworn (end of the year symp-
toms or they needed watering); the changers were enjoying the performance (hers and Dan's as well as the
table's).

Brann shivered. The wind was more than chill this
morning, it was cold. If those clouds ever let down their
load, it would fall as sleet rather than rain, a few degrees more and the Plain might have this year's first

snow. "Yaro, collect us two or three of those quilts, please? And here," she tossed two golds to Yaril, "leave these somewhere the farmwife will find them but a thief would miss. I know we're gifting the farmer with three fine mules, but he didn't sew the quilts and he doesn't use the table we're walking off with. I know, I know, not walking, flying. You happy now, Dan? Shuh! save your ah hmm wit until we're somewhere you can back it up. If you need something to occupy you, figure for me how long our flying table will need to get us to Deadfire."

Danny Blue danced his fingers over the sensors; the table lowered itself smoothly to the flagging. He got to his feet, stretched, stood fingering a small cut the sorcerously sharpened knife had inflicted on him when he used it to shave away his stubble. Ahzurdan jogged my hand, he told Brann, he keeps growling at me that adult males need beards to proclaim their manhood, it's the one advantage he had over Maksim, he could grow a healthy beard and his teacher couldn't, the m'darjin blood in him prevented, but I can't stand fur on my face so all old Ahzurdan can do is twitch a little. He fingered the cut and scowled past Brann at the wooden fence around the kitchen garden. "It's hard to say, Bramble. Last night, who was it, Yaril, she said we'd reach the mountains late afternoon today, say we were riding, that's . . . hmm . . . what? Sixty, seventy miles? Jay, from this side the hills, how far would you say it is to Deadfire Island?"

Jaril kicked his heels against the pot. "Clouds," he said. "We couldn't get high enough to look over the hills." He closed his eyes. "Before we left on the Skia Hetaira," he said, his voice slow and remembering, "we wanted to get a look down into Maksim's Citadel, we weren't paying much attention to the hills . . . Yaro?" Yaril dumped quilts and pillows onto the table, walked over to him. She settled beside him, her hand light on his shoulder. They sat there quietly a moment communing in their own way, pooling their memories.

Jaril straightened, opened his eyes. "Far as we can remember, those hills ahead are right on the coast. You just have to get through them, then you're more or less

at Silagmatys. About the same distance, I'd say, from
here to the hills, from the hills to Deadfire. Maybe a
hundred miles altogether, give or take a handful.''

Dan nodded. "I see. Well . . ." He clasped his hands
behind him and considered the table. "If the sled goes
like it's supposed to, flying time's somewhere between
hour and a half, two hours.''

"Instead of two days," Brann said slowly. She looked
up. The heavy clouds hid the sun, there wasn't even a
watery glow to mark its position, the grayed-down light
was so diffuse there were no shadows. She moved her
shoulders impatiently. "Jay, can you tell what time it
is?''

Jaril squinted at the clouds, turned his head slowly
until he located the sun. "Half hour before noon.''

Brann thrust her hands through her hair. Her stomach
was knotting, there was a metallic taste in her mouth.
Instead of two days, two hours. Two hours! Things rushing at her. Danny was cool as a newt, the kids were
cooler, but her head was in a whirl. She felt like kicking
them. They were waiting for her to give the word. She
looked at the table, smiled because she couldn't help it,
charging through the sky on a kitchen table was pleasantly absurd though what was going to happen at the
end of that flight was enough to chase away her brief
flash of amusement. She wiped her hands down her
sides. "Ahh!" she said. "Let's go.''

16

THE BEGINNING OF THE END.

SCENE: Deadfire island. Taking color from the clouds, the bay's water is leaden and dull; it licks at a nailparing of a beach with sand like powdered charcoal; horizontal ripples of stone rise from the sand at a steep slant in a truncated pyramid with a rectangular base. About halfway up, the walls rise sheer in a squared-off oval to a level top whose long axis is a little over half a mile, the short axis about five hundred yards, with elaborate structures carved into the living stone (the dominant one being an immense temple with fat-waisted columns thirty feet high and a central dome of demon-blown glass, black about the base, clear on top, the clear part acting as a concentrating lens when the sun's in the proper place which happens only at the two equinoxes). On the side facing Silagamatys a stubby landing juts into the bay; a road runs from the landing through a gate flanked with huge beast paws carved from black basalt, larger than a two-story house, three-toed with short powerful claws; it continues between tapering brick walls that ripple like ribbons in a breeze, then climbs in an oscillating sprawl to the heights.

Settsimaksimin stands in the temple garden, leaning on a hoe as he watches a narrow stream of water trickle around the roots of bell bushes and trumpet vines. Most of the flowering plants have been shifted from the flowerbeds into winter storage, but there are enough bushes with brilliantly colored frost-touched leaves to leaven the dullness of the surroundings. Behind him Amortis in assorted forms is flickering restlessly about the temple, her fire alternately caged and released by the temple pillars; she is working herself into a fury so she can forget her fear.

Maksim scratched at his chest, then scratched some dirt into the channel to redirect the water. When he was satisfied, he swung the hoe handle onto his shoulder and strolled to the waist-high wall about the garden. Sliding between Deadfire and Silagamatys, glittering ferociously, shooting those glitters at him, the Godalau swam like a limber gem through the gray matrix of the sea. Tungjii was nowhere in view, no doubt heesh was around, watching for a crack where hisser's thumbs could go. Past noon. Divination said they'd be here in an hour or so, riding Danny's little toy. He had a last look around, took the hoe to the silent brown man squatting in a corner sipping at a straw colored tea and went back across the grass to the minor stairs that led to a side door into the temple.

The Dome Chamber was an immense hexagonal room at the heart of the temple, it was also an immense hexagonal trap set to catch Brann, Danny Blue and the changers. A complicated trap with overlapping, reinforcing dangers. In each of the six walls, two arched alcoves bound by quickrelease pentacles, twelve cells holding different numbers of different sorts of demons, fly-in-amber-waiting. A blackstone thronechair on a dais two thirds the length of the room from the entrance, massive, carved with simple blocky fireforms, unobtrusive lowrelief carvings that decorated every inch of the chair's surface, caught the constantly shifting light and changed the look of the chair from moment to moment until the surface seemed to flow like water, a power-sink, a defensive pole, not dangerous in itself, only in its occupant. Pentacles everywhere, etched into the basalt floor like silverwire snowflakes widecast about the dais, some dull, some glowing with life, some punctuated with black candles awaiting an igniting gesture, some left bare (though scarcely less dangerous), some drawn black on black so only sorceror's sight could see them. Between the pentacles, sink traps scattered hapazardly (the unpattern carefully plotted in Maksim's head so he wouldn't trap himself), waiting for an unwary foot, a toe touch sufficient to send the toe's owner into a pocket universe like the one that held the Chained God only not nearly so large. Other traps written into the air itself, drifting on the eddying currents in that air. Amortis, shape abandoned, a seething fireball, floating up under the dome filling the space there with herself, keeping herself clear of the traps, waiting for her chance to attack and destroy the midges who'd dared to threaten her, waiting her chance also to sneak a killing hit at Maksim, waiting for him to forget her long enough to let her strike, not knowing he'd made her bait in another trap; if the changers tried to tap her godfire, they tipped themselves into a far reality, removing themselves permanently from the battle.

As Maksim moved through the forest of columns, he tugged the clasp from his braid, pulled the plait apart until his hair lay in crinkles about his shoulders, unlaced the ties at the neck of his torn wrinkled workrobe. He turned aside before he reached the Dome Chamber, entering a small room he'd set up as a vestry. Humming in a rumbling burr, he stripped off the robe, dropped onto a low stool and planted one foot in a basin filled with hot soapy water. With a small, stiff-bristled brush he scrubbed at the foot, examined his toenails intently then with satisfaction, wiped that foot and began on the other. When he had washed away the dirt of his play at gardening, he buffed his fingernails and toenails until he was satisfied with their matte sheen, then he started brushing his hair, clicking his tongue at the amount of gray that had crept into the black while he was busy

with Brann and the Council. He brushed and brushed,
humming his tuneless song, vaguely regretting Todichi
Yahzi wasn't here to do the brushing for him (it was one
of his more innocent pleasures, sitting before the fire
on a winter evening while little Todich tended his hair,
brushing it a thousand strokes, combing it into order,
until every hair end was tucked neatly away, braiding
it, smoothing the braid with his clever nervous hands).
Maksim clicked his tongue again, shook his head. No
time for dreaming. He plaited his hair into a soft loose
braid, pressed the clasp about the end, pulled on an
immaculate white robe, touched it here and there to
smooth away the last vestige of a wrinkle. Standing before a full length mirror, he drew the wide starched
collar back from his neck, brought BinYAHtii out and
set the dull red stone on the white linen. He weighed
the effect, nodded, reached for his sleeveless outer robe.
It was heavily embroidered velvet, a brownish red so
dark it was almost black. He eased into it, careful not
to crush the points of his collar, settled the folds of the
crusted velvet into stately verticals, slid heavy rings onto
the fingers of both hands, six rings, ornamental and
useful, invested with small but deadly spells shaped to
slip through defenses busy with more massive attacks.
Holding his hands so the rings showed, he closed his
fingers on the front panels of the overrobe and studied
the image in the mirror. He smiled with satisfaction
then with amusement at the vanity he'd cultivated like
a gardener experimenting with one of the weeds that
came up among his blooms. He licked his thumb and
smoothed an eyebrow, licked it a second time and
smoothed the other, winked at his image in the mirror
and left the room.

His staff was leaning against a column beside the
broad low arch that was the only entrance to the Dome
Chamber; he'd left it there because he'd need it to move
around the chamber without getting wrapped in one of
his own traps. He went through the arch at its center,
turned sharply left, moved along the wall to the first of
the cells then began a careful circuitous almostdance
across the floor, staff held before him to sweep aside
the air webs. He reached the chair intact and immacu-

late, with a memory of heat close to him. Having seated himself in the greatchair which was ample enough to hold him with room to spare and more comfortable than it looked, but not much, he laid his staff across the arms and settled himself to wait.

A whitish waxy muzzle nosed slowly, awkwardly, through the low arch. He waited. When the thing emerged a bit more, he was amused to see it was an inverted table with Brann and Danny Blue crouched between its legs. Floating a yard above the floor, it inched forward until it was clear of the arch then stopped, rocking gently as if blown by summer breezes on a summer pond. The changers followed it in, twin glimmerspheres so pale they were visible only as smudges of light against the blackstone wall as they hovered one on each side of the table.

For a breath or two he considered calling to them, working out some sort of compromise, but Amortis was seething overhead, ready to seize and swallow at the first sign of hesitation, not caring whom she took, him or them, BihYAHtii trembled on his chest, hungrier and more deadly than the god, and, beyond all this, he remembered the thousands of landfolk who'd left home and harvest for him, trying to interpose their bodies between him and those on that table. There was no room left for talking. There never had been, really. He swung the staff up, knocked its end against the dais three times and took all restraints off his voice. "I give you this warning," he roared at them, "This alone. Leave here. Or die. There is nothing for you here." While he was still speaking, before the warning was half finished, he fingered the staff and loosed a sucking airtrap, throwing it at the table. There were many ways of managing that lift effect; it didn't matter which Danny Blue had chosen, for the trap would negate the magic behind the effect, send the table crashing to the floor and prison it with its riders in one or another of the stonetraps.

Nothing like that happened. Danny Blue didn't even try to counter the trap. While it twined about the table and withered futilely away, Dan spat into his palm, blew at the spittle. It flew off his hand, elongated into a blue-white water form that arrowed at Maksim, a water elemental (which surprised Maksim quite a lot since Ahzurdan's forte had been fire and fire-callers, like earth-singers, seldom could handle water at all, let alone handle it well; this was either the Godalau's work or the Akamarino melded with him, which made one wonder what else he could do and what his weaknesses were); Maksim drew briefly on the chair's power, channeled it through his staff and twisted a tunnel through the air that sucked in the elemental and flung it into the bay.

The table moved a hair or two forward. Dan was frowning, trying to read floor, air, ceiling, walls as if he had forty eyes not two. The Drinker of Souls knelt beside him, silent, frowning, one hand resting lightly on his shoulder. The changers drifted beside the table, waiting. For what, Maksim did not know, perhaps they wanted to get closer before they came at him; one thing he did know, he did not want them anywhere near him. He prodded a reluctant Amortis, ordered her to stir herself and start attacking, wanting her to draw the changers into striking back at her, thereby taking themselves out of the game. While she shaped and flung a storm of firedarts at the sled, he scanned his prisoned demons, chose the players for his first demon gambit.

Third cell on the right: small bat-winged flyers with adamantine teeth and claws, a poison dart at the tip of whippy tails. He released the pentacle and sent the flyers racing at the sled.

Third cell on the left: one creature there, a knotty tentacled acid spitter, capable of instantaneous transfer across short distances, capable also of terrific psychic punches when it was within touching distance. He tripped the pentacle on this one a few seconds after the other, waiting until Danny Blue was focused on the first set of demons, fishing for the release call that would send them home.

Demons in the remaining ten cells, waiting to be loosed to battle.

In two separate cells, two vegetative serpents thirty feet long and big around as a man's thigh, immensely powerful with shortrange stunner organs that they can use to freeze their prey before they drop on it.

In three separate cells, three swarms of Hive demons each three inches long, they suck up magic like flies suck up blood, hundreds of units in each swarm.

In three separate cells, three tarry black leech things, eyeless, with feelers that they extrude and withdraw into themselves, each with a rhythm of its own; like the hivers they drink magic rather than blood, they are capable of sensing traps and avoiding them and nothing but death or dismissal will take them off a trail they're started on.

A mist creature, a subtle thing, slow, insinuating; given sufficient time it can penetrate any shield no matter how tight; once in, it consumes whatever lives inside that shield.

A roarer, a swamp lizard mostly mouth and lungs, it attacks with sound, battering with noise, stirring terror with subsonics, drilling into the brain with supersonics.

Dan shouted the release that flipped the flyers to their home reality a micro instant before the tentacled demon slammed into the shield sphere, gushed acid over it and wound itself up to punch at the people inside. As the sled rocked and groaned under the added weight, before Dan had time to shift his focus, Brann had the stunner out of his pocket; she thumbed the slide back and slashed the invisible beam in a wide X across the creature.

It howled in agony, pulled its tentacles into a tight knot and tumbled off the shield, crashing to the floor inside one of the pentacle traps which locked around it and held it stiff as a board against stone that sucked at it and sucked at it, slowly slowly absorbing the demon into its substance.

The changers wheeled above the shield, catching the firedarts and eating them. Amortis stirred uneasily in the dome and stopped wasting her substance for no result.

Danny Blue shivered the shield to rid it of the remnants of the acid, then he scraped the sweat off his brow and peered into the air ahead of him, searching out the airtraps, inching the sled between them, gaining another foot before he stopped to catch his breath and prepare another attack.

Maksim frowned. That shield should be costing Danny Blue more than he could afford—unless he had something similar to BinYAHtii feeding him. Her. Had to be her. Forty Mortal Hells, I have to get to her. How, how, how . . . ah! The sled had whined and dropped lower under the weight of the demon. If he could crash it, if he could put them on foot. . . .

Second gambit. Complex. Crushing weight, pile stone elementals on that shield sphere, attack on every side with everything I can throw at them, distract the changers, tempt them once more to attack Amortis.

Settsimaksimin tripped the pentacles, flipped the serpents and the roarer at the sled and left the others to make their own way; he goaded Amortis into attacking again, instructing her to slam the sled about as much as she could while she flooded it with fire; he reached deep into the stone, wakened the elementals sleeping there, sent them boiling up (bipedal forms with powerful clumsy limbs, forms altering constantly but very slowly, growing, breaking off into smaller versions like a glacier calving icebergs, gray and black and brown and brindle, stone colors, stone flesh, stone heavy), standing on each other, climbing over each other until they were up and over the shield sphere, saving only where the serpents were. Once they were in place, they swung their arms and crashed their fists into it, pounding it, pounding. . . .

The Roarer crouched on its bit of safe ground and hammered at them with with great gusts of SOUND, blasts so tremendous they seemed to shake the temple, threatening to bring the columns crashing down around the chamber. The effect of this SOUND was diminished slightly by the insulating effect of the crawling stone bodies of the elementals, but not enough, not nearly enough. The serpents tightened their grip on the shield, flat sucker faces pressed against it, sensors searching for life within, stun organ pulsing, ready to loose its hammer the moment it had a target. . . .

Danny Blue cursed and fought the numbing of that SOUND and searched through Ahzurdan's memories for the names and dismissals he needed. Brann tried the stunner again, but she couldn't get at the Roarer and the serpents were stunners themselves with a natural immunity that bled off the field before it could harm them. She felt something like tentacles moving over her, slimy, cold, nauseating, closing around her; force like a fist blow raced through them, struck at her, almost took her out, but Dan found one reality he wanted, one name he needed, shouted the WORD at the serpents and banished them.

He pulled more and more energy from her as the pressure on the shield increased and she was beginning to wilt as the drain on her resources intensified. "Yaril," she cried. A tentacle of light snaked through the shield, touched her. *I need help, I'm nearly empty.*

Gotcha, Bramble. Just a moment. Yaril merged briefly with Jaril. When they separated, Jaril dived at the elementals, swept through and through them, stealing energy from them, sloughing what he couldn't contain, Yaril expanded into a flat oval, a shield over the shield, absorbed the fire from Amortis, sent some of it along a thread to Brann and flared off the rest, doing her best to splash the overflow toward Maksim.

As the godfire poured into her, Brann gasped, closed her eyes tight, tears of agony squeezing out the sides. She contained the fire, controlled it, transmuted it and fed it into Dan to replace the energy flooding out of him.

The hivers sucked at the weave of the shield, softening it, draining it. The slugs were still a few yards out, oozing their way warily past the traps on the floor, but Dan could already feel them. The roarer battered at him, it was impossible to think with that noise drilling into his brain, plucking at his nerves, making him shudder with dread. After more frantic searching, he chanced across another NAME and another WORD, and with a sigh of relief he banished the Roarer and its SOUND.

The shield softened further and he couldn't stop it, no matter how much strength he poured into the weave, he could only slow it a little. He scowled at the buzzing hivers, trying to get a closer look at them, chilled inside because nothing he remembered came close to matching them, and if he didn't get rid of them soon. . . .

He didn't attempt to do anything about the elementals; earth was Maksim's forte and this close to him no one, not even a god, would wrest them from his control, Jaril was distracting them, weakening them, that was all anyone could hope for.

He was furious and frustrated. Maksim hesitating to attack, HAH! he'd kept them on the defensive from the moment they reached the chamber. His ground. No doubt he'd been preparing it for days, perhaps for decades, not specifically for them but for anyone who thought to challenge him. He shook off his malaise. "Brann, the swarms, see if the stunner will knock them down. Ahzurdan doesn't know them, I can't. . . ."

"I hear." She began playing the stunner along the undersurface of the sphere, an undersurface clearly marked by the stony bodies of the elementals. Dan made a little sound, a combination gasp and involuntary chuckle as the hivers fell away from the shield, pattering to the floor with tiny clatters like wind driven seeds against windowpanes.

More elementals came out of the earth and crawled onto the shield, closing the last interstices so he could not longer see the slugs. The sled groaned and shivered and sank lower until it was only six inches off the stone, in minutes it was going to touch the floor, it was bound to land in one of the pentacles or sink into a trap. The elementals stopped pounding on the shield, they were weakened by Jaril's raids, but that didn't help, it was the weight of them that did the damage. Water, he thought, water, somehow I've got to get water in here, some . . . how. . . . The slugs pulled harder at him, they were going to swallow him if he didn't do something. Where where did Maksim get them, I seem to remember . . . Magic Man, where where . . . ah! He spoke the NAME, he spoke the WORD, the pressure diminished so suddenly, so sharply, he almost fell on his face, his skin felt too thin as if he were about to explode, his grip on the shieldweave wavered. His hands

snapped into fists as he caught hold of the shield and
tightened it again. He forced himself to sit up, pressed
a fist against his thigh and straightened the fingers one
by one, working them carefully until he had some control over them. Bending over the sensor panel, he started
the sled forward, got a little momentum and was able
to break away from the elementals still boiling up
through the floor, though the ones already clinging to
the shield sphere stayed with him and he couldn't gain
height. He didn't have to worry about airtraps any more,
the bodies of the elementals protected him from those.
He felt the sled jolt and knew that Maksim was hammering at him. The jolting grew harder, came faster
without any pattern to it. Amortis was slamming at them
too, her blows amplifying or interfering with Maksim's,
she wasn't concerned with that, she screamed her hate
and fury as she put all her strength into those clouts.
The sled rocked precariously, tilted far to one side,
bucked and twisted, throwing Danny Blue and Brann
against the legs, threatening to whip them through the
shield into the arms of the elementals. This wasn't
something he planned for, the sled was reasonably stable but even its prototype wasn't built for this kind of
strain; the table groaned and whined, rocked wildly,
one moment a corner scraped against the stone; luck
and luck alone kept them from trap or pentacle. He
fought the sled level again, managed to squeeze more
forward speed from the field, hoping as they got closer
to Maksim that Amortis would have to take more care,
giving him a chance to think a little. Somehow he had
to strip away the elementals so he could see Maksim,
as long as he was blind all he could do was hold his
defenses tight.

Maksim watched the mound of oozing stone forms
surge, tilt, shudder, heard the sled scrape the floor,
ground his teeth when he was sure it had touched down
in one of the few clean spaces. It labored on, creeping
toward him; so far nothing had worked to stop it. He
glared up at Amortis, shouted at her to stop wasting
fire, she was only feeding the changers, to concentrate
on slamming the sled about. A mistake, that fire, it

meant the changers didn't have to draw from the source.
He'd misread the events in Amortis' first attack, he saw
that now, and he'd made other mistakes in play;
shouldn't have hit them so hard from so many directions, he wasted the demons that way (though he hadn't
expected all that much from them since Ahzurdan knew
them as well as he did, except the hivers, too bad about
them, that cursed weapon Akamarino brought with him,
the mist demon was still in the game, Ahzurdan knew
its form and home, but Danny Blue would have to see
it before he could do anything about it). Wasted his best
trap too, there was no one clear danger, he should have
made Amortis the clear danger, then the changers might
have attacked her, they were too busy defending the sled
to be tempted that way. The mist demon finally reached
the sled and began oozing among the elementals, the
overflow from the fire was bothering it, he could feel it
whining, he snarled at Amortis again, subsided as the
flood of fire choked off and the sled tottered as she put
muscle into her immaterial arm and her immaterial fist
slammed into it.

He pulled more elementals from the stone and threw
them atop the pile. The sled groaned and dropped an
inch lower, but still kept coming. He wondered briefly
whether Danny Blue meant to slam into the stairs of the
dais, or didn't know he was getting close to them; the
elementals flowed so thickly about him, there seemed
no way he could see where he was going. Unless the
changers were piloting him. They went through the rind
of elementals and that peculiar shield as if neither existed. That shield, it was like nothing he'd seen before;
he assumed it was an amalgam of the knowledge held
by Ahzurdan and Akamarino. It was certainly effective.
Fascinating, what the Chained God had done with those
two men. He moved his staff, sent a ram of hardened
air at the sled; it swung and shuddered, then came on
even faster. He scowled, deflected a splash of earthfire
slung at him by one of the changers as it drained strength
from the elementals and pried bits of the elastic stone
from the shield sphere, thumped the sled once more.
He didn't want to give up the trap woven round Amortis, but if that thing got too close he might have to; he

began shifting his intent, began gathering himself for one last grand effort.

The sled swerved sharply, picked up yet more speed and began running at the wall on Maxim's right, rocking, sliding, tottering under the increasing force and speed of the whacks from Amortis' immaterial fists. It must be hellish inside there.

The sled swerved again, scooted behind the chair and stopped. The changers sucked great gulps of energy from the earth elementals and washed it across the back of the thronechair. The obsidian chairback exploded in a spray of molten stone; part of the energy in that eruption came from his own power which he'd stored in the chair, part from the stone life in the elementals, stone against stone, stone melting stone. Maksim jumped to his feet, did a hasty dance with his staff to shunt the melted obsidian away from him, cursed, then laughed, appreciating the irony in this interweaving of chance and intention. He leaped onto the chairseat, drew what remained of the stored power into himself and flung the fire back at the changers and the sled.

Hampered by the narrow space and nervous about getting too close to Maksim, Amortis struck at them, hit the sled hard enough to slam it into the backwall, hit it again when it rebounded. And again.

The elementals kept trying to crush the shield, pushing that futile attack because Maksim wouldn't release them. They pressed more substance into their fists and beat on the shield, they grew knife-edged talons on feet and hands, gouged at the shield, they oozed themselves up toward the top of the shield sphere, oozed back down again when they couldn't get a hold on it, their stony substance stretching and flowing like cold taffy.

The changers went wheeling and whipping through the elementals, they scooped huge gouts of earthfire out of them and flung it at Maksim, flung it with such power it seemed to reach him almost before it left their hands. He deflected it, but he was linked too closely to the elementals to escape their pain, their fury, the heat got at him, the fire raised blisters on his face and arms.

The exchange went on and on, neither side seriously affecting the other. Maksim kept waiting for the mist to

act, but nothing seemed to be happening on the sled. It
slammed against the wall, bounced against the back of
the dais, it groaned and whined, it came close to cap-
sizing, but the shield never faltered. He cast up a de-
flector of his own to carry the changers' attack away
from him and away from the chair so its stone wouldn't
melt from under him, he slapped his right foot on the
stone, slapped his left foot on the stone, yelled a wordless defiance that filled the chamber, set himself firm as
stone, set himself for a last throw, unknotting the trap-
web about Amortis, dragging it back into himself, dragging an unwilling Amortis down from the dome, holding
her shivering on the dais beside him, her mass compacted until she was a mere ten feet tall, a vaguely bipedal shape of red-gold white-gold light. Sullen light.
He muttered to himself, pulling from his sorceror's
trickbag the preparatory syllables that would set the
points for the wild web he was planning to spin.

Sometime later he happened to glance round, no particular reason for it, it was just something he did; he
saw black, dull black shirt and trousers, threadbare,
wrinkled, a round graceless form silhouetted against the
flare of the deflected earthfire. Tungjii. Watching. It
jolted him. What's that one doing here? Never mind.
Concentrate, Maksim, don't give himmer a crack for
hisser thumbs. Forget himmer, you've got them in your
hands, you can throw them anywhere you want once
you're ready. Ready ready, almost ready . . .

His voice boomed in a reverberant chant, filling the
chamber with sound so powerful it was a tangible
THING, the intricately linked syllables weaving a fine
gold web about the sled. . . .

SEY NO TAS   SEY NO MENAS
   DAK WOLOMENAS WOLOMENAS
SEY NO TAS   SEY NO MENAS
   DAK AMEGARTAS GARTAS GAR TASSSS
SEY NO TAS   SEY NO MENAS
   PAGASE PAGASE AMEGARTA GAR
SEY NO TAS   SEY NO MENAS
   KNUSI AIKHMAN

SEY NO TAS   SEY NO MENAS
  IDIOS NOMAN
HROUSTITAKA HREOS
SEY NO TAS
HREOS MEGARITAN. . . .

Danny Blue grunted as he slammed into one of the
legs, then into Brann; he rolled across the table, con-
torted his body to avoid the sensor panel, finished for
the moment stuffed into the corner where the windbreak
curved round one of the front legs. The sled shuddered,
scraped against the wall, stone shrieking as it rubbed
against stone. He ignored the battering and focused on
water; the shield he'd woven about the sled wasn't difficult to hold in place, it just required a steady flow of
power which Brann and the changers supplied. A tube,
that was what he needed, a tube and some molecular
pumps. Tube, hmm, same weave as the shield, don't
want Maksim cutting it. . . .

Brann wrapped one arm about a table leg and reached
for Dan's ankle so she could keep up the feed. It was
hot and stuffy and darkly twilight inside the sphere, the
sensor panel provided a dim bluish glow and the feed
pipe was a soft yellow, neither of them made much impression on the darkness. She and Dan weren't choking
on fouled air because Yaril and Jaril fed them fresh
along with the godfire, but that only kept the atmo-
sphere bearable, it didn't make it pleasant. The godfire
feed was spasmodic now (she smoothed it out before
sending it on into Dan); the changers were moving too
fast and too erratically to maintain a constant flow. They
took turns as they'd done that time on the mountain,
plowing through the elementals, collecting from them,
splashing earthfire at Maksim, snapping the feedpipe
down to Brann, pumping her as full as she could hold,
doing this over and over. When the earthfire flooded
into her, when it sat seething in her, it wasn't quite as
agonizing as godfire, but it was bad enough, it was like
gulping down mouthfuls of boiling acid and it never got
easier. She endured the pain because she had to, Danny
Blue depended on her, young Kori had called in a promise—and most of all she was no longer ready to die,

there were too many other promises she had to keep, promises she had made to herself. She endured and grew stronger not weaker as the torment went on.

Her eyes began to burn. She blinked repeatedly, tried to focus, but she could see less and less as the minutes passed. Her skin burned. She touched her face, held her fingertips close to her eyes and saw that they were stained. She touched them to her tongue, tasted warm salty wetness. Blood. Her tongue began to burn. The pain from the earthfire was hiding . . . what? She fought to set that internal burning aside and feel about with immaterial fingers for what else was happening.

Smoky rotting vegetation smell, faint but there. A feeling of humidity, swampiness. Hunger. Now that she was listening, it shouted at her. HUNGER. "Dan," she cried. Her voice was hoarse, her throat felt as if something was scraping it raw. "Dan, there's something in here with us. What is it? DAN!"

Danny Blue heard Brann saying something, but he had no time nor attention to give her. He Reshaped the Pattern of the spherical shield (maintaining the shield in place and carefully separated from his other activities), and used the new Pattern to construct a closed cylinder; he poured more energy into it, lengthening it. He inserted the lead end into the shield, eased it through, then began the exacting and difficult task of forcing the cylinder through the thick elastic rind of earth elementals.

Brann realized he wasn't listening and dropped the attempt to reach him. She took her hand from his ankle and clamped it briefly around her own arm, felt something like a greasy film spread around it. Scowling, she wiped her hand on her trousers, then closed it around Dan's ankle so she could maintain the feed. She's got a reading from the thing: an intensification of that feral hunger, no sense of intelligence behind it, only will, a predator's will. Cautiously she reached out, pulled life from the thing, drinking it in as once she'd drunk the life of a black malouch, there was the same sense of wildness, greed, hunger. And fear as the thing felt the danger from her.

It wrenched free of her and Danny, fled toward the

top of the sphere. The air curdled up there as it compacted its misty substance, as far from her as it could get.

Brann broke from Danny again. Holding the table leg she struggled to her feet and reached for that mist.

With a kind of silent scream it flowed desperately away from her hand until it managed to ooze down between the windshield and the shieldsphere where she had no way of reaching it. Satisfied for the moment, she dropped back, settled herself as comfortably as she could while the table continued to rock wildly, to judder like a worm with hiccups, to slam between the wall and the dais. Her legs wrapped about the table's leg, she spared a moment to heal the damage from the mist, Dan first, then herself, then she went back to feeding fire to him. She didn't know what he was doing, only that it must be important if the intensity of his concentration meant anything.

Danny felt the small pains but ignored them. Sometime later he felt the upheaval when Brann interfered with his body as she healed the skin burns and the eye-damage; he ignored that too. He drove the tube up until it was clear of the elementals, bent it in a quarter circle and expanded it swiftly toward the nearest wall, holding it steady despite the careening of the sled. When it jammed against the stone, he heated the head end hotter than Amortis' fire and melted the tube through; his Sight was cut off by the elementals, but he could See down the tube and expand that Sight a few degrees as soon as one end was outside the temple. He sent it arching down over the edge of the island, down and down until it reached the gray seawater. When it dipped below the surface, he felt the cold shock of that water, shouted his triumph, "I've got you, Maks, I've got you now." He heard Brann's exclamation, ignored it and grew side pipes along the tube in an ascending spiral; grinning, he popped in the tiny pumps and started them sucking. "Brann, tell the changers there's going to be a lot of water in here in just a moment. I don't know exactly what's going to happen, but it'll be wild."

He reached again, sending an imperious call for water elementals, felt an immediate, almost frightening surge

as they answered him. Answered him in the hundreds.
Came compressed, swimming up the tube with the water the pumps were hauling.

Water and water elementals spurted from the side-
pipes, sprayed copiously over the earth elementals
crawling weak and angry over the shield sphere. Converting them to a slippery mindless sludge that dripped,
ropy and viscid, off the sphere.

Light flared through the shield, red light, gold light,
light hard and bright as diamond.

Settsimaksimin and Amortis stood together, dais and
chair, Maksim half sunk in her shimmering translucent
female body. Black sorceror body, Black Heart in that
Rose of Light, chant reverberating thunderously through
the great chamber. . . .

SEY NO KRISÊ   SEY NO KORÔN
KATAMOU NO KATAMOOOOU

Lines of light webbed around the sled, closing on it.
They were caught like fish in a tightening purse
seine. . . .

SEY NO KATALAM   SEY NO
   PALAPSAM   EKHO EKHO PALAPSAM

Dan shuddered under the power of that chant. Amortis and BinYAHtii and Settsimaksimin plaited like a
gilded braid, their unstable meld building to a climax
that was terrifyingly close. For a moment he sat pas-
sive, helpless, Ahzurdan exhausted riding up hill to the
Chained God and the trap inside the ship. . . .

SEY NO EKHO   SEY   SEEY UUHHH
   EY NO NO NO. . . .

The water elementals flowed up the dais, pressed
around Maksim and the Fire, not quite touching either,
disturbing him so much it broke into the drive of the
chant. Didn't stop it, but the chant faltered and some
of the power went out of it. BinYAHtii's dull red glow
flickered.

A smallish dark figure strolled up the burning air,
moved easily and untouched through the ring of water,
the shell of fire and stepped onto the half-melted chair

arm. Tungjii balanced there a moment, then rested hisser hand on Maksim's arm near the wrist, that was all, then heesh was somewhere else.

Settsimaksimin's body jolted, his voice broke; he gave a small aborted cry, crumpled, tumbling off the chair and down the stairs to land sprawled on his face on the floor.

Ball lightning and jagged firelines snapped across and across the Dome Chamber, rebounding from the walls, bouncing from the floor and ceiling as Maksim's stored magic discharged from stone and air and his tormented flesh, squeezed its tangible elements into hot threads that braided themselves in a rising rope of fire that went rushing up and up, bursting through the dome, shattering it into shards which fell like glass knives onto the stone, glancing off the shield Dan kept in place about the sled until the worst of the storm was past. Amortis solidified into her thirty meter female form, looking wildly about and fled after the fleeing remnants of Maksim's magic.

——— 17 ———

THE END OF THE END.

SCENE: Maksim sprawled on the floor, dead or dy-
          ing. The changers stood beside him, once
          more in their bipedal forms. The table set-
          tled to the floor. Brann and Danny Blue,
          bruised, battered, weary, climbed off it and
          started around the ruined dais.

Danny Blue stood beside the crumpled body. "Looks
like his heart quit on him. Old Tungjii found his crack."

Brann frowned, disturbed as much by the dispassion-
ate dismissing tone of those words as by the words
themselves. She touched Maksim's hand with her toe,
feeling manipulated and not liking it very much. She'd
helped destroy a man she might have liked a lot if things
were other than they were. Before the eidolon appeared
(a hollow image, yet with enough of his personality in
it to intrigue her) she'd known him mostly through Ahzurdan's comments, yes, and his attacks on her, which
seemed to give her no choice; if she wanted to live she
had to stop him, but the rise of the landfolk had shaken
her badly. Abandoning a harvest only half-gathered with
the winter hunger that might mean? leaving their houses
open to plunder, their stock handy for the nearest light-
finger? doing it to protect one man, the man that ruled
them? In all of her travels, in all of her reading, she'd
never heard of a king (not even the generally mild and
intelligent kings of her home island Croaldhu), emperor, protector of the realm, whatever the ruler called
himself, whose peasantry volunteered (volunteered!)

their bodies and their blood to keep him from harm. Nobles certainly, they had a powerful interest in who sat the local throne. Knights and their like, for gold, for the blood in it, for what they called their honor (being a true son of Phras, Chandro boasted hundreds of those stories about this one and that one among his ancestors and she'd heard them all). Armies had fought legendary battles but not for love of their leaders; they had their pay, their rights to plunder, their friends fighting beside them and the headsman's axe waiting for the losers. Peasants though! What peasants got from a war was hunger and harder work, ruined crops, dead stock, burnt houses while their landlords refilled war-starved coffers out of peasant sweat and peasant hide. She frowned down at Maksim, caught her breath as the fingers by her foot moved a little. She dropped to her knees beside him. "Dan, help me turn him over."

"Why?"

"Because I damn well refuse to be some miserable meeching god's pet executioner. If you don't want to help, get out of the way."

He shrugged. "It's your game, Bramble. You take his feet, I'll get his shoulders."

When Maksim was on his back, the velvet and linen robes smoothed about him, Brann eased BinYAHtii's gold chain over his head and tried to lift the talisman away without touching the stone; this close, it seemed to radiate danger. It rocked a little but wouldn't come free. She laid the chain on his chest, the heavy links clunking with oily opulence; she looked at them with distaste, then used both hands on the broad gold frame fitted around the stone, pulling as hard as she could. The pendant lifted away from his chest with a sucking sound, a smell of burned meat. She swallowed, swallowed again as her stomach threatened to rebel, thew the thing away, not caring where or how it landed. "Yaril," she said, "take a look inside, will you? I think I'd better not try this blind."

"Gotcha, Bramble, just a sec."

Yaril shifted form and flowed into the body, flowed out a moment later. She didn't bother talking, she leaned against Brann's side, transferred images to her that

Brann used as she bent over Maksim, planted her hands on his chest and worked to repair the extensive damage inside and out, heart, arteries, brain, every weakness, every lesion, tumor, sign of disease, everything Yaril had seen and passed on to her.

Dan watched her for a while until he grew bored with the tableau whose only change was the slow shifting of Brann's eyes. He strolled around behind the wreck of the dais, brought the table back, parked it close to Brann's feet, looked around for something else to kill some time. Jaril was pacing lazily about, sniffing at things, a huge brindle mastiff. Yaril was glued to Brann and didn't seem likely to move from her. The clouds must have begun breaking up outside because a ray of light came through the jagged hole in the dome and stabbed down at the floor, the edge of it catching the pendant, waking a few glitters in it. He walked across to it and stood looking down at it. The thing made him nervous. That was what the Chained God sent him to fetch, good dog that he was. He didn't want to touch it, but the compulsion rose in him until he was choking. Furious and helpless, he bent down, took hold of the chain and stood with the pendant dangling at arm's length. He looked at it, ran the tip of his tongue over dry lips, remembering all too clearly the hole burned in Maksim's chest.

There was a subdued humming, the air seemed to harden about him, the chamber got suddenly dark. "OHHHH. . . ."

. . . SHIIIT!" He stumbled, went to his knees before the control panel in the starship, caught his balance and bounded to his feet. His arm jerked out and up, the talisman was snatched away, the chain nearly breaking two of his fingers. BinYAHtii hung a moment in midair, then it vanished, taken somewhere inside the god. And I hope it gives you what it gave Maksim, he muttered under his breath. "Send me back," he said aloud. "You don't need me any more."

"I wouldn't say that." The multiple echoing voice was bland and guileless as a cat with cream on its whiskers. "No, indeed."

Dan opened his mouth to yell a protest, a demand, something, was snapped to the room where he had lived with Brann and the others. He was conscious just long enough to realize where he was, then the god dumped him on the bed and put him to sleep.

Bran sat on her heels, sighed with weariness. "Done," she said, "He'll be under for a while longer." She rubbed at her back, looked around. "Where's Dan?"

Jaril came trotting over, shifted. "He picked up BinYAHtii and something snatched him. If I guessed, I'd say the Chained God got him. The god really wanted that thing."

"Looks like it didn't want us."

"Luck maybe. Old Tungjii wiggling his thumbs in our favor for once. Say the god couldn't grab us all, we were too scattered."

"Hmm. If it's luck, let's not push it." She got to her feet. "What about the table? Will it fly again?"

"Sure. Where do you want it to go?"

"Give me your hand." She closed her fingers around his, said silently, *Myk'tat Tukery. Jal Virri. Not much can get at us there.* Aloud, she said, "Help me load Maksim on the sled."

"That's like bedding down with an angry viper, Bramble. Leave him here, let him deal with the mess he made for himself. It's not your mess. When he wakes, he's going to be mad enough to eat nails. Eat you."

"So we keep him sleeping until we go to ground and have some maneuvering room. I mean to do this, Jay."

"Ayy, you're stubborn, Bramble. All right all right, Yaro, give us a hand here." He scowled at the table. "Hadn't we better pick up those quilts and pillows we dumped outside? The sky's clearing, but it'll be chilly when you hit the higher air."

Brann smiled at him. "Good thought, Jay. There are people living here, a few anyway, that gardener for one. See if you can find some food, I'm starved and I'll need supplies for the trip; going by how long it took us to reach here from the farm, it'll be eight to ten days before we get umm home."

The changers darted about the island collecting food, wine and water skins, whatever else they thought Brann might need, then they helped her muscle the deeply sleeping sorceror onto the table. They settled him with his head on a pillow, a comforter wrapped about him, tucked the provisions around him and stood back looking at their work.

Brann shivered. "I've got an iceknot in my stomach that says it's time to be somewhere else." She swung round a table leg, settled herself in a nest of comforters and pillows; tongue caught between her teeth, she ran the sequence that activated the lift field, gave a little grunt of relief and satisfaction when the sled rose off the floor, moving easily, showing no sign of strain (she'd been a bit worried about the weight of the load). When it was about a yard off the floor, she stopped the rise and started the sled moving forward. She eased it through the arch, wound with some care through the great pillars beyond, starting nervously whenever she heard the stone complain.

Outside, the gray was gone from the sky, the bay water was choppy and showing whitecaps, glittering like broken sapphire in the brilliant sunlight. She took the sled high and sent it racing toward the southeast where the thousand islands of the Myk'tat Tukery lay. Behind her, the massive temple groaned, shuddered, collapsed into rubble with a thunderous reverberant rattle; part of it fell off the island into the sea. Brann shivered, sighed. She stretched over, touched the face of the man beside her, wishing she could wake him and talk to him. She didn't dare. She sighed again. It was going to be a long dull trip.

18

KNOTTING OFF.

Kori.
The School at Silili.

Kori glared at the flame on the floating wick, trying to narrow her focus until she saw it and only it, until she heard nothing, felt nothing, knew nothing but that erratically flickering flame. The small room was dark and quiet, no sounds from outside to distract her, but she felt the stone through the flimsy robe Shahntien Shere had given her, she heard every scrape her feet made when she had to move or suffer torments of itching, she felt the chill draft that curled round her body and shivered the flame. It seemed to her she was getting worse not better as she struggled to learn the focus her teachers demanded. Talent! He was dreaming, that man. She had no talent, nothing. She scratched an itch on a buttock and began running through the disciplines for the millionth time. . . .

Something watching her. The small hairs stirred along her spine, her mouth went dry. She fought to keep her eyes on the flame but couldn't, she jumped to her feet, turning with the movement so she faced the open arch.

Shahntien Shere stood there, eyes narrowed, fury rolling off her like steam. "Maksim's dead or destroyed," she said softly. "Your doing." She smiled. "He set a geas on me to teach you, it doesn't stop me making you one sorry little bitch. Contemplate that a while, then do me a favor and try leaving." A last glare, then she whipped around and stalked off.

Drinker of Souls, Kori thought, she did it. She sighed.

Nothing had turned out the way she planned. Ten years, she thought, I'm safe for ten years, but after that I'd better be a long, long, way from here. She dropped to her knees and began going through the disciplines again, contemplating the flame with grim determination; she had to learn everything and be better at it than anyone else before her. Maksim said she had talent, talent didn't count if you couldn't use it. Ten years. . . .

> Trego.
> The Cave of the Chained God

Sealed into the block of crystal, the boy slept. Now and then he dreamed. Mostly he waited unknowing in the midst of nothingness.

> Danny Blue.
> The Pocket Universe.
> The stranded starship.

After an interval whose length Dan never knew, he was allowed to wake because the god wanted someone to talk to. The god couldn't leave the pocket universe, he/it knew that now and it was Dan who told him/it. He/it couldn't change that verdict without dying, but he/it could punish the messenger who brought the bad news. And Dan could be converted easily enough into a blood and bone remote who could do things the god wanted done in that other universe. He/it wasn't about to lose his services. The mortal could sulk and rage and plot all he wanted, he lived and breathed because the god willed it, he was going to do whatever the god wanted done.

> Todichi Yahzi.
> Settsimaksimin's Citadel.
> Silagamatys.

When Maksim vanished from the scene, Todich took the drop from around his neck and looked at it for a long while, then he shook his head, packed his things

and started off to look for the man he knew was still
alive somewhere.

Brann.
Myk'tat Tukery. Jal Virri.

Maksim coughed, opened his eyes.
"Jal Virri."
The voice came from behind him, amused and wary.
Brann. Sooo. He sat up. The sky was blue, the air warm,
a silky breeze wandered past him, stirring the pendant
limbs of a weeping willow. The tree grew by an artesian
fountain, where water bubbled from a vertical copper
pipe, sang down over mossy boulders into a pond filled
with crimson lilies and gilded carp and out of that into
a stream that rambled about the garden. He was sitting
on a gentle slope covered with grass like green fur. *This
has to be south of Cheonea, I can't have slept completely through winter.* He looked at his arms. *He'd lost
flesh and muscle tone. Maybe not all winter but more
than a day or two.* "Jal what?" He got to his feet, moving slowly to camouflage his weakness.
Brann was sitting on a stone bench beside a burst of
ground orchids. "Jal Virri. Isn't that what everyone
asks? Where am I?"
Maksim moved uphill and eased himself onto the far
end of the bench. "Where's Jal Virri?"
"Myk'tat Tukery. One of the inner islands."
"How long was I out?"
"Ten days."
"Why bother?"
"I loathe being jerked around."
"I was a fool."
"You were."
He folded his arms across his chest, narrowed his
eyes, grinned at her. "You were supposed to appreciate
my humility and disagree with courteous insincerity."
She gave him a long look; eyes green as the willow
leaves smiled at him. "I'd rather beat up on you a bit.
Why didn't you talk to me? You swatted me like I was
a pesty fly. That sort of thing is bound to upset a per-
son."

"It seemed easier, a surgeon's cut, quick and neat, and a complication was gone out of my life."

"Wasn't, was it."

"Doesn't seem like it. Sitting here on this dusty bench, I can see half a dozen ways we might have managed some sort of compromise. Hindsight, hunh! bad as rue and twice as useless. Seriously, Brann, all I needed was maybe ten years more. I was buying time."

"For what?"

"For Cheonea."

"You say that so splendidly, so passionately, Maks. Such sincerity."

"Sarcasm is the cheapest of the arts, Bramble all thorns, even so, it needs a scalpel not an axe."

"Depends on how thick the skull is. Seriously, Maks, you've made a good start, but my father would say it's time to let the baby walk on its own. Otherwise you'll cripple it. Hmm. Are you thinking of heading back there?"

"That rather depends on you, doesn't it?"

"No."

"What?"

"I pulled you out there because I wouldn't trust the Chained God as far as I could throw it. Amortis either. And you weren't in any shape to defend yourself. I take no more responsibility for you than that. If you want to go, good-bye."

"And if I wish to stay for a while?"

"Then stay."

"Hmm." He fiddled with the charred hole in the linen robe he still wore, looked down at the smooth flesh under it. "What happened to BinYAHtii?"

"I took it off you, threw it away, foul thing, it'd eaten a hole almost to your heart. Jay told me this: when Yaro and I were working on you, Dan went over to it, picked it up and vanished. Chained God probably."

"Good-bye Finger Vales, eh?"

"Seems likely."

"So Kori got what she wanted. Her brother safe and the Servants tossed out."

"You know about that?"

"Had a talk with her."

"Where is she now?"

"The Yosulal Mossaiea in Silili. Do you know it?"

"She's talented? Slya's teeth, why am I surprised, she's Harra's Child. You sent her?"

"Why are you surprised? You expected me to eat her?"

"Well, feed her to BinYAHtii."

"That ardent soul? BinYAHtii was hard enough to control with ordinary lives in it. Besides, I liked her."

"So. What will you be doing next?"

"So. Resting. Here's as good a place as any. Will you be staying?"

"For a while."

"The changers?"

"Yaro says this place is pretty but boring." She looked wary again, smiled again. "I probably shouldn't tell you this, but they've gone off exploring, they've got a lot of things to get used to, the changers have changed. I suppose the next thing for me will be finding a way to get them home. I don't want to think about that for a while yet. I'm tired." She got to her feet, held out her hand. "I'm glad you're staying. It'll be pleasant having someone to talk to. Come. Let me show you the house. I haven't the faintest notion who built it, I stumbled across it the last time I was here. It's a lovely place. Friendly. When you step through the door, you get the feeling it's happy to have you visit." Her hand was warm, strong. She seemed genuinely pleased with him, in truth she seemed in a mood to be pleased by almost anything. As she strolled beside him, she slid her heels across the grass, visibly enjoying the cool springy feel of it against the soles of her bare feet. She'd had a bath before she woke him, she smelled very faintly of lavender and rose petals, the silk tunic which was all she wore was sleeveless and reached a little past her knees, the breeze tugged erratically at it, woke sighs in it. I'll need clothing, he thought, he touched the soiled charred robe, grimaced. She didn't notice because she was looking ahead at the odd structure sitting half shrouded by blooming lacetrees. "There's something I've never been able to catch sight of that bustles around, cleans the house, weeds the garden, prunes things, generally keeps the place in shape, I don't know how many times I've hid myself and tried to catch it working. Nothing. Maybe you can figure it out, be something to play with when you feel like exercising your head. To say truth I hope it eludes you too, that gives me a chance to stand back and giggle.''

"Myk'tat Tukery," he murmured, "I've heard a thousand tales about it, each stranger than the last.''

"Maksim mighty sorceror, I'll show you a thing or two to curl your hair, a thing or two to draw it straight again." She dropped his hand, ran ahead of him along the bluestone path, up the curving wooden stairs; she pushed the door open, turned to stand in the doorway, her arms outspread. "Be pleased to enter our house, Settsimaksimin, may your days here be as happy as mine have been.''

Laughter rumbling up from his heels, he followed her inside.

KNOTTING DONE (for the moment).

DAW

DAW Presents
The Fantastic Realms of
JO CLAYTON

DAW

Savor the magic, the special wonder of the worlds of
Jennifer Roberson

☐ **SWORD-DANCER**
Here's the fast-paced, action-filled tale of the incredible
adventures of master Northern swordswoman Del, and her
quest to save her young brother who had been kidnapped and
enslaved in the South. But the treacherous Southron desert
was a deadly obstacle that even she could not traverse alone.
Then she met Tiger, a mercenary and master swordsman.
Together, they challenged cannibalistic tribes, sandstorms, sand
tigers, and sand sickness to rescue Del's long-lost brother in a
riveting story of fantasy and daring.   (UE2152—$3.50)

CHRONICLES OF THE CHEYSULI

This superb new fantasy series about a race of warriors gifted
with the ability to assume animal shapes at will presents the
Cheysuli, once treasured allies to the King of Homana, now
exiles, fated to answer the call of magic in their blood, fulfilling
an ancient prophecy which could spell salvation or doom for
Cheysuli and Homanan alike.

☐ SHAPECHANGERS: BOOK 1   (UE2140—$2.95)
☐ THE SONG OF HOMANA: BOOK 2   (UE2195—$3.50)
☐ LEGACY OF THE SWORD: BOOK 3   (UE2124—$3.50)
☐ TRACK OF THE WHITE WOLF: BOOK 4 (UE2193—$3.50)
☐ A PRIDE OF PRINCES: BOOK 5   (UE2261—$3.95)

NEW AMERICAN LIBRARY
P.O. Box 999, Bergenfield, New Jersey 07621

Please send me the DAW BOOKS I have checked above. I am enclosing $_____
(check or money order—no currency or C.O.D.'s). Please include the list price plus
$1.00 per order to cover handling costs. Prices and numbers are subject to change
without notice.

Name _____

Address _____

City _____ State _____ Zip _____

Please allow 4-6 weeks for delivery.

DAW

A New Superstar in the DAW Firmament!

Mercedes Lackey

THE VALDEMAR TRILOGY

☐ **ARROWS OF THE QUEEN: Book 1**   (UE2189—$2.95)

Growing up in a repressive, puritanical environment, young Talia dreams of serving as a Herald—one of the Queen's elite special guard, who act as lawgivers, peacekeepers, and even warleaders. Chosen by one of the mysterious and powerful Companions, Talia is awakened to her own unique mental powers and magical abilities, and assumes a vital role in the attempt to save the kindgom from disaster.

☐ **ARROW'S FLIGHT: Book 2**   (UE2222—$3.50)

Talia, a full Herald at last, must face new and greater challenges as she rides forth on Patrol, dispensing Herald's Justice throughout the land. But in this realm, beset by dangerous unrest, enforcing her rulings will require all the courage and skill Talia can command—for if she misuses her special powers, both she and Valdemar will pay the price!

☐ **ARROW'S FALL: Book 3**   (UE2255—$3.50)

As Talia, the Queen's own Herald, undertakes a dangerous diplomatic mission, she is plunged into a sorcerous trap . . . a trap which may keep her from ever warning Valdemar and the Queen of the marching armies and sorcerous destruction which are even now reaching out to engulf them.
